THE ESCAPE

Gabriel's plan was for each of us to walk straight into the bushes, one by one, while the others kept lookout along the beach. His order was me, Luis, Uncle Ramon, and then himself.

When the moment came, I headed into the bushes without hesitation. But a few strides into the thick brush, I had to reset my bearings to sidestep a branch full of sharp thorns. When I did, I found myself standing in the middle of a cloud of mosquitos. They were hitting my arms and legs like I was the last warm meal on earth. And every time I'd slap at one spot, five or six of them would bite me somewhere else. So I bolted forward, praying I was still going in the right direction. I shoved aside branch after branch that either snapped back at me or cracked beneath my weight until I finally arrived at the clearing.

First, I saw the green body of a Buick automobile. There was something strange attached to the grille—a wide, pointed front that looked like the bow of a ship. I searched for a boat, maybe one on a small trailer behind the car. But there wasn't any. Then I saw the weld marks, sealing the car's four doors shut, and the supplies tied down in the backseat.

That's when it hit me: we'd be sailing to the US in a floating car.

OTHER BOOKS YOU MAY ENJOY

GAME SEVEN

PAUL VOLPONI

speak

SPEAK
An imprint of Penguin Random House LLC
375 Hudson Street
New York, New York 10014

First published in the United States of America by Viking,
an imprint of Penguin Group (USA) LLC, 2015
Published by Speak, an imprint of Penguin Random House LLC, 2016

THE LIBRARY OF CONGRESS HAS CATALOGED THE VIKING EDITION AS FOLLOWS:
Volponi, Paul.
Game seven / Paul Volponi.
pages cm
Summary: "A sixteen-year-old shortstop in Cuba who dreams of playing with the pros must
choose between his country and his father who defected to the U.S."—Provided by publisher.
ISBN 978-0-670-78518-6 (hardcover)
[1. Baseball—Fiction. 2. Fathers and sons—Fiction. 3. Emigration and immigration—Fiction.
4. Defectors—Fiction. 5. Cuban Americans—Fiction. 6. Cuba—Fiction.]
I. Title.
PZ7.V8877Gam 2015
[Fic] —dc23
2014000118

Speak ISBN 978-0-14-242429-2

Printed in the United States of America

This text is dedicated to the loving memory of my mother,
Mary, who was ejected from the stands during several of my
baseball games by blind umpires with adequate hearing.

◆ ◆ ◆

GAME
SEVEN

THERE ARE 108 stitches on a baseball. I should know. I've run my fingers over every one. The first and last stitches are hidden beneath the surface. But believe me, I've felt those, too.

I was up on my toes, shifting my weight from side to side. It's important for a shortstop. You don't ever want to get stuck in one spot, unable to move. So you learn to stay light on your feet. As our pitcher went into his windup, I was focused on the baseball in his left hand, following it all the way through his release.

Spinning out of his hand, it was just a seed of white to my eyes. A split second later, off the hitter's bat, it had turned into a scalding line drive headed right at me.

On instinct, I raised my glove in front of my face, almost in self-defense. The baseball stuck in its pocket, stinging my palm through the soft brown leather. Then I reached inside, gripping the ball by the seams before I tossed it around the infield diamond.

Six years ago, on my tenth birthday, Papi gave me this glove as a present. At the time it was brand-new and way too big for me.

"Don't worry. You grow into a glove. Then you'll have it the rest of your life," Papi said as I struggled to keep it on my hand. "We'll play lots of catch together, every day. That'll help you break it in."

Before I went to bed that night, Papi oiled the glove's pocket. He put a stone that was slightly bigger and heavier than a baseball in its center. Then he tied the fingers tightly closed around it, using string from Mama's kitchen.

"Do this every night and the ball will feel like a feather when it hits your glove," Papi promised.

So I did.

Back then, every kid I knew was jealous of me. That's because baseball is practically a religion in my country. And Papi walked through the streets of our hometown, Matanzas, like a god, with me trailing behind. He'd been an all-star pitcher for almost a decade. Not only for the Matanzas Crocodiles, but also for the Cuban National Team—the Nacionales—in all the big international tournaments.

Fans called him El Fuego, for his blazing fastball, which no batter could touch. The only way Papi could have been more respected was if he'd been a general in the military or a high-ranking government official. But most of *that* respect would have come out of fear.

A few months after my birthday, though, everything changed.

The Cuban National Team traveled to play an exhibition in the US. I was so excited. Papi promised to bring back lots of presents, like blue jeans for Mama and my younger sister, Lola. And Papi said that if he could find a way, he'd bring me a brand-new ten-speed racing bike. I would have gladly settled for a pair of new tires and a chain for my old bike—more than most of my friends' fathers could get for them.

Every night while Papi was gone, I dreamed about that bike while the stone sat tied inside my glove.

When the Nacionales swept all three games of the US exhibition—against the Baltimore Orioles, St. Louis Cardinals, and Chicago Cubs—it made the front page of every government-run newspaper in Cuba. Only Papi's name wasn't mentioned in any of the stories. I figured he might have injured his arm, or the team's manager decided to use other pitchers. Either way, I was completely disappointed and didn't know how to explain it to my friends.

The day the team arrived back in Cuba, I was waiting for Papi at home with Mama and my sister. We'd put up red, white, and blue streamers—the colors of the Cuban flag—

along with a big congratulations banner that read, FELICI-
DADES! Mama even made Papi's favorite dish, fish casserole
with sweet onions, green peppers, and yellow rice, for our
victory feast. But the hours dragged past with no Papi and
no celebration.

Mama must have screamed at us a dozen times about
picking food off the plates. And as her dinner turned cold,
the shadows slowly climbed the pink and purple walls of
our single-story concrete house, touching our wooden
front door.

Finally, there was a knock.

It was one of Papi's teammates.

Mama let him in, and I could tell by the way his eyes
were focused on the floor that the news was bad. Maybe Lola
could tell, too, because she buried her shoulder in the side
of Mama's chest, waiting to hear. Only I stood on my own,
pushing my toes hard into the ground, bracing myself.

"In Baltimore, the hotel lobby," he said, "El Fuego
walked out the revolving door, got into somebody's car, and
drove off with them. He never came back."

"Defected?" Mama asked with a twinge in her voice that
sounded like a combination of amazement and fear.

Papi's teammate nodded his head. Then his eyes rose up
and looked out the window, as if to check if he'd been followed to our house.

"Dios mío," she said, letting go of my sister just long enough to cross herself.

That's when I realized Papi was never coming home. He couldn't. Not without going to prison for being a traitor.

I was in total shock. I could feel an earthquake starting inside of me. My legs got so shaky I had to lock them at the knees to stop the trembling from taking over my entire body.

"Right before he left," Papi's teammate continued, "El Fuego whispered to me, 'Tell my family I'll find a way for us to be together.'"

That night, the three of us cried in each other's arms. There were tears of joy for Papi's freedom and wondering what *our* future might be with him in the United States one day. But there were tears of worry, too, over what might happen to us in Cuba as the family of a defector. To make those worries even worse, the very next morning police officers confiscated Papi's car before we could even think about selling it.

In all the time that's passed since then, we haven't heard a single word from Papi: no letter, no phone call, no message delivered by a friend—nothing.

It took more than a year of waiting for this empty feeling to completely come over me. When it finally did, it ached more than anything I could imagine. It was like we didn't exist to Papi anymore, like we weren't his family, and like I wasn't really his son.

There are no professional baseball players in Cuba. All the Nacionales have other jobs. Papi had been given a good one, coaching baseball at a nearby school. But without his salary, we couldn't afford to live in our house anymore. Instead, we had to move into a one-bedroom apartment with sinks that sometimes back up and a toilet that overflows. Now Mama works as a maid, cleaning tourists' hotel rooms. And I stopped attending school this year to bus tables in the hotel's restaurant.

Meanwhile, I heard on free radio from the US that Papi signed a second multimillion-dollar deal to pitch in the major leagues for the Miami Marlins.

Whenever I cry now, it's always tears of bitterness.

A few days ago, the Marlins made it into the World Series against the New York Yankees. Game One of the Series was played in Miami, and Papi came in to pitch in relief. I sat alone on a dark staircase in our apartment building with a small transistor radio pressed against my ear, listening to every pitch thrown by the great El Fuego—something the police could have punished me for.

Papi threw a perfect ninth inning for the save, striking out a pair of Yankees as the Marlins won, 5–4.

When the game was over, with my blood beginning to

boil, I ran into our apartment and snapped the string around my glove. Then I grabbed the stone from inside it and marched down to the shore.

It's ninety miles from Cuba to the coast of Florida. That didn't matter to me. I reared back and fired that stone as hard as I could toward Papi. And after it left my hand, all that remained was an intense burning sensation in my right arm.

1

MY NAME IS Julio Ramirez Jr., and baseball is my whole life.

With two outs in the top of the ninth inning, we were ahead by just one run. It was an all-star game between the best junior players from here in Matanzas and the best from Colón. Winning meant getting on a bus the next morning and traveling to play a series against other all-star teams in the city of Cárdenas. And that's exactly what I wanted: a chance for the coaches of the Junior Nacional Team to see me play more.

The name RAMIREZ JR. across the back shoulders of my uniform already gets me a lot of attention. It opens people's eyes and it closes them on me, too—all because of Papi.

I turned sixteen this year. That means this is my last chance to make the team, to become a junior Nacional, representing Cuba against the best young players from other countries. For me, it's not about politics or national pride. It's strictly about baseball.

The team from Colón had a fast runner on first base.

He was tall and lanky, like a baby giraffe, with knees that almost reached to his chest when he was in full stride.

I could tell by the way he was leaning that he was looking to steal second. That would put him in scoring position, to try and tie up the game. From shortstop, I used my glove to partly shield my face so the other team couldn't see. Then I turned toward our second baseman and closed my mouth. It was a signal, letting him know I'd be covering the bag on a steal attempt.

Our pitcher was working from the stretch instead of a full windup, determined not to give the runner a head start. He was a lefty, just like Papi. And he had copied all of Papi's moves on the mound—the way he snorts like a bull ready to do battle, the way he straddles the pitching rubber with his spikes, and the way he practically glares through a runner who thinks he can steal a base off him.

It doesn't matter that the government erased Papi's name from the baseball record books the day he defected. Kids from Matanzas still remember El Fuego. They talk about their hero all the time. They want to pitch like him. Most of them want to play in the major leagues like he does, collecting megachecks. And watching our pitcher work was like seeing a highlight film of Papi from twenty years ago, from before I was even born.

I kicked hard at the dirt beneath me. Then I pounded a fist into my glove, waiting for the next pitch. But after our pitcher came set with his hands, he hesitated for a few seconds, stopping the base runner from timing the rhythm of his pitches. Only that hesitation froze me in my tracks, too, with my feet nearly glued to the ground.

As our pitcher strode toward home plate with the ball, out of the corner of my eye, I saw the runner explode out of his shoes. I held my position as long as I could. Then I broke for the bag, leaving a huge hole behind me at shortstop.

The batter swung and missed.

Our catcher leaped out of his crouch, and the iron bars of his mask spun around his face as his shoulder flew forward.

He threw a perfect strike, just a few inches over the head of our ducked-down pitcher. I could feel the runner bearing down on me, going into his slide feet first, with his spikes pointed up.

There was a *pop* as the ball hit the center of my glove.

I swiped the tag at the runner's feet. His spikes caught leather, tearing at the glove's fingers. Then I pulled my glove away, showing the umpire that I still had control of the ball.

"*Fuera!*" the umpire cried, punching the air with a closed fist.

The runner was out and the game over.

My cousin Luis raced in from center field, jumping on my shoulders to celebrate. I carried his weight for a few steps before we both tumbled onto the infield grass, laughing and smiling like little kids.

"Now we show those teams going to Cárdenas what hungry Crocodiles can do—take a bite out of their behinds," said Luis, chomping at the grass with a big grin.

Luis is a year younger than me. He was still in school and probably wouldn't have been an all-star if his father, my uncle Ramon, hadn't been our hometown coach. But Luis already knew that and didn't have any crazy dreams that he could be chosen as a Nacional.

"A few more games in this uniform, off from classes— that's all I'm asking for. I don't even care if I ride the bench," he said as we picked ourselves up off the ground and started toward the dugout, surrounded by our teammates. "But you were terrific today—three base hits and some slick plays in the field. You know those big coaches are making notes on you, and everything they're writing is good."

"I just need to keep my mind straight. Stay focused on the game in front of me, not anywhere else," I said, tossing my glove, end over end, into the dugout.

"Maybe you should forget about listening to that radio for a few days," said Luis. "Let the Series go."

I nodded my head to his advice, even though I knew that wasn't going to happen.

Over the last five years, Luis and I had become much closer, almost like brothers. His mama died of pneumonia about eleven months after Papi defected. That left us like two puzzle pieces that suddenly had a need to fit together—

him without a mother and me without a father.

"The two of you, get your gear together. Let's go home," said Uncle Ramon, his attention seemingly split between us and someone in the stands. "We've got traveling to do tomorrow. Get some rest. No partying."

"I'll be at a party, but it's not for me. I have to work tonight at the restaurant," I said, trying to give him a high five as I walked past.

Only I don't think Uncle Ramon even noticed, because he never took his hands from the pockets of his red Windbreaker. He just left me hanging.

Uncle Ramon is Papi's younger brother. They played together for the team in Matanzas for a while. Now Uncle Ramon works at one of the big sugar mills and coaches part-time at the school where Papi once did. He's tall and thin, with a pair of strong legs that are usually rooted to the ground. And when his brown hair blows around, Uncle Ramon reminds me of a palm tree that refuses to bend in the breeze.

I changed out of my cleats, packed away my glove and bats, and then slung my equipment bag over my shoulder.

On the walk out of the field house, our lefty pitcher threw an arm around me and said, "I can't believe the Marlins lost last night! Now the Series is tied one game apiece. They're not playing tonight, right? They're traveling to New York."

"I know," I said, trying to keep any emotion out of my response.

"Of course you know. Better than me," he said. "I hope El Fuego gets into the next game, shuts down those damn Yankees. Imagine a pitcher from our town with a World Series ring!"

"That would be something," I said.

"That's your genes, your blood," he said, before patting my back and then turning me loose. "Be proud."

"Without a doubt," I said, slowing down and letting him go on ahead.

That's when Uncle Ramon nearly walked up on my heels from behind.

"Sorry, Julio," he said. "My mind was somewhere else, thinking about things down the road."

In a quiet voice, I asked my uncle, "Did I make a big enough impression today?"

He stopped in his tracks. So I did, too.

"This is what I overheard some powerful people say," he answered in a tone even quieter than mine. "Senior defected. How do we know Junior won't do the same his first trip outside of Cuba? Is he so good it's worth the potential embarrassment?"

Hearing that was like getting smacked across the teeth with a baseball bat.

"So I have to pay for *his* freedom? For *him* abandoning his family?"

"If some people get their way, yes," Uncle Ramon said,

nudging me forward to start walking again. "Nothing's written in stone yet. I'm working on lots of solutions. You just concentrate on playing even better, nothing else."

I carried that heavy load out to the parking lot, where there were more beat-up bikes chained to fences than cars, including mine. Uncle Ramon suddenly veered off to the right to shake hands with an old friend of his named Gabriel, who'd been hanging around our games and practices for the past couple weeks. Luis told me that he'd even slept over at their house a few nights.

Uncle Ramon had introduced Gabriel to us as somebody he used to play baseball with. Gabriel sort of nodded his head to that with an honest enough smile. But when a ball got away from some kids playing catch, I watched him toss it back. Gabriel's form was awful, with a huge hitch in it. I would have believed he'd never thrown a ball before in his life. Besides, his hands were cracked and calloused. And the lines of his palms were embedded with grease, like he'd done more fishing than playing sports. I never mentioned it to anyone.

"See you tomorrow, boys," Gabriel called out, waving to me and my cousin after a short conversation with Uncle Ramon.

"Really?" I asked. "You're driving all the way to Cárdenas to watch us play?"

"Not so far for me. That's where I live," he said, getting into an old Chevy. "I'm hitting the road right now. I'll meet you there. Maybe show you around."

It all seemed strange. But I had too much on my mind to think any more about it as my cousin climbed into the passenger seat of my uncle's car, and I unchained my bike.

2

I RODE STRAIGHT home to take a quick shower and change my clothes. Two old men in straw hats were sitting in the shade outside our building, playing dominoes and chewing raw sugarcane. I smiled at them as I slowed down enough to throw a leg over the seat of my bike, balancing myself on one pedal.

Coming to a stop, I lifted the bike off the ground. Then I leaned back to get some momentum in my legs and started with it up the steep flight of stairs in our building.

Opening our apartment door, I got hit with a blast of hot air, as if the walls had been absorbing every bit of heat from that day, refusing to let any of it go.

Mama was at work, but my sister, Lola, was there, studying at the kitchen table. She was still dressed in her school uniform—a white blouse and yellow skirt—with textbooks spread out all around her. And every few seconds, a rotating floor fan from the living room would make it seem like a page from one of her open books was almost turning by itself.

We had no air conditioner. We could barely afford our electric bill as it was.

"How are your math calculations, Julio?" she asked, turning a pencil over and nearly rubbing a hole in her notebook paper with the pink eraser at the other end.

Lola and I actually shared an old laptop, though we didn't have a license to be on the Internet. We couldn't come close to making the kind of payments needed to become connected.

"Why aren't you working on the computer?"

"It just makes me feel even hotter. Never mind that," she said, with a hint of impatience. "Now, how are your calculations?"

"Okay, I thought, until they started mixing letters in with the numbers," I answered, dropping my equipment bag to the floor and hearing the bats inside rattle. "But no matter what, two and two still equals four. Unless your father's a defector; then they try to tell you it's something different."

"What's that mean?" she asked, sounding irritated, with a bead of sweat starting down her right temple. "Please. I can't get distracted. I have nothing but exams for the next two weeks."

"Uncle Ramon told me I might not get picked to be a Nacional, because of Papi."

I suppose there was sympathy inside of Lola somewhere. But she didn't seem interested in showing me any. Maybe it was the stifling heat or tension over her tests that put a charge into her voice.

"That's exactly why I'm going to a university one day, to become a teacher," she said, burying her head inside a book. "I'm going to make my own history, not be stuck with his. You need to do the same."

"That's good for *you*. But I'm not a student. I play baseball," I snapped, heading toward the shower. "They're always going to compare me and him."

"Then jump in the ocean and swim for Miami! Follow Papi!" Lola shouted after me, a second before I slammed the bathroom door shut.

Turning the faucets up high, I caught a glimpse of my anger in the mirror. It made my eyebrows look even sharper, as they arched at an angle, and my thin lips pulled back at the corners. Only I didn't want to face it. So I yanked the plastic curtain closed. Then I stood in the shower with my head down and the water rushing off the bridge of my nose, like it was a spout. The temperature changed from hot to cold a couple of times without warning. Lola had always said there were ghosts in the shower. But I knew it was just other tenants in our building running water at the same time.

When I finished, I dried myself and wrapped a towel around my waist. The mirror had fogged over with steam. But I'd seen enough of myself and didn't even consider wiping it clear.

Stepping outside into the hall, I saw that Lola had walked away from her textbooks. She was standing by an open window, brushing her straight black hair.

I guess we could both feel a little bit of breeze now.

"Done with your swim?" she asked, behind a half smile.

"For now," I answered. "I'll probably take another one after the game tomorrow in Cárdenas."

"Well, make sure you don't drown," she said. "I'd miss you. You're my only big brother."

"Thanks, I won't," I said, letting her words sink in as I grabbed a fresh towel from the closet and began to dry my wet head.

— — —

I put on a white shirt, black pants, and a pair of Papi's old leather shoes. Then I headed back down the stairs and walked the five blocks to the restaurant where I bussed tables. It's part of the hotel where Mama cleans. It's called El Puente—"The Bridge." That's because Matanzas is the City of Bridges, with seventeen of them crossing the three rivers surrounding us.

My shift ran from five p.m. to midnight. I got there just

a few minutes before it started. It's my job to take away the dirty dishes from the tables, make sure all of the water glasses are kept full, and deliver any part of the meal the customer wants to take home wrapped in tinfoil. The pay by the hour isn't good. But the waiters and waitresses give me and the other two busboys a small percentage of their tips every night. That adds up. The only problem I ever had was with a waiter named Horatio, who constantly hides his biggest tips by burying them in a different pocket. He gets away with it because he's the nephew of the restaurant's manager. Otherwise I'd grab him by his black bow tie, turn him upside down, and then shake him until it rained money.

The customers are mostly tourists. Lots of them are from the US, even though there's a travel ban from the States to Cuba. They go someplace like Canada first and then fly here. The US ban is because we're not a democracy and don't have any real human rights, just the ones our *presidente* and his soldiers decide to give us.

Living in a country without freedom is like being stuck at the birthday party of someone who believes he's much better than you. It doesn't matter that the party stinks and you're having a bad time. You can't leave because there are guys guarding the door with guns. And you'd better sing "Happy Birthday" with a smile when the cake comes out, even though you can't have a piece, or else you could wind up in prison.

During my shift, six or seven customers came in wearing New York Yankees caps or T-shirts. Every time I saw one, my stomach churned with acid over Papi and the World Series. Then, around nine o'clock, the manager called me over to a table and introduced me to a customer as El Fuego's son.

A man in a Yankees cap shook my hand. Then the manager translated his English for me, even though I understood some of what he was saying.

"Pleasure to meet you, Julio. I'm normally a big fan of your father's, just not right now. I'd rather see *my* team win. But you must be so proud of him," he said.

I nodded and said, *"Sí. Sí."*

The man stood next to me so his wife could take a photo. It was his idea for us each to make a fist. We lined them up, knuckles to knuckles, as if we were fighting over the Series. An instant before the camera's click, I saw Mama standing in the doorway of the restaurant. She was dressed in her blue maid's uniform and apron. Her tired eyes caught mine and I looked away from the lens.

His wife wanted a better photo, so we posed again.

Mama jutted her chin in the direction of our apartment and mouthed, *See you at home*. Then she walked out the door.

After the second photo, the man smiled and stuffed ten pesos into my shirt pocket. That was more than two weeks' salary for me.

"Gracias," I responded, feeling better about the whole encounter.

A few minutes later, that river rat Horatio asked about the tip I got.

"Shouldn't that be for you and me to share?" he asked. "It happened in my section of tables."

I couldn't believe his nerve.

I looked Horatio square in the eye and said, "It's in my shirt pocket. Why don't you stick your hand in there and take it."

Only he never tried.

That same couple had me wrap up a pork chop for them to take home. It was a beautiful one that neither of them had even touched. I brought it back to their table, but they forgot it and left the bag behind.

Workers aren't supposed to take food out of the restaurant for any reason. But I kept thinking how good that pork chop would taste on the bus ride to Cárdenas. So I hid it in a small alcove, beneath a wicker breadbasket. And when my shift was finally finished, I made sure no one was watching as I tucked it beneath my arm and headed out the kitchen door.

— — —

I turned the key in the lock. Then I stepped inside our apartment. Mama was sitting on the far end of the couch in her pink seashell bathrobe. There was a single lamp lit over her left shoulder. She had a newspaper spread open on her lap, reading it while she worked at her fingernails with a small file.

I figured my sister was already asleep in the bedroom.

"A pork chop from El Puente. No lecture, please," I said, showing off the silver tinfoil like a prize before making a quick detour to put it into the fridge.

When I circled back, Mama had a serious look on her face. But it didn't have anything to do with taking food from my job.

"Lola told me your name might stop you from becoming a Nacional."

"Maybe. But my name didn't hurt me tonight," I said, taking the ten-peso note from my shirt pocket, then pulling it tight from opposite ends with a snap. "That photo I was posing for."

I placed it on a small table beside some bills that needed to be paid, like rent and electricity. There was also a bill for the two cell phones the three of us shared, making calls only when it was something really important.

"Your father lives like a king while we struggle," Mama said. "Sometimes I think money was the reason he defected."

"Not baseball? Not a World Series ring?"

"He wants a *ring*? How about this one?" she asked, pointing to her gold wedding band. "Know why I still wear this?"

"No," I answered, closing the distance between us.

"It's all I have left," she said, as her temper began to flare. "This way, I'm the wife of a sports hero who gave this government the middle finger for the whole world to see."

"And without it?"

"Then I'm just the woman he abandoned."

"He abandoned me and Lola, too."

"But he'll always be your father, no matter what," Mama said. The newspaper fell to the floor as she stood up. "He won't always be my husband. I'm not stupid, Julio. You're old enough to hear this. The great El Fuego has not been alone for six years, not without a woman by his side—one probably ten years younger than me."

I'd never heard her talk like that before, and now the shadows fell across her face.

"See these fingernails?" she asked, holding her hands out. "Maybe I can't tell you the name of the woman he's with. But I'm sure her nails aren't chipped from cleaning hotel rooms and scrubbing toilets. They're probably perfect and polished at a salon."

I didn't know what to say. I just knew that suddenly I was even angrier at Papi.

"You need to make your own life now. Take that money. It's yours," Mama said, becoming calmer and kissing me good night on the forehead. "Treat yourself to something nice. His *name* owes you that, for having to carry it this long."

Then she went into the bedroom, closing the door behind her.

For almost a half hour, I paced the living room, cursing Papi to myself until I was too exhausted to keep going. Finally, I took the cushions off the couch and folded out the bed inside. Then I lay there for a while with the light on, staring up at every crack in the ceiling over my head.

3

BY SIX THIRTY a.m., I was on my feet again. The sunlight was just starting to push past the curtains as I packed up my baseball gear and got myself ready to go. Only I didn't touch the tip money from the night before. And I didn't go near the refrigerator either. Instead, I left that pork chop where it was, for my mother and sister, who were both still sleeping.

The team was meeting in the parking lot outside our field. That was more than a mile away. So I lugged my bike down the stairs. Then I tied my equipment bag to the back before I rode out into the street.

Almost all the cars on the road here are American, built in the 1950s—Chevrolet, Plymouth, Ford, and Dodge. They're huge cars with wide bodies, fancy grilles, big headlights, and shining chrome everywhere. Some have windshields that wrap all the way around. Others have sleek fins or wings in the back, with long red taillights that make them look like rocket sleds ready to blast off.

It's been that way since the US stopped selling cars to

Cuba in 1962, to protest our government. It's like living in some kind of time warp. We see modern sports cars like Porsches, Jaguars, and BMWs in contraband magazines and pirated DVDs of movies. Everyone here knows about them, what they look like. But I guess we're supposed to pretend they don't really exist. We know about the Chevy Nova, too. In Spanish, *no va* means "doesn't go," so we all thought that was pretty funny. But I don't think anybody here would turn down a new car, no matter how stupid its name.

There aren't any spare parts coming into Cuba either. That doesn't matter. People here will use anything to keep their cars running, like leather belts that once held up pants and electric fuses from toasters. When cars break down totally, people keep them in their yards behind locked fences and make money selling off the parts one by one. And if I had known the police officers were going to confiscate Papi's car, a 1958 Dodge Royal in good condition, I would have pulled out the brakes to sell and left those officers rolling off the road, straight into the surf.

Pedaling closer to the field, I saw a big yellow school bus parked in the lot. The morning sun was getting stronger, glistening off its roof. As I sped through the gate, I noticed the driver inside that bus walking the length of it, opening all the windows before it became a big metal hotbox. Lots of our players were already there, and more were arriving right behind me, by bike and on foot. Just one other vehicle was there. It was a Russian-made car and almost like new, maybe from the 1980s. There was no doubt it was for the top tier of the Junior Nacional coaches to ride in.

Uncle Ramon was standing inside a small circle of those coaches, talking. His back was to me. Just to his right, I could see the bloated face of Coach Moyano, the one responsible for picking the players. Moyano was short and overweight, wearing pants that were baggy enough for two people to use as a tent on a camping trip. I'd seen him a dozen or more times. The bottom half of his eyelids were always puffed out, like he'd never had a good night's sleep in his life. And except for the red Nacionales cap on his head, you probably would have figured him for a butcher or a sanitation worker before a baseball coach.

I was getting off my bike and resting it against a fence when Moyano's eyes settled sharply on mine. I felt like he was looking right through me, judging me inside and out, as he chomped away on an unlit cigar. From the corner of his mouth, he spit a stream of brown saliva onto the ground. Then he said something, and Uncle Ramon turned to look in my direction. That's when I quickly turned away from them both.

A few feet away from me, Luis was lying flat on his back on the paved asphalt. His eyes were closed, his bag beneath his head as a pillow. He was surrounded by six or seven of our teammates, looking equally exhausted after a night of partying. Only most of them were up on their feet.

"Junior," said one of our guys, reaching out to connect his fist with mine. "I'm glad our best player looks like he's ready to swing for the fences right now."

"You could wake me up in the middle of the night to hit. I wouldn't care," I said, bringing my hands and wrists together in front of me, as if I were gripping a bat. "But listen, no more 'Junior.' From now on it's just Julio."

"Got it," he said, before lowering his voice to nearly a whisper. "Man, if you're not picked starting shortstop for the Nacionales, it's a crime."

I didn't say a word back. But I extended my fist one more time to bump with his again.

"Hey, Cuz," Luis called up to me from the ground. "My pop didn't want to leave his car here overnight. So we walked all the way. Guess who carried the equipment?"

"Don't have to guess," I answered. "The sweat stains by your armpits say *you* were the donkey—Uncle's little *burrito*."

"That should be my official position on this team," he said, smiling. "You know it's true."

Uncle Ramon was twice as hard on Luis as on any other player. He had to be. That way the other guys didn't resent Luis being an all-star. In fact, Luis got less playing time than anyone. And his was usually the first name out of my uncle's mouth whenever he needed somebody to take a bucket and gather up over a hundred loose baseballs in the outfield.

The day he picked Luis as part of the team to represent

Matanzas, Uncle Ramon had told me in private, "A father needs to do this for his son—find a way to keep him by his side. Right or wrong, that's a father's job."

That struck a raw nerve in me. And I went home feeling more jealous of their relationship than I could ever remember.

The driver started up the bus with a *ggrrrr-rrrr-rrr*. Then the doors folded open and players began piling inside. I gave Luis a hand, pulling him to his feet. Beneath him, on the gray asphalt, he'd left behind a damp imprint of his body that the sun was already starting to fade.

As I climbed the bus's steps, a dark-skinned man with a bushy mustache and goatee, sitting in the driver's spot, turned up the volume on a boom box jammed between the dashboard and his seat.

"*Muchachos*, my name is Paulo. It's fifty-three miles to Cárdenas," he bellowed down the rows of seats with a big grin, as salsa music drowned out the sound of the engine. "There's no bathroom on this bus. So take care of your personal business now, before it becomes my business."

"We pee out the window!" somebody called out.

Everyone cracked up laughing, including Paulo.

"If you do, be very careful," Paulo replied, without missing a beat. "Birds are hungry to eat little *inchworms* this time of the morning."

That got an even bigger laugh. Suddenly, it seemed like no one was interested in sleeping anymore. I parked myself by a window in the row right behind Luis. On the open seat next to me, I put my bag with all of my baseball gear. That's when I noticed Uncle Ramon walking toward the bus, while that car with Moyano and the other coaches inside was pulling out of the lot.

"I must be loco to want to ride in this hunk of junk instead of that air-conditioned dream," announced Uncle Ramon as he climbed aboard. "But I just love to be around baseball players."

That got a huge cheer, and even Paulo raised his voice in approval.

Then, as the bus jerked forward, I looked out the window and saw that Luis's imprint on the asphalt was almost gone. As we rolled to the gate, I realized the chain on my bike was unlocked. I didn't want to cry out like a baby for the bus to stop. I just hoped the bike would still be there, with its handlebar stuck through the chain-link fence, when I got back.

Since those Nacional coaches had been hanging around, kids were careful whenever they talked about El Fuego being in the World Series. They didn't want to be overheard glorifying a traitor, hurting their own chances of being picked for the junior traveling team. But with Moyano and his crew out of earshot, and Uncle Ramon riding with us, the conversation turned to that subject fast.

"I heard it might be raining at Yankee Stadium. That the

game tonight could get postponed," said one of our players.

I tapped at the transistor radio in my pocket, making sure it was still there.

"It would have to be enough rain for Noah and his ark," replied another player. "That's a World Series game you're talking about."

"Tonight's game is a huge one," said Uncle Ramon. "One team is going to take a two-to-one lead in the Series."

"Still, it's not Game Seven. When it's tied up, three to three," said our left-handed pitcher, who stood in the aisle mimicking Papi's windup, "that one's for all the marbles. Everything. With the whole world watching."

Then he followed through, releasing an invisible base-ball in my direction.

My heart jumped a little as I almost put my hands up to catch it.

"Imagine making millions of US dollars to play," our pitcher added. "Money. Freedom. Baseball. That's the life."

I let that sink deep inside of me. Meanwhile, a steady *hummm* vibrated up through the wheels and into my seat as we passed over the metal grating of the bridge, leaving Matanzas. Out the window, I could see the river below. And without a shred of wind, the blue water looked smooth as glass, with the bus's yellow reflection sailing across.

"It's not about the money. I guarantee it," responded

Uncle Ramon. "I used to be El Fuego's catcher, before there was *any* money or fame. That was when we played for pride on fields littered with broken bottles, in shorts and T-shirts. We were both crazy for the game. Anyone here know what they call the catcher's equipment—the mask, shin guards, chest protector?"

"I know," answered Manuel, our catcher. "Tools of ignorance."

"That's right—because you take an unholy beating back there. You have to be half-stupid to even want to play the position," said Uncle Ramon, knocking a fist against his own skull, before displaying his two crooked pinkies. "You break fingers, block pitches in the dirt with your chest, and take foul tips off every part of your body. And don't even think about going behind the plate without wearing a cup to protect your jewels."

"I got hit *there* once," said Manuel, cringing a little bit. "Even with a cup it hurts."

"But catchers know the game better than anybody, because we see the whole field in front of us," said Uncle Ramon. "I used to start out to the mound in the middle of an inning, to tell *El Fuego* what I was thinking. He'd wave me off, saying, 'The only thing you know about pitching is that you can't hit it.'"

"What did you say back?" asked Manuel.

"Nothing. He was my older brother," answered Uncle Ramon. "But there was one league game when an umpire from Havana was squeezing the strike zone on him really bad, calling all of El Fuego's pitches on the corner of the plate balls. I turned around to look at him and that umpire says, 'I'll tell you what a strike is and what's not. Look at me again and you're ejected.'"

"What happened?" asked one of our players.

"The next pitch, I called for one high and outside, just above my right shoulder, where that umpire was squatting behind me. At first El Fuego shook me off. But I called for it a second time, until he finally nodded his head," said Uncle Ramon. "He put that pitch exactly where I asked for it—his best fastball. Then I lowered my mitt a few inches."

Luis glanced back at me. We'd heard this story plenty of times growing up.

"The pitch hit that bastard in the middle of his mask— *ping*," said Uncle Ramon. "Knocked him out cold."

"Did you get in trouble?" Manuel asked, excitedly.

"They called us both to appear in front of the local sports commissioner. Right after the game, before we could get our stories straight," he continued. "El Fuego said it was *his* fault. That he crossed me up by reading my signals wrong. That I was expecting a curveball. The commissioner screamed at us for twenty minutes. Then he let us go with just a warning. My brother was pissed at me for a few hours, for causing all that trouble. But later on, he slapped my back and said, 'Screw that umpire for trying to take away what's mine. He got exactly what he deserved.' We laughed the rest of the night over it."

Papi's version of that story wasn't exactly the same as Uncle Ramon remembered it. Some of the facts of who did what were a little different. Only the conclusion didn't change: nobody would ever again take away what belonged to El Fuego.

4

MORE THAN AN hour later, we reached Cárdenas. The bus rolled along the coastline, past rocky beaches, the bay, and empty docks where fishing boats had probably been out on the water since before sunrise.

Then our driver, Paulo, turned the wheel inland, into the countryside. On his lap, he began unfolding a paper map until it looked like there was no way on earth it could ever become a neat rectangle again. Eventually, we pulled up to a baseball field behind an old boarding school with a one-story, flat-roofed dormitory.

The Nacional coaches, including Moyano, who was still chomping on that unlit cigar, were already there, waiting beside their car.

"This is it—the place where you're going to make your mark," Luis said to me. "Outplay those other shortstops for a spot on the junior team."

"How about you?" I asked, as Paulo brought us to a stop

and the bus's doors opened with a belch of air. "What are you going to do here?"

"Maybe play a few innings. Catch some rays in the out-field," he answered with a widening grin. "Then hit the beach in my uniform top. Impress the local senoritas. That's my plan—like a little vacation."

Uncle Ramon was the first one off the bus. He was talk-ing with those big shots while the rest of us unloaded the gear and gathered outside. A few dark clouds were hanging low in the sky over our heads, covering up the sun.

A moment later, Moyano, with his hand on Uncle Ramon's shoulder, spoke to us. "When this tournament is over tomor-row, some of you will be playing for me as Nacionales," said Moyano, through the chewed-up cigar in the corner of his mouth. "Other teams are here from Cárdenas, Santa Clara, and Puerto Padre. They're your competition. We only want the best of the best. Cuba's best. Our proudest. I won't accept anything less. You know who you are. How you have to per-form. You only let yourselves down when you fail, because we'll find someone hungrier to take your place. Remember that. Now your coach will give you instructions."

As a sprinkle of rain began to fall, Uncle Ramon cleared his throat and stepped forward from Moyano's grasp.

"Dormitory number four, that's ours. It's two players to a room. Breakfast is in the cafeteria, and then we're on the field for practice at eleven o'clock. We play Puerto Padre at twelve thirty. I'll post the lineup inside our dugout soon."

He seemed to be done talking, so most of us started toward the dorms, including me. Then Uncle Ramon spoke again and my feet came to a halt, gripping the gravel below them.

"For lots of you, this is a dream. But it's a dream that can slip away with age faster than you think. I know all about that," he said, touching a few gray hairs around his temple. "Don't let this chance pass you by without a fight. Approach it with passion. At least then you'll always be able to live with yourself, no matter what the outcome. Now, go prepare yourselves."

Walking to the dorms, I felt a kind of electricity revving up and pulsing through me from Uncle Ramon's words. And I could feel that same energy jumping off most of my teammates.

As another raindrop tapped my forehead, I separated myself from the others by falling back a little bit. Then, instead of entering the dorm, I walked behind a large wooden shed filled with gardening tools. I looked around in every direction. When I was sure no one could see me, I took the transistor radio out from my pocket.

I wanted to know about the weather for the World Series.

The reception from the US stations during the day isn't nearly as good as at night. It's constantly cutting in and out.

So I pressed the blue plastic radio with the black dials up against my ear, struggling to hear.

> *Nightly forecast . . . intermittent showers . . . Yan-*
> *kee Stadium . . . Game Three of the Series . . . tied at*
> *one . . . the visiting Miami Marlins . . . under way at*
> *eight . . . clearing later tonight . . . now a word from . . .*
> *all your lumber and hardware needs. . . .*

Luis and I shared a tiny room with two single beds in it. They were perfectly made up, covered in worn-out comforters and pillowcases. A see-through plastic tub, to store belongings, peeked out from the floor beneath each one. There was a nightstand with a lamp on it between the beds. And the one bathroom was down the hall for the entire team to use.

I thought of the fancy hotel suite that Papi was probably staying in, after arriving in New York on the Marlins' private jet. But I wouldn't give him the satisfaction of wanting to trade places.

My cousin grabbed the bed closest to the door.

"Sometimes I need to *go* in the middle of the night," he said. "This'll make it easier. I won't wake you."

"That's fine," I said, pulling the tub out from under my bed. "This is better than sleeping on a foldout couch. That's all I care about."

Before Luis unpacked, he put a small framed photo of his mother, Blanca, on the nightstand. He crossed himself. Then, with a click of the lamp, the warm, bright light shone on her face.

Nobody expected my aunt to die. She was completely healthy before getting pneumonia. The doctors said my aunt was so strong that she'd walked around with it for two weeks doing her normal chores—laundry, cooking, a weekend shift in the sugarcane refinery. So when the phone call came from the hospital that Aunt Blanca had died, none of us believed it. We thought there had to be some mistake. But there wasn't.

I swear, Luis cried for a week straight. His eyes would water everywhere—home, church, the funeral, and school. And it didn't look like he had one bit of shame over it either. When Papi left, I cried a lot, too. Only I wouldn't do it in front of anyone. I didn't even want people to see that my eyes were red.

Since then, we've had plenty of sleepovers together, both at my house and his. Luis would always say his prayers before bed. Like a little kid, he'd get on his knees with his hands clasped in front of him and close his eyes. Then his mouth would move with no sound coming out, until he was finished. I never poked fun at him over it. I'd just stay quiet and try to be respectful.

"My son has faith in his prayers," Uncle Ramon once

told me. "I quit praying a long time ago. I believe God already knows what we want. Why should I bother *Him*? I'll work on those things myself."

I stopped believing in a lot of things when Papi turned his back on us. And if I ever have any praying to do, I save it for when I'm rounding third base, hoping to be safe at home plate.

The cafeteria was packed with more than a hundred players and coaches. We were stuck in a long line of people holding red plastic trays and moving slowly between two silver rails along a glass counter. Older women wearing paper hats that looked like sailboats were serving breakfast. There were scrambled eggs and bacon, waffles, cold cereal, fruit, and tostada—toasted bread—to dunk in milk or *café con leche*.

I'd been drinking coffee for a few years, and liked it most in the morning.

"That stuff's nasty," said Luis as I poured myself a cup. "Too bitter."

"Stick to chocolate milk, little boy," I needled him. "When you're ready to put some hair on your chest, I'll let you try some of this."

"I've had it before. Makes me jumpy. I'm hyper enough," he said, biting into a strip of bacon as we moved forward. "But I like coffee ice cream."

As we came off the line, the cafeteria looked like it was divided into four separate camps. That's because the all-star teams were sitting at their own tables, dressed in different colored uniforms. But there were only three players who weren't from Matanzas who had my attention. Those were the other shortstops I was in competition with. The most important one was Chico López from Puerto Padre, our opponent that afternoon. He was a show-off with a big ego. They called him "Matador," because he used his glove like a bullfighter wields a cape. He tried to make even the most routine plays look flashy that way. And on his feet he wore a pair of spikes painted gold, just to stand out.

Once I reached our section of tables, my eyes went searching for Matador.

Only his eyes found me first.

"Behind you, coming off the breakfast line," Luis said, tapping my shoulder. "That hotdogger's looking right at you."

His gold spikes were hanging around his neck like a pair of boxing gloves. And the closer he got, the more his eyes riveted onto mine.

"That's a challenge if I ever saw one," said Luis, sounding insulted. "A challenge to my family."

"Calm down. He's grilling me, not you."

Matador stopped a few feet from our table.

"All those millions and your pop can't buy you a decent

pair of shoes," he said, spying my beat-up cleats on the floor beside me while balancing his tray on the fingertips of one hand. "What a pity."

Luis cursed at him. But I just focused on the black pupils of his brown eyes.

"Nope, no Nike shoes," I said, dunking bread into my coffee. "Just that glove I wear. You want to try it on one day? See if it fits?"

He sucked his teeth at me with a sharp *thhh* and walked off.

"Want me to knock that tray out of his pretty little hands? I will," steamed Luis. "I've got nothing to lose. They suspend me, I'll have more time for the beach."

"That's tough talk coming from somebody with a chocolate milk mustache," I said.

Then I stared down Luis until he was almost forced to smile.

"Let Matador run his mouth," I said, poking my eggs with a plastic fork. "He doesn't understand how much it motivates me. None of them do, especially those coaches for the Nacionales."

After breakfast, we all grabbed our gear and headed for the field house. We changed in a damp locker room, behind and a few steps below our third-base dugout.

I looked into the one mirror there, tightening the belt on my red uniform with the green crocodile swinging a baseball bat. Then I pulled my cap down low over my eyes.

"Crocodiles, let's take the field together!" shouted Uncle Ramon from the doorway, with a clap of his hands. "One team! One mind! Matanzas!"

We moved through a short hall, with our spikes scratching the floor, and then into the dugout. That's when I first caught sight of the field. Maybe it was something that had been building up inside of me, begging to be released—the pressure, the anger. I wasn't sure. But for a moment, seeing that field was like walking out into a brand-new world. Every dark cloud in the sky had burned off beneath the sun. The grass was the brightest green I'd ever seen, still glistening from the rain. There wasn't a single rock or even a pebble on the base paths. And I didn't know how a baseball could ever take a bad hop on a diamond that perfect.

So I stepped out onto the grass. It was cut about an inch high all the way across in two different directions, looking like a checkerboard. The soft cushion felt great beneath my feet. It reminded me of walking on the thick carpet in the hotel lobby where Mama worked.

I decided to loosen up my legs by jogging in the outfield. Soon Luis was running beside me. The outfield fences were a few feet lower than the ones back home.

"I love these low fences. Watch this," said Luis, increasing his speed.

Luis headed straight for the fence in full stride. Then he

planted his foot at the bottom and scaled it with a flying leap. He threw his arm way over the top, as if he were bringing a home run back into the park.

"I could have jumped right over if I wanted," said Luis, grinning and hanging on top of the fence by his armpit.

He seemed so happy to be up there, I went sprinting for that fence myself. Then I leaped and took flight, joining him. The two of us just hung there for a while, laughing and looking over both sides. It wasn't until Uncle Ramon called the team together for fielding practice that I even thought about coming down.

I put my glove on and took about twenty ground balls at shortstop, firing a half dozen of them over to first base. A few minutes later, Uncle Ramon walked to the mound to pitch batting practice. So I raced into the dugout to grab a bat and take my swings. Pinned to the wall was the starting lineup. In the leadoff spot, Uncle Ramon had written my name in thick black marker.

PLAYER POS.
1. Ramirez Jr. SS

As I stepped back outside with a bat on my shoulder, I heard my name—"Julio!"—and clapping from the stands. Maybe forty or fifty people were already there, watching practice and waiting for the first game to begin. The voice sounded familiar, but I couldn't place it. Following the echo of the last few claps, I saw it was Uncle Ramon's friend Gabriel. He was wearing a flower-print shirt, shorts, sandals, and sunglasses. And I couldn't help thinking he looked as out of place there as that fat slob Moyano did being a baseball coach.

5

SOON IT WAS Matador and his Puerto Padre teammates' turn on the field. I sat in our dugout watching him take ground balls. The growing crowd in the stands was really into it. There were oohs and aahs every time he flashed leather, and even I was impressed with his glove.

Then Matador finally booted a ball, trying to be too slick.

"Why are your spikes *yellow*? So you can have some mustard on that hot dog?" Luis, who wasn't in our starting lineup, shouted. "I hope that one tasted good!"

The players on our bench loved that remark.

"Bueno," said Uncle Ramon, clapping quietly. "I knew there was a reason I picked you for this team, son."

Luis was grinning from ear to ear. Matador glanced into our dugout, spitting sunflower seeds from his mouth and pointing to the ground with his middle finger. Most of our guys were pissed at that. So was I. Only I kept my expression blank, not wanting to show any emotion or get involved in that nonsense.

After the players from Puerto Padre took batting practice, a professional-looking grounds crew came onto the field. I guess they worked for Moyano and the Nacionales. They used a bucket of chalk dust to mark the lines between fair and foul territory, and a rigid template to draw the batter's box. Then they cleaned the footprints from all the bases and home plate, leaving them sparkling white. Their work was almost perfect, except for a few inches down the right-field line. That's where their straight line bent a bit, becoming uneven. None of the coaches or players complained about it. But I saw it plain as day, and deep down, it really bothered me.

Uncle Ramon went out to home plate, to meet with the umpires and exchange lineup cards with the coach from Puerto Padre. For some reason Moyano was out there, too. That blowhard was dominating the conversation. And everyone there seemed to be listening intently, as if all of the baseballs in Cuba belonged to him.

A few minutes later, Puerto Padre took the field. A bunch of younger kids marched out in their school uniforms. One of the boys held the Cuban flag and two others had drums hanging from their necks. The instant they started to beat the rhythm of our national anthem, everyone took off their caps and hats. Then those kids started singing. So did lots of people. I just moved my mouth without any words really coming out.

"Hasten to battle . . . do not fear a glorious death . . ."

My mind was mostly on the game. But for a few seconds, I thought about how Papi took his cap off now to the US anthem and sometimes the Canadian one whenever the Marlins played there.

Our anthem was written by a general during a war. Eventually, he was captured by the Spanish, and he sang it while they lined him up in front of a firing squad.

"To live in chains is to live in dishonor . . . hear the call of the bugle . . . hasten, brave ones . . ."

When the singing was finished I stuffed my cap into my back pocket. Then I put on a protective batting helmet.

I moved closer to the plate, taking a few practice swings with a weighted donut on my bat. It was like whipping around a heavy tree branch. But once I popped that donut off, my swing felt lightning-fast.

"Be a hitter, Julio," said Uncle Ramon, coaching third base.

Their pitcher took his final warm-up toss before I stepped into the batter's box. Digging my heels into the dirt, I purposely wiped out the chalk line behind me. That way I could plant my back foot where I wanted, and not be trapped inside that small space.

No pitcher wants to begin the game by falling behind in the count. So I was sure he'd throw me a first-pitch strike. I stayed loose and relaxed during his windup, zoning in as the ball escaped his hand.

With that pitch halfway to home plate, time seemed to slow down. I could see the baseball clearly—the white covering and every red stitch across its seams. An instant later, I heard the *crack* of the ball off my wooden bat. It was slicing over the second baseman, heading for the gap between center and right field.

Sprinting down the first-base line, a split second before I made the turn toward second base, I heard a horn blow from the stands, maybe a trumpet or a bugle. The sound of it jolted me forward a step. Picking up my head, I saw that the right fielder had cut off the ball. But the decision inside my head was already made for me.

The voices and crowd noise filled my ears as I streaked for second, reaching with every stride.

"Rápido! Rápido!"

A few feet from the bag, I dove headfirst, with my arms out in front. I went sliding through the dirt until I was almost swimming in it.

My hands grabbed the base before Matador slapped his tag on my shoulder.

I stood up as fast as I could, even taller than Matador

now with that base safely beneath me. Then I smacked the front of my uniform clean, creating a cloud of dirt that settled on Matador's gold spikes.

That's when that horn in the crowd blew again.

My eyes searched the stands, trying to find it. There were probably close to four hundred people there now. It sounded like it was coming from where Gabriel was. Only I could see that he didn't have one.

The next batter ripped a base hit into the right-field corner, more than a foot inside that crooked foul line. I steamed around third base with Uncle Ramon's right arm spinning like a windmill to urge me on. I scored the game's first run and didn't slow up until three strides past home plate.

Waiting on the top step of the dugout, Luis was the first one to give me a high five.

"That's how to start things," he said as I plopped myself down on the bench, trying to catch my breath.

My heart jumped at another blast from that horn. Only I was too winded to get up and see where it was coming from.

We scored two more runs that inning to take a 3–0 lead.

In the bottom of the first, Matador came to the plate for Puerto Padre. He was a slap hitter who choked up on the bat with a tight, white-knuckled grip. He'd step partly out of the batter's box after every pitch and go through his usual routine. First he'd tap at his gold spikes with the bat. Then he'd lean back and readjust his helmet. Finally, he'd hold his hand up to the umpire to show that he wasn't ready yet, while he reset his stance.

"That whole show of his is about calling attention to himself," Uncle Ramon once told me. "If Matador ever tried that with your father on the mound, he'd get drilled in the rib cage with a fastball."

Matador chopped down on the ball, sending a two-hopper my way. I could see him motoring down the line. I knew I had to charge the ball and get to it as quickly as possible. The thick grass slowed it up, and I was running out of time. So I made the decision to forget about my glove and barehand the ball. It spun sharply into my palm, biting at my skin. Then I positioned my fingers around the seams and, in one motion, gunned the ball to first on a frozen rope.

I heard the *pop* of the first baseman's mitt an instant before those gold spikes hit the bag. I was already smiling in Uncle Ramon's direction when the umpire called Matador out. If there's anything Papi handed down to me, it's this cannon I have for an arm. But for the next few minutes, inside my right hand I could see and feel the imprint from the stitches on that ball.

I came to bat in the next inning with two runners on base. Puerto Padre's pitcher had been getting roughed up, and I could see how angry he was. Matador called something to him, too low for me to hear.

It didn't take long, though, for me to guess what he'd said. Not after the first pitch knocked me back off the plate with a whistle. It was chin music, meant to make me start thinking instead of reacting. Only I wouldn't bend to anything like that, and just dug my heels in even deeper. I slammed his next pitch over the center fielder's head, up against the wall Luis and I had climbed.

There was no hesitation as I rounded first. I was intent on at least a triple. Hitting second base, I was in full flight as I passed Matador, who'd drifted into the outfield, waiting for a relay throw.

Flying for third, my head rose up and the breeze took my helmet off. As I felt it go and saw Uncle Ramon giving me the stop sign—to come in standing up without having to slide—I dropped my hands behind my back, catching my helmet before it hit the ground.

Confidence was soaring through me. I stood on third base like I owned it, as if no one could ever take it away. Not Matador. Not an umpire. Not even Moyano. I felt like Superman in a baseball uniform. Then Uncle Ramon pointed to the helmet in my hands. I wanted to toss it aside. Only something in me thought better of it. I spread the earflaps wide and put it back on my head.

Three innings later, we were leading 9–0 when Matador came to bat with two outs and the bases loaded. I wanted to whisper to our pitcher to drill him in the ribs. But that would have given Puerto Padre their first run. And I liked looking at their row of goose eggs on the scoreboard.

Instead, I pounded a fist into my glove, keeping ready on my toes.

The next pitch was a mistake. It was a slider, left up and out over the middle of the plate. I swear I saw Matador's eyes light up as his bat rushed forward. He hit a lined shot headed straight for me.

It was rising in a hurry and I had just a fraction of a second to set my feet.

I leaped straight up into the air.

I was up so high I would have believed there were springs on the bottom of my shoes and not spikes.

My left elbow nearly came out of its socket as I thrust my arm skyward, with only my glove to trust in. The ball caught the very top of the webbing, and I squeezed my fingers. I crashed to the ground with my arm still in the air, away from my body. Then I heard a roar from the crowd. The bottom half of the ball had stuck inside my glove, with the top half peeking out. It looked like an ice-cream cone. And I gently carried it that way to our dugout as my teammates slapped me on the back to celebrate.

"This is for you," I said to Luis. "Here's that ice cream you wanted."

It looked like Uncle Ramon was putting him into the

game, because he had a helmet on and a bat in his hands. Luis stuck his tongue out and took a big pretend lick.

"Thanks, Primo," he said. "Tastes even better knowing who you robbed for it."

Then Uncle Ramon, with a face as serious as a stone statue's, took the ball and glove from my hand. I thought he might be taking me out of the game. But that wasn't it.

"Someone wants to speak to you," he said, pointing to the hall that led to the locker room behind our dugout. "Go now. See what it is."

All I could think was that even Superman had Kryptonite to worry about. So I took a deep breath and a hesitant step in that direction, trading a sparkling baseball diamond for the shadows inside that doorway.

6

I **DESCENDED SOME** stairs and turned the corner into the damp locker room. No light was on. But several small streams of sunlight were seeping in through the slatted wall, from the field outside.

In the center of the room, Moyano was sitting on a tabletop. His stubby legs, dangling beneath him, didn't even reach the floor.

"Junior, please enter," he said, drenched in shadows. "We need to have some conversation."

"My name's *Julio*," I replied, adding more bass to my voice so it would carry in that near-empty room.

"Of course it is. Just like your papi's."

Moyano's fingers struck the side of the table. The next moment, they seemed to be on fire. Then I saw him cup the long wooden match inside his hands and finally light the cigar that had been in his mouth since we'd left Matanzas.

"I understand you want to represent Cuba, as a Nacional," he said, through a cloud of smoke that was already drifting in my direction. "Give me a good reason. Why should that be?"

"Because I'm the best shortstop my age," I answered, with more emotion than I was comfortable with. "Baseball's my life. I live it, breathe it."

"I can sympathize. This game is my life as well," he said. "Not playing, but assembling a team that brings our leaders glory. That also includes choosing players who will safeguard them from embarrassment and shame—the kind your traitor father brought upon them."

I wanted to charge Moyano right there, knocking him off that table and onto his fat ass. It was all right for me to think and feel anything I wanted about Papi. I didn't want to hear a negative word about my own flesh and blood from that ugly toad.

But I understood that he basically held my future in his hands. That's when I steadied myself, thinking this might be part of some test, to see how I'd react.

I wasn't sure what to say, so I decided to keep quiet.

"You must have felt that shame. At how he abandoned you, your family," he said, turning his eyes, with their bulging lower lids, toward my locker. "Look at your clothes hanging there. How old are they? How many times has your mama used a needle and thread on those pants? I know your father doesn't dress that shabby. You don't look like a millionaire's son."

The smoke from his cigar reached me, and I could feel a burning inside my nostrils.

"If you become one of *my* players, I'll dress you. You'll be wearing a uniform that *I* give you. I'll be your new papi."

I didn't want to charge Moyano anymore. Instead, I wanted to strangle him with my bare hands. That way he'd never open his mouth again.

"Maybe you're listening to him pitch in the World Series," he said. "I've heard that a few players from Matanzas still have some misguided pride in El Fuego."

I shook my head no. I'd been smart enough to leave my transistor radio in the dorm room, beneath the mattress of my bed.

Suddenly, the locker room rattled with the stamping of feet from our dugout. We were probably scoring more runs, and I could hear the echo of Uncle Ramon's voice cheering the team on.

"It's hurt him, too, you know—your uncle," said Moyano.

"What has?"

"Your papi's actions," he answered. "He's a good coach. Maybe even Nacional material. But he can never be trusted to travel off this island. Could be he disappears while we're playing in Amsterdam or Japan. Why not? His wife is already dead."

I couldn't believe he was talking about Aunt Blanca that

way, as if her death was just another circumstance for him to make decisions.

"Maybe El Fuego sends someone for him. Ramon decides to leave his son behind. It happens. True?" he continued on, like I was a pincushion for his jabs. "I enjoy my job. I can't risk those things, not for a coach."

That remark started me thinking. In my mind, that meant there was a chance Moyano might risk it for a *player*, a star shortstop.

Moyano took a long pull on his cigar, causing the tip to glow a bright orange. Then, for the first time, I saw him take it from his lips. He held the cigar out in front of him, tapping it with a finger. The ashes silently fell to the floor and flickered out.

"So, speak for yourself," said Moyano, acting as judge and jury. "I want to hear."

The last thing I wanted to do was sound like I was pleading. But I felt like I needed to defend myself.

"No one's better than me. Not Matador, no one. I make all of my teammates better. I hit, field, throw, run the bases—all the tools are mine. I just want to compete at the highest level."

"That's it? Nothing more?"

"I'm a baseball player, not a public speaker."

"No, you're a busboy," said Moyano, the smoke billowing from his lips. "You're only a baseball player if I say you are."

"Just let me go."

"*Go?* Or do you mean *defect?* To where, the United States? So you can fill your belly with McDonald's and Pepsi, on your papi's money?"

"What do you want to hear?" I asked, with my voice cracking. "That I hate my papi? That I'd rather see him in hell than the World Series?"

"How about your country?" He batted the questions back at me as a fly buzzed around his head. "No love for Cuba? For El Presidente? No desire to represent your homeland with honor? To wear its name across your chest?"

The smoke from his cigar was starting to make me sick and dizzy.

"There are players who would fall to their knees and kiss the ground for this opportunity," he said, pointing toward the field. "Pledge their undying support for the motherland. All *you* do is talk about yourself, how great you are. The truth is you're *nothing* without Cuba. And you're nothing without *me.*"

In one surprisingly swift move, Moyano snatched the fly from midair. He shook it inside a closed fist, like he was getting ready to roll dice. After he threw it to the floor, that fly's wings quivered at my feet and then went still.

"You can hit all the triples you want, Junior. Make all the plays with your glove," he said with more fire in his eyes than in the tip of that cigar. "Unless you are obedient, compliant, loyal, you will not be permitted to succeed."

Part of me felt like that lifeless fly. I understood that my dream of becoming a Nacional was dead. Not because Moyano wouldn't eventually choose me, but because putting on his uniform would be the same as playing inside a prison, wearing invisible handcuffs every moment of the day. And I had a real glimpse into what Papi might have been feeling when he got into that car in Baltimore and left his whole world behind.

Everything Moyano said after that barely had any meaning to me.

I wouldn't wish his type of slavery on my worst enemy. But if Matador wanted to sell his soul to Moyano, to flash his glove and golden spikes to the world, I wouldn't waste my breath trying to talk him out of it.

"I'll tell you something. I'm going to sit here and finish this fine cigar. Take my time with it. You know, it's part of the privilege of living in Cuba. How this tobacco is grown beneath our sun, then cut and rolled special. People come from all over the world for these cigars," said Moyano, puffing away. "When I'm done, I'm going to make my decision about who will be my next shortstop. That decision will be

the *right* one. I won't announce it until tomorrow night, after
the tournament is completed. Until then, you'll just have to
live with the fact that only I will know your fate, who you'll
become."

Then Moyano pushed his face toward the door as a signal for me to leave.

My lungs didn't fill with fresh air again until I left that
darkness behind and stepped outside into the light of the
dugout.

Uncle Ramon looked me up and down from the third-
base coaching box. He seemingly nodded his head in approval, and I wondered if he could see the change in me.

Luis was standing on second base, giving everyone in
our dugout two thumbs-up. One of our teammates told
me that he'd just stroked a double down the first-base line.
There was a look of pure joy on Luis's face, like he'd finally
justified his place on the team.

My cousin took a walking lead off second. On the next
pitch, he took off. Luis took Puerto Padre's pitcher by total
surprise, easily stealing third.

We were far ahead on the scoreboard, and Matador was
pissed at Luis, barking that he was trying to rub it in by taking the extra base. Luis just clapped his hands, looking even
more satisfied. That's when Uncle Ramon leaned in close
and said something to his son. He probably told him not to
try to steal home, or he could cause a riot on the field. After

that, Luis stayed put on third. But I would have loved to see him break all the rules and go streaking for the plate.

I had a hard time shaking off that meeting with Moyano. Everything he'd said stayed with me. Even the smell from his cigar clung to my uniform. So I went out into the field for the next inning with my nose pointed up in the air, trying to avoid the stink.

I tried to concentrate on baseball and nothing else. But I couldn't.

The rest of the game was a blur to me. I just know that Luis and I each got another hit, while Matador never reached base. Right before Puerto Padre made their final out, I watched Gabriel rise to his feet and begin cheering for us. From a section of seats right behind him, once more, I heard the sound of that horn.

This time, I saw a little, chunky man in a white T-shirt marching down the aisle with it, tooting away. Behind him, a bunch of grade school kids followed along, like they were having the greatest time in the world. They disappeared through an open gate by the bleachers, and I didn't see them again.

When the game was over, Luis and the rest of our players celebrated on the diamond. They were all congratulating me. But I had a tough time managing any kind of smile. A minute later, as the teams lined up to shake hands, I practically glared straight through Matador, knowing that even if he became a Nacional, he'd never have a thing in this world that I'd be jealous of.

Turning away from the line of Puerto Padre players, I saw that fence in center field. The thought of running over there and hanging from the top of it crossed my mind. I even considered jumping over it in one big leap, like Superman over a skyscraper.

"I know just what you need to relieve the pressure you're feeling," said Uncle Ramon, his hand dropping down onto my shoulder, grounding me where I stood. "Go change out of that uniform. I've got some relaxation planned for the whole team, a real reward."

I held my breath as I walked into the locker room behind Luis. This time the lights were on. Moyano was gone, but that fly was still in the same spot on the floor. Then, without noticing, one of my teammates accidentally kicked it beneath a locker. I was probably the only one in the room who knew it was there. And I wondered how many players Moyano had crushed that way in his career, or made invisible.

"All right, *winners*. Get into beach clothes as quick as you can," announced Uncle Ramon from the door, with Gabriel standing beside him. "The bus is out front, ready to go. Five minutes. That's it. Otherwise Paulo says he'll leave without you."

That set off an excited buzz among my teammates.

"That driver leaves us behind, we'll chase his broken-down bus all the way to the beach," said Luis, pulling a clean shirt over his head. "You with me on that, Cuz?"

"All the way," I answered, starving to trade the dampness of that locker room for the feeling of warm sun on my bare back. "Maybe we'd even get there ahead of him."

7

I COULDN'T TAKE a chance on how long we'd be gone. So I sprinted over to our dorm room for my transistor radio. I quickly pulled it out from beneath my mattress. As I moved toward the door, a splinter of sunlight reflected into my eyes, freezing me in my tracks. It had shone down from that lamp, bouncing off the face of Aunt Blanca's photo. From where I stood, it looked like there was a halo surrounding her. Then I shifted the angle of my head, and just as suddenly, it was gone. I crossed myself and bolted for the bus.

Outside, Luis was standing between the bus's folding doors, making certain that Paulo couldn't pull away without me. Gabriel's Chevy was parked beside it with the engine running. Uncle Ramon was busy talking to Gabriel through the driver's side window before he followed me onto the bus.

"Paulo, take the team to the beach about a half mile past the big stone jetty. They'll like it there best," said Uncle Ramon, slipping past both Luis and me, blocking us from getting to a seat. "I understand there are lots of teenagers at that section. I'll meet you there later. I'm going with my friend to a beach near his house first."

I couldn't believe Uncle Ramon wasn't going to celebrate with us.

"It's quarter to four now. What time are we coming back?" asked Paulo. "Dinner in the cafeteria starts at six thirty."

"Don't be concerned with that," answered Uncle Ramon, handing Paulo some pesos. "There's food at the beach. Treat the team to whatever they want. You, too. No curfew either. Don't bring them back until they're too tired to party anymore."

"All right, my pops is letting loose for a change," said Luis.

Paulo grinned. "For a few more pesos, I'll give the players piggyback rides to the dorm one by one whenever they're ready."

"What about our game tomorrow?" I asked Uncle Ramon. It seemed as if a brain other than his usual coaching one had been moving his mouth. "Are we going to stagger through that?"

"We'll deal with those consequences when they come," he answered. "Right now, we're going to revel in this opportunity. Some of us may never be at this point in our lives again."

Then Uncle Ramon fixed his gaze down the rows of players in their seats.

"You earned this reward, worked hard to get it!" he shouted to them. "Take what belongs to you! Embrace it!"

The players let out a roar, and Paulo turned up the music on his boom box.

I was even more surprised when Uncle Ramon said, "Luis, Julio, you'll ride with Gabriel and me. There are some things here in Cárdenas I want you to see before you join your friends."

"Everything I want to see is at the beach where *they're* going, the one with all the girls," Luis protested to no avail, as Uncle Ramon took us both off the bus. "This isn't fair. It's no reward."

Uncle Ramon rode shotgun, next to Gabriel, in the front. Luis, still complaining, was in the backseat with me.

"Follow me," Gabriel called to Paulo. "I know the area very well. I live here."

Then Gabriel put his Chevy into drive, and the bus pulled out behind us.

"What did Moyano say to you in the locker room?" Uncle Ramon asked me.

"That he owned my future," I answered.

"I know that feeling," said Uncle Ramon, with his eyes on the road ahead. "I've dealt with it longer than you."

"I only know from watching him, how he stands, acts,"

said Gabriel, turning the wheel toward the coastline. "There are many officials like Moyano in Cuba. They want you to be dependent on them. They want to be your god, like you owe them your life."

"Is Moyano the reason my party's on hold?" asked Luis, annoyed. "That fat swine?"

Gabriel and Uncle Ramon both began laughing at that.

"Officials like him, they're the reason everyone's good time is delayed," said Gabriel. "Ballplayers, fishermen, farmers, factory workers—everyone. The island is littered with Moyanos, from the top of the government down."

"Did he want something from you, Julio?" Uncle Ramon asked.

"He wanted to hear me say that I love Cuba and I would never embarrass it."

"We all love our country—the land, the people," said Uncle Ramon. "What he really means, what he really cares about, is that you would never disgrace *him* by defecting."

"Do you want to give Moyano that kind of power over you?" asked Gabriel.

"I'd rather quit playing baseball," I said.

"Even if you don't play baseball, they'll be another Moyano waiting," said Gabriel. "You'll encounter them all your years here. That's from experience."

Suddenly, the confines of that Chevy began to feel like a secure space where I could speak my mind about anything.

And I started to wonder exactly who Gabriel was, and why we were sharing so much with him.

Ten or twelve minutes later, I saw that big jetty coming up. It looked like a long stone bridge, extending out into the ocean until it vanished beneath the distant waves. There was a kid with a fishing pole carefully walking on it, stepping from rock to rock, maybe sixty yards out into the surf. Just one misstep on those slippery stones and he'd be up to his neck in rough water, swimming for his life.

We drove for another couple hundred yards before Gabriel stopped the Chevy beside a sandy lot filled with a half dozen cars and a ton of bikes. That got me to thinking about my unlocked bike back in Matanzas, if I'd ever see it again. Or would I be wearing out Papi's good leather shoes, walking back and forth from my job at El Puente?

The bus pulled over and Gabriel pointed inside the lot.

"Paradise, that way!" he called out above Paulo's music.

Paulo honked his horn in response, and then Gabriel leaned on his own a little longer and louder before we drove off.

Luis uttered a groan as he watched the bus get smaller out the rear window.

"Two base hits I had today—a perfect pickup line to meet girls," Luis said, shaking his head. "I wouldn't have even had to lie."

"You won't be missing much, just a few hours of fun," said Uncle Ramon. "Your time is just beginning. There'll be better days than this in your future."

But Luis continued to sulk.

The odometer spun for nearly another three miles. Then Gabriel parked just off the roadside, in a small clearing beside a trio of huge boulders. There was one other car there and just a handful of bikes.

"Boys, unload what's in the trunk while Gabriel and I find a good spot on the beach," said Uncle Ramon, stepping out of the car.

Gabriel got out and turned his key in the trunk lock, opening it a few inches for us. Then the two of them headed toward the sound of the ocean. Soon as they disappeared around the corner, Luis followed far enough after them to see who else was there.

"Two girls a little older than us. They're sitting on blankets, reading. They look all right, but they're not even wearing swimsuits," reported Luis. "Besides them, there's a couple of families, some younger kids hanging out, and a few old folks."

"Not exactly a party waiting to happen, huh?"

"I say we give it ten minutes. Then we walk back if we have to."

In the trunk, there was a small barbecue, a bag of charcoal, blankets, folding chairs, and an ice cooler. We loaded ourselves down, taking it all in one trip.

"Guess I've joined you as Uncle's *burrito*," I said, with the chairs on my back and both hands full.

"How about that cooler you're carrying? Think there are any cold beers inside?" Luis asked. "Maybe that could be our reward."

"I wouldn't argue against it," I said, laboring through the hot sand with every step.

Thirty yards from the water's edge, Uncle Ramon pointed to a spot beside him, and we began to build a little camp. Except for kids running past, playing tag, we were far enough away from the other people there to have privacy. But not so far as to look like we didn't want to be anywhere near them.

Gabriel opened the bag of charcoal, poured it into the barbecue, and then struck a match to start it burning.

"Luis, look inside the cooler," said Uncle Ramon. "Gabriel brought us something special."

There weren't any beers, but that didn't stop Luis's eyes from lighting up.

There were five huge swordfish steaks. I recognized them because they were on the menu at El Puente. Only these were thicker and pinker than any I'd ever seen. That cinched it in my mind that Gabriel was some kind of fisherman.

"We're going to cook these steaks and have some important conversation," said Uncle Ramon in a serious tone, pointing to the close circle of chairs in the sand.

"Conversation? About what?" I asked.

"Your papi," Uncle Ramon said, his eyes fixed on mine for a second. "And the future. All of our futures."

My hand tapped at the transistor radio in my pocket. Just to feel that it was still there.

"What do you mean?" I asked, with my arms and legs almost trembling. "You've heard from him?"

Luis took a step closer to me.

"About a year ago," Uncle Ramon said. "Via a messenger."

"And you didn't say anything?" I shot back.

I looked hard at Luis. Only he seemed as surprised at the news as I was.

"Julio, your papi's the reason that Gabriel is here," said Uncle Ramon. "We never played baseball together. He's not an old friend. We've only met in the last few months."

"El Fuego has trusted in me to help his family," said Gabriel, stretching a fresh sheet of tinfoil over the bars of the smoking grill and then putting the steaks on top of it. "When you hear what I have to say, Julio, you'll decide for yourself if you have trust in me, too."

"Who are you?" I asked, point-blank.

"Just a man. A Cuban," replied Gabriel. "But before this

is over, you might consider me family. That's how it happens on a journey like this. I know. But for now, listen to Ramon. Let's sit while he speaks, before we have our good meal."

As I lowered myself down into one of the chairs, I couldn't help but think of Mama and Lola, back home in Matanzas. In my heart, I didn't believe anything I was about to hear was going to include helping them.

8

FROM HIS CHAIR, Uncle Ramon kicked his shoes off and dug his feet deep into the sand.

"Your papi was able to get a sum of money into Cuba through a Canadian *turista*," he said, as the smell of swordfish filtered through the salty air. "That money was given to Gabriel."

I was pissed. My family had struggled for every peso, just to meet the bills. No wonder Gabriel could afford steaks like these.

"Why?" I demanded. "How come *our* money went to *him?*"

"So Gabriel can get us out of Cuba," Uncle Ramon replied, before popping the top on a can of soda with a *tsssp*.

Those words seemed to hang in the air for a moment—*get us out of Cuba.*

I only felt the weight of them when Luis grabbed hold of my arm and gasped, "Holy crap."

My heart began beating harder and harder inside my chest, and I had to actually think about taking my next breath.

"And that's his payment?" I asked, hoping to steady myself.

"Payment?" repeated Gabriel, turning the steaks on the grill with a long metal fork. "No. There's nothing for me. That money covered the entire cost of building—"

"Look! Down the beach!" interrupted Luis. "Police!"

There were two officers on a motorcycle with a sidecar. It had three wide wheels, meant to power its way over the sandy shore. They were slowly making their way from the far end of the beach toward where we'd camped.

"Just act naturally. Remember the truth: you're baseball players from Matanzas celebrating a victory over Puerto Padre. Nothing more," instructed Gabriel. "Besides, I know these two, what they're all about."

"You *know* them?" asked Luis.

"I make it my business to," answered Gabriel, through the smoke from the barbecue.

The policemen rolled past the families and kids without any interest. But they took a long glance at the two girls reading on their blankets. They seemed about to pass us, too, before Gabriel called out to them, "Officers! A moment, please!"

I shot Uncle Ramon a concerned look, already feeling the sweat on my palms.

"I've learned to trust him," Uncle Ramon said quietly, barely moving his lips. "There's no other way."

Gabriel took one of the steaks on a paper plate down to the officers, who were maybe ten yards from the water. They had some conversation. Then one of the officers gave us a thumbs-up and called out, "I used to play baseball myself."

A minute later, they were gone with their steak.

"They'll pass this way again in a few hours, just before sundown," said Gabriel, who'd walked back to us. "Their last patrol of the day. That's when we'll be packing up."

"We're going to sit here that long?" asked Luis. "And do what? Talk?"

"How much of this does my mama know?" I asked Uncle Ramon.

"She knows enough," he answered. "That there's a plan, and that it's happening sooner rather than later."

"How soon?" I asked.

"Tonight," answered Gabriel, handing me a steaming plate of fish.

"What about her and Lola?"

"Your mother thinks the trip is too dangerous for Lola," answered Uncle Ramon. "And she won't leave her daughter behind. Your sister knows nothing of it."

"They're both *staying*?" I asked.

"Your mother's made her choice," my uncle said. "Now you need to make one."

"How about me?" asked Luis.

"I'm your father," said Uncle Ramon. "You go where I go, and we're leaving Cuba."

Luis nodded his head, taking a plate of his own.

I turned to my cousin and said, "Besides, you don't want to be the son of a defector."

Then Uncle Ramon looked at us both and said, "I'm sorry about all the deceptions, for keeping you in the dark so long. But the fewer people who knew, the better our chance of making it this far without being arrested."

"Papi's *money*," I repeated to myself in disgust.

"I know you're angry at him, Julio. But your papi does love you. He wants you to be free," said Uncle Ramon, peeling off a chunk of fish with his fingers. "And if you decide to stay, well, Moyano will know that he can trust you. He'll make you a Nacional for sure."

With all of that churning inside my stomach, Gabriel sat down, making four of us in a tight, seated circle.

"Before we make any decisions, let me be honest with you boys. Tell you what I know of a journey like this one," Gabriel said. "When I was eight years old, from this beach, I boarded a raft for the US."

My uncle stopped him and said, "If it's too painful, you don't need to go through all the details again."

"Thank you, amigo," said Gabriel, who took a deep breath before he continued. "Both my parents were dead and my grandfather was getting too old to take care of me. Our neighbors were planning an escape. It wasn't much of a raft, just wood and rubber tied together with ropes. They made oars from fish boxes. My grandfather gave them the rubber from some old car tires he had. So they agreed to take me along. There were eight of us—three grown men, two young women, one very old woman who could barely walk, me, and their family dog. Before the trip, we all went to church together."

"To pray?" asked Luis.

"Yes," he answered. "The priest even gave me my first Communion—the body and blood. As soon as it got dark, we put the raft into the water. The moon was cut like a sickle—thin and sharp. Everything went smoothly that night. But the next morning, instead of sun, there were black storm clouds and ripping winds. First, our food and water got washed overboard. Then, piece by piece, the raft started to come apart."

A pair of kids chasing each other, kicking up sand behind them, did a close lap around our camp.

"Hey, watch it!" Luis hollered. "Keep—"

Uncle Ramon stopped Luis cold, showing him a single finger over his lips, followed by a long look.

Gabriel resumed his story. "We all huddled in the middle of the raft. At some point, the dog spotted something in the water and jumped in after it. I heard him barking for a while.

But I never saw that dog again. The others tied the old woman and me to the raft. The waves pounded us. I couldn't open my eyes. They were stinging from all the salt water. When the sun finally came out and the waters calmed, there were only five of us left. Over the next eight or ten hours we floated in the middle of nowhere. Then the raft broke apart even more. I was clinging to the old woman. She was dizzy by that point, seeing things that weren't there. The others each had their own section of raft. We were floating within fifty yards of each other when we heard an engine in the distance. It was a boat. Unfortunately, it was Cuban."

"So they brought you back here," I said.

"They did, to the docks in Cárdenas," he answered. "But before they pulled us from the water, the old woman asked me about the boat. 'Who is it?' she wanted to know. I'd already recognized the flag on its side. All I said to her was, 'We're saved.'"

"What did they do to you all?" I asked.

"The surviving adults went to prison. I got sent to an orphanage and never saw my grandfather again," answered Gabriel, setting down his plate in the sand. "The old woman, I believe she died happy, because she never made it back to shore."

"For almost thirty years now, Gabriel has worked as a fisherman in these waters," said Uncle Ramon. "He knows these currents like the back of his hand—where they run, how swiftly they can change."

"And thanks to El Fuego, now I have a vessel of my own to captain," added Gabriel. "One that will hopefully sail us to freedom."

I stood up and silently walked down to the shoreline, alone. I stared at the northern horizon, that distant point where the water and sky touch. I thought about what it would take to reach it. To be in a place where the higher-ups in Cuba didn't have control over me. Would it be worth maybe never seeing Mama and Lola again? Would it be worth risking my life?

For all his tough talk on the pitcher's mound, Papi never risked his life for freedom. He walked through a revolving door in a hotel lobby and into a waiting car. But now he wanted me to take a chance on practically swimming to Miami.

I dropped my eyes down to the whitecaps, watching them roll all the way to shore. One after another, they turned to foam on the beach until they disappeared back into the surf. And after a minute or two, my heartbeat seemed to be in sync with the rhythm of the breaking waves.

At the water's edge, there was a horseshoe crab turned upside down. It was stuck on its back. Its legs were moving a mile a minute, going absolutely nowhere. And its spiked tail kept whipping the damp sand, trying to flip its round shell upright. Finally, I walked over and picked it up, water seeping into my sneakers.

Despite all its armor, that horseshoe crab was lighter

than I'd imagined. I was gentle enough with it, tossing it underhand into the ocean, where it vanished beneath the surface with a *plunk*.

When I turned back around, Uncle Ramon was standing a few feet behind me.

"This is all happening too fast. It's not a decision about *me*. It's about my whole family. I'm not going to have an answer for you, not without talking to Mama first. I'm not leaving her and my sister behind without a word, the way Papi did. That's not who I am, or who I'm ever going to become."

9

GABRIEL PRODUCED A cell phone that looked like it had never been used. I guess the government couldn't trace or listen in on any calls if it was brand-new. He held the phone out to me, and I took it from his hand. Then I turned my back to the three of them before I dialed. In the few seconds those numbers were changing into tones, a thousand moments went racing through my mind—from the time I could first remember following Papi around in short pants until right now. I didn't know exactly what I was going to say. I just knew that my tongue was waiting to start in motion.

I heard Mama's voice say, "This is Luz Ramirez."

My heart jumped.

I said, "Mama, I'm in Cárdenas with—"

That's when the rest of Mama's message greeting began talking over me.

I hit the "end" button fast, without even thinking about leaving her a message.

"You'll have time to call back," said Uncle Ramon from

over my shoulder. "There's a two-hour window for you to make a decision."

I turned back around and Gabriel said, "Your papi would be crushed if we made the crossing without you."

"I'm not living my life for *him* anymore," I said, standing on a small mound of sand. "I'm sorry to possibly disturb *his* plans."

"Julio, you see that man with his family over there?" asked Gabriel, pointing about forty yards away. "He's not here by accident. Twenty minutes before sunset, he's going to walk off this beach. He'll bring back my vessel and leave it in a small clearing past those thick bushes. Then his family will pile into my car and take it home to keep."

"What Gabriel means is there's a structure to *our* plan. There has to be," said Uncle Ramon. "Being dependent on a single phone call can't destroy its timing."

I started dialing another number.

"Lola?" Luis asked me.

Uncle Ramon put his hand over the phone, shutting it. I tried to yank it away, but his grip slid down to my wrist, holding me there like a vise.

"Remember, she doesn't know," said Uncle Ramon. "This isn't the time for her to find out. She's very emotional and talkative. That could hurt us."

"I wasn't going to tell her. I'm not that stupid or mean," I said as Uncle Ramon loosened his grip.

A moment later, Lola picked up the cell we'd shared.

"Listen, Mama's not answering her phone at work. I need you to go down to El Puente and let her know I'm trying to call."

Lola pitched a fit and I waded through every one of her complaints.

"I know you're studying, that it's hot outside. But I need to speak to Mama. Do this for me. Please. What? No, it's not about me becoming a Nacional," I told her. "I just may be away longer than I expected, to train some more. I need her permission. It's important. When? All right, but as fast as you can. Listen, I don't say it enough, but you're a great sister, much smarter than I'll ever be. Okay. Thank you."

As I closed my hand around the phone, Uncle Ramon nodded his head to me, and I took it as an apology. Then I turned toward Luis. I hadn't noticed it before, but I could see the growing panic in his eyes. Luis said he wanted to go for a walk on the beach, just to "stretch his legs." I decided to go with him.

"Sure. Walk. Relax. Just stay within our sight," said Gabriel, who seemed calm as could be. "The four of us shouldn't get separated for any reason. We'll discuss this more when you get back."

When we got out of earshot, walking along the water's edge, Luis said, "Julio, you know that I can barely swim, right? I should have practiced my whole life for this."

"Don't worry," I said. "There'll be at least one life pre-server on Gabriel's boat. If I'm there with you, it's yours. I promise."

"What would we even do in the US?"

"I can't put myself in that situation yet. But *you'll* escape the Moyanos on this island. I'm sure."

"You have to come. I'd be lost without you," Luis said.

"You're stronger than you know. I've seen it," I said, kicking the broken seashells at my feet.

"I keep thinking of that photo. The one I left in our dorm room," said Luis. "If we leave, I won't have a single picture of my mother. I'd give a hundred pesos to have it with me right now."

"You still have your memories."

"But I have to close my eyes to see her that way."

"Sometimes that's better," I said. "Then your memories can never change."

"Maybe your mama and sister will bring me a photo, the day they leave Cuba."

"Yeah, maybe," I said, squeezing the phone tighter inside my hand.

That's when I started thinking that if I did go, I'd most likely never see Mama and Lola again. That they'd become images in my mind. The same way Aunt Blanca had become for Luis and Uncle Ramon.

Luis stopped us about fifteen yards from those two girls

reading. They were probably twenty years old. But that didn't discourage Luis from running a hand back through his jet-black hair.

"Who knows what could happen tonight. A big wave might drown me," he said. "I'm going over there. Turn on the charm, see where it gets me. You coming?"

"Not worth the effort," I answered. "Either way, we'll never see those two again."

"That's the point. I've got nothing to lose," he said, walking off toward their blankets.

The sun was sinking in the sky. Maybe it was down half a thumb's worth since I'd last noticed. Everything else in my life seemed to suddenly stop. It was like I was alone on my own island, waiting for a sign to move in some direction. And hanging over that ocean in front of me was Papi's shadow.

I didn't know what I wanted or where I belonged. I just knew that I'd had enough—six long years of trying to make sense of an empty feeling.

After a few minutes, Luis came back flashing a strip of paper with a phone number on it.

"I told them there was going to be a party after we won the tournament tomorrow. That I'd personally get them invited," he said, leading me back in the direction we'd come. "And that you were too shy to talk to them. They thought that was cute."

"What are you going to do with the number?"

"Maybe put it in a bottle, like a note. Throw it overboard from Gabriel's boat."

"Why did you even bother talking to them, then?"

"Think of the story. Two girls waiting for me to call. Then they find out I'm either in the US or in prison or dead," said Luis.

"Something to tell their friends?" I asked.

"Bigger. It could become famous, like a folktale."

Suddenly, the phone inside my hand began to vibrate. It felt like an earthquake starting in my palm and spreading through my entire body. I flipped open the phone and it stopped. But I could still feel a rumbling in the pit of my stomach, shaking me to the core.

"Who is this? I don't know this number," Mama said in a defensive voice.

"Mama, it's me. I'm in Cárdenas, on a borrowed phone," I answered, with Luis's eyes glued to mine. "Didn't Lola tell you?"

"No, I took a break at work and saw the missed call. Is everything all right?"

"Mama, I'm on the beach, with Luis and Uncle Ramon, and someone else. They say that it's time. Time to—"

"*Shhh*. Don't speak it," she interrupted. "Do what you need to do, Julio. This is *your* life. Live it."

"Mama, I don't—"

"Julio, you *need* to go. Find what you're searching for."

"Are you sure?"

"Wait, I see Lola coming."

"Mama?"

"Julio, make your decision and know that I love you. I'll always love you, no matter what."

"I love you, too, Mama," I said, before I heard Lola's out-of-breath voice and then the connection cut off.

"So?" asked Luis nervously, as I closed the phone.

"I guess those girls are going to have some story to tell about meeting *us*."

"Yes!" exclaimed Luis, throwing both arms around me and hugging me tight. "But remember, you were too shy to talk to them."

The rest of the way back, I walked on the damp, hard-packed sand closest to the water. I didn't want the ground shifting beneath my feet. At some point, I saw the tracks we'd left behind heading toward us. I stopped for a second to look down at them. It was a strange feeling, like suddenly being present in my past. Then I picked my head up and kept right on walking into my future.

When we reached camp I handed Gabriel his cell phone.

"A journey like this makes people family—that's what you said," I told him. "Well, I've already got an uncle and cousin here. But I'll give you a chance to earn your way in."

"I accept that," said Gabriel, reaching out to shake my hand. "I can't ask for anything more."

"No one can. That's the highest bar there is," said Uncle Ramon, who looked as if a huge weight had just been lifted off him.

"There's still lots to talk about and little time," said Gabriel, glancing at the sun.

"Before any more talk, let's pray," said Luis.

Nobody argued with that. We all knelt in a tight circle, bowing our heads, even me and Uncle Ramon.

10

92 • PAUL VOLPONI

OVER THE NEXT half hour or so, we each downed two sixteen-ounce bottles of water to hydrate ourselves for the trip. Gabriel couldn't say exactly how long we'd be at sea. Instead, he was more like a weatherman giving a forecast he wouldn't stake his reputation on.

"Depending on the currents, we could reach the coast of Florida inside of two days," he said, before putting both hands out in front of him as if to halt any hopes of a guarantee. "But the weather can change in minutes. Even storms miles away can have an impact, driving us off course, spinning a small vessel in endless circles."

"You have a compass, don't you?" asked Uncle Ramon.

Basically, the only reason to have a compass in Cuba is to help you defect. So you could get into serious trouble being caught with one.

"Think I'd take you and two young boys onto that ocean without one? I'm not the devil," Gabriel countered, with a twinge of annoyance. "As a kid I experienced what happens when it's tried that way."

That was the first time I'd seen Gabriel tense. It didn't seem like much to get upset over. Maybe his nerves were getting tighter as the sun slipped lower.

"I've got other supplies, too," Gabriel continued, his voice leveling out. "Food, water, flares, and an extra can of gasoline."

So I figured his boat had a motor. I felt better knowing that, like we could choose our own direction if the currents didn't cooperate.

"Ramon and I will sit in the front. Julio and Luis, you'll be in the back," he added. "Oh, and we're going to be low to the water, very low. That's by design, to avoid being detected on any radar. If it's choppy we'll get slapped in the face by a few waves. Be prepared to get soaked."

That's when I took the transistor radio out. I wrapped it in a pair of plastic bags to keep it from getting wet, as the others eyed it.

"We might need this way out there. You never know," I said, trying not to make a fuss.

"You're right. Could come in handy," said Uncle Ramon, reaching into his shirt pocket and handing me a new 9-volt battery. "We could hear a World Series game on it, too. Give us something else to focus on."

— — —

The tide rolled in and the water's edge kept creeping closer to our camp. From a distance, those two girls waved good-bye to Luis as they walked off the beach. He didn't return the wave, though. Instead, he just glanced their way like somebody they should have been starstruck to meet. Then that man got up and left without his family, just the way Gabriel told us he would.

"I want you boys to take the barbecue and cooler to my trunk," said Gabriel, giving us his car keys. "But leave the chairs behind. It'll look better when we hang around *to see the stars.*"

Even with the charcoals emptied, I could still feel the warmth from the barbecue as I carried it back. I closed my eyes for a moment, imagining Mama and Lola in my arms for one last embrace.

Gabriel's car was the only one remaining behind those rocks.

"When we walked off that baseball field today, I wasn't thinking about anything like *this*," said Luis. "Things can change fast, huh? My mother passing, your papi—thought I was all through growing up for a while."

"Maybe it never stops," I said as he opened the trunk. "In a few hours, we might be looking back at right now, thinking we didn't know shit."

"I just hope my next learning curve is about life in the US, not how to shower in prison," said Luis, stowing away

the cooler and leaving enough room for me to fit the barbecue next to it.

"No, I hope the next curve I see comes out of a pitcher's
hand. That I'm waiting on it to break, right before I drive it
over some center-field fence and round the bases."

Luis slammed the trunk lid down and then gave me a
high five.

"Amen to that, Cuz," he said.

A minute later, I saw those two police officers slowly
rolling back down the beach on their motorcycle. Only this
time, because of the tide coming in, they were going to be
much closer to us.

"Act like we're packing the chairs up next," said Gabriel,
casually folding one.

Suddenly, I heard the rev of an engine, and the officers'
motorcycle turned in our direction.

"I don't trust these two," Uncle Ramon said, barely
moving his lips. "What if we have to jump them?"

"Easy, Ramon," whispered Gabriel. "They're probably
looking for more food, or beer."

I was wishing I had a baseball bat in my hands. I'd be
more comfortable wielding one of those than any weapon in
this world.

Their wide tires kicked up a ton of sand before the officer
driving pulled back on the throttle, four or five feet from
where we were standing.

The one sitting in the sidecar of that three-wheeler said, "So you boys are baseball players, huh? When I played, shortstop was my position. I had a lot of range with my glove and a good stick, too. I even dreamed of one day becoming a Nacional, representing Cuba. Now I wear *this* uniform."

"This is *our* star shortstop. My nephew," said Uncle Ramon, who'd moved to the outside of the officer's right hip, where his pistol was holstered.

"I'm not surprised. I used to have a build like yours, like a whip. That was before I put on an extra twenty pounds sitting around," he said to me. "Where are you from? Not Cárdenas. I've been stationed here for three years. I would have seen you play."

"I'm from Matanzas," I answered, taking a step closer to the one on the motorcycle, in case I had to defend my uncle.

"Ahh, the Crocodiles," he said, turning to his partner.

Meanwhile, Gabriel had slipped an arm around Luis. I guess to stop him from doing anything stupid.

"These boys are very dedicated," said Gabriel. "Baseball is all they dream about."

"What's your name?" the officer asked me. "I'll keep an eye out for you in the future."

"My name's Julio."

About thirty yards behind those officers sat that last family on the beach, minus their father. And maybe another forty yards farther down the beach, I saw the bushes start to shake and shimmy a little. Then they went completely still.

"What's your last name?" he asked.

Ramirez was on the tip of my tongue. But I bit it back, thinking he'd probably heard of Papi. And that might make him suspicious about us being here.

"Sanchez," I said, giving him Mama's maiden name and praying he wouldn't want to see any kind of ID. "My name's Julio Sanchez."

I felt sick to my stomach at having to deny my own name. But that was all on Papi, and the politics of Cuba.

"Very good," the officer said, nodding to his partner, who put the motorcycle in motion. "Remember, the beach closes at sundown. You have to be on your way soon."

"Thank you, officers," said Gabriel. "We appreciate your concern."

In the distance, that father had just reappeared from the bushes. The officers were traveling in his direction. He began pulling at his pants zipper, as if he'd gone off from his family to pee. Then the motorcycle rolled right on past him without slowing down.

"That's one obstacle out of the way," said Uncle Ramon.

"Men are a small obstacle compared with what we'll be facing," said Gabriel. "But you're right."

That entire family walked off the beach together. A minute later, I heard Gabriel's car starting up from behind the trio of huge rocks that separated us from the sandy lot. Once it pulled away, and the echo of it faded, everything that was about to happen felt even more real.

The sun was in flames now, burning orange and yellow in the red-blue sky as it went sinking into the horizon. It reminded me of one of Papi's fastballs blazing into a dark catcher's mitt.

Gabriel's plan was for each of us to walk straight into the bushes, one by one, while the others kept lookout along the beach. His order was me, Luis, Uncle Ramon, and then himself.

"That clearing I mentioned, it's small and about thirty paces straight into the bushes," emphasized Gabriel. "Don't get yourself moving sideways. You'll miss it completely."

When the moment came, I headed into the bushes without hesitation. But a few strides into the thick brush, I had to reset my bearings to sidestep a branch full of sharp thorns. When I did, I found myself standing in the middle of a cloud of mosquitos. They were hitting my arms and legs like I was the last warm meal on earth. And every time I'd slap at one spot, five or six of them would bite me somewhere else. So I bolted forward, praying I was still going in the right direction. I shoved aside branch after branch that either snapped back at me or cracked beneath my weight until I finally arrived at the clearing.

First, I saw the green body of a Buick automobile. There

was something strange attached to the grille—a wide, pointed front that looked like the bow of a ship. I searched for a boat, maybe one on a small trailer behind the car. But there wasn't any. Then I saw the weld marks, sealing the car's four doors shut, and the supplies tied down in the backseat.

That's when it hit me: we'd be sailing to the US in a floating car.

For some insane reason, I reached my arm inside the open driver's side window. I was about to tap the horn, as if I needed to hear how it sounded. Then Luis came stumbling through the bushes. His eyes focused on the car/boat in astonishment, and then on mine.

11

ONCE WE ALL got into the car/boat through the open windows, Gabriel turned the key in the ignition. I don't know what he had done to that Buick's engine. Or maybe it was just my own motor going full throttle. But it felt like there was enough horsepower under the hood to climb Pico Turquino, the highest mountain in Cuba.

"Buckle your seat belts!" cried Gabriel, his voice blaring over the engine.

There was nothing to see through the windshield but dense brush.

An instant later, as we jolted forward, leaves were flying everywhere. Three of them, on a tiny brown branch, landed on my lap. Then the air was filled with sand and I could hear the tires straining for traction on the beach.

"Hold on tight!" shouted Uncle Ramon.

The Buick struck the water with a *thud*. I guess we were doing almost thirty miles per hour. It was like hitting a low brick wall that only partially moved. Suddenly, there was nothing in front of us but ocean and a darkening sky. The pointed bow attached to the front sliced through the waves, and I was praying its tip would lead us straight to the States.

"Should I roll up my window?" asked Luis, in a near panic. "I'm getting wet. Are we leaking?"

"That's just the spray from the surf," answered Gabriel, grabbing for what looked like an air pump. "I'll get us higher up."

Then he flipped the switch on the pump and two long inner tubes on either side of the Buick began to inflate, lifting us.

"Any more big surprises?" asked Uncle Ramon, who sounded like he'd had no idea Gabriel's boat would be a Buick.

"Only if the rubberized seams don't hold and she takes on water," replied Gabriel, who now had a compass in his hand as he turned the wheel. "Then I'll be the one surprised."

"You can control this thing?" asked Luis, with a voice wavering between wonder and fright.

"There's a rudder on the back. It's synced up to the steering wheel," answered Gabriel, despite his intense focus on the direction we were headed.

I exchanged a quick glance with Luis. This was like that roller coaster ride we took in Havana last summer. It was all happening so fast we didn't know where or when the next sharp turn was coming. But this wasn't any amusement park.

The ocean muffled most of the engine noise. We were all breathing hard, even Gabriel. I don't know how much adrenaline four people could possibly have pumping. But right then, inside that floating car, it was probably a world record.

Gradually, our questions and conversation died down. There were stretches of silence between us when all I could hear was the water rushing by and the sound of my heart beating hard. Eventually, I looked out the back window and I couldn't see any trace of Cuba. Everything I knew, everything I was raised on was gone, except for the three leaves on that tiny branch.

It was strange to be without a country, without borders or boundaries. I was feeling small and lost, like I was too insignificant to be a new mark on a map. Fears piled up inside me until I almost started bawling right there. Then we hit the first big wave. For an instant, I believed we were actually airborne.

"*Wooo!*" hollered Uncle Ramon, as if he were riding a wild bull. "If that's what freedom feels like, I'll have some more!"

I'd seen him smile before. But this wasn't the same smile he wore after winning a baseball game. It was completely different. This one was etched deeper into his face, like no one could ever take it away from him. That got me to feeling bigger, stronger, and I raised my spine until the top of my head nearly touched the roof of that car/boat.

My entire life I'd lived under some kind of authority— El Presidente, his generals, political ministers, police. Almost all of them were like Moyano, and some much worse. I realized this was the first time I didn't have to watch my words. There was no one in power lurking in the shadows. No one I was forced to respect out of fear.

Right then, I thought about Papi—about the moment he walked out the revolving door of that hotel lobby in Baltimore. How he probably experienced these exact same feelings. I guess that was something we shared now, no matter how I felt about his leaving.

The Buick was practically our own country—a floating metallic island. It didn't matter that it was made in Detroit, USA, or kept running for decades with spit and glue on Cuban soil. Until we either got caught or washed up on somebody's shore, we didn't have to answer to anyone. It was only God who was above us, however He laid out the currents and weather in our path.

"I think I'm getting seasick," said Luis, his complexion turning nearly as green as the paint job on the Buick.

"Maybe that's why Gabriel left the windows open," I

said, shoving his head outside into the stream of salty air. "Breathe deep and try not to puke."

"Your cousin's right," said Uncle Ramon. "You don't want to lose any fluids. Water's precious on this trip."

I stuck my head out the opposite side. There was more light than I would have imagined. I could see for about fifty feet in every direction, as a constantly moving curtain of darkness kept an even pace with us. But there was no limit when I looked straight up. A crescent moon was shining, partly lighting the way. And the stars around it were burning bright, like someone had punched a thousand holes in the nighttime.

That's when I reached my arm over Gabriel's shoulder. I hit the horn in the center of the steering wheel, and it let out a long *beeeeeep!* I swear it was like music to my ears—better than any salsa, merengue, reggae, or rock. So I punched the horn again. And this time when I did, I hollered out, "Freedom!"

Then Gabriel said, "Everyone together: one, two, three."

The four of us screamed "Freedom!" until his hand lifted from the horn.

I grabbed the branch with the leaves from my lap. I thought about my family as I pulled the first leaf off. I remembered how we used to be, when Papi was a Cuban hero. When we walked around Matanzas with our heads held high, like El Fuego's fastball would never lose its velocity. Then I tossed it out the window.

Plucking the second leaf, I thought about all the baseball I'd played in Cuba, my teammates, and every drop of sweat I put into becoming a Nacional. I'd barely opened my hand when the wind outside sucked that leaf away.

"If I started my own version of the Nacionales, right here, would you play?" I asked Luis, only half kidding.

"You'd want *me*?" he replied, looking much less green now. "Sure. What would we call ourselves?"

"I don't know. Maybe Tortugas Marinas."

"Why not? I'll be a sea turtle," said Luis. "I was a crocodile this morning."

"Count me in," said Uncle Ramon. "And I don't want to coach. I'm coming out of retirement to play catcher."

That was good by me. But I didn't even consider asking Gabriel to play, not even to be polite. I'd already seen him try to throw a baseball.

I pulled away that third leaf, thinking about Moyano and everyone in power like him. Then I crumpled it up inside my palm and heaved it into the waves.

All that was left of my homeland was that small piece of branch. I put pressure on it at both ends, watching it bend from the middle. It had a lot of strength for its size. Only I made sure to back off before it snapped. That had me thinking about the people of Cuba—the farmers, factory workers, fishermen, maids, and busboys. How they had to deal with the system there every day of their lives, especially Mama and Lola. So I carefully dropped that branch into the water, hoping with all my heart that it would eventually find a place to put down roots and grow even stronger.

12

WE'D BEEN ON the water for more than two hours, thankfully without a police boat in sight. Then Gabriel got us into a swift-moving current and turned off the engine to save gas.

"This is where I hoped we'd be, with a *chance* to make it," he said. "We're probably past the first ring of security. With any luck we won't run into one of our navy ships on an exercise."

"How would we know if one's coming in the dark?" asked Uncle Ramon.

"Three red beacons about fifty feet apart, riding way over our heads," answered Gabriel. "We're small enough, though, that we shouldn't show up on their radar. So even if one happens by, it might not see us and could steam right on past."

"Or it could plow straight through us," said Uncle Ramon. Gabriel gave him a hesitant nod.

Luis kept checking the wristwatch hanging from a belt loop on his shorts, telling us how long we'd been at sea.

"It's supposed to be ninety miles to Miami," said Luis.

"A car can go at least forty-five miles an hour. How come we can't make it there in two hours?"

"The ocean's not a paved highway, and the currents don't run in a straight line," said Gabriel, eyeing his compass to make sure we were still headed north and a few degrees west. "And we're not moving at anywhere close to forty-five miles an hour. But if the wind keeps blowing from the south, it'll only help speed us up."

Luis's watch was a birthday present from his mother just a few months before she died. On its face, it had Mickey Mouse, with his two white-gloved hands pointing to the numbers. It was a cheap kiddie watch, but Luis treated it like it was made of gold. He'd worn it on his wrist for nearly five years, even after the cracked leather band had gotten way too small for him. Sometimes it had looked like it was cutting off his circulation. And if he'd ever flexed his forearm, it might have gone flying off, like he was the Incredible Hulk or something. So about a year ago, Luis started wearing it on his belt loop.

"When we get to Florida, I'm going to take you to see the real Mickey at Disney World," Uncle Ramon told his son. "Then you can ask why he only has four fingers."

"Okay, but I'd rather meet those cute Disney princesses," said Luis. "Besides, I thought Mickey lost that other finger in a mousetrap."

"No, that was his Cuban cousin, Eduardo Mouse," said

Uncle Ramon, in a biting tone. "He was reaching for a crumb of cheese in El Presidente's palace. Then, *wham!*"

We all laughed loudly over that. And I swore to myself, if we got dragged back to Cuba in handcuffs, I'd tell that joke to the judge *before* he sentenced me.

Gabriel started eating sliced pieces of raw squash, and offered us some. With a look of disgust, Luis shook his head. Then he went looking through one of the supply boxes in the backseat.

"This is more like it," said Luis, opening a small bag of potato chips. "These should settle my stomach."

Luis shoved the bag at me and I took a few.

"I thought we'd save those for a celebration, when Florida was in sight," said Gabriel, as I sucked the salt off a chip without breaking it inside my mouth. "But I'll take one, too."

"Speaking of celebrations," I said, "do you think the team's back at the dorm yet?"

"They should be," answered Uncle Ramon. "It's about that time, when Moyano will realize something's wrong."

"I'd like to see his face when he figures out we're gone," I said. "Maybe he'll swallow a lit cigar."

"Don't forget," said Uncle Ramon, "your teammates and Paulo will be there to experience his anger firsthand. Moyano will bring the police in and have them questioned half the night."

"Of course, the Cárdenas beach patrol will report they saw the four of us at a different beach," added Gabriel. "That will get the players and your bus driver off the hook."

Uncle Ramon and Gabriel quietly exchanged a satisfied look, as if they'd planned that chess move in advance.

I guess every adrenaline rush, no matter how big, has to subside eventually. And after a few more time-checks by Luis, with the water completely calm, it began to feel like we were just hanging out in a parked car overlooking the ocean. So I took out the transistor radio, tuned in to the game, and turned the volume up for everyone to hear.

Bottom of the sixth inning here at Yankee Stadium, in pivotal Game Three of the World Series. The Miami Marlins lead the Bronx Bombers four to three, with two outs and the bases empty.

Our ears perked up at that. Because with the Marlins ahead in a tight game, Papi could be coming in soon to pitch the final few outs and shut the door.

It's been an unusually warm and humid fall night in the Bronx. The sweat continues to cascade down the face of the Marlins' starting pitcher. He's worked in and out of trouble all game. Here's his one-hundred-and-third pitch of the evening already. Oh, that's way high and outside to the Yankees' power-hitting second baseman. That's an indicator the Marlins' starter may be feeling fatigued. The most pitches he's thrown in a game so far this season has been one hundred and twelve. And that was in a nine-inning, complete-game performance. Now he checks the signs. He's into his windup. Fastball, low and outside. That one registered just eighty-eight miles per hour on the radar gun. Prior to that pitch, he's consistently been in the low to mid-nineties all night with his heater. Two balls, no strikes the count. The Marlins' pitcher to the bill of his cap with his hand, wiping away the perspiration. Here comes the pitch. It's drilled deep into right field. There's no doubt about this one. It's going, going, gone! And we're tied up at four apiece.

Uncle Ramon punched the dashboard. Gabriel quickly grabbed his still-clenched fist so he couldn't hit it again.

"You don't want to break your hand," said Gabriel. "We may need all of your strength to survive."

"Sorry, I get stupid over baseball," said Uncle Ramon.

I saw a movie once where an air bag popped out at a guy who'd punched the dashboard, smacking him in the face like a big pillow. But this Buick was made probably twenty years before air bags were put into cars.

The fans are still on their feet here. That home run has also sparked quick action in the Marlins' bullpen, as a pair of middle relievers are beginning to warm up.

Papi is the Marlins' closer. So he most likely wasn't coming in to pitch unless Miami regained the lead or the game was on the line.

"Don't worry, Julio. Miami is going to jump back out in front. I can feel it," Luis said to me, between crunches on a chip.

I knew Luis didn't mean anything by it. But for some reason, his words got me riled.

"What do I care if Miami wins? I'm not on that team!" I snapped. "You think because he sent money for this floating car that I have to live and die by what he does? I don't. This is *his* game, not mine."

I could see the surprise in Luis's eyes as he backed off.

After a moment of silence, Uncle Ramon calmly said, "Understood, Julio. But we're headed to Miami. There's a huge Cuban community there. We're not going to root for the New York Yankees, are we? They just buy up free agents like they've got more money than God. I prefer a little Latin flavor to my baseball, a little humbleness."

It was the sound of Uncle Ramon's voice, and not his words, that mattered. It was as if he'd thrown me a life pre-server in the middle of the ocean. His speech gave me a few seconds to stop struggling, to think, to breathe.

"There's another reason, too," Uncle Ramon continued. "A few seasons back, the Marlins' manager, a loudmouth Hispanic who loves to hear himself talk, said he *respected* Fidel Castro, because he was tough enough to survive as a dictator. Well, the Cubans in Miami protested by boycotting the team. Eventually, the Marlins fired that idiot manager's ass over the remark. And I respect *that*."

I let that all sink in for a few seconds. Then I said, "You're right. Why would I ever root for those Yankees over the Marlins?"

13

OVER THE NEXT hour the waters turned choppy. We rode into an almost continuous flow of short, strong waves that hit us head-on. Then they started coming from the sides—*tap, tap, tap.* And that Buick began to feel like a punching bag being worked by a heavyweight boxer who was just warming up.

A bank of clouds rolled across the moon, blocking out a lot of our light.

"It's getting even darker out there," said Luis.

"Don't worry. We don't need to see," said Gabriel. "As long as we follow this compass, we're headed toward freedom."

"How about following the North Star? It's supposed to be the one burning brightest. I learned that in science class," said Luis, ducking his head out of the window to look straight up. "I think I see it—the one with the twinkle."

"That's good, but we need to head north and a little bit

west, Son," said Uncle Ramon. "Let Gabriel do his job. I have faith in him."

I wished I had that kind of blind faith. But I would have given anything to see exactly where we were going, to follow a bunch of clear markers to Florida. Instead, my cousin, my uncle, and I were risking everything on the direction of a compass needle pointed inside the palm of Gabriel's hand.

I thought about holding that compass myself, to see if it would point the same way for me. But I didn't want to take that kind of responsibility and maybe even screw us up.

The game was still going on. It was the top of the eighth inning, and the Marlins got a runner to third base with two outs. Their scrappy leadoff batter had worked a walk after fouling off six or seven straight pitches. He advanced to second on a sacrifice bunt, and then over to third on a ground-out to the Yankees' second baseman.

"That's what I love about this team," said Uncle Ramon. "These Marlins will scratch, claw—whatever it takes to get a run across. They don't have the same power in their lineup as the Yankees—no superstars. But they've got the passion to succeed and the fire in their bellies to do it."

"You think heart beats talent?" I asked him, as we absorbed another quick blow in that chop.

"Not always," he answered. "But talent *without* heart—that talent's just a waste of a God-given gift."

Here's the pitch. Fastball, low in the dirt. And the ball kicks away from the Yankees' catcher! It's rolling to the backstop, and here comes the go-ahead run from third base. Across home plate and the Marlins regain the lead, five to four. We'll have to see how that's scored—a passed ball on the catcher or a wild pitch on the pitcher. Either way, the Marlins are back on top.

"See, they manufactured that run out of nothing. Did it without a single base hit," said Uncle Ramon, extending a fist to bump with both Luis's and mine. "Of course, if I had been the Yankees' catcher, that ball would never have gotten by me. I would have blocked it with my chest, knee, foot—any part of my body. And I would have done that for a sandlot game. For the World Series? I would have gotten down low enough to eat dirt if I had to."

"I'd eat dirt to be at Yankee Stadium right now," said Luis.

"That would be the taste of freedom," said Gabriel, turning his attention away from the steering wheel for a moment to look at us. "And I'd have delivered my *three crates of fish* safely."

"Was that your code word for us?" I asked.

"Maybe 007 could have come up with something better," answered Gabriel. "I tried to keep it simple."

"So you never talked directly to my papi?"

Gabriel shook his head and said, "Just his representative."

I felt satisfied with that, knowing Papi didn't speak to Gabriel instead of me.

In the bottom of the eighth inning, the Marlins brought in their setup man to pitch. The announcer said that Papi was throwing in the bullpen, getting ready to pitch the bottom of the ninth. The Yankees' first two hitters made weak outs. But momentum in baseball can change fast, especially in a one-run World Series game. The next batter slashed a double into the right-field corner. That was followed by an infield single to put runners on first and third.

"What are they waiting for?" asked Luis. "Why don't they bring in El Fuego?"

"Because everyone's a damn specialist these days," said Uncle Ramon. "The Nacionales play it the same way. They want their closer to only pitch in the ninth, like his arm could get tired doing any more than that."

The Marlins' setup man walked the next batter to load the bases. Then he lost the strike zone completely, starting off the next hitter with two straight balls that weren't even close to the plate.

The Marlins' manager is walking out to the pitcher's mound. He looks at the bullpen and signals

*with his left arm. He can wait no longer. We're
going to see Julio Ramirez, otherwise known as
El Fuego, who recorded a club-record forty-eight
saves this season.*

Luis whistled and clapped, as if he was really at the
game. He even tried to stand on his feet, until his head hit
the roof of the Buick. But I sank deeper into the backseat,
tightening my grip on the transistor as the chop outside got
a little heavier.

*This is Ramirez's sixth season in the majors. He
was one of Cuba's all-time great pitchers until he
defected and signed with the Miami Marlins. He's
lost a little bit on his fastball over the last few years,
but he still throws smoke. Ramirez claims to be
thirty-seven years old. Many doubt that number,
however. His age is uncertain, since he arrived in
the US without documentation.*

"Thirty-seven, huh? That makes me a year older than
my *older* brother," said Uncle Ramon. "I understand his
thinking, though. No team wants to give an old man a
long-term contract. The younger, the better. Anyway,
he was already cheated out of millions when he was the

best pitcher in the world and all the Cuban government gave him was a few more hours coaching schoolkids."

Ramirez finishes his warm-up tosses on the mound. He's ready. I don't know how to describe the look in his eyes as he stares down the Yankees' center fielder, who reenters the batter's box. I suppose the only appropriate word would be intense. The crowd is on its feet. Listen to them, more than fifty thousand strong. Ramirez inherits a two-and-oh count on the hitter. The bases are filled with Yankees. There's absolutely nowhere for the Marlins' closer to put him without forcing in the tying run.

"Does he challenge him with one down the middle?" I asked Uncle Ramon.

"Not just *challenge* him. That guy's about to see smoke," he answered.

Here's the pitch. Swing and a miss. That one registered ninety-nine on the radar gun.

"To be called World Champion, believe me, your papi will turn back the hands of time," said Uncle Ramon. "As if he's twenty-one years old again. That kind of desire."

That made me wonder what Papi would do to be with me. And why he hadn't done anything.

Strike two! Ramirez painted the outside corner with that one. The plate's seventeen inches wide, and he nicked the very edge of it—that eighth-of-an-inch black border. The batter wisely took that one, because he probably wasn't going to hit it. Maybe just foul it off. That's expertise on both ends, and a masterpiece of a pitch.

"This batter's toast," said Uncle Ramon. "He might as well start walking back to the dugout now."

Ramirez from the stretch. Here's the pitch. A swing. Strike three! Punched him out with high heat. And look at the reading on the gun—one hundred and one miles per hour!

If the government had planted secret microphones on the ocean floor, we probably would have been taken to prison. Because we let out a roar so loud and so long, the Cuban navy could have followed the sound right to us.

14

IN THE TOP of the ninth inning, the Marlins scored another two runs, adding to their lead. Then, in the bottom half of the inning, Papi shut the door, setting the Yankee hitters down in order—one, two, three—and giving Miami a two-games-to-one lead in the best-of-seven series.

Every time I'd listened to Papi pitch before, I was sitting alone. Lots of times it was as dark as it was right now. That was because I was usually in the stairwell, hiding the transistor radio and the fact that I wanted to hear anything about him at all.

"God willing, we'll be in Florida before the team flies back," said Uncle Ramon. "They could sweep the next two games in New York. Then they'd arrive in Miami as World Champions. That's how I'd like to see my brother after all this time: walking off a plane as a World Series winner, maybe even MVP. We'd be waiting in the crowd, right up front. I wouldn't want him to know we were coming. That moment he first saw us, I know the look on his face would be priceless."

I tried to imagine that scene the way Uncle Ramon described it. Only every time I did, it changed when Papi's eyes met mine. That's when the crowd disappeared, and it became just me and Papi. I could see him opening his mouth to speak. But before he ever did, that vision froze up solid and then faded to black.

"Maybe they'll have a big parade," said Luis. "It would be like a double celebration, the Marlins winning and our freedom. We could all ride in a brand-new convertible, waving to the fans along the streets. And I mean *new*—as in this century, not from the 1950s. What do you think, Julio? What a way to raise our cool factor, first week in the States. Girls will treat us like pop stars."

I loved Luis. But sometimes he was absolutely clueless as to what was going on inside of me.

"All of that sounds great," said Gabriel. "But Julio and his father may need some space, some privacy to resolve whatever the time apart has put between them."

Uncle Ramon quickly jumped in with his take on things.

"I want to make it clear to you, Julio," he said. "What your papi did in leaving, that was all about family. It was about *you*, your sister, and mama. It wasn't a selfish thing. It was about your future, all of our futures. He did the hard work, took the chances. Now it's our turn. He never abandoned you or any of us."

I could tell that Uncle Ramon believed every word he

was saying. I could hear the pride he had in being Papi's brother. And I didn't want to insult him by not having the same pride in being Papi's son.

"I know he still loves me," I said, turning off the transistor.

"That's right," said Uncle Ramon. "Remember, Julio, he gave you his name. I'm sure he looks in the mirror and sometimes he sees you staring back."

I glanced into Gabriel's rearview mirror. For some reason he'd left it hanging over his head, maybe to convince people this '59 Buick wasn't going to be traveling anywhere else but down a dirt road in Cuba. Staring back at me was my own face, in a small, wide frame. There was nothing to see behind us anymore. There was nothing outside the windshield up front either, except for the hope of where we were headed.

"How come *I* didn't get *your* name?" my cousin asked his father.

"Because your mama, since the time she was young, dreamed of having a child named Luis," he answered.

After a few seconds of silence, I looked Luis up and down and said, "It's a good thing you were born a boy. With that name, you would have made an even uglier girl."

Uncle Ramon burst into laughter.

"Oh yeah? You never heard of *Luisa*? That would have been my name," said Luis, beginning to blush a bit.

"Sure, we'll call you that from now on," said Uncle Ramon, wiping a tear from the corner of his eye. "Just make sure to shave the fuzz on that upper lip."

"Don't worry, *muchacha*, there are plenty of razors in Miami," quipped Gabriel, with a widening grin. "Waxing parlors, too."

"Ha-ha. That's so funny," Luis muttered, sulking.

That put an end to all the talk about me and Papi.

My legs were starting to cramp from being in the tight space of that rear seat. There were shooting pains in both my hamstrings. I didn't have room to completely straighten them, though. So I clenched my teeth and dealt with it, feeling like they were two giant rubber bands about to snap. I kept changing positions, putting one leg over the other and then back again. Only it didn't help.

Finally, I found a tiny comfort zone with my left elbow resting against a wooden box of supplies and my right knee jammed up against the back of Gabriel's seat.

Luis was complaining that his foot had fallen asleep.

"Everything's pins and needles," he said, leaning back until he was practically shaking his foot in my face.

That forced me to rearrange myself, losing my good position.

"I hate the feeling of being numb," Luis said.

"It's better than cramps," I told him, annoyed.

Then I went searching desperately for that comfort zone

again. But no matter which direction I contorted my body, I couldn't find it.

The choppy waves continued to slap at us. And after a while, the rocking they delivered started to take on a rhythm. I'm not sure exactly when I drifted off. I just remember opening my eyes sometime later with everything quiet inside the Buick and my legs feeling stiff as boards.

Luis was sleeping across from me, his two hands tucked beneath his head like a makeshift pillow. In the front seat, Uncle Ramon's head looked heavy, sinking lower every few seconds as he gazed into the darkness beside Gabriel.

I didn't want to disturb any of them. So I pressed the transistor up to my ear, keeping the volume as low as possible. I was hoping to hear some of the postgame comments and maybe even an interview with Papi. But that was all over with, and there was just a deep-voiced announcer wrapping things up.

The Marlins' clubhouse was positively brimming with confidence after tonight's game. The feeling in there was electric. Coming into the Series, there was a lot of bravado on the part of the Miami players. The wild-card team talked big about taking down the mighty Yankees—baseball's Goliath—with a slingshot of slap hitters and a single stone. But now

I think they truly believe it's possible. A lot of Miami's younger players are gaining confidence and poise under pressure from the leadership displayed by the team's veterans. Reliever Julio Ramirez was keeping the team loose by having his three-year-old son, "Little Smoke," stamp his feet on a Yankees cap. Then there was . . .

I couldn't listen to another word after hearing that.

I closed my eyes tight, shutting off the radio. Suddenly, it felt like there was a crushing weight on the center of my chest. Without looking, I would have believed it was Papi inside that Buick, jumping up and down on me in a pair of new spikes.

Pretending to be asleep, I sat there in silence, struggling to keep my tears on the inside. I already understood that this weight belonged to me alone. And that if I told Uncle Ramon about Papi's kid, it would fill up every moment of us being out here, sinking me to the bottom even faster.

15

THE NEXT TIME I opened my eyes it was light outside. The sun was blasting through the windshield. I needed to put a hand in front of my face to cut the harsh glare. Luis was already awake beside me, leaning over into the driver's seat. But it took me a while to realize that it was Uncle Ramon behind the wheel.

"Look, Julio, my father's the captain of a ship," Luis said, as Gabriel caught some shut-eye. "I'm going to steer next."

Uncle Ramon reached up and adjusted the sun visor before he said, "Son, this isn't a *ship*. It's a floating car. And the only way you're going to navigate is if you swallow the compass and your nose points north."

"Why? You let me drive *your* car in plenty of parking lots," Luis said, sounding hurt. "I don't need a stinking license. We're outlaws."

"Your job's to keep track of time, Luis," said Uncle Ramon, softening his words a bit. "You're the only one with a good watch. We need to know how long we've been out here so we don't run out of gas. There isn't exactly a service station around."

"How long has it been?" I asked.

"Almost thirteen hours," answered Luis, checking the watch on his belt loop.

"With any luck, one more day at sea for us," said Uncle Ramon, his hands positioned solidly at ten and two o'clock. "Forget the transistor, Julio. We could be watching the next World Series game in color, on a big flat-screen TV. Maybe even in your papi's new house. I'll bet he has a two-car garage, five or six bedrooms, swimming pool, a butler, and a housemaid."

"Housemaid, huh?" I muttered, with the image of Mama in her maid's uniform filling my head.

I remembered Mama's words about Papi. About how there was no way he was alone, living without a woman. Now I knew she was absolutely right. And that could have been the reason she didn't want to come with us.

"If he doesn't have one, maybe he could hire Mama. She has experience at that job now," I sniped.

"Julio, put that anger aside," Uncle Ramon said. "Your mama did what she needed to do to support her children. I don't know why my brother didn't send her money. But I'm sure he had reasons."

I used to want to believe that, too. Sometimes, especially in the first few years after Papi had gone, I'd talked myself into it. Now I knew what Uncle Ramon didn't—that I had a half brother. And he didn't just magically appear. The stork didn't drop him on Papi's doorstep one day. He got here by Papi doing my mama wrong.

"I've said enough. I'm done with it," I told him. "I need to stretch out. I can't sit here anymore. My legs feel like they're in knots."

So I started to climb out the window.

"You going for a swim?" asked Luis. "There could be sharks."

"Careful, Julio," said Uncle Ramon.

I wasn't going into the water. Instead, I made my way across the roof of the Buick and slid down the rear windshield. I sat on the back bumper between the two tail fins, looking at where we'd been, at where I came from. It was the closest thing I could find to being alone. For a second, I thought I heard Luis climbing out his window. But Uncle Ramon probably fished him back, knowing I needed some privacy.

I sat there for maybe twenty minutes, thinking, as I watched the rudder and the wake of white-capped water slipping behind us. Then, before I climbed back inside, I unzipped my pants and took a long piss into the ocean.

Gabriel wiped sleep from his eyes and checked the compass.

"You're a natural-born navigator," he told my uncle.

"We're right on course. Why don't you keep the wheel for a while?"

"It's pretty simple stuff," said Uncle Ramon, deflecting the praise. "All there is to do is keep a straight line just left of the needle. The rudder does the rest."

The words were barely out of his mouth when Luis gave him a long stare.

"Is that so?" my cousin asked.

Uncle Ramon quickly had a response on his tongue. But I could see him pull up short on what he was about to say. Then he hesitated for a moment and took a deep breath, as if he was preparing to swallow his pride.

"I don't see why you can't steer for a while later on," he said, before he exhaled. "As long as the waters stay calm."

"You mean the way they are right now?" asked Luis, with his eyes lighting up like he'd just lined a pitch into the gap between outfielders.

Uncle Ramon shifted his gaze to Gabriel, who nodded his head. I laughed at watching my uncle try to climb into the backseat as he and Luis switched places. But once we were sitting side by side, the shape and color of Uncle Ramon's eyes reminded me too much of Papi's and I stopped laughing.

For the next half hour or so, Luis held the wheel with Gabriel guiding him. Uncle Ramon broke out a supply of PowerBars he'd "borrowed" from Moyano's secret stash behind the counter in the players' cafeteria. I enjoyed every bite. Then I used the silver wrapper to reflect the sun into Luis's eyes as he steered.

"Go on, keep distracting your cousin like that," Uncle Ramon warned me. "A few degrees off and we could wind up in the Bahamas instead of Miami."

"That might not be the worst thing in the world," I said, focusing on the waves in the distance. "We'd still be free, wouldn't we?"

"Yes, but it would be one more obstacle to your papi's helping us," he answered.

"I don't know how much *help* I need," I countered. "I already know how to be a busboy."

Over the next few hours the sun got much stronger. There wasn't a single cloud in the sky or a shred of wind. After a while, that Buick started to bake. The temperature inside must have gone up at least twenty degrees, with the windshield acting like a giant magnifying glass, intensifying the rays. The air got so heavy I could barely breathe.

Bathed in sweat, I tried to climb onto the roof outside to escape that oven. But as soon as I touched my hand to the green metal, I yanked it back, my fingers burning.

"It's on fire up there," I said, pouring some of our drinking water on my hand to ease the pain.

"It's a piece of sheet metal. You could fry an egg on that roof right now," said Gabriel, in a tone that suggested

I should have known better. "That's why I brought along what's under the rear seat."

I reached down and felt the big plastic tarp. With Luis and me working from opposite windows, we unrolled it across the roof of the Buick. Meanwhile, Uncle Ramon grabbed a bucket meant to bail out the car/boat in case it leaked. He leaned outside and filled it with ocean water, before dumping it onto the tarp. Then my cousin and I stretched ourselves out on the roof, like we were on a beach blanket back home in Matanzas.

Gabriel passed up to us a tube of heavy-duty sunblock, and we rubbed it into our faces and bare chests. It was beautiful riding on top of that Buick, with nothing in sight but the horizon up ahead. Then, out of nowhere, a school of flying fish put on a show for us, jumping out of the water and taking flight before vanishing beneath the waves.

"This is what it's going to be like in Miami," Luis said. "The two of us sitting on top of the world like a pair of princes."

"You think?"

"Of course. Who else is your papi going to spend his time and money on?"

"That's a good point," I replied, as the heat building up below that tarp started to seep through to the surface.

16

I WAS LYING flat on my back with my eyes closed when I heard a splash. Then I thought I heard Luis's voice laughing and full of joy. But after I opened my eyes and the sun's glare cleared, I realized Luis was still beside me on the roof of that Buick.

"The water feels amazing!" shouted Uncle Ramon, swimming alongside the car/boat. "It's cold, but it feels great! Did you see my cannonball?"

"No, I missed it," Luis called back in excitement.

Uncle Ramon's voice sounded so much younger, and almost exactly like Luis's, as he floated in the ocean.

"I saw your cannonball!" said Gabriel, laughing out loud from behind the wheel. "You should have seen it, Luis! Your father made a huge splash, bigger than El Presidente lowering himself into his bathtub."

Uncle Ramon looked so satisfied and free, I couldn't stay on that roof for another second. So I took off my sneakers, lifted my arms up over my head, and then dove in.

A chill hit every part of me. A million goose bumps tingled on my skin. My eyes were closed as I went down deeper, straight as an arrow. Then my momentum stopped. I knew that I couldn't be anywhere near the bottom. So I opened my eyes, craning my neck upward. I saw a glimmer of light above me. As a long stream of air bubbles escaped from my nostrils, I propelled myself toward it. I broke the surface and took a deep breath, with the taste of salt water dripping from my lips.

"Neither of you are worried about sharks?" asked Luis.

Uncle Ramon shook his head and said, "There's no fear in me today. I won't allow it. And I'm here to protect your cousin."

"Sharks want whales and barracuda. Not little guppies like us," I said.

"This is *our* ocean now," said Uncle Ramon. "We'll enjoy it. Right, Julio?"

"We should *all* be enjoying it," I answered, swimming toward the Buick.

"I'd love to be out there," said Luis. "But I'm a terrible swimmer."

Climbing back into the car/boat, I grabbed the long nylon rope beneath the front seat. I already knew that Uncle Ramon wasn't getting out of the water if Luis jumped in. So the rest had to be on me.

I took the rope and tied it around Luis's waist before he

handed me the watch from his belt loop for safekeeping.

"This is crazy," said Luis as I doubled the knot.

"Fishermen in China teach their kids to swim this way," said Gabriel.

"We're not going to China. We're going to Miami," said Luis, still hesitant. "Are you sure about this?"

Without warning, I shoved Luis into the water.

He came back up to the surface with a cough, spitting out seawater and flailing his arms.

"Relax and you'll float naturally," Uncle Ramon told him.

I wouldn't leave any slack in the rope. At some point Luis stopped swimming and just held on to it.

"I feel like you're fishing and I'm the bait," said Luis.

"Do you want me to pull you in?" I asked.

"Not yet. I want to be as brave as my father," he answered.

"No fear. *Verdad*, Luis?" asked Uncle Ramon.

"*Verdad*," replied Luis.

Gabriel showed no interest in swimming.

"I've been in the water too much in my life," he said, from the driver's seat. "If I had my choice, I'd rather learn how to fly. It's always been a dream of mine."

Within a few minutes, Luis and Uncle Ramon got out of the ocean. We were all back inside the Buick, looking to escape the sun for a while.

"Enough fun," said my uncle, with beads of salt water clinging to his bronze shoulder blades. "Now this ocean needs to take us to the States. We must be getting much closer."

"Maybe halfway," said Gabriel, studying the horizon.

"It's been almost twenty hours," said Luis, before he reached into his pocket and pulled out a slip of paper that was completely drenched. "The girls from the beach at Cárdenas, their phone number—it's ruined. I can't read this."

"Forget about the girls you knew in Cuba," Uncle Ramon told him. "I know it's hard to think about at your age, boys, but the women in your future, the ones who are going to have your children one day, they're what's important now. Because your own sons are going to be born *free*. That's a gift I couldn't give to you, Luis—a gift my brother's trying to give us now."

Deep down, I understood that speech made plenty of sense. But right then, I didn't want to hear about any gift Papi was giving me. Because I knew now I was at best second-in-line behind his new son. I might have been even third or fourth, if Papi had been super *busy* since he'd gone. And I resented the fact that I had to risk my ass for freedom while some kid called Little Smoke had it before he took a dump in his first diaper.

A few hours went past, and the waters were getting choppy again. The hottest part of the day was over. But I got a reminder of how intense those rays had been when my back and shoulders touched the seat. I hadn't used any of Gabriel's sunblock on those spots. And I could feel the stinging burn now.

"Look out there!" cried Luis. "What's that floating?"

It looked to me like a little island, barely big enough for one person to stand on. For an instant, I thought about jumping in and swimming to it. Only I didn't need to. Instead, the waves brought it right to us.

"It's three coconuts connected to some palm leaves," said Uncle Ramon, who scooped them out of the water.

"They had to fall off a tree somewhere," I said. "Maybe one that's close by."

"It's possible," said Gabriel, with the horizon still empty. "Or maybe they've been out here longer than we have."

"Think we should keep them?" Uncle Ramon asked, after he stripped the palm leaves and held up the coconuts, which were still in their green casings. "If so, somebody's going to have to do the hard work of splitting them open."

"Of course we should keep them," said Luis, taking them into the backseat. "There's milk inside. What if we run out of drinking water?"

"Do whatever you want," said Gabriel. "Personally, I wouldn't waste the energy. If we're out here long enough to run out of water, a few ounces of coconut milk aren't going to save us."

But Luis held on to them anyway, and started cutting

away at their casings using a small knife that Gabriel gave him from the glove compartment.

Later on, we had dried apricots and figs for dinner. I could have eaten each one in a single bite. Only I decided to take my time, making our meal last, like we were a real family sitting around a kitchen table at home. Then I thought about Mama and Lola. How I might never share another meal with them again. And even though I was still hungry, I told Luis, "You can finish my figs, Primo. I know they're your favorite."

A few minutes before sunset, a commercial jet roared through the sky maybe three or four miles to the west. That's when Gabriel and I exchanged a look, like we both wished we had wings to fly.

"We've only been out here twenty-three and a half hours. Less than a whole day," said Luis. "How could it be sunset?"

"That's a good thing," replied Gabriel. "It means we're making progress, moving north. Night falls in Florida before it does in Cuba, because of the curve of the earth."

The darker it got, the more the wind and the waves picked up. A ton of clouds moved in. That left us with less than half the light we had from the moon and stars the night before. So Gabriel's compass became even more important.

Sooner or later, I knew it was coming. I wouldn't mention it first for anything. But after a couple of hours, Uncle

Ramon said to me, "Take out the transistor. Let's hear the game. It should be in the fourth or fifth inning by now."

I was just happy to miss the pregame stuff, when an announcer was more likely to mention something about Papi's new son again.

It's the bottom of the second inning here at Yankee Stadium....

"Second inning?" Luis said, checking his watch. "Maybe they were delayed by rain."

"No, it's more than that," said Uncle Ramon. "Listen to those fans cheering. They're wired."

It's been an offensive onslaught early on. And it's been all Yankees. The Bronx Bombers are living up to their nickname. They lead it eleven to nothing already, scoring seven runs here in the second inning, adding to the four runs they scored in the first. Still, runners on second and third for the Yanks with just one out here.

"Turn it off, Julio. I can't listen to any more," said Uncle Ramon. "We'll turn it back on later. Maybe Miami will make the score closer, salvage some self-respect. But *this* game's over."

"It's all about tomorrow night now," added Luis, still hacking away at the trio of coconuts. "About who'll win Game Five, and go up three games to two."

I was happy to turn off the transistor. I was even happier the Marlins were losing big. That way there'd be practically no chance of Papi getting into the game. So whenever I did turn it back on, the announcers would be talking about the personal lives of other players instead.

HOURS PASSED AND the waves started to get stronger. The
Buick began to really rock. I was bouncing around in the
back, worse than in any school bus I'd ever ridden on.

"I feel like an American cowboy in one of those rodeos,"
said Luis, bouncing as much as me. "Only their rides last just
ten seconds or less."

"Better hold on to your coconuts then," I told him.

"That's right," said Uncle Ramon. "Ten seconds is nothing to us. We're Cuban cowboys. We've got major-league
cojones, made of steel. We'll take this ride for days if we
have to. There's no quit in us. That's why the Marlins are
going to win the Series. They'll ride out their rough patch,
too. Julio, check the game."

"What's the use?" I asked.

"I want to see if they've closed the gap," said Uncle Ramon. "What kind of guts they have."

"They're just ballplayers," I said. "We've got the guts.
We're the ones defecting."

"You mean, like your papi?" he countered.

I didn't want to argue anymore. So I turned on the transistor, waiting to hear if things would get bumpier.

Seventh-inning stretch and what a night it's been for the Yankees. They lead the Marlins by an American football score, fourteen to three. They've pounded every Miami pitcher to take the mound tonight, and I don't believe the Marlins will be wasting any of their better bullpen arms in this one. I think they've already conceded....

Uncle Ramon waved his hand in disgust, and I took it as a signal to put the radio away. After that, there was nothing but the sound of the waves crashing. And I was satisfied in keeping my secret for at least another night.

I was the only one who hadn't steered the Buick yet. I wasn't about to ask now, though. Not in heavy seas. But I was sitting right behind Gabriel, watching him grip the wheel and imagining how it would feel to set my own course. Then I squeezed my own hands tighter, as if they were wrapped around a wooden baseball bat.

I closed my eyes and could see myself walking up to home plate. I'm not sure when things blurred for me, but they blended from a daydream to a sleeping dream. As I settled into the batter's box, wiping out the chalky back line with the heel of my spikes, I could hear the voices of the crowd echoing from the stands. It wasn't the sound of cheers. But there weren't any boos either.

A catcher was in a deep crouch behind me. I could see him out of the corner of my right eye, and hear him pounding his mitt. I wasn't sure whether there was a home-plate umpire or not. And I wasn't about to turn around to find out, instead keeping my concentration on the left-handed pitcher on the mound.

The bases were loaded, and the runners took their leads. The pitcher glared in for the catcher's sign. As he lifted his head, beneath the brim of his cap, I saw that it was Papi. Either he didn't recognize me or he didn't care. He nodded his head to the sign and was practically breathing fire. I didn't have any choice. I knew what kind of heat was coming. So I steeled myself, with all of my senses ready to react.

Papi toed the pitching rubber. Then he brought his hands together, set, with the baseball hidden inside his glove. I could even read his name stitched along the thumb in script—*El Juego*.

His right leg kicked out. Then he dropped his weight down, and drove forward with the lower half of his body. His left arm whipped over his head. And suddenly, the white baseball was in my eyes. It was flying at me so fast the red seams looked as sharp as razors. So I started my wrists forward and brought around the bat head.

First I heard the *crack* of the ball off the bat. Then I felt the vibrations traveling through my hands. It was like the sting of bees, wrenching my fingers from the inside.

The baseball rocketed right back at Papi.

For an instant, we were both frozen in time—me at home plate and him on the mound—with that ball lined directly at his chest.

When I realized he'd never get his hands up in time, I felt an immense surge of satisfaction. But as the ball struck him, Papi disappeared in a puff of smoke.

I lurched forward in my seat, waking up with a start.

"Julio, are you all right? You were asleep," said Uncle Ramon.

"I'm fine," I said, with my heart still pounding.

"Were you dreaming about girls or defecting?" asked Luis.

"Neither," I answered, still trying to get my bearings. "It was baseball."

"That's dedication," said my cousin, who was working on freeing the second coconut from its casing. "If I had your natural talent, I wouldn't be dreaming about baseball. I'd be dreaming about everything baseball could get me, like a fat contract full of US dollars."

"Believe me, son, if you had a connection to the game like Julio," Uncle Ramon said, "it would take over your life. Part of it would be pleasure. The other part would be fear of not making it. That what you have inside isn't good enough, especially when you have to live up to a legend like his papi."

I looked my uncle square in the eyes and said, "I don't need to live up to anything Papi's done. He's not my hero."

"Men aren't supposed to be heroes. They're supposed to be *men*," said Gabriel, still glued to his compass with the waters getting even rougher. "That means they're going to have flaws, sometimes serious ones. Even the legends."

"It's been six hard years. Perhaps you feel like you don't know him now," said Uncle Ramon, returning my gaze until a jolt from a wave broke our eyes apart.

"I *don't* know him," I said, with some gas to my voice. "Neither do you."

"I know he's not a stranger. He's my brother, my blood, just like you are."

Then Luis came between us with some stupid comment about his own special talent.

"Having a girl on every beach in Miami. That's what I'm going to be known for," he said.

Gabriel laughed loudly over that, while Uncle Ramon scoffed at his son's so-called purpose in life. Luis took it all with an easy smile, rolling with the tide. That's when I started to wonder if my cousin's *real* purpose at the moment wasn't to get me out of that conflict with Uncle Ramon.

A few minutes later, Luis said to me, "I never took baseball too seriously. But there is something I really love about it."

"What's that?"

"There's no clock. No time limit," he answered. "A game could go into extra innings and take forever to play out. Other sports, you know when the end is coming. Time runs out. Baseball's got some magic to it that way. No one can say exactly when it's going to be over. So things can always change."

I nodded my head, surprised that Luis even thought about such things.

Sometime around midnight, the wind picked up enough that we had to close all the windows. It was the first time I started to feel boxed in inside that Buick. None of us had showered for more than a day, and there was a growing funk in the air.

I turned on my side, away from the rest of them. Then I tucked my mouth and nose into the crook of my arm, preferring the smell of my own stink to anyone else's.

18

SUNRISE CAME. ONLY it was still dark outside. The sky was a dense gray, while the clouds were black and multiplying.

"Those are storm clouds—violent ones," said Gabriel. "I've got lots of experience with them on the ocean, and none of it's good."

A moment later, the first jagged bolt of lightning ripped through the sky. A few seconds after that, a booming clap of thunder pounded at my eardrums.

"Can we get electrocuted out here?" asked Luis nervously. "What if lightning hits the car or the water around us?"

"That's the least of our worries," replied Gabriel, who was suddenly in a struggle with the steering wheel attached to the rudder. "We're in a big metal box—that'll protect us."

"And that's enough?" Luis followed up.

"Electricity will run through the metal and into the water, grounding us. That's science. Sometimes you just have to trust in it," Gabriel said, as another thunderclap echoed inside the Buick.

"When I was young, my mother told me thunder was the angels bowling in heaven," said Uncle Ramon. "That it was the sound of them knocking down all ten pins, getting a strike."

"Mama told me that story, too," I said.

"Angels bowling?" mocked Gabriel. "I've never heard of such a thing."

The next coupling of lightning and thunder was almost simultaneous.

"I think that means we're moving closer to the center of the storm," Uncle Ramon said.

"Or it's moving closer to us," I added.

"Well, we've had thirty-seven good hours. We can deal with some rough weather," said Luis. "How long could a storm like this last?"

Gabriel didn't offer him an answer.

– – –

I thought I knew what big waves were before that day. I didn't. Every time I believed that Buick couldn't rise any higher on a crest, it did. Then we'd fall off the top and into the watery canyon below. It was like a bad ride at an amusement park that had gone out of control and wouldn't stop.

"They must have used broom handles for shock absorbers on this thing," said Luis as we bounced around the cabin.

Then Luis started to get sick to his stomach again. Only this time there was no open window for him to hang his head out of, not without us getting flooded by those waves.

Uncle Ramon had one hand pressed up against the ceiling, trying to steady himself. In his other hand he held the compass, while Gabriel wrestled with the wheel to keep us on course.

"We're headed west now! Turn right!" shouted Uncle Ramon, an instant before he passed me the compass.

There were four hands on the steering wheel now, as Gabriel and Uncle Ramon both did battle with it.

I watched the needle and called out directions to them: *Right! Left! Straight!* That must have gone on for fifteen minutes. In the middle of it all, one of those damn coconuts flew across the cabin and clonked me in the head.

"Luis, you idiot! Get rid of those things!" I screamed.

But with the windows closed, it was all he could do to shove them down beneath the rear seat.

The sweat was pouring down Uncle Ramon's face. He was leaning so far over, he was almost on Gabriel's back. That's when his right arm must have caught a cramp.

"Augh!" Uncle Ramon cried, letting go of the wheel.

Suddenly, we were spinning in circles. There were no more directions for me to call out, because we were headed in every one. The compass needle was turning as fast as we were. And I couldn't look at it without getting dizzy.

I reached for my seat belt, but I couldn't get it into the buckle.

Then, for an instant, everything went black as a wall of water swallowed the Buick. I don't know if I was praying. But *oh God* were the only words I could find until we came out on the other side of it, still in one piece.

Bang! Bang! Bang! The Buick began to vibrate, like a steel hammer behind us was striking it from side to side.

"That must be the rudder coming loose," said Gabriel, gauging his words. "Don't worry. It won't hurt us too bad."

In my mind, I kept seeing the Buick splitting in two and the four of us being separated on the ocean. It wouldn't have even mattered who could swim and who couldn't, because the waves were going to take you wherever they wanted.

Every time I heard Gabriel's voice, I thought back to the story he'd told—about surviving that storm on the raft when he was a kid. I couldn't imagine what was going through *his* mind at that moment. And if he wasn't scared out of his wits, then he was putting on a good show to keep the rest of us from going into a complete panic.

The water outside was churning with whitecaps. It felt like someone had just tossed the Buick into a giant washing machine. I could feel the tide pulling us down and then the inflatable rubber balloons on each side of the car/boat buoying us back up.

It went on that way for probably three or four hours. I can't say for sure, because Luis didn't give us a time-check once. Maybe he couldn't read his watch as we spun. Or maybe he didn't want to torture us with knowing how long we were being tossed around. At some point, though, I felt almost immune to it, like my body had adjusted itself through some kind of internal gyroscope.

— — —

The first hint that it was ending came when the wind's howl died down. Not long after that, spears of sunlight broke through the cloud cover, reaching the water. Then the waves got smaller and came farther and farther apart.

"Is it over, or do you think we just sailed through it?" asked Uncle Ramon.

"Either way, it's put us somewhere," answered Gabriel, who looked completely wiped out from the battle.

My uncle, who hadn't shaved in probably three days, didn't look any better. And it was the first time I'd noticed gray hairs in his budding, sandpaper beard.

"You think the storm pushed us forward or back?" I asked, before I rolled open my window and swallowed a big breath of fresh air.

"There's really no way of telling," answered Gabriel, as

I handed him back the compass. "All we can do is keep heading north and slightly west."

With the sun's return, the heat started to build again. Luis went back to work on that last coconut. I shot him a glare while I rubbed the lump on my head.

"Don't worry," he said to me. "If we need to split one open, we'll use my noggin this time."

I didn't comment back, but it was exactly what I was thinking.

A few hours later, Uncle Ramon broke the calm.

"Ship!" he shouted. "Off to the right! There's a ship on the horizon!"

"Where?" I asked.

"I see it!" screamed Luis, pointing in that direction. "Way out there. See? It's small. It looks like a smoking cigar on the water."

It was maybe ten or twelve miles off, steaming away from us.

"Should we shoot the flares?" asked Luis. "Signal that we're here?"

"Can you make out any markings on it?" Gabriel asked Uncle Ramon. "A flag? Anything?"

"No, I can't," he answered, with his voice dropping low in disappointment. "And I know what you're thinking. The storm could have pushed us anywhere. That ship might even be Cuban."

"It couldn't be," I said. "We've been out here too long."

"Forty-five hours," said Luis. "Nearly two whole days."

"If it's not a US ship, it's risky to give ourselves up," Gabriel said, continuing on our course. "Captains from other countries might get orders to turn us over to Cuban authorities, just to make it easy on themselves."

That seemed to end any potential argument. And within a few minutes, that ship had sailed out of sight.

When the Buick was almost out of gas, I grabbed the extra ten-gallon container and climbed out onto the trunk. I leaned over the tail fin, connected the spout to the opening of the fuel tank, and tipped the red plastic container back.

Out of nowhere, a seagull started circling. I watched him make four or five passes, with his eyes seemingly glued to mine. Once the container was empty, I took a half-eaten energy bar from my pocket and broke off a small piece. Then I tossed it onto the roof. Without ever touching down, the bird scooped up the morsel with its beak.

I was hoping he'd fly off in the same direction we were headed. But he flew from the glare of the sinking sun into a thick bank of clouds before I lost him.

"Nephew, we have less than half our food and water left," said Uncle Ramon. "Are you going to waste even a single crumb on a seagull?"

"Maybe Julio was luring the bird in. So we could eat him," said Luis.

"That wasn't it at all," I said. "I was trying to bribe him."

"*Bribe* him?" asked Uncle Ramon, confused.

"I was thinking he might give Gabriel flying lessons one day."

"That's nice of you, Julio," Gabriel said, with a widening grin. "But that's something every man has to learn for himself."

Inside of the next hour, the sun went down over the horizon.

"That's three minutes earlier than yesterday," said Luis, excitedly.

"So the storm didn't push us back," said Uncle Ramon.

"No, but it could have blown us sideways," said Gabriel.

Still, we hadn't moved toward Cuba. And that was enough to send us into a celebration where we each ate and drank more than was rationed out for that night.

I put off tuning into the game for as long as possible. But eventually, Uncle Ramon wore me down.

Top of the fifth inning here at Yankee Stadium in a swift-moving contest. The Marlins lead Game Five by a score of one to nothing on a solo home run back in the second inning. Other than that, the pitch-

ers have dominated this evening, with a brisk wind blowing in from right field....

"See, it's a pitcher's night," said Uncle Ramon. "Your papi's probably going to play a big part in this one. Maybe save it. Mark my words."

Over the next four torturous innings, the Marlins had base runners everywhere. They even had a man on third base with less than two outs—twice. But they couldn't get either of those runners home, while the Yankee hitters went down quietly, one after another.

If the Marlins were going to win, I wanted them to blow the game wide open. I didn't want to hear a single word about Papi saving the day. I didn't want him to be the hero. Not mine and not anybody else's. But when the bottom of the ninth inning finally arrived, the score hadn't changed.

To a chorus of sustained boos from Yankees fans, Julio Ramirez completes that long walk from the bullpen to the mound. If El Fuego, perhaps Cuba's greatest pitcher ever, can shut the door on the Bombers, the Marlins will take a three-games-to-two lead back to Miami. They'll be just one game away from a World Series Championship. And even as Ramirez kicks at the dirt around the rubber with his spikes, that much-talked-about intensity and passion appear to be already at full throttle....

"That's his Cuban blood running hot," said Uncle Ramon. "Where we come from, you either have desire or you die a nobody."

"Matanzas!" cried Luis.

"Victory!" shouted my uncle.

I nodded my head and clapped my hands. But somewhere in the darkest part of my heart, I was rooting for Papi to get hammered on that mound.

19

AS THE GAME played on the transistor, I yanked the third coconut from Luis's grasp. I wedged the fingers of both of my hands into the opening he'd made. Then, using all my strength, I tore away the green casing with a grunt.

"There, now all three of them have their shells exposed," I said, shoving it back at him. "Crack them open anytime you want."

"Yeah? I thought you wanted me to chuck them," said Luis. But I wouldn't get into it with him, and didn't respond.

Ramirez ahead in the count, no balls and two strikes, on the Yankees' right-handed-hitting third baseman. Here's the windup and the pitch. Swing and a miss. El Fuego blew it right by him for strike three. One out in the bottom of the ninth....

"My brother's untouchable in situations like this," said Uncle Ramon, his voice ringing with confidence. "And

when you add on the thought of being World Champion? I
wouldn't want to be any of these hitters right now."

"He's bringing the fire," said Gabriel.

"That's because it's burning inside him," said my uncle.
"Since he was a kid."

*Strike one to the Yankees' right fielder. The former
Japanese all-star standing in against the former Cuban National. Ramirez right back to the rubber. He
gets his sign from the catcher and quickly goes into
his windup. The pitch—an absolute BB on the outside
corner, strike two. That registered one hundred and
one on the radar gun. No wonder the batter let it go
by. Ramirez ready to go again. But the hitter steps
out of the batter's box, asking for time, trying to dis-
rupt Ramirez's rhythm. He's back in now. El Fuego
focused and into his delivery. Oh, and Ramirez got
him to chase one out of the strike zone. Strike three!*

"Uno mas," said Uncle Ramon, pumping a fist in the air.
"Just one more out!"

All I knew was that Papi was about to be a hero in front
of the whole world, and I didn't want to hear it happen.

*Here's the first pitch to the Yankees' left fielder. He
swings and it's a high chopper over the pitcher's*

head. Ramirez spears at it. Oh, it deflects off his glove. The runner's safe at first. And suddenly, the Yankees have life. If Ramirez had only let that ball go. His second baseman was right there. It looked to be a sure out. Now the tying run is on first base....

"Come on, my brother. Trust in your teammates to do their jobs," said Uncle Ramon, as if the transistor was a one-way microphone feeding directly into Papi's ears.

The crowd's into it now, and here's the Yankees' first baseman stepping to the plate. Ramirez working from the stretch. He deals. First-pitch swing. And there's a long drive to left field. It's off the wall and right back to the left fielder. Here's the relay throw. The runner's being held up by the third-base coach. The batter chugs into second with a double. And listen to the voices of the Yankee faithful in the stands....

"Can you pray for an out in a baseball game?" asked Luis. "Is that allowed?"

"If it isn't, I earned a ticket to hell before I was fifteen," said Uncle Ramon flatly.

Then Gabriel turned away from the wheel and said,

"You can pray for whatever moves you. And Ramon, I don't believe your passion for baseball will bring you to the gates of hell."

The designated hitter to the plate for the Yankees now. The tying run is at third. The winning run at second....

The vibrations from the sound of the radio ran through my arm. I gazed out the window into the darkness. Then my eyes settled on a star—one almost off by itself, one that seemed to be burning around its edges.

Ramirez undoubtedly wishing he'd kept his glove off that chopper up the middle. That was the error that began this potential Yankees rally. But it's a decision he'll have to live with, and here we are with high drama in the Bronx. El Fuego goes into his stretch. There's one high and tight. Ball one. The crowd booing as Ramirez brushes the Yankees' DH back. Ramirez glaring in. He quickly comes set again. Here's the next pitch. He swings. It's ripped into right center! It's rolling back to the wall. Both base runners score. And the Yankees win! The Yankees win! They now own a three-games-to-two lead in this best-of-seven series, with the scene shifting back to Miami in two days. Oh, how fortunes can change in the space of just a few pitches....

Sinking into the backseat, I shut off the transistor. I struggled to keep any expression at all off my face. Part of me was smiling on the inside, thrilled that Papi had blown the save and taken his lumps. But another part of me felt like a complete traitor—a traitor to my family, and to whatever ties I had left to Cuba. And I kept feeling both of those opposing sides as the Buick rose and fell with the waves.

Uncle Ramon was quiet for a good while after that loss. Then, finally, he said, "Don't worry, Julio. Your papi will be all right. There are still two more games left. And pitchers like him, they have a short memory. They need to. It's the only way they can move forward. Wipe the slate clean and go out to the mound next time and be focused."

Those words—*short memory*—stuck with me like a huge boulder tied around my neck. I thought about sharing that weight with Uncle Ramon, telling him about Papi's new son. But in the end, it was my burden to carry.

"I think you described Papi perfectly," I said. "I don't believe he has any problem putting things behind him."

"Life's always into the future, never backward," said Uncle Ramon. "There's no stopping that."

"The world could spin ten times faster," said Luis. "I'd never forget my mother."

Uncle Ramon nodded his head in silence.

After a moment, Gabriel said, "It's where we've been and what we take with us that count."

"You sure you're a fisherman, and not a philosopher?" I asked him.

"There's lots of time to think on the ocean. The way it pushes and pulls you," Gabriel replied.

"Maybe that's what the tides and currents are all about," said Luis.

That's when I looked at my cousin like he might have been a professor, if he'd had the chance to go to school without any females around to distract him.

Sometime around midnight, Luis announced, "It's been fifty-three hours."

"Your papi's probably on a plane home already," Uncle Ramon told me. "I wonder who's closer to Miami right now, him or us?"

I didn't have an answer. But for a while after that, I was drawing lines in my head on an imaginary map—one line for Papi's plane, and one for the Buick. Sometimes those lines intersected in Miami. Other times they were miles apart. Only no matter what, none of them ever took a straight course.

Later on, around three o'clock in the morning, I was drifting in and out of sleep. On the surface, the waters were calm. And except for the muffled sound of the engine, everything inside the cabin was quiet.

Then, out of nowhere, the Buick was broadsided. I felt a blast of power shake me from left to right. For an instant, we were up in the air, and I swore we were going to flip over, like a turtle on its back.

"Hold tight!" screamed Gabriel, from behind the wheel.

I could hear the cries of my uncle and cousin, too. But I couldn't make any sense of them. My brain was shaking inside my skull. And all I could think was that another car had run a red light, slamming my passenger door. Then I remembered where we were, and thought maybe a huge ship had collided with us.

The Buick splashed back down, right side up. And just as suddenly, everything was peaceful again.

Uncle Ramon reached into the rear, grabbing Luis and me by the arm.

"Are you boys all right?" he asked.

We both nodded before looking out the windows for the lights of whatever had pounded us. Only there was nothing at eye level except darkness.

"What the hell was that?" Uncle Ramon asked Gabriel.

"Maybe it was some kind of sea monster," said Luis, who sounded like he was only half joking.

"My best guess is a rogue wave—a small one," answered Gabriel, still getting himself together. "A big one would have capsized us for sure, and then buried us beneath a ton of water."

"A *rogue* wave?" I asked.

"Strong currents and winds, even miles away, can cause them. Those pressures clash head-to-head, building, until all that force rises up. And when it does, you don't want to be in its path."

"Like a wave on steroids," Uncle Ramon said. "One with 'roid rage?"

"Sounds right," said Gabriel.

"But everything was so smooth and calm," Luis said.

"It's a reminder of where we are. Of what can happen at any moment," said Uncle Ramon. "It's not that different from living in Cuba."

"It *is* a reminder," I said, "that sucker punches like that can come no matter where you are."

20

THE BACK OF my eyelids were filled with orange light. So even though my eyes were still shut, I knew that the sun had come up. I hadn't brushed my teeth in days. The worst taste in the world was living inside my mouth. I opened my lips a crack to suck in some fresh air, trying to diffuse it.

Suddenly, someone grabbed my upper arm in a frenzy. I figured we were about to be slammed by another monster wave, and my entire body tensed.

It was Luis, and he shouted, "Land! I think that's land!"

He was pointing straight ahead into the distance. It took a few seconds for my eyes to focus. Uncle Ramon was awake now, too, jumping up and blocking my view. But when I finally was able to see over his shoulder, I saw that Luis was right.

There were tall buildings and a beach, maybe four or five miles away.

Only Gabriel was sitting calmly behind the steering wheel.

"When were you going to let us know?" Uncle Ramon asked him excitedly.

"At first, I wanted to make sure it wasn't a mirage. That I wasn't dreaming," answered Gabriel, with a look of satisfaction. "Then I decided that I didn't want to cheat you out of that moment of seeing it for yourselves."

"Is it Miami?" I asked.

"We won't know for sure until we're there," answered Gabriel, pressing the gas pedal to the floor.

"Pinch me, Julio," said Luis. "I want to know that this is for real, not a dream."

"All right, but you don't need to pinch me," I replied. "None of my dreams have been this good lately."

Getting closer, we could see windsurfers on their boards. Luis and I climbed up onto the roof of the car/boat and started waving. Then a cluster of windsurfers gathered, before turning their sails around and heading toward us.

"Think they're excited to meet Cuban refugees?" Luis asked.

"No, I think they've never seen a green fifty-nine Buick before," I answered.

That's when I heard the siren. There was a big gray ship, probably a mile off, closing in from our right. I could see the US flag on its side.

Gabriel hit his horn in return, and the sound waves vibrated through the soles of my feet.

"You see the red, white, and blue?" asked Luis.

I nodded my head, thinking how it was the same three colors as the Cuban flag, only with fifty small stars instead of a single giant one.

A voice came over the ship's loudspeaker in Spanish.

"This is the United States Coast Guard!" it bellowed, with an echo. "You are in US waters! Shut off your engine! Put your hands on top of your head!"

"Have we made it far enough to stay?" I asked my uncle, leaning down into the cabin. "Not to get sent back?"

Uncle Ramon climbed onto the roof with us, while Gabriel kept driving with the engine still running.

"Gabriel *thinks* this is good enough," said Uncle Ramon.

"How could it be better?" I asked.

"If we were standing on US soil," he answered.

The voice on the loudspeaker repeated its demands. Then that ship launched a smaller, faster boat, full of uniformed men.

"I'm not taking any chances," I said. "I'm going to swim for the beach."

Luis told his father, "You go, too. Maybe it'll help us all."

"No way I'll leave you here," my uncle said, an instant before I dove into the water.

I was swimming in a straight line, as fast as I could, riding every wave to pick up speed. Gabriel finally shut off his engine. Glancing back, I could see them all with their hands on their heads.

That smaller boat reached the Buick, and now a second one was motoring after me. I was kicking my legs harder, reaching with every stroke. I was already exhausted. But there was no way I was going to stop.

Ahead of me, one of the windsurfers had broken away from the others, coming in my direction. He reached out a hand, like he wanted to pull me onto his board. But I kept on swimming.

"Behöver hjälp?" he asked, lowering the sail and paddling alongside me.

I didn't know what language that was. All I knew was that it wasn't English. And that really freaked me out, like I might be swimming toward the wrong shore.

That boat was getting closer, and I'd reached a group of windsurfers, maybe a hundred yards off the beach. I was so focused on going forward that my brain couldn't link together their words. But my ears understood they were speaking both English and Spanish to me.

My arms felt like limp rubber bands, and my lungs ached until I thought they were going to explode. Then, about fifty yards out, I heard the cheers from the people on the beach. And that sound gave me an added surge of strength.

I heard the motor of that boat getting closer. So I turned

my head to see where it was. That's when a wave broke over-
top me and I swallowed a mouthful of seawater.

I was closer to the shore than that boat was to me. I was
choking and gagging now. Someone grabbed me around the
shoulders and started dragging me in. But as soon as it was
shallow enough for my feet to touch the bottom, I got myself
free from that person's grasp and propelled myself toward
the sand.

Before I knew it my chest was out of the water, and then
my waist. I staggered onto the dry sand, falling to my knees.
I touched the ground like it was home plate and I'd been
rounding the bases. Only I wasn't safe. I was *free*.

The applause and the motor were ringing in my ears.

I collapsed face-first into the sand, and it stuck all around
my lips and mouth. I'd seen photos of people kissing the
ground, grateful to be somewhere. But this was different. I
could *taste* it.

Then someone in the crowd turned me over, putting
something ice-cold into my hand.

"Drink. Drink," a woman said in English.

I looked and it was a can of Pepsi.

The sound of the motor stopped and the circle of people
around me opened. A man, maybe in his early thirties, with
a complexion that looked like mine, came walking through.
He was wearing a blue uniform and hat, with a holstered
pistol strapped to his right hip.

I put the can down into the sand, before I ever took a sip. Then I held out both my wrists, expecting him to handcuff me.

He stood over me with his hands on his hips. Then in Spanish he said, "I'm Chief Petty Officer Sebastian Rodriguez. You sail from Cuba? Looking for asylum?"

I nodded, with the salt water dripping from my chin.

"You didn't have to swim so fast. Once you hit the water, I wasn't going to stop you from reaching shore. I'm just glad you didn't drown. Do you need a doctor?"

I shook my head. And when I finally caught my breath, I asked, "You won't send them back, my family in the car/boat?"

"It's not up to me," he answered. "There's a government agency—Immigration and Naturalization Service. They take care of that. But unless you're terrorists, you'll probably all be allowed to remain. Basically, it's your reward for surviving the trip."

"I'm not a terrorist," I said. "I'm a shortstop."

"That's always better," he said, smiling from the corners of his mouth.

I couldn't believe it. I was actually here, alive and in one piece. It was like being reborn. Every breath seemed new, and even the sun felt different on my skin.

Suddenly, there were more sirens, this time from the street beyond the beach, and the sound of another motor on the ocean in front of me.

Uncle Ramon, Luis, and Gabriel were coming ashore with some officers in a small boat. Then a pair of ambulances and three carloads of agents in blue Windbreakers with the letters INS across the front and back arrived.

Luis leaped onto the sand. He ran up and threw his arms around me.

"How long?" I asked him.

"Sixty-two and a half hours," he answered through his hug.

"That's a long trip in a Buick," said Officer Rodriguez. "Who put that thing together?"

"That was our guardian angel here," answered Uncle Ramon, kissing Gabriel once on the forehead. "We made it on a wing and a prayer, right?"

"Always," answered Gabriel, with his hands clasped to heaven.

"My men are checking it over from top to bottom now," said Officer Rodriguez. "If it's clean, you're probably in good shape to stay."

"Don't worry. No drugs. No guns," said Uncle Ramon.

"Just three coconuts waiting to be cracked," added Luis, lightly punching my arm.

People all over the beach were taking photos of us with their cell phones. But Officer Rodriguez wouldn't let any of them pose with us.

"Buena suerte con su beisbol," said Officer Rodriguez, wishing me well before handing us over to a Spanish-speaking INS agent.

"Good *luck?*" questioned Uncle Ramon. "This is the son of El Fuego, soon-to-be World Champion. He was born with skills."

That statement brought more cheers and photos from the crowd.

I couldn't tell by the look on Officer Rodriguez's face if he'd ever heard of Papi or not. But for some reason, I almost wished he hadn't.

"Family's important," said Officer Rodriguez, with his brown eyes on mine.

Then he turned away and gathered his men, before walking back to his boat.

We didn't want any medical treatment. So that INS agent took us to his car.

"Excuse me, but what year model is this?" Luis asked him as we got in.

"I believe it's a twenty-twelve," he answered.

"Can you imagine that, Cousin? A two thousand and twelve," Luis said in awe. "I'll bet you it rides like a dream."

21

GAME SEVEN ● 171

RIDING IN THAT car, I couldn't take my eyes off the faces of the people on the streets of Miami. The INS agents wouldn't let me open any windows. But even through the tinted glass, I could see the light in people's eyes, and how much less weight they carried here. They were young and old, black, white, brown—a few even had hair dyed crazy colors, like orange and purple. But none of them seemed afraid of being who they were. And I just knew that back in Cuba, people would think twice about standing out from the crowd, thinking there was always a chance of getting in trouble over it.

"Julio, what if we see your papi walking around?" asked Luis. "We could jump out of the car and yell, 'Surprise!' I swear I'd kiss his feet for getting us here."

Before I had to come up with a reply, Uncle Ramon said, "El Fuego's not going to be walking in the streets, not today. He's going to be at home, resting for the game tomorrow night."

But I began to wonder—what if we *did* see Papi on the

street? Would he be holding the hand of his new son? Or would he be walking alone, forgetting about his family, the same way he did to Mama, Lola, and me?

Then I noticed the GPS built into the car's dashboard. I tapped Luis on the shoulder, pointing at it. His eyes opened as wide as mine. Part of me felt like we were finally living in all of those modern movies I'd seen, while another part was already feeling guilty that I was here without my mother and sister.

"We could have used that on the ocean," Luis said.

"Why? Such little faith in me to guide you?" replied Gabriel, behind a wry smile.

The agent who was driving must have been impatient. Because instead of waiting at a red traffic light, he tapped a switch and the siren let out a short *whhaaaa* before we went through the intersection. One block later, we turned into an underground parking garage beneath a tall office building. Then an elevator took us up to a third-floor processing center.

The scent of the place tickled my nose. It was unbelievably clean, like someone scrubbed it down with bleach every hour.

Once you got past a long hallway of offices, there was a big open room with hundreds of fluorescent bulbs shining down. Maybe a dozen other refugees were there. And one of the agents said a small group of them had washed ashore from Cuba just a few hours before we had, but that most of them were at a hospital, and in bad shape.

"I have a phone number I need to call," Gabriel told an agent. "We already have representatives and a sponsor here."

"I'll pass that on to my superiors," said the agent, walking away. "For now, just relax and get comfortable. Your processing will take a while."

The windows nearly stretched from the floor to the ceiling, letting in lots of light. Only those windows wouldn't open. Cool air was being pumped in through vents.

Round tables, plastic chairs, and cots dotted the room. The refugees were spread out among them, talking, looking at paperwork, and sleeping. Against the far wall, beneath a framed picture of the Statue of Liberty, there was a table filled with free food. It had coffee, juice, bottled water, and fruit. There was also a tray of packaged treats, including Twinkies, Sno Balls, Suzy Q's, and Ding Dongs.

I saw those treats and couldn't help thinking about Lola, who was practically addicted to them. Papi used to buy them for her on the black market—in illegal stores the government didn't know about—before he defected. After that, we didn't have the money to waste. But every year on her birthday, Mama and I would scrape up enough to buy her a whole box.

"Hey, Primo. Who would be crazy for one of these?" asked Luis, a moment before shoving an entire Twinkie into his mouth.

"I know," I answered, losing my appetite.

The agent came back and handed Gabriel a cell phone. I watched as he dialed the number by heart.

"Is that my brother's number?" Uncle Ramon asked him.

"I'm not sure," answered Gabriel as it rang. "I've never called it before."

I saw Gabriel's shoulders lift as someone on the other end picked up. I moved closer to him, trying to hear.

"We're here. Everyone's safe, in good health," Gabriel said. "We're at the immigration building in Miami."

I couldn't make out the voice as Gabriel listened to the short response. Then he gave the agent back his phone and said, "Someone will be here for us very soon."

"*Someone?*" asked Uncle Ramon.

Gabriel nodded.

A few minutes later, the agent brought us into an exam room, where a woman doctor in a white lab coat was waiting. She listened to our heartbeats with a freezing-cold silver stethoscope. Then she used a tongue depressor and a tiny flashlight to look down our throats. After that, she asked about any diseases we'd ever had, like measles or chicken pox.

"Julio, this is just like taking a physical to play baseball," said Luis, who then lowered his voice to a whisper and asked, "Think she'll hold our nut sacks and make us cough?"

I cracked a half smile over that, but wouldn't answer.

Finally, she gave us each a small plastic container to pee in. They were numbered from 189 to 192.

"That's how many people we've processed this year," she answered, after I asked what the numbers meant.

It didn't seem like a lot. But I understood it didn't reflect all the people who weren't as lucky as us. The ones who'd died trying to get here, or who got caught and were rotting in prisons.

We went back to the main room, waiting to fill out our paperwork and be interviewed. There was a Cuban family—a mother, father, and small daughter—at a table near us. The mother had a wide bandage on the right side of her forehead. Gabriel went over to ask about it.

"My little girl was falling out of our raft. By the grace of God I caught her," she said, crossing herself and then raising her eyes toward the fluorescent lights above. "I hit my head on a wooden oar. It made a big gash. But I'm all right."

"We're from Havana. Pleased to meet you," said her husband, shaking Gabriel's hand, as Uncle Ramon walked over as well. "Two days we made it here. The wind was pushing us the whole way."

"You arrived this morning?" asked my uncle.

"No, five days ago," he answered. "We've been trying to get placed in a refugee house. So we don't wind up sleeping on the streets and finding trouble."

"What kind of house is that?" Luis asked the man, going over by the little girl, who was playing on the floor with toy soldiers and animals battling on either side of a blanket hanging down off a cot.

"Maybe fifteen people living together in a few rooms—different families sharing food, looking for work," he answered. "Houses like that are spread out all over Miami. But they're hard to get into. You'll see when you try."

"Not us. My uncle's famous," scoffed Luis, picking up one of the girl's toys. "We'll probably be living in a mansion and—"

That's when Uncle Ramon gave him a swift kick in the behind.

"I'm sorry. My son thinks he's more important than he is," Uncle Ramon explained to the man, with a sharp glare for Luis. "Good luck to you and your family finding an opening in a house."

Luis knew that he'd screwed up, acting obnoxious. So he tried to be extra nice to that girl, making a helmeted soldier fight a striped tiger for her, including sound effects.

"Get ready to shoot," Luis told her, before putting an empty Ding Dong wrapper to his mouth and puffing it up with air. "One, two, three!"

Then Luis slammed the wrapper between his palms, producing a loud *pop!*

Nearly everyone turned around to see. Even though it was just a kid's game, it got quiet for a while, and I could feel the anxiousness in the room until it slowly faded away.

We were stuck there for the next seven hours, watching TV on a Spanish news station and listening to music on my transistor. The signal came in much better now that we were in Miami.

"Very soon?" Uncle Ramon nudged Gabriel. "Is that what the voice told you?"

"You waited almost forty years to be free," Gabriel replied. "A few hours in the US and now you're impatient?"

I guess we all were, especially once the sun went down.

Luis even stopped checking his watch after a while. But I think the impatience was getting to me the most. I wanted to see Papi face-to-face. And I wanted the freedom I'd risked my life for to become something more than four beige and blue walls and a tray full of free Hostess cakes.

Then, just as I was about to lose my mind in that room, we were called into a small office. On a table were four pens and four forms to fill out.

A Spanish-speaking agent introduced himself to us. He was about to walk us through the forms when the phone on his desk rang.

"Un momento, por favor," he said, and then picked up the receiver.

A few seconds later, he turned his attention back to us

and said, "Someone has just arrived to represent your party. May I invite that person to join in?"

"Yes, absolutely," answered Uncle Ramon.

"Send him in," the agent said into the phone.

Suddenly, against the hallway wall, by the open door, I saw the immense shadow of a tall figure. I rose up in my seat a little. Then I swallowed hard at the thought of what might happen next.

22

THE SHADOW SLID forward, turning razor thin. My eyes had to refocus as it rounded the corner, going from shadow to substance. And when my brain finally caught up to my eyes, I realized that it wasn't Papi.

Instead, it was an older Hispanic man in a suit and tie, carrying a sharp leather briefcase. He introduced himself to the INS agent first.

"I'm Antonio Oliva, attorney for Julio Ramirez Sr.," he said, before turning to us. "I'll be representing each of you in this process. Now, which one of these young men is Julio Jr.?"

"I am."

"Your father wanted me to express his great relief and answered prayers that you're finally here," he said, reaching out to shake my hand. "He's focused on the World Series right now, with his obligations to the Miami Marlins. That's why I'm here in his place. But he'll be with you soon. He promises."

Mr. Oliva wouldn't turn my hand loose until I nodded, acknowledging his speech.

"You mean, as soon as he *wins* the World Series," added Uncle Ramon.

"From your mouth to God's ears," said Mr. Oliva. "But what else would I expect from El Fuego's brother? I can see and *hear* the resemblance."

Right then, I was willing to bet anything that Papi hadn't sent a replacement to read his new son a bedtime story that night.

"I have their forms already filled out. All they need to do is sign," said Mr. Oliva, producing the pages from his briefcase. "How quickly can these gentlemen be released to Mr. Ramirez?"

"Released to my brother," said Uncle Ramon in a reverent tone.

"I take it that Mr. Ramirez is willing to clothe, house, and feed them?" asked the agent.

"Absolutely," said Mr. Oliva. "Employ them as well. In a manner of speaking, Gabriel is already on his payroll. And obviously the young men will be enrolled in school."

"I know what happens in US high schools," Luis whispered to me. "I've seen lots of movies. Students can do anything they want here—sing, dance, hang out in the halls."

"I'll go through the paperwork," said the agent. "If it's correct, they should be released shortly."

Mr. Oliva gave Uncle Ramon his card and said, "When everything's in order, call that number. I'll arrange the rest from there."

I didn't know what there was to *arrange*. This was starting to seem more like a business meeting than a family reunion. And I hadn't thought it was possible, but the closer in miles I got to Papi, the farther away from him I felt.

I picked up the pen and found the blank line with the *X* next to it. I wanted the signature that let me walk free on the streets of the US to look amazing. But I guess my hand must have been shaking, because when I was finished, it looked like I'd signed that paper in the dark.

When we walked back into the big room, some of the refugees who were gathered around a TV in the corner began pointing to us. A Spanish news station was showing a video of our Buick on the water from this morning. Then on a split screen, side by side, they showed photos of Papi and me—him in his Marlins uniform and me on the beach.

"Less than a day in the States and you're on TV," said Luis. "Maybe we could get our own reality show together. It'd be perfect—two hot young Cuban guys, their first year here. Your papi could pull some strings."

I shook my head at Luis like he was insane.

"Your cousin doesn't need that kind of publicity," Uncle Ramon said. "His ability to hit a baseball will get him everything he needs in life."

The idea that I *couldn't miss* as a big-time baseball player sounded just as crazy to me.

The hours crept past and we were all exhausted. But none of us wanted to sleep.

It was a few minutes after midnight when Uncle Ramon said, "The first time I wake up in America, I don't want it to be here, guarded by agents. I want it to be in a place where I can walk out the door whenever I like and *really* be free."

"I want to wake up in a king-size bed in my uncle's house," said Luis, leaning back on a cot with a rolled-up blanket beneath his head as a second pillow. "No more foldout couches for Julio. Right, Cuz?"

"I'd sleep on the floor if I had to," I said, glancing over at that family we'd met from Havana. "If it was worth it to me."

The three of them were asleep on two cots pushed together—the man and woman on either side of the small girl tucked safely in between them.

"We all make our own beds," said Gabriel.

"Is that right?" I questioned. "It never happens that someone else makes it for us?"

"You said it yourself, Julio," he quickly countered. "You can always get up and go sleep on the floor."

"Gabriel, how about you? Where are you going from here?" asked Uncle Ramon.

"I haven't given it a lot of thought," he answered. "My job of safely delivering the three of you isn't completely over. Not yet, at least. Until it is, I don't have to think about what's next for me."

Then Luis said, "I thought that lawyer, Oliva, was taking over now."

"Not in my mind," replied Gabriel. "He might walk us out the front door. That's one thing. I promised to bring Julio to his father."

"Seems like Game Six and Game Seven are standing in the way," I scoffed.

"I believe it's more than that, at least from your side," Gabriel said, without sounding like he was judging anyone. "Six years can bring a lot of baggage with it."

I didn't respond to that.

It was almost three o'clock in the morning when the agent who'd been processing our paperwork appeared. He handed Uncle Ramon a cell and said, "Congratulations. You can make that phone call now."

Ten minutes later, a black limo pulled up outside the INS building.

Mr. Oliva wasn't anywhere to be seen. And as we walked out to the car, a driver in a small round cap came around and opened the door for us.

Out of nowhere, a woman holding a tape recorder called my name. She had red hair and her Spanish wasn't great. But I understood her well enough.

"Julio, I'm Cadence Myers, ESPN. How does it feel to be in America? To be free?"

I looked at Uncle Ramon, to see if he thought I should speak. But he seemed as interested in my answer as she was.

"I hope it will be worth everything, leaving behind my family," I said, talking into the machine.

"And your father? How will it be? Sharing love with him again?"

My eyes became fixed on the two tiny wheels slowly turning inside that recorder as I answered, "It will probably change my life. Maybe both our lives."

"*Mucho gusto,*" she said, an instant before those wheels came to a stop.

Then we climbed into the car with no idea where we were headed.

I'd counted seventeen traffic lights when Marlins Park first came into view.

"There it is. That's the baseball stadium," Luis said excitedly.

It was so big I couldn't believe my eyes. It looked like a giant flying saucer. And even though there'd been no game that night and it was mostly dark, it still shone with plenty of turquoise and white lights.

"I think those red flashers on top are so anything flying low to the ground doesn't hit it," said Gabriel.

"It's beautiful," said Uncle Ramon. "Julio, that's where your papi pitches. That's something special. Maybe one day, you'll play there, too."

"If Uncle pitches long enough, it's possible you'll both play on the same team," said Luis. "Like Ken Griffey Jr. and his pops once did."

But right then, that idea sounded crazier than any reality TV show Luis could have concocted.

23

THE LIMO PULLED up to the gates of a two-story apartment complex. There was a uniformed guard stationed out front in a little booth, and our driver needed to get a parking pass from him to enter.

"See that guard? It's his job to keep the wrong people out," said Uncle Ramon.

Even when Papi was the most famous baseball player in Cuba, anybody could walk up to our door and knock.

"The *wrong* people?" I asked. "You mean, like busboys and factory workers?"

"No, I mean autograph hounds and favor seekers," he emphasized. "The salary ballplayers get paid in the States makes it so they won't leave you alone."

Inside the complex, there were six buildings laid out in a circle, with manicured lawns, shrubs, and palm trees in between.

"Look in the middle—there's a huge swimming pool with a twisting slide," said Luis. "And all of those lounge chairs. That must be where the honeys go sunbathing in bikinis. Maybe even topless."

We slowly rolled up to building number four. I could see Mr. Oliva standing in the glow of our headlights, his red tie still knotted tight.

Getting out of the limo, Luis asked him, "Is this the apartment where El Fuego lives?"

Mr. Oliva put a finger to his lips and murmured, "Please, keep your voices low. It's close to four in the morning. The people on the ground floor are probably sleeping. We're up-stairs. Follow me."

So we did. The keys in Mr. Oliva's hand looked shiny and new as he opened a trio of locks on the heavy wooden door.

We walked into the living room, which was connected to a large open kitchen on one end and an outdoor balcony overlooking the lighted pool on the other. The apartment was spotless and the air was a little musty, as if no one had been living there for a while.

"Are we staying here for a few days?" asked Uncle Ramon.

"No, this is your new home," answered Mr. Oliva, hand-ing him the one set of keys. "It was rented once the plan to defect became a reality. That's how much faith Mr. Ramirez had that you'd make it."

"How big is this place?" asked Luis, beginning to explore.

"There are three bedrooms—for Ramon, Luis, and Julio," Mr. Oliva continued. "Gabriel, of course you're welcome to stay until your business with Mr. Ramirez is complete."

Uncle Ramon and I exchanged glances. We didn't need any words. We both quickly understood that Papi didn't want me in his house.

"So where does my uncle live?" asked Luis.

"Mr. Ramirez owns a modest home in South Beach," answered Mr. Oliva.

"*Modest*, in South Beach?" questioned Luis. "I heard that place is packed with mansions."

But Mr. Oliva started toward the front door and said, "I'll call tomorrow to see if you need anything. There are boxes of new clothes in the bedrooms. I hope they fit. There's lots of Marlins gear, too."

At that moment, I couldn't see myself wearing a Marlins shirt.

Standing just on the other side of the door, Mr. Oliva turned around. He finally loosened his collar and tie, and then said, "I know this hasn't exactly been a family reunion so far, especially for young Julio. I'm sure that in the coming days, you'll find the connection you're looking for. For heaven's sake, the World Series is on the line."

Maybe that was as personal as somebody's lawyer could get. After all, we weren't *his* family. He was just paid by Papi to do a job. But his speech didn't change the way I was feeling.

Then Mr. Oliva left, along with the limo outside.

I turned to Gabriel and said, "Why don't you take one of the bedrooms? I'll sleep on the couch. I'm used to it."

"No, that's not my place here," he said.

I opened the sliding glass door to let in some fresh air. Then I walked out onto the balcony overlooking the pool. I rested both hands on the iron railing, staring at the little cuts and ripples on the surface of the light-blue water.

"Quite a change from twenty-four hours ago," said Uncle Ramon, walking out behind me.

"There are waves out there," I said, trying to see through to the bottom of the pool. "How's that possible? There are no currents or winds. No kids splashing."

"Maybe it's the pull of the moon, or the way it just has to be," he answered. "Listen, Julio, my brother is a man of family, ever since we were young. I know the last six years have been hard on you. But remember, he's the reason we're standing here."

"The reason *I'm* standing here is freedom," I said.

"That's only partly true," said my uncle. "Now you have to deal with the rest of it. And there's going to be no easy road."

Luis walked out onto the balcony. He was wearing a Marlins home jersey with the tags still hanging from it, along with a huge smile. I figured we were about to hear all his plans for tomorrow—for turning Miami into his personal playground, before anyone got the bright idea of sending us back to school.

I was surprised when he called Gabriel to join us, and then said, "Before we left Cuba, we prayed on the beach to make it here alive. Now that those prayers have been answered, I think we should give thanks."

We all bowed our heads in silence. But what jumped into my mind was the thought of my half brother. I didn't know him or his name. But I was positive he followed Papi around the way I used to—like he was some kind of superhero. So after giving thanks, I prayed the kid would never lose faith in Papi the way I had, even if I was going to be jealous of that.

After everyone else was gone, I stood on the balcony a while longer, watching those little waves in the pool. I decided that I really didn't care how they got there. That if I wanted things smooth I would have sat in my bathtub back in Cuba, instead of crossing the ocean in a '59 Buick.

By the time I went back inside, Luis and Uncle Ramon had claimed their bedrooms. Walking into the remaining one, I saw the huge bed, dresser, boxes of clothes, and private bathroom. Right away, I thought how Lola would die for a bedroom like this. And if we were still living in the same house, how *I'd* do anything for Lola to have a bathroom of her own. That way I could actually get some time on the toilet.

But deep down, I knew it was more than that. The truth was that I was going to miss being her big brother every day. Because even when she was a royal pain in my behind, she was still my sister—someone I'd shared losing Papi with.

I got into the bed, but I just couldn't get comfortable. Despite being bone tired, I kept tossing and turning. Then I remembered what I'd said to Gabriel about someone else making your bed. So I got up and pulled the blankets down to the hardwood floor. And that's where I slept.

24

WHEN I OPENED my eyes it was a few minutes before noon. I picked myself up off the floor and walked straight into the shower. I turned the water on full force, paying no attention to the HOT or COLD. I dealt with whatever came——the freezing and scalding ribbons of water.

It was the strongest shower I'd ever felt in my life. Without moving a muscle, I let the powerful stream pour over my head. It ran across my eyelids and down the corners of my mouth. I stood there for a long time, letting it soak into every part of me. All at once, I felt clean enough to move on, to face anything.

I found a shirt and pants that fit from the boxes of clothing Papi had sent. I wouldn't even waste my time at a mirror. Then I went out into the living room. Neither Gabriel nor Luis was anywhere to be seen. Uncle Ramon was seated in the kitchen. He was on the cell phone that Papi's lawyer had left him. At first, I figured that's who he was talking to. But just before he ended the call, Uncle Ramon said, "I can't wait to see you again either."

My uncle put the cell down on a granite countertop as his eyes met mine.

"Was that Papi?" I asked.

Uncle Ramon nodded in response. Then there was a long silence, and I could sense the weight he was suddenly carrying—much heavier than not putting me on the phone with my father. And there was a look in his eyes, one that seemed to say, *I was wrong about a lot of things*.

That's when I understood that Uncle Ramon knew.

"What's his son's name?" I asked, in a tone that probably sounded like an accusation. "And don't tell me it's Julio."

My uncle appeared absolutely stunned.

"You knew?" he asked, from the opposite side of the counter. "How?"

"The transistor."

After a moment, Uncle Ramon said, "Milo. He's named for your grandfather."

"And that's the reason we're here in this apartment? So we don't intrude on his new life?" I said.

"I can't say that for sure," said Uncle Ramon. "It sounds too harsh."

"Does it? Why didn't he talk to me? Were *you* supposed to break the news about this instead of *him*?"

"No. My brother said he wanted to tell you himself, in person."

"Well, it's too late for that, isn't it?"

"Your papi says he'll be here as soon as the Series is finished."

"And maybe I won't be," I said, before walking out the apartment door.

I didn't know where I was going. I didn't have money, food, or a phone. I decided to stay clear of that guard in the little booth out front. So I started wandering between the buildings of the complex for a while. I walked off a lot of frustration in the midday heat, before finally settling in the shade of a palm tree behind some shrubs. I was about forty yards from the pool, where it looked like Gabriel was giving Luis a swimming lesson.

At my feet, I saw a small green lizard with a long tail. As it moved from the leaves of the shrub to the trunk of the palm, its bright color began to fade. Given enough time, I suppose the lizard's scaly skin might have turned brown to match. But before it ever did, I kicked at the surrounding dirt, sending that lizard scurrying in another direction.

I didn't remember much about my grandfather. I was only five or six when he died. If Uncle Ramon hadn't told me his first name, I probably would have been hard-pressed to recall it. I knew that he loved baseball, too, yelling words at umpires that Mama would never let me repeat. And he was always trying to feed me hot peppers, to see how much I could take before I screamed for a glass of water.

Off to the side of me, there was a big patch of grass. A mother walked past with her two little boys. She was headed toward the pool in a terry cloth robe. But her kids had on baseball caps and were carrying a yellow plastic bat and a white Wiffle ball. The two of them started running around that open space, chasing each other in circles. Then the one with the ball began pitching. The other kid knew how to swing all right. Only his hands were too far apart on the bat, and he was nearly corkscrewing himself into the ground. So I walked over to where they were playing. They saw me coming and froze up a little bit.

In English, I asked them, "Brothers?"

They smiled wide and said, "Yes."

I reached out for the yellow bat and the kid gave it to me.

Pushing my hands close together on its narrow neck, I said, "This way."

I took a swing. The bat sliced through the air with a *whoosh*, and both kids seemed really impressed. Then I handed the bat back. On the next pitch, the kid swung with his hands in the right position. He blasted one over his brother's head and started running a diamond shape around imaginary bases.

Their mother noticed me. It looked like she was about

to walk over, probably to find out who I was. Only Gabriel, who was out of the pool now, said something to her first. After that, she sent a little wave in my direction instead. Then she settled back into her lounge chair.

Those kids seemed to be having the time of their lives. It wasn't even real baseball. But that didn't matter. They were laughing and smiling at everything they did. That's how I used to feel about baseball—before Papi defected, before Moyano tried to run my life, and before the World Series became more important to Papi than me. And suddenly, I was jealous of those two kids just learning to play.

I looked up and Luis and Gabriel were almost right on top of me.

"One more lesson and I should be swimming like a fish," said Luis, standing barefoot on the grass in his trunks, drying himself with a towel. "I want to look good on the beach. No more being bait, with a rope tied around my waist."

"I didn't know you were a teacher, too," I told Gabriel.

"Not me," he said, leading us back toward the apartment. "I'm a student, always learning."

"I'd like to be a teacher one day," said Luis, already grinning at some joke that was coming.

"Why's that?" I asked, as if I was grooving him a pitch at batting practice.

"So I could get one of those books with all the answers in it," he said proudly.

"I'm right behind you on that," I said, pulling the towel from his hands and snapping it at his butt cheeks.

Just as we got back, a delivery man was coming down the apartment stairs.

Uncle Ramon was still at the door and said, "Now we have a refrigerator full of food. And right before that, a messenger came and left an envelope."

"Maybe there are tickets for tonight's game in it," said Luis excitedly.

"Gabriel's name is on the envelope," said Uncle Ramon, pointing to the counter where it sat. "If there are tickets inside, he'd have to invite us."

"Open it, please," said Luis.

Picking it up, Gabriel seemed to weigh it in his palm. Then he slowly ripped the envelope's edge from top to bottom, before blowing inside to make it open. From over Gabriel's shoulder, I caught a glimpse of the check he pulled out. I didn't see the exact amount. And I didn't care. But there were enough zeros to end any money worries Gabriel might ever have.

"I take it you won't be sleeping on the couch tonight," Uncle Ramon said to Gabriel.

"I told you I wasn't leaving until my job here was done," he said, sliding the check back inside the envelope. "And Luis needs another swimming lesson."

Over the next few hours, I realized that we had plenty of food, but no cash, and no car. That was probably the way Papi wanted it, with his new family sitting behind the dugout at Marlins Park and us anchored to this apartment, watching on a flat-screen TV.

From the living room window, I could see the top of the stadium. I tried hard not to look at it, or even acknowledge it was there. But when the sun went down and a halo of lights glowed around its crown, I could barely take my eyes off of it.

25

IF THE MARLINS lost Game Six, the Series would be over one day earlier. That would put pressure on Papi to see me sooner rather than later. In my mind, I was tossing coins— heads or tails—over what I really wanted to happen.

From the first second of the pregame show, Uncle Ramon, Luis, and Gabriel were camped out in front of the flat-screen watching ESPN Deportes. They were snacking on three different kinds of chips, pizza rolls, and ice-cold Pepsi. None of us had ever used a microwave oven before. So I picked my head up to watch it melt nacho cheese in less than a minute.

"I can see every blade of grass on that field," said Uncle Ramon. "This high-definition TV is incredible."

"I'd still rather be there," moaned Luis. "Why couldn't Uncle get us tickets?"

"Son, this is the World Series—maybe a once-in-a-lifetime chance to go down in baseball history," answered

Uncle Ramon. "El Fuego doesn't need any distractions right now. He has to stay focused like a laser beam."

Uncle Ramon understood those were only half-truths. He didn't even sound convincing. I realized that I didn't need to hide the truth from Luis and Gabriel.

"The *real* reason is that my papi has another family, another son," I said, hitting the mute on the remote. "He's not ready to face me, or have his families mix together."

Luis looked upset, maybe even as much as I was when I found out.

"Does your mama know?" my cousin asked.

"In her heart she does," I answered. "She was smarter than me about it."

"Smarter than me, too," conceded Uncle Ramon. "But that doesn't change anything. He's still my brother and your papi."

I'm not sure why, but I asked Gabriel, "What do you think?"

"You don't need my advice," answered Gabriel. "I'm not here to judge—his actions or your response. And it doesn't sound to me like you're judging either. It sounds more like you just want answers. It's been a long journey. I think you're almost there."

I wasn't sure what to make of that. So I just let it sit with me, and I restored the volume on the TV.

*Here in Miami, Marlins Park is rocking with antici-
pation. The retractable roof is closed and the noise
level is high. There's a distinct energy among the
crowd, with the start of Game Six only moments
away. Will the visiting Yankees be crowned World
Champions here, or will the home team, the Miami
Marlins, force a deciding Game Seven tomorrow
night? The Bronx Bombers, built on hitting, and the
Marlins, built on pitching, are about to collide. . . .*

The first three innings flew past without a single run being scored. Then, in the bottom of the fourth inning, the
Marlins' cleanup hitter hammered a hanging curveball more
than 418 feet over the center-field wall. That gave Miami the
lead, 1–0.

That's when the camera zoomed in on the Marlins' huge
home run sculpture, just over the left-center-field fence. It
had pink flamingos shaking their feathers, blue marlins div-
ing beneath waves, and white doves sailing across the sky.
Whenever a Marlin hit a home run, all the pieces moved.

"Look at that thing go," said Luis. "It's like a giant pin-
wheel spinning. Maybe one day I could get the job pressing
the button to set it off."

A burst of water shot from the sculpture's base up into
the air, followed by the piercing sound of a horn.

Right away, I thought about that stranger at our baseball game in Cuba—the one blowing his horn as he marched
through the crowd. Then I thought about how it felt to hit
that horn on the '59 Buick once we were free. How its vibrations tingled up my spine.

In the next inning, the Marlins added on a pair of runs,
pushing their lead to 3–0. When the bottom of the fifth was
finished, Papi walked across the field from the dugout to the
Miami bullpen inside the right-field stands. It wasn't a close-
up camera shot. He was looking down at the ground ahead
of him with his cap pulled low. So I couldn't even see his face
clearly.

*There's the great El Fuego making his usual
midgame trek to the bullpen. That's where he'll
ready himself, getting his legendary left arm loose
in case he's needed by the Marlins late in the game.
Our best wishes go out to Ramirez and his family.
Several of them, including his teenage son, undertook the perilous sea journey from Cuba just days
ago, defecting to the US. They're undoubtedly having a splendid reunion....*

"These announcers know everything," said Luis, in a
sarcastic tone.

"Listen, I understand the *real* reunion hasn't taken place yet. But it will," countered Uncle Ramon. "Look around, Son. We're not living in one of those refugee houses, right? What was it, seven families in three bedrooms, the kind of house those poor people stuck at the INS building were begging to get into? Don't we have it a hundred times better?"

Luis hung his head and said, "Now I feel like a spoiled baby, making a fuss over not getting Series tickets."

"Hey, you're not a baby anymore," I smiled at him. "Not since we left Cuba."

Between innings there were commercials for everything—beer, sports cars, insurance, energy drinks, and even pills to keep older guys ready for sex. They seemed like fairy tales, filled with talking animals. There was a pig driving a convertible, a duck that could quack a company's name, and a gecko with an accent who figured out math percentages in his tiny head.

"Don't be fooled by those ads," said Uncle Ramon, after another round of slick commercials. "You don't need money to enjoy freedom."

I guess that was true, because none of us had a single dollar in our pockets. Gabriel had a paper check. But there wasn't a bank in sight. And he didn't appear to be in any hurry to cash it.

The Marlins' starting pitcher had pinpoint control. He

was changing speeds on his pitches, painting the corners of the plate, and hitting the catcher's target every time. The Yankees hadn't had a runner past second base all night, and their batters looked completely baffled.

At the start of the eighth inning, Papi began warming up in the bullpen.

"This Marlins pitcher's having the game of his life," said Luis. "Does the manager take him out for El Fuego?"

"I wouldn't," I said firmly. "Not unless he puts two runners on, and the tying run comes to the plate."

"Of course he's going to bring your papi in to pitch. Soon as the ninth inning comes," said Uncle Ramon. "It's not even a discussion."

"What makes you so certain?" asked Gabriel.

"Because Julio Ramirez Sr. was born to pitch the ninth inning," he answered, confidently. "God blessed his left arm. Gave him the ability to blow away three straight batters and leave the other team feeling helpless. And in a series like this one, that feeling will carry over to tomorrow."

In my heart, I didn't think God had much to do with anything Papi did.

When the ninth inning came Papi strode to the mound. The cameras zoomed in as he delivered the last of his warm-up pitches. Uncle Ramon and I both moved closer to the TV screen to see him better. He looked a little heavier than I remembered, and his face was fuller. Then I focused in on his left hand and saw that he wasn't wearing a wedding ring.

Maybe forty feet behind home plate, there was a beautiful glass aquarium built into the backstop. It was filled with pink coral and all kinds of tropical fish.

"If a fastball got away from El Fuego, think he could crack that aquarium?" asked Luis. "Imagine fish flopping all over the field."

"They must have tested that glass," answered Uncle Ramon. "It's probably unbreakable."

"No, I'd bet he could break it," I said, without hesitating.

Papi was nearly unhittable that night, except for the two pitches that Yankee batters fouled off into the stands. He struck out the three hitters he faced. Now the World Series was tied at three games apiece. And that put me another whole day away from facing Papi myself.

26

I SLEPT ON the floor again that night. I didn't have a single dream, or at least not one I could remember. The next morning, I woke up early. The sheets and blanket had slipped out from beneath me, and my face was flat against the hardwood floor. When I got to the bathroom, I watched in the mirror as the pressed crease in my right cheek slowly faded.

I hadn't played *real* baseball in nearly a week. My body was aching to compete, to be in motion. No one else was awake yet. Luis and Uncle Ramon were in their bedrooms, and Gabriel was still asleep on the couch. I got dressed and headed out the apartment door without locking it behind me.

There was no one in the pool. But swimming didn't interest me. I'd had enough of treading water to last a lifetime. That's when I started bouncing forward off my toes—building from a fast walk to a jog to a run. I did six or seven laps around the complex, gaining more speed and momentum with each one. After a while, the soles of my feet were itching to break out of that same circular path. So

I turned toward the gates and flew past the guard inside that little security booth.

Suddenly, I was on the streets without a plan or destination. The sweat was pouring down my forehead, stinging my eyes. But that didn't matter. I was reaching with every stride. My arms were driving forward in perfect rhythm with my legs. And I'd never felt more free.

I ran past schoolkids with book bags, old ladies pushing shopping carts, men in business suits, and couples holding hands. Some were headed in the same direction as me. Others were going the opposite way. I was in the US, with no dictator or corrupt police to hold me back. I could run as far as my strong legs would take me. On one block, I flew by a coffee shop, a clothing store, and a Burger King. I felt powerful, like one day, if I worked hard enough, I might own all three. Because there was no one with an army behind him to tell me I couldn't.

But in my heart, I would have traded anything for Mama and Lola to be running by my side. And almost every time I blinked I saw their faces.

Then, just as my thigh muscles were beginning to burn, I caught a glimpse of the back side of the apartment complex. I made my way there and leaped over its waist-high fence before I slowed down to a jog.

Luis was in the pool. But it wasn't Gabriel giving him a swimming lesson. It was Uncle Ramon instead. I didn't want to interrupt, so I stayed in that grassy patch where I'd coached those two little boys playing Wiffle ball, and I started stretching. After that, I did five sets of two hundred crunches, and then fifty push-ups on my bare knuckles.

I walked back to the apartment, picking blades of grass off the back of my sweaty hands. Gabriel was inside, packing himself a bag.

"You're leaving?" I asked. "What happened to Luis's swimming lesson?"

"Ramon's got that covered. He's here for your cousin. Besides, this was never going to be forever—not unless we drowned at sea," Gabriel answered, winking.

"Where you going?"

"I'm already where I want to be: in a country with freedom," he said, closing the bag with a *zip* and then slinging it over his shoulder. "The real question is, Where are *you* going?"

"I don't know," I answered, with my feet flat on the floor.

"I can't imagine it's going to take you too long to find out," he said. "I know what you're made of. You've got a big heart. I've seen it. Just listen to whatever it tells you."

"Hey, didn't you say you weren't leaving until your job was complete—until you delivered me to my papi?"

"I see you've got a handle on that now. I'm not worried."

Gabriel gave me a big hug before he headed out the door. From the balcony, I watched him stop by the pool to say his good-byes to Luis and Uncle Ramon. A few minutes later, Gabriel was gone. And I didn't think that huge check in his pocket was ever going to weigh him down.

At around three o'clock, another messenger arrived, leaving a second envelope with Uncle Ramon.

"I'm not getting my hopes up that those are tickets for Game Seven," said Luis.

Uncle Ramon shook the envelope one time, and then he opened it.

First, he took out a blue credit card and said, "Well, now we can go to the store for things we need. But Luis, I think you'll be pleased at what else is here."

"Let me see," said my cousin, taking the envelope from his father's hand.

As Luis looked inside, his entire face lit up. I knew right away it was something even better than World Series tickets. Only I had no idea what it could be.

That's when Luis pulled out a small photo of his mother. She was standing beside Uncle Ramon on their wedding day. Luis pressed the picture to his lips.

"The day your uncle defected, he had that picture in his wallet," said Uncle Ramon. "He had pictures of everyone in his family."

I wasn't about to ruin Luis's moment. But in my mind I was thinking, *He cared so much about his family that he replaced us with a brand-new one.*

"Win or lose tonight, when I finally see my uncle I'm going to kiss him on both cheeks," Luis said, holding that picture close to his chest.

By quarter to four, Uncle Ramon and Luis wanted to go out for food.

"Primo, let's test this credit card. We'll go to a restaurant where you're not the busboy," Luis said to me. "We'll be back in plenty of time for the game tonight."

"Not me," I said, shaking my head. "I'll stay here."

"You sure?" Uncle Ramon asked.

"I've got a lot on my mind. You guys go."

"We'll bring you something back," said Luis. "One of those big racks of pork ribs with french fries, like I saw on the TV commercials."

Five minutes after they left, I was at the living room window, focused on what I could see of Marlins Park. Even standing still, I could feel the momentum building inside of me. And before my feet were ever in motion, I knew I'd be heading out the door.

I left the complex and started walking north. Whatever compass I had inside of me was set. I could feel a force almost dragging me in that direction. I walked for more than a half hour, and the closer I got to the stadium, the stronger I felt the pull.

The streets and sidewalks were getting more crowded. A half dozen blocks from Marlins Park, I began to see police on every corner, directing traffic and keeping people on foot moving. They weren't about to have a problem with me, because I didn't have any intention of stopping.

Two guys around my age came up on either side of me. One of them flashed a ticket, trying to sell it. I didn't have any money. But in my mind, I'd already paid enough to see Papi. So I shook my head no and walked faster.

As I approached the stadium, there was a band playing on the corner. It was four older men wearing straw hats with red-and-white-striped jackets. They had a banjo, bass, drum, and trumpet. They were in the shade, looking cool as anything, except for the man with the trumpet, whose puffed-out cheeks seemed like they were about to explode.

It was probably three and a half hours before the game when I found the players' entrance. There was already a crowd around it, with plenty of security. I pushed my way close to the front, watching as some of the players arrived.

Every time one of the Marlins showed up, there'd be cheers and people begging for autographs. There were boos for a taxi full of Yankees. But fans wanted autographs, too. I was glued to that one spot for maybe an hour. Only there was no sign of Papi. Then the crowd started to thin out. And I understood that most of the players were already inside.

It was hard for me to stand still. My feet just wanted to move forward. But another part of me was willing to wait until midnight, or whenever the game was finished, to finally confront Papi.

Then someone called my name: "Julio."

For an instant, I was frozen solid. Then her hand touched my shoulder and I was able to move again. It was that woman from ESPN, Cadence Myers—the one who'd interviewed me outside the INS building.

In broken Spanish, she asked, "Why you out here? No ticket?"

She wasn't holding a tape recorder. But I didn't really want to answer any questions. So I shrugged and said, "I'm just waiting. That's all."

She must have been able to see through me, because there was suddenly sadness in her eyes.

"Wear this," she said, taking off one of her TV credentials and then placing it around my neck. "Stay behind me. I'll talk for you."

A moment later, we were walking through the press entrance together. She said something to security about me working with her. The next thing I knew, we were inside the stadium's offices. She guided me down a series of halls, first left and then right.

I tried hard not to make eye contact with anyone, and

mostly stared down at the blue carpeted floor. When we came to a stop, we were standing in front of a door with a sign on it that read, MARLINS CLUBHOUSE: PLAYERS ONLY (PRESS AT DESIGNATED TIMES).

Cadence showed our tags to a guard at the door. Then she walked me inside. My entire body was on pins and needles as my eyes darted from player to player. The instant I saw him, it was like ice water had suddenly filled my veins. Chills shot up my spine. He was sitting on a chair, alone in front of his locker, tightening the laces on his cleats.

I took a hesitant step forward. Maybe he sensed me coming, because he suddenly looked up and his dark eyes zeroed onto mine.

27

PAPI RUSHED ACROSS the room. With my legs suddenly weak, I managed just another half step forward.

"Junior," he said, as his chest thumped against mine.

He was holding me so close I could feel his breath and smell the soap he must have used to shave.

Then he took a step back, with his arms extended, holding me by the shoulder blades. In Spanish, he asked, "How did you get inside here?"

His voice was like a weight bearing down on me. My mouth had gone bone dry. And even if I'd had an answer on my tongue, I wasn't sure I could have gotten the words out. I couldn't believe I was actually seeing Papi in the flesh, not on TV or hearing him described on the radio. I'd never been this tall before, standing beside him. The pores on his face looked huge, and there was a blemish beneath his right eyebrow. Then Papi noticed the press credential around my neck, and shot a fiery look at Cadence.

"Did *she* bring you?" he asked, nearly seething. "To do a story about my family?"

I shook my head and said, "I came on my own. I was stuck outside. She brought me in. To help."

"*Gracias,*" Papi told her, an instant before he pulled me away toward his locker.

A pair of Papi's Hispanic teammates came over, trying to find out what was happening.

"This is my son," Papi introduced me.

"His oldest," I added, hoping he would feel the sting.

I could tell he was embarrassed by how this was playing out. Both his teammates gave me huge hugs, congratulating me on escaping from Cuba. They'd seen the TV footage and had all kinds of questions about the trip and the Buick. But Papi cut them off. Then he told one of the clubhouse workers to get me a Marlins jacket.

"You're going to need one to stay with me," he said.

I didn't know what to make of that.

Cadence waved good-bye to me, without trying to disturb us. But as I put my arms into the jacket's sleeves, other reporters gathered around us. They were mostly older men with long yellow notepads and chalky faces. Papi blew off their questions, ushering me past them without a word. I thought I was going to bawl. I could feel my eyes welling up and the dam about to break. But just as the first tear started to escape, I sucked it all back inside.

Papi led me down a short tunnel, through the dugout, and then onto the field.

For a few seconds, my senses were overwhelmed. It was like stepping into some kind of baseball video game. There were thousands of people in the stands already. Most of them were dressed in either bright orange or black Marlins T-shirts. I could see the aquarium built into the backstop behind home plate and that giant home run sculpture beyond the outfield fence. The stadium's roof was rolled open, and the clouds in the sky looked like cotton candy.

"Junior, come," said Papi, bringing me back to reality.

He started jogging around the perimeter of the field, next to the stands.

I was still a half stride behind when I said, "I don't go by that name anymore. Call me Julio."

"So, *my oldest*. Then you know about your half brother? Did Ramon tell you?"

"No, I found out on my own. Does Mama know?"

"Not from my mouth," he answered, as we made the turn along the outfield fence.

Some of Papi's teammates who were loosening up in the outfield started over toward us. But Papi went from a jog to a sprint, leaving them behind. Only I stayed right with him.

"I'm much faster now," I said. "The days of you running away from me are over."

As we slowed back down to a jog, passing the Marlins'

bullpen beneath the right-field stands, Papi caught his breath and said, "I can't explain my feelings right now, especially what it's been like not seeing you all these years. I need to stay focused. People are depending on me—my teammates, the fans—"

"Your *new* family?" I said, interrupting. "So you can get another million-dollar contract? Keep them living in a mansion while Mama and Lola scrape to get by?"

Papi came to a stop and looked me square in the eye.

"I already told you, I can't explain my feelings now. I have to be ready to pitch. You're a baseball player. You should understand that," he said, with the muscles in his face pulling tight like a stone statue's.

Staring down at Papi's bare left hand, I said, "You know, Mama still wears *her* ring."

"It's out of respect for her that I don't wear mine," he snapped, before he started jogging back toward the dugout.

I wasn't convinced that I wanted to follow him. But I didn't know where else to go. When he entered the dugout, somebody handed Papi a towel and he wiped the perspiration from his face. When he was finished, Papi grabbed me and put me down on a seat near the end of the dugout, by a door leading back to the clubhouse. I was almost out of sight from everyone else, and a few feet behind the TV camera in the corner.

"Julio, you stay here," he said. "Don't move without me."

Then he disappeared through the door. I guess word spread fast, because I didn't have to explain who I was to any of the players, coaches, or trainers. The Marlins' manager even walked past and gave me a big thumbs-up.

A few minutes later, Papi came back. He was holding his glove and had his game face screwed on supertight.

"Ramon says you're a shortstop. Still using the glove I gave you for your birthday?"

"It's back in Cuba," I answered. "Along with my old bike."

"Easy to replace them both," he said, opening a package of sunflower seeds.

"Yeah, I guess everything's *easy* to replace," I sniped.

A voice on the PA system announced the lineups to the crowd. The umpires and managers met at home plate. They talked for a while there, going over the ground rules of Marlins Park. Then someone led a blind man with a guitar to a stool and microphone near the backstop. Everyone stood as he began to play the American National Anthem. Papi took his cap off and we were almost shoulder to shoulder.

For that moment, whatever private war we were having didn't matter to me. And I don't think it mattered to him either. We were two Cubans who'd risked everything to be free. Him in a car outside a Baltimore hotel and me in a '59 Buick on the Atlantic Ocean.

The blind man sang in English, with a thick Spanish accent. I swore he started out the song with the words, "*José* can you see." At his final note, the crowd went wild with applause. And I clapped my hands together so hard that they hurt.

Three fighter jets roared over the stadium in a tight formation, leaving a trail of white smoke across the sky.

"Those are US navy jets," Papi told me. "They're called the Blue Angels."

They reminded me of Gabriel. I was thinking how he would have loved to see them, and maybe even learn to fly one.

The Marlins' starting pitcher finished his warm-up tosses, before an umpire wiped the dirt away from the corners of the plate with a small brush. Then the first Yankee stepped into the batter's box. Papi already had a mouthful of sunflower seeds. He was chewing on them and spitting the empty shells onto the dugout floor.

"Here," said Papi, holding out the open package and pouring some into my hand.

The Yankees' leadoff hitter took a fastball down the middle for strike one. That's when I realized that Uncle Ramon and Luis must be back at the apartment in front of the flatscreen. I knew that Uncle Ramon wouldn't be too worried about me, because he probably had a good idea where I was.

I popped some of those seeds into my mouth, and the salt from them sat on my tongue until it started to burn at the cracks of my closed lips.

28

I HEARD THE *crack* of the ball off the bat. Papi jumped to his feet at the sound and so did I. It was a long fly smacked to deep center field. Papi was bending his body with the flight of the ball, like maybe that could influence it. Only it couldn't. The baseball vanished over the 418-foot mark on the fence. The Marlins' home run statue stayed silent, though. Most of the crowd did, too. That's because it was a Yankee who'd homered. They'd had a runner on first base at the time. And after the top half of the first inning, New York was ahead, 2–0.

Papi gave the Marlins' starting pitcher some words of encouragement as he came back to the dugout. Then he turned to me and said, "Those Yankees think Game Seven belongs to them, because of all their tradition. They think this moment's too big for us. It's not. We're not afraid of their uniforms or anybody wearing them."

We'd gone more than six years without speaking. Not a single word. I couldn't believe that Papi was actually talking to me about the Yankees' stuck-up attitude.

The Marlins went down in order in the bottom half of the first inning. When they took the field again, their shortstop made a slick play on the first Yankee hitter, robbing him of a base hit.

"Ramon tells me you were the best young shortstop in Cuba this season," said Papi. "Is that true?"

"If they'd let me play."

"Explain that."

"You defected," I said, spitting out the last of my seeds. "They wanted to punish me for that, afraid that I'd do the same."

"Those bastards were right," said Papi, as if he were teaching me something.

"*You* explain *that*," I said, annoyed.

"Well, would you rather I'd stayed? Or that I left, so one day we could both be free?"

I didn't know how to respond. Part of me wanted to curse him out for leaving us behind. Another part wanted to say thank you, for making me walk that long, hard road to right here. And when the grateful part started to win that tug-of-war in my heart, I became angry with myself.

After a few more pitches, Papi said, "I don't blame you for not having an answer. Sometimes I don't have one either."

Both teams put up goose eggs on the scoreboard in the

second inning. Then Papi left the bench and walked back to the clubhouse. This time I refused to sit still.

He was on the floor in the middle of a hurdler's stretch, with the fingers of his left hand reaching for the toe of his right cleat, when I walked in. The game outside was being shown on a pair of huge flat-screens at either end of the room. That's when it came to me that Luis was watching the game on TV with his father, and now I was watching it the same way with mine.

"How's the apartment you're living in? Nice enough?" asked Papi, as he popped off the floor and started to do a set of jumping jacks. "I've never seen it."

"Uncle and Cousin really love it," I answered, measuring my tone. "What's your place look like? Full of tricycles and kiddie toys?"

"No, I live alone," answered Papi, beginning to run in place with his knees coming all the way up to his chest.

"What do you mean?"

"Julio, I'm not with Milo's mother. We were never a real couple or going to get married. This baby was a surprise. But Milo's my son and I love him. So I provide for him and his mother."

Suddenly, I was less jealous of the kid. But I still had plenty to challenge Papi on.

"So how come you never—"

"No more!" demanded Papi, who stalked over to a huge trunk full of equipment. Searching through it, he pulled out a right-handed glove. "Here, take this. You're going to need it."

I remembered the last time Papi gave me a baseball glove. It was for my tenth birthday. He'd promised to play catch with me every day until it got broken in. That was a promise Papi never kept.

I took the glove from him. But I didn't even want to put it on my hand. So I tucked it beneath my armpit.

"Come on. I have to get back out there and support my teammates," said Papi.

All I could think was that he'd spent a lot of effort supporting everyone except Mama, Lola, and me.

The hallway between the clubhouse and the dugout was covered in a collage of hundreds of photos, reading like a history of the Marlins' franchise. But there was a blank space in the corner, where there was just blue wall.

Papi stopped right in front of it and said, "There used to be a picture here of me and my former manager. He told some sportswriters how he admired Fidel Castro for being so tough."

"Uncle Ramon told me about him on the trip over."

"From the moment I read that quote, he lost my respect—even after he apologized," said Papi. "Because my children were stuck in Cuba, without the freedom to follow me here."

"What happened to the photo?" I asked, as the crowd outside let out a roar.

"The day he was fired, I told the general manager to get rid of that picture. He gave me some excuse about how they'd have to redo the whole wall. So I came here with a putty knife and I cut it out myself. That way I never had to ask about it again."

When we got back to the dugout, Miami had a runner on second base with just one out. That's when the Marlins' shortstop came to bat. He hit a high chopper to the left side of the infield, with the runner holding at second. The Yankees' third baseman had to wait for the ball to come down, and then gunned his throw across the diamond. I could hear the sound of the runner's foot striking the bag an instant before the ball hit the first baseman's mitt. It was like the rhythm of a song—*swish-pop.*

Only the umpire called, "Out!"

The Marlins' manager charged onto the field. He got between the umpire and his player, who was already arguing the call. That way his shortstop wouldn't get tossed. The umpire was acting smug as anything, like he could never blow a call. The Miami manager completely lost it. He spun his cap around. And without the brim in front, he could get his face about a quarter of an inch from that umpire's. Before he got ejected from the game, he really had his say. I didn't know all of those words in English. But I could guess.

The manager was supposed to leave the dugout. Instead, he hid in the doorway right behind me and Papi at the end of the bench. That way he could manage the team from there.

"He was safe," said Papi, with his eyes glued to the slow-motion replay on a TV monitor. "I hate when umpires become more important to the game than players."

I didn't need the cameras to slow it down. I'd heard the music of that bang-bang play and knew he was safe.

The shortstop was standing right in front of me, looking at the monitor. I was watching him watch himself, being present in his past. It reminded me of those two sets of footprints I'd left on the beach in Cuba—one coming and one going—before I decided to defect.

All that emotion the manager showed on the field had an effect on the crowd and the players in the Marlins' dugout. Even I was up on my feet. I had my thumb and pointer finger jammed into the corners of my mouth, emptying my lungs into one long whistle. Papi was blowing just as hard with a sharp *tsssspp!* But the next Marlins batter struck out to end the third inning. And that surge of emotion was suddenly gone, like the air escaping from a punctured balloon.

Neither team scored over the next two innings. After the Marlins made the final out in the bottom of the fifth, I could see them starting to get really tight. The Yankees' starting pitcher was sailing along. The Marlins had just four innings left—twelve outs—to put a crooked number on the scoreboard. It was either be winners—World Series Champions—or losers. As a baseball player, *that* I understood.

"Let's go. Come with me," said Papi, walking out of the dugout and beginning his jog to the bullpen in the right-field stands.

I was on his heels in front of that huge crowd, with the glove he'd given me still stuffed under my arm.

That's when I heard a high-pitched voice from the first row calling, *"Papi! Mi papi!"*

29

I TURNED TO put a face with that voice. When I spotted who it was, I knew it had to be Milo, Papi's son. He was the right age, standing on a seat next to a woman who was probably his mother. There was a cascade of dark curls flowing from beneath his baseball cap. He wore a Marlins jacket like mine and smiled from ear to ear, waving a huge foam finger that read, #1. The woman was much younger than Mama, maybe thirty years old, with bleached blond hair. She was clapping her hands over her head, with lots of silver and gold bracelets on both wrists. And from where I stood, her fingernails looked perfect and polished, just like Mama said they would be.

Papi never looked in the boy's direction. I guess he was too focused and didn't hear. I wasn't about to bring his attention to it.

Seeing them was like a swift kick in the ass. I knew they existed. I just didn't know that they were standing practically right behind me.

But I felt sorry for the boy, too. Because I'd called Papi's name plenty of times myself without getting an answer.

A security guard opened the bullpen gates for us, and we walked inside. The Marlins' bullpen is beneath the right-field stands. It has a long bench, a telephone connected to the dugout for the manager to call, and a pair of pitching mounds for the relievers to warm up. There were several other relief pitchers there, two bullpen catchers, and a coach.

The view of the game wasn't nearly as good, because you had to watch through a chain-link fence. It felt a little bit like some kind of baseball jail—one Moyano probably would have loved to run. And with that security guard on the gate, it reminded me of being locked inside Cuba.

Before we ever sat down, Papi said, "Help me get my arm loose."

So I finally put the glove on my hand. It was almost new, and the leather was still stiff. It fit me. But I wasn't happy with the feel. I started pounding its pocket with my right fist, like I was beating up on it.

Papi stood about fifty feet from me. He came overhand with an easy, relaxed throw. Even getting loose, he had enough steam on his ball to sting my palm through the leather. It was the first time I'd played catch with him in six years—since the days when he was my hero, and his only other child was Lola.

While that ball was going back and forth between us, my mind was everywhere. For the moments when it was safe inside my glove, I'd close my eyes and see images—Mama's face, Lola studying, our old house, and my bike in that parking lot by the field.

I glanced up and the image of Papi and me playing catch was up on the stadium's video screen. It must have looked to the whole world like some picture-postcard moment of a father and son being reunited.

Other than that baseball, I had no idea what Papi was seeing, or exactly how clearly he saw me.

Papi ended our catch when the Yankees made the last out in their half of the sixth inning. I took a seat at the end of the bullpen bench, with Papi standing behind me, continuing to stretch his muscles.

"We just need one spark to start a fire," said Papi, as Miami still trailed, 2–0. "A relief pitcher like me—my whole job depends on us scoring runs. We don't get a lead or tie the game, nothing I do can make a difference. If I could do it over again, I'd become a shortstop like you, control my own destiny."

"That's what I want more than anything," I said, making sure that he heard me. "To control my own life and not have it dictated by what *other* people do."

Papi nodded his head to that, as if my thinking was just like his.

The Marlins had a runner reach first base in the bottom of the sixth. But that wasn't enough of a spark, as they failed to put a run on the board. Now they were just nine outs away from getting blanked in the biggest game of their lives.

Miami's starting pitcher was due to bat in the bottom of the seventh. Two Marlins relievers began warming up on the mounds behind us, ready to go into the game in case their manager decided to pinch-hit for his pitcher.

Papi watched them throwing for a moment. Then he told me, "These guys are important. They're the bridge to me. But if they go in and get pounded for five runs, I might as well take an early shower."

If I had a bucket of cold water, I would have poured it over Papi's head. I wanted to hear how important *I* was to him, not his setup men.

"I know all about teammates," I said. "I've had plenty pass through my life already. Coaches, too. My cousin Luis and Uncle Ramon, they're the only ones who've stuck with me—*mi familia.*"

"I was sorry to hear about Blanca," said Papi, showing a small crack in his game face. "Ramon says that Luis took it very hard. That you were a huge help to him."

I wondered what Papi would have done if Mama or Lola had died after he defected. Would he have sent a card? Money for their funeral?

The Yankees left a pair of men on base in the seventh.

Only I couldn't say that I was jumping for joy when they didn't score.

Miami's leadoff batter drew a walk. That got a pair of pitchers up in the Yankees' bullpen, opposite us, beneath the left-field stands. The Marlins' manager pinch-hit for his pitcher, who was due up next. Then he decided to really make something happen. He played hit-and-run on the first pitch, sending his runner toward second base and committing his hitter to swing.

"Our manager's got guts, faith in these guys," said Papi, deciphering the signs the third-base coach was giving to the batter. "More than I would have."

Protecting the runner, the hitter swung at a low pitch, golfing it into center field for a single. Now there were runners at first and third with nobody out.

Suddenly, the stands above our heads were rocking. Everyone must have been stamping their feet. It felt like we were in the middle of an earthquake. Then that stamping fell into a rhythm, punctuated by a clap of hands: *Bum, bum, bum—clap. Bum, bum, bum—clap.* And my heart seemed to be beating the same way.

The next batter was the Marlins' shortstop.

"He's going to deliver for us," said Papi. "He's going to get me into this game."

Earlier, he'd been cheated by the umpire on that close

call at first base. So I wanted him to do something good. As he set himself in the batter's box, I could almost feel the bat in that shortstop's hands. And when he started it forward on the first pitch, the muscles in my forearms twitched.

He hit a lined shot over the right fielder's head, almost directly at us. The ball hit the bullpen gate on one bounce. I didn't hear the noise it made, because the crowd was roaring like thunder. Both base runners scored. Game Seven was tied at 2–2, and the shortstop steamed into second base with a double.

For a brief moment, Papi and I were in each other's arms. Then he left me to grab a bullpen catcher and begin to warm up his left arm for real.

The Yankees' manager changed his pitcher.

Papi was up on the bullpen mound, just starting to make the catcher's glove *pop*.

The next Marlins batter fouled off five pitches in a row. The crowd started and restarted its rhythmic clapping with every pitch. My pulse was rising and falling with them, while my feet were dancing off second base with that shortstop.

I saw a curveball hang over the middle of the plate. An instant later, I swore that baseball had wings. It soared so high into the left-field stands that I didn't think it was ever going to come down. The home run statue was spinning like a giant merry-go-round, and somewhere in my mind I could see Luis hitting the button to start it.

The Marlins had the lead, 4–2. Now the Yankees were six outs from elimination. I glanced over at Papi in the midst of all that noise and emotion. There was a glint in his eyes as he stood even taller on the mound. He seemed completely focused on the catcher's target. And he looked like there was nothing in the world more important to him than being El Fuego.

30

A MARLINS RELIEF pitcher left the bullpen to start the eighth inning, but it wasn't Papi. It was Papi's regular setup man. The team's bridge to him to close out the game.

Papi was throwing even harder now. He'd fire four or five pitches in a row, building a rhythm, and then take a short blow. When Papi wasn't throwing, he snorted around the edges of that mound like a bull waiting for something to charge. And if my jacket was red instead of blue, I probably would have run for cover.

That sequence kept up until the Yankees went down quietly in their half of the eighth inning. Then Papi put a jacket on to keep his arm warm and a good sweat going.

The bullpen phone rang. A coach answered it, listening for a few seconds.

"El Fuego!" he hollered, hanging up the phone in the same motion.

That was no surprise to anyone. I would have believed the moon over Marlins Park was green and made of cheese before I thought Papi wasn't going to pitch the ninth.

I was standing by the bullpen door when Papi walked over and said, "I know you have plenty of reasons to hate me."

I was shocked to hear those words come out of his mouth. Maybe he was so stoked right now, over the chance to save Game Seven, that there was nothing he could hold back.

"I don't hate you," I said. "I just don't know if I should ever trust you again."

He took those words like a batted ball ripped back at his head, barely flinching. Then he stalked off to pace the bullpen.

For a moment, I felt good over what I'd said to him. But once those words disappeared into the atmosphere, so did my satisfaction. After that, I just felt empty.

The Marlins didn't add to their lead in the bottom of the eighth.

Just before their final out was made, Papi came back to me.

"I deserved that," he said, with his voice wavering in a way I'd never heard. "I know how selfish I can be. That's who I am. Baseball's in my blood. So is being the best at it. You, your mama, your sister—you're all in my heart, too."

"Yeah, but how far behind?"

"You love this game, too. That's why you left Cuba," he said, a tear welling in the corner of one eye.

"That's all good for *me*. But what if your new son never plays baseball? How will you ever explain it to *him*?"

That's when the last Marlins hitter was retired. The bull-pen gate swung open, salsa music started playing loudly over the PA system, and the crowd began chanting, "El Fuego!"

Papi made a fist, holding it out in front of himself. Then I did the same and touched mine to his, completing the connection.

"I'm going to win the World Series for me *and* my family—all of them," said Papi, his voice becoming rock solid again.

Then Papi pulled his fist away and pounded it to the center of his chest.

"I promise. You won't be far behind in my thoughts," he said, striding onto the field to a huge ovation.

When the gate closed, I stood with my face pressed against the chain-link, my fingers locked tight around it. If I had my way, I would have broken that fence down. Not to be free—I already had that gift. But to be on that field, playing and backing up Papi.

The Yankees sent up their switch-hitting center fielder, who dug his heels into the right-side batter's box against Papi.

From a full windup, Papi blazed a fastball past him for a called strike. The scoreboard flashed the speed of that pitch—ninety-eight miles per hour. The noise was near deafening as Papi went into his next delivery.

I didn't hear the ball explode off the bat. But I saw it.

Crushed over the left-center-field fence, it hit the Marlins' home run sculpture with a *clang*, as the crowd went silent. Now the Yankees were within a run at 4–3.

Papi never turned around to watch that ball sail out of the park. He just put his glove up for the umpire to throw him a new one. Then Papi rubbed the ball inside of his bare hands until I thought the cover might come off.

The noise was beginning to build again when the next Yankee batter tattooed Papi's pitch off the face of the left-field fence for a stand-up double.

For an instant, Papi hung his head on the mound. It was something I'd never seen him do before. He didn't seem like the same pitcher who'd been breathing fire in the bullpen. Maybe he just didn't have it tonight—his arm was tired or his age was catching up to him at the end of a long season. Or maybe I was the cause, making him lose focus. And I felt sick to my stomach thinking about it.

The Marlins' pitching coach walked out to the mound. I wouldn't have been surprised if Papi had waved him off. But he didn't. The infielders gathered around them, too, probably discussing what to do if the next Yankee tried to bunt the runner over to third. When that meeting was over, and the pitching coach was on his way back to the dugout, the Marlins shortstop lingered there for some extra words with Papi. Then he tapped Papi once on the backside with his glove for encouragement before going back to his position. Only I wished for the world that could have been me.

Papi was pitching from the stretch now, straddling the rubber beneath him. That was meant to keep the runner closer to second. So it would be harder for him to score on a hard single.

The shortstop was up on his toes, shifting his weight from side to side. And so was I, almost feeling his rhythm.

The next Yankee batter laid down a beautiful bunt, sacrificing himself to get the runner over to third base with just one out. Now the tying run was just ninety feet away from home plate. That meant the runner could score on an out—a ground ball to an infielder or a sacrifice fly.

Papi needed a strikeout in the worst way. He picked up the rosin bag from behind the mound, running it through his fingers for a better grip on the ball. Then I swear he tried to throw that rosin bag through the ground.

The Marlins decided to play their infield in, to try to keep the runner on third from scoring. That put the shortstop maybe twenty-five feet closer to the batter than normal, limiting his range to the right and left. That was a call that had to come from their ejected manager, who was probably still hiding himself in that dugout doorway.

I picked my glove up off the ground and put it on my hand.

Back in the windup, Papi nicked the outside corner of the plate with a ninety-nine-mile-an-hour fastball.

"Steeee-rike!" rang the umpire's voice.

Papi got the ball back, took a deep breath, and was ready to go again. But the batter stepped out of the box, asking the ump for time.

The instant he was back inside, Papi started his windup. His entire body was behind his delivery, driving low and forward with his legs.

The hitter swung. Only he was a half mile behind a one-hundred-mile-an-hour fastball.

Papi seemed to have his delivery back in sync and his focus again.

The catcher put down his signs for the pitch he wanted. Papi shook him off. But that had to be all for show, because everybody in the park knew that El Fuego wasn't going to throw anything except more heat. With a runner on third, Papi probably wasn't going to bounce one in the dirt—to make the batter go fishing—risking a wild pitch that could roll all the way to the aquarium in the backstop.

My heart was starting to beat hard as I bent slightly at the knees, just like the Marlins shortstop, who was practically staring down the barrel of that hitter's bat.

Now Papi was taking his time, glaring at the batter. That Yankee was waving his bat, just off his shoulder, looking for a rhythm of his own.

The second his bat went still, Papi started his delivery.

I didn't see a baseball leave Papi's hand, just a blur. But I heard the crackle of the catcher's mitt and felt the explosion in the stands as the batter swung and missed. Then I needed to look twice at the scoreboard when it posted that pitch at 103 miles per hour.

Papi gazed into the stands, from the seat where Milo was sitting all the way to me behind the bullpen gate. He took his fist and pounded his chest, before he let it hover for a moment over his heart. Despite the distance between us, when his eyes met mine I felt a spark of electricity, and nothing but pride and love for Papi.

I could only imagine what my half brother was feeling. I'm sure he thought that look from Papi was his alone. Maybe one day, I would explain to him exactly what we'd shared.

Turning toward home plate, Papi windmilled his left arm as if he could throw a pitch even faster than he just did. With two outs, the shortstop and the rest of the infielders moved back to their regular depths.

The Yankees were down to their final out. Papi was one batter away from fulfilling his dreams.

He was snorting on the mound, kicking at the dirt beneath his cleats. My fingers and palm inside the leather glove were sweating.

The hitter crossed himself and kissed the gold medallion hanging from his neck before he stepped into the batter's box.

Papi went into his windup, coiling his body like a snake.

Then he sprang forward with the same motion he'd used for all of his fastballs. That's when time seemed to slow down for a second. Things were suddenly clearer to me and everything was in better focus. Somewhere inside that brief instant, my brain recognized that Papi hadn't thrown his fastball. Instead, it was a changeup—probably eight miles an hour slower than that Yankee batter or anyone else ever expected. And I held my breath.

I don't know what motivated Papi to put his trust in that particular pitch, to make that kind of change with so much hanging in the balance. But he did.

The hitter's front foot was way out in front. Totally off-balance, he swung and popped the ball high into the air above the infield.

My lungs filled themselves with air.

Now, it was only a matter of gravity for Papi to realize his dream, and for the Marlins to win.

Papi pointed straight up into the night sky, past the halo of lights that encircled the stadium and all the way to the stars.

The shortstop settled himself beneath the ball, waiting. When it nestled into his glove, he squeezed both hands around it tight and the crowd went crazy.

As the shortstop leaped into Papi's arms, the bullpen gate opened and I was the first one to charge out onto the field. By the time I reached Papi, he was being swarmed by his teammates from the diamond and the dugout. I pushed past them all and found *my* place in his arms.

I could feel the tears of joy running down Papi's face. I wanted to say something to him. Only I couldn't speak. I just held on tight as bursts of fireworks filled the sky. Then my own tears started to flow.

I wasn't sure what the future was going to bring. All of my resentment over Papi leaving us behind wasn't going to disappear because of a baseball game. But deep inside, at least I had the satisfaction of knowing one thing: a pitcher who once walked the streets of Matanzas like a Cuban god, with me trailing behind, had just saved Game Seven of the World Series.

He was a World Champion. And he was my father.

ACKNOWLEDGMENTS

Special thanks to April, Sabrina, Carlos, Marc, and Eva.

HOME FREE

THE STORY BEHIND THE STORY OF *GAME SEVEN*
Originally published August 2015 in *VOYA* magazine

The seeds of *Game Seven* started with an empty doorstep. Our new newspaper delivery person had decided that getting up early in the morning wasn't his calling in life. So after several weeks of near-10 AM late deliveries, I angrily cancelled my subscription. That pushed my wife to order the newspaper online to takes its place—guaranteed to be on your computer screen by 6 AM. That was great for my wife and daughter but bad for me, considering I liked to clip the newspaper most days for bits and pieces I might use in future novels.

After a few months of these electronic deliveries, I woke up one morning with the outline of a photo burned into my brain. I had probably seen it for only a brief second while scrolling through the newspaper on a tablet. But suddenly, I couldn't shake the somewhat fuzzy image from my memory. It was a photo of a green car on the water. That's all I knew. I couldn't recall if it was caught in a flash-flood, rolled down an incline while launching a boat lakeside, or accidentally driven into somebody's swimming pool. All I knew for sure was that I needed to see it again. Nearly an hour later, after entering dozens of combinations of key search words on Google Images, I finally found it.

It was an amazing photo of a green 1959 Buick that had been transformed into a car/boat (fitted with a pointed bow to slice through the sea waves), and was sailing off the shore of Key West, Florida, with several Cuban refugees aboard. I sat mesmerized by it, trying to decipher the facial expressions of the refugees resting on the roof of the floating car as the US Coast Guard approached them. One thing was crystal clear to me, however—I needed to write their story. Of course, not exactly *their* story, but *my* vision of how they arrived at that moment.

I had long been moved by the stories behind Cuban baseball players in Major League Baseball—players such as the Hernández brothers (Liván and Orlando, both pitchers and the subjects of a fascinating ESPN documentary entitled *Brothers in Exile*), Rey Ordóñez, Luis "El Tiante" Tiant, Tony Oliva, and current superstar players Yasiel Puig (Los Angeles Dodgers), José Abreu (Chicago White Sox) and Yoenis Céspedes (Detroit Tigers). Most of these players were forced to leave their loved ones behind when they defected, with family members often facing retribution from the authorities in Cuba. And in the case of Yasiel Puig, brought to the US/Mexico border by cutthroat smugglers who then held him for ransom—physically threatening his well-being for days—the flight for freedom was terrifying from both sides of the equation.

Though most of my sports related novels have been about basketball (*Black and White, The Final Four* and *Rucker Park Setup*), baseball was the first sport that captured my heart. I played catcher. As a kid, I used to go down to the diamond alone with a bucket of baseballs, throwing out of a crouch from home plate to an invisible shortstop covering second base. That was until I realized I could throw from second base to the backstop behind home plate instead, without having to chase those balls into the outfield.

Surprisingly, as the plot of *Game Seven* started to take shape in my mind, it was wasn't about who defected from Cuba, but rather whom was left behind—sixteen-year-old Julio Ramirez Jr., Cuba's best young shortstop. Six years prior, Julio's father was praised as Cuba's greatest pitcher. That was until Julio Sr. defected to the US while the Cuban National team was playing an exhibition tournament here.

Back then every kid I knew was jealous of me. That's because baseball is practically a religion in my country. And Papi walked through the streets of our hometown, Matanzas, like a god, with me trailing behind. Fans called him El Fuego, for his blazing fastball, which no batter could touch. The only way Papi could have been more respected was if he'd been a general in the mili-

tary or a high-ranking government official. But most of that respect would have come out of fear.

Papi has now signed a multi-million dollar contract to pitch for the Miami Marlins, while Julio, his mother, and younger sister are plunged into poverty. Julio is also being blackballed from the Cuban National team by the government, which believes he would undoubtedly defect as well. So Julio has been robbed of both his father (whom he is angry at for leaving) and the opportunity to play the game that he loves at the highest level.

Now, exactly how is a novelist from New York City going to write a book about a teenager from Cuba? It's funny how fate helps things fall into place. My mother was suffering from the onset of dementia. She would sometimes disappear early in the mornings, and I would comb the streets looking for her. I began to find my mother sitting in a Cuban coffee shop. I became friends with the owner, who would help look after her when I wasn't around. That marked the beginning of our many conversations about daily life in Cuba, both present and past.

With that spark lit inside of me, I went on a mission to find as many people as I could who could talk to me about their own personal odyssey. I also discovered several detailed on-line accounts of the 90-mile journey on the open ocean. Then I stumbled across Cuban baseball fans and recent tourists to the island who had sat in the rowdy and raucous stands during baseball games there. And almost right from the start, the research and writing never felt like a chore. It seemed more like a privilege to represent these brave and passionate people on the pages that were taking shape before me.

No matter how much love and joy the Cubans I encountered had shining inside of them, they all seemed to display a bit of a hard edge, having dealt with the reality of their harsh home government. That's why I chose to begin *Game Seven* with this preamble recited in the first-person by Julio Jr.

There are 108 stitches on a baseball. I should know. I've run my fingers over every one. The first and last stitches are hidden beneath the surface. But believe me, I've felt those, too.

When I was thirteen years old, I had a Cuban baseball coach named Hugo, who headed up the local traveling team. More than a dozen of us would pile into his beat-up station wagon, weighing down the shock absorbers until the tail end almost scraped the ground. Hugo always had a cigar rolling between his lips. He was also extremely competitive, even when he was driving or looking for a parking space with that oversized wagon.

During one of my at-bats, the opposing pitcher fired a

fastball inside at my ribcage. I barely jumped out of the way. But the umpire signaled that I was hit and should proceed to first base. When I arrived there Hugo asked if I was injured and I whispered to him, "The ball never hit me." He put a huge grin on his face. After the game, he pulled all of our players together for a private speech.

Hugo said, "I go down to first base thinking I might need to drive Paul to the hospital with broken ribs. But that sneaky SOB never even got hit. That's how I want the rest of you to play ball, cutthroat, like it means everything in the world to you to win."

Actually, what Hugo had ascribed to me wasn't any part of my motivation or thinking. But I accepted his colorful praise all the same, and he treated me to lemon ices for the rest of the season. In *Game Seven*, I modeled the evil and manipulating Moyano, who dictates the roster of Cuba's Junior National team, upon what I remembered of Hugo's many mannerisms.

Here's Moyano addressing Julio Jr. alone in the locker room:

Moyano took a long pull on his cigar, causing the tip to glow a bright orange. Then, for the first time, I saw him take it from his lips. He held the cigar out in front of him, tapping it with a finger. The ashes silently fell to the floor and flickered out.

"So, speak for yourself," said Moyano, acting as judge and jury

"I'm a baseball player, not a public speaker."

"No, you're a busboy," said Moyano, the smoke billowing from his lips. "You're only a baseball player if I say you are."

In one surprisingly swift move, Moyano snatched [a buzzing] fly from midair. He shook it inside a closed fist, like he was getting ready to roll dice. After he threw it to the floor, that fly's wings quivered at my feet and then went still.

At its roots, Cuba is predominantly a Christian country. That's why the character Gabriel plays an important role in this novel. Gabriel is a longtime fisherman who knows the ocean currents surrounding the island like the back of his own calloused hands. He is the one who converts the 1959 Buick auto into a seaworthy vessel, and operates on a good amount of faith that the car/boat will not sink or be capsized. Gabriel is based on the Biblical (both the old and new testaments) angel Gabriel, a messenger who blows his horn. In *Game Seven*, Gabriel's famed horn is found on the steering wheel of the Buick, and it signals the group's departure from oppression.

That's when I [Julio Jr.] reached my arm over Gabriel's shoulder. I hit the horn in the center of the steering wheel, and it let out a long beeeeeep! *I swear it was like music to my ears—better than any salsa, merengue, reggae, or rock. So I punched the horn again. And this time when I did, I hollered out "Freedom!"*

Then Gabriel said, "Everyone together: one, two, three."

The four of us [in that car/boat] screamed, "Freedom!" until his hand lifted from the horn.

There was also a need for a bus driver in the novel. Someone to drive Julio Jr.'s teammates on the Matanzas Crocodiles to the baseball tournament in Cardenas. I named that bus driver Paolo (Paul in Spanish), because, after all, I am the one at the wheel of this story, choosing a direction and driving it forward.

As a kid, I was a staunch fan of the World Champion 1969 "Miracle" Mets and the 1973 "You Gotta Believe" version of the New York Mets. Through both of those summer pennant drives and October World Series appearances, I usually had my transistor radio to my ear, listening to all of the action. The transistor radio, which first found popularity in the mid-1950s, saw approximately 1 billion units manufactured by the 1970s, using a 9-volt battery as a power source.

Julio Jr. had hidden such as transistor radio to hear his father pitch for the Miami Marlins in the World Series against the New York Yankees. Unlike myself, Julio wasn't worried about his teachers discovering the radio during a math lesson. Instead, he needed to be more concerned about the Cuban government finding out that he was using it to gain information from the outside world.

I sat alone on a dark staircase in our apartment building with a small transistor radio pressed against my ear, listening to every pitch thrown by the great El Fuego—something the police could have punished me for.

Of course, I did learn something about modern US teens and the transistor radio while I was in the midst of writing *Game Seven*. My wife and I had the car radio on when Van Morrison's *Brown-Eyed Girl* jumped out of the speakers. There are some lines in the song that mention going down a mine with a transistor radio. That's when our sixteen-year-old daughter, Sabrina, asked from the backseat, "What's a transistor radio?" It hadn't initially occurred to me that today's teens wouldn't know about them. But I guess that iPods and MP3 players have put them far into the rearview mirror. So I went back to the novel's text and made sure to describe the transistor radio in much greater detail.

There needed to be a substantial link between Julio Jr. and Papi. That important family connection comes in the form of Julio's two traveling companions on the ocean voyage from Cuba—his fun-loving cousin Luis and his uncle Ramon, who is Papi's brother and his former catcher. Luis's only real interest in the sport lies in the potential girls, parties, and popularity that a teen wearing a baseball uniform might be accorded. He serves as the perfect counterbalance to the ultra-serious Julio, who is trapped inside an intense pressure cooker of emotion and circumstance.

My cousin Luis raced in from center field, jumping on my shoulders to celebrate. I carried his weight for a few steps before we both tumbled onto the infield grass, laughing and smiling like little kids. "Now we show those teams going to Cárdenas [for the big tournament] what hungry Crocodiles can do—take a bite out of their behinds," said Luis, chomping at the grass with a big grin.

Uncle Ramon, however, is a coach and a former hardcore baseball player.

"An umpire from Havana was squeezing the strike zone on him really bad, calling all of El Fuego's pitches on the corner of the plate balls. The next pitch, I called for one high and outside, just above my right shoulder where that umpire was squatting. Your papi put that pitch exactly where I asked for it—his best fastball. Then I lowered my mitt a few inches. The pitch hit that [umpire] in the middle of his mask—ping," said Uncle Ramon. "Knocked him out cold."

Of course, Uncle Ramon passionately believes that his brother still loves his family, despite abandoning them.

"It's been six hard years [of separation]. Perhaps you feel like you don't know [your papi] now," said Uncle Ramon.

"I don't *know him,"* I said with some gas to my voice. *"Neither do you."*

"I know he's not a stranger. He's my brother, my blood, just like you are."

Crafting the character of Papi, the great El Fuego, was probably the most difficult thing I ever had to do as a novelist. He only appears in name, backstories, and remembrances for more than the first two-thirds of the book. He needed to be imposing on the pitcher's mound and in life——the kind of competitor who would put a 100-mph fastball into your ribs for smiling too much in the batter's box. Still, he'd have to be a compassionate and loving father in his own way. The character of Papi is partially based on several real-life pitchers who carried this ultra-competitive mantle through their lives. Among them are Cuban great Luis Tiant, aka El Tiante, as well as American Hall of Famers Bob Gibson (St. Louis Cardinals 1959–75) and Don Drysdale (Brooklyn and Los Angeles Dodgers 1956–69).

The first time the pair are together in the novel is when Julio Jr. is smuggled into the Miami Marlins' locker room prior to the electrically charged atmosphere of Game Seven of the World Series.

The instant I saw him, it was like ice water had suddenly filled my veins. Chills shot up my spine. He was sitting on a chair, alone in front of his locker, tightening the laces on his cleats. I took a hesitant step forward. Maybe he sensed me coming, because he suddenly looked up and his dark eyes zeroed onto mine.

Papi rushed across the room. With my legs suddenly weak I managed just another half step forward. "Junior," he said, as his chest thumped against mine. He was holding me so close I could feel his breath and smell the soap he must have used to shave. Then he took a step back, with his arms extended, holding me by the shoulder blades. In Spanish, he asked, "How did you get inside here?" His voice was like a weight bearing down on me. My mouth had gone bone dry. And even if I had an answer on my tongue, I wasn't sure I could have gotten the words out. I couldn't believe I was actually seeing Papi in the flesh, not on TV or hearing him described on the radio. I'd never been this tall before, standing beside him. The pores on his face looked huge, and there was a blemish beneath his right eyebrow.

Throughout the writing of this novel, I kept myself insulated from the real story of any of the refugees in that inspiring photo of the 1959 Buick car/boat sailing into Key West, Florida. But once *Game Seven* was published, I was more than eager to discover what I could about those brave freedom seekers.

It turns out that eleven refugees were jammed in that

car/boat. It was a vessel that cost $4,000 to make sea-worthy, a staggering amount for poor Cubans. Among the passengers was a family of three—Luis Gras Rodriguez; his wife, Isora; and their son, Angel. The US Coast Guard intercepted the Buick at sea and stopped all involved from coming ashore. If the refugees had actually reached US soil, however, the refugees would have most likely been granted the opportunity to stay.

There was a public outcry about the pending fate of Luis Gras Rodriguez and his family. Two years prior, Luis had tried to get his loved ones to the US in a floating truck/boat without success, before they were sent back to Cuba. Many people, including relatives back on the island, believed that the trio would suffer severe punishment from the Cuban government for this second attempt.

A US District Judge then stepped in, sending the family to the US-controlled Guantanamo Bay facility in Cuba, instead. The family remained there for some ten months, with Luis even participating in a brief hunger strike in protest of their captivity. Eventually, the family was granted refugee status in Costa Rica.

I knew how important it is for refugees to actually reach the shore. So in *Game Seven*, Julio Jr. is presented with that very situation.

A voice came over the ship's loudspeaker in Spanish. "This is the

United States Coast Guard!" it bellowed, with an echo. "You are in US waters! Shut off your engine! Put your hands on top of your head!"

"Have we made it far enough to stay? . . . Not to get sent back?" I asked my uncle, leaning down into the cabin.

"How could it be better?"

"If we were standing on US soil," he answered.

The voice on the loudspeaker repeated its demands. Then that ship launched a smaller, faster boat, full of uniformed men.

"I'm not taking any chances," I said. "I'm going to swim for the beach."

I was swimming in a straight line, as fast as I could, riding every wave to pick up speed. Glancing back, I could see that the smaller boat had reached the Buick, and now a second one was motoring after me. I was kicking my legs harder, reaching with every stroke. I was already exhausted. But there was no way I was going to stop.

My arms felt like limp rubber bands, and my lungs ached until I thought they were going to explode. Then, about fifty yards out, I heard the cheers from the people on the beach. And that sound gave me an added surge of strength.

I heard the motor of that boat getting closer. So I turned my head to see where it was. That's when a wave broke over me and I swallowed a mouthful of seawater. I was closer to the shore than that boat was to me. Before I knew it my chest was out of the water, and then my waist. I staggered onto the dry sand, falling *to my knees. I touched the ground like it was home plate, and I'd been rounding the bases. Only I wasn't safe. I was* free.

I feel privileged to have had that news photo seemingly choose me. For it to jump inside my brain and take root there until I could give birth to this novel. I know that this novel's publication in 2015 came at a very important time, with the US's renewed interest in starting conversations with the Cuban government. I hope that *Game Seven* will serve teachers, library media specialists, and most importantly, young adult readers in considering the value of family, loyalty, and freedom.

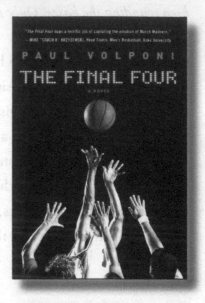

BY
PAUL VOLPONI

MYSTERIES AND
SECRETS OF
MAGIC

THE SORCERERS

From a wood engraving by Hans Baldung Grien. XVI century.

MYSTERIES AND SECRETS OF MAGIC

C. J. S. THOMPSON

SENATE

Mysteries and Secrets of Magic

This edition published in 1995 by Senate,
an imprint of Senate Press Limited,
133 High Street, Teddington,
Middlesex TW11 8HH, United Kingdom

Cover design © Senate Press Limited 1995

3 5 7 9 10 8 6 4

ISBN 1 85958 156 0

Printed and bound in Guernsey by
The Guernsey Press Co Ltd

" Shew me the secrets of the magical art and sciences and the sacred operation of hidden mysteries."

Manuscript of the XVI century.

CONTENTS

CHAPTER I

CONTENTS

CHAPTER VII

CHAPTER VIII

CHAPTER IX

CHAPTER X

CHAPTER XI

CHAPTER XII

CHAPTER XIII

CHAPTER XIV

CONTENTS

CHAPTER XV

CHAPTER XVI

CHAPTER XVII

CHAPTER XVIII

CHAPTER XIX

CHAPTER XX

CHAPTER XXI

CHAPTER XXII

CONTENTS

CHAPTER XXIII

CHAPTER XXIV

CHAPTER XXV

CHAPTER XXVI

CHAPTER XXVII

CHAPTER XXVIII

CONTENTS

CHAPTER XXIX

CHAPTER XXX

CHAPTER XXXI

LIST OF ILLUSTRATIONS

LIST OF ILLUSTRATIONS

IN THE TEXT

LIST OF ILLUSTRATIONS

THE MYSTERIES AND
SECRETS OF MAGIC

CHAPTER I

THE GENESIS OF MAGIC—MAGIC AND RELIGION

MAGIC has been described as the pretended art of influencing the course of events, and of producing marvellous physical phenomena, by methods which were supposed to owe their efficacy to their power of compelling the intervention of supernatural beings, or of bringing into operation some occult force of nature. The fundamental purpose of magic was therefore in opposition to the laws and principles of natural phenomena.

It has exercised a profound influence upon mankind throughout the ages, and has either formed part of the religion of a country, as in Babylonia and Egypt, or has been carried on in conjunction with it.

The roots of the belief in magic, as with superstition, seem to be grounded in fear, for man has ever dreaded the unknown.

Hegel remarks concerning what he calls the " Religion of Nature," or fear of the powers of Nature—of the sun, of thunderstorms and other natural phenomena—it was not the fear that might be called religious fear, for that has its seat in freedom. The fear of God is a different fear from that of the natural forces.

The priest-magician in ancient times, by claiming to be able to control the powers of the unseen deities, thus worked on the fears and imagination of the people.

The instinct of mystery, common to mankind among civilized and uncivilized communities, appears to have arisen primarily from ignorance or limitation of knowledge and fear of the unknown future.

These faculties men of greater intelligence than their fellows soon recognized, and turned belief in the mysterious to their own account.

As the practice of magic meant interference with the regular operations of Nature, the magician had first to appeal to some deity and propitiate it by prayers, offerings and perfumes that would render his appeal acceptable, and then call in the aid of supernatural powers, good or evil.

Some authorities are of the opinion that magic was the primary form of religion ; that it has existed among all peoples and at every period, and that faith in magic is probably older than a belief in spirits.

The whole doctrine of magic, according to Wiedmann, formed not a part of superstition, but an essential constituent of religious faith, which to a great extent rested directly on magic and always remained closely bound up with it.

On the other hand, Frazer observes, that in the evolution of thought, magic, as representing a lower intellectual stratum, has probably everywhere *preceded* religion.

It has also been suggested that in man's emotional response to his environment, in his interpretation in the terms of personality of the objects which encumbered his attention, and in their investiture by him with potentiality, we have the common root of magic and religion.

The practice of magic involved certain rites which may be regarded as traditional acts that embodied the idea of a wonder-working power, but magical rites not forming part of an organized cult came to be regarded by the society concerned as illicit.

" There is but one mythical idea at the back of all rites," says Wundt ; that is, " the idea of the soul, and from it are generated three forms of cult—magic, fetishism and totemism."

Thus magic in its primary form consisted in the supposed direct action of soul on soul, as where the " evil eye " is dreaded. The secondary form consisted in supposed action from a distance, when the soul influence made itself felt by means of a symbol.

As time went on, those of higher and wiser intelligence no doubt came to perceive that magical rites, ceremonies and incantations did not really produce the effects they were supposed to ; and so gradually there came a separation in the belief. The ignorant still clung to superstition and faith in magical powers, while the more intellectual saw the hand of a power greater than that of man, and began to see his dependence on a God above all.

Robertson Smith states that, it was the community, and not the individual, that was sure of the permanent and unfailing help of its deity, so much so, that, in purely personal concerns, the ancients were apt to turn to magical superstitions. Thus man had no right to enter into private relations with supernatural powers that might help him at the expense of the community to which he belonged.

Frazer considers that the principles of thought on

3

which magic is based are : first, that like produces like, which he calls imitative magic, from which the magician assumed that he could produce any effect he desired by imitating it ; secondly, that magic is contagious, from which he inferred that whatever he did to a material object, would affect equally the person with whom the object had once been in contact, whether it formed part of his body or not.

In practice, the two branches are often combined, to which he gives the name of sympathetic magic, since both assume that things act on each other at a distance through secret sympathy.

The attempt to injure or destroy an enemy by inserting nails into his image in the belief that just as the image suffers so does the man, and that when it perishes he must die, is an instance of one of the earliest forms of imitative magic.

It was practised by the ancient Babylonians, Egyptians, Hindus and other races at a remote period, continued throughout the Middle Ages, and is employed among the magical practices of many barbaric races at the present day.

The same form of charm was also practised for a more benevolent purpose, to gain the love or affection of a person. As the wax figure melted before a fire, so the heart of the individual desired was supposed to be softened and his love obtained.

Contagious magic is shown in the magical sympathy which was believed to exist between a person and any portion of his body, such as the hair, teeth or nails.

The idea that whoever gained possession of such things may work his will upon the person from whom

4

they were taken, at any distance, is one of considerable antiquity.

The old custom of placing an extracted tooth in a hole where it could be found by a rat or mouse, in the hope that, through sympathy, the person's other teeth might acquire the same excellence as those of the rodent, probably originated in this belief. On the other hand, an extracted tooth was sometimes thrown on the fire so that no one should find and keep it and so work magical power on the person to whom it originally belonged.

Another example of contagious magic is evidenced in the ancient belief that there is a connexion between a wounded person and the weapon that caused the wound, and that what may be done to the agent will correspondingly affect the injury.

Pliny says : " If you have wounded a man and are sorry for it, you have only to spit on the hand that gave the wound and the pain of the sufferer will cease."

Francis Bacon thus alludes to this belief : " It is constantly received and avouched, that the anointing of the weapon which maketh the wound will heal the wound itself."

This practice was revived in the seventeenth century by Sir Kenelm Digby, whom Dr Walter Charlton describes as " a noble person, who hath built up his reason to so transcendent a height of knowledge, as may seem not much beneath the state of man in innocence."

His theory, " touching the cure of wounds by the powder of sympathy," was delivered at great length before an assembly of nobles and learned men at Montpellier.

Digby's " Sympathetic Powder," which was applied

to the weapon that caused the wound, consisted of copper sulphate in powder, prepared when the sun entered the sign of Leo.

It is probable that the professional magician was originally one who, in the course of the evolution of society by birth, study and practice, acquired a powerful influence over his fellows. The priest by similar means, or by prayer and fasting, obtained the favour of the imaginary personages believed to influence or control the affairs of men, and thus the union of the priest-magician was probably fundamental. The magician always supplicated a power greater than his own, thus the help of the gods was invoked by incantation, and so magic and religion were again associated.

From the primitive rock carvings found in the Trois Frères cave near St Girons, Ariège, in France, there is some evidence of the practice of magic by prehistoric man. There Breuil discovered in a little chamber at the end of a long cave, the walls of which are covered with engravings on the rock, the figure of a man, masked, with antlers, as a stag with a tail, which dominated all the others.

" Close by this figure and equally prominent in the chamber below, is a kind of natural pulpit accessible from behind, whence it is thought the magician or sorcerer officiated."

If such was the case, the dim and mysterious surroundings of the cave must have helped to influence the minds of those who witnessed his proceedings.

With reference to the use of a stag's hide in this figure, it is interesting to note the story of the witch of Berkeley in the early part of the twelfth century, related by William of Malmesbury. He states, that when dying, she begged the monks and her children who were with her, "to sew her body in the hide of a stag, then place it in a stone coffin and fasten in the covering with lead and iron, so that her body might be secured from the hands of the demons."

In Egypt the magician claimed the power of com-

PREHISTORIC SORCERER.
At the Trois Frères Cave, France (after Breuil).

pelling the highest gods to do his will, and in India the great triune deity, Brahma, Vishnu and Siva, was subject to the spells of the sorcerers.

"The rites celebrated on special occasions," says Oldenberg, "are complete models of magic of every kind, and in every case the forms of magic bear the stamp of the greatest antiquity."

Even witchcraft formed part of the religion, and penetrated and became intimately blended with the

7

holiest Vedic rites. The Samavidhana Brahmana is in reality a handbook of incantations and sorcery.

" In ancient Egypt," states Maspero, " the faithful who desired to obtain some favour from a deity had no chance of succeeding except by laying hands on the god, and this arrest could only be effected by means of a certain number of rites, sacrifices, prayers and chants, which the god himself had revealed and which obliged him to do what was demanded of him."

The belief that the priest owing to his office possesses a certain power to put a spell on an offender, or—as termed in Ireland—" to put a curse upon him," survives till the present day.

" Magic as the enemy of an organized cult or the social organization as a whole," says Robertson Smith, " came to be worked in dark and secret places and grew by adoption of degraded and scattered rites from various cults." Thus we shall find that later and in the Middle Ages it imitated religious ritual to the verge of the blasphemous.

Religion, on the other hand, developed an ethical conception of the Godhead, in which the action of mere power is gradually converted into that of a power that makes for righteousness.

Having thus briefly considered the theories advanced by various authorities on the genesis of magic, it will be of interest to study its development and its practice among the early civilizations.

CHAPTER II

SUPERNATURAL BEINGS

THE belief in certain supernatural beings of diminutive size, but of charming appearance and with generally a benevolent influence, is common among various races and peoples.

In the Far East they have formed part of romance and story from early times and, according to an ancient Hindu tradition, they inhabited the earth before the creation of man.

In Persia the peris counteracted the malevolent influences of the divs and lived in enchanted palaces and castles.

In Europe the superstition is generally ascribed to the Celtic races, while the Gothic people introduced the elves and gnomes, the more malignant types of spirits.

In the poetical mythology of southern Europe they appear in the early Middle Ages, and are alluded to in the romantic stories of Italy, Spain and France. In ancient Erin, the belief in fairies was general, and their appearance is described as being " beautiful miniatures of human beings."

The fairies and their king and queen appear in early mythology, and later on, as Diana and her nymphs. Oberon is alluded to in the early French romances,

9

in which he is described as a "tiny creature of great beauty, wearing a jewelled crown, and a horn which when he blew set all dancing." Their power of making themselves invisible when they wished was typical.

Joan of Arc was charged with frequenting the tree and fountain near Dompré, which was the reputed haunt of fairies, and with joining in their dances and accepting their aid in the cause of delivering her country.

In the Middle Ages fairies were frequently associated with charges of witchcraft, as in the case of Ann Jefferies, who was said to have been fed for six months by "a small sort of hairy people called fairies." According to her statement, "Six small people, all in green clothes, came suddenly over the garden wall one day, when she was knitting stockings," in a garden at St Teath in Cornwall. They threw her into convulsions but endowed her with extraordinary powers of healing the sick, which eventually led to her being haled before the magistrates and committed to Bodmin Gaol for witchcraft. The Scottish fairies were not so amiable in character from accounts given by Scott. They are described as being "diminutive in form, and were to be found in the interior of green hills, on the surface of which, the rings which mark their moonlight dances may often be seen. They are clad in green, heath-brown or grey and are fond of riding invisible horses and occasionally real ones whom they force to a great speed."

The idea of a fairy king and queen is made use of by Chaucer, who alludes to the Queen and her land in the "Rime of St Thopas" and, in the "Wife of Bathes Tale," as holding her Court with great splendour in the time of King Arthur. In the "Merchante's Tale" the spirits of evil are mentioned as presiding over the country.

> " Proserpine and all her fayrie."

Allusion is also made to

> " Pluto, that is king of fayrie."

Oberon is first mentioned in a play written in 1594 entitled " The Scottishe Story of James the Fourth slain at Flodden, intermixed with a pleasant Comedie presented by Oberon, King of the Fairies."

According to Reginald Scot : " Fairies do principally inhabit the mountains and caverns of the earth, whose nature is to make strange apparitions on the earth, in meadows and in mountains, being like men and women, souldiers, kings and ladyes, children and horsemen, cloathed in green, to which purpose, they do in the night steal hempen stalks from the fields where they grow, to convert them into horses as the story goes.

" Such jocund and facetious spirits are sayd to sport themselves in the night, by tumbling and fooling with servants and shepherds in country houses, pinching them black and blue and leaving bread, butter, and cheese sometimes with them, which if they refuse to eat, some mischief shall undoubtedly befall them by means of the fairies."

John Webster, another early writer, says : " In a few ages past, when Popish ignorance did abound, there were in discourse nothing more common (which is yet continued among the common people) than of the apparition of certain creatures which they call fayries ; that were of little stature and when seen would soon vanish and disappear."

11

In his opinion, "fairies are pigmy creatures which really exist in the world, and are and may be still in islands and mountains that are inhabited, and that they are not real demons. But that either they were truly of human race, endowed with the use of reason and speech, or, at least, that they were some kind of little apes or satyres, having their secret recesses and holes in the mountains."

Some magicians claimed to be able to summon a fairy at will and, in a manuscript of the fifteenth century in the Ashmolean Collection, the following method is said to be " An excellent way to get a Fayrie." " First get a broad square christall or Venus glasse, in length and breadth 3 inches : then lay that glasse or chrystall in the blood of a white Henne, 3 wednesdays or 3 Fridays, then take it out and wash it with Holy Water and fumigate it. Then take 3 hazel sticks or wands of a years growth, peel them fayre and white and make them so long as you write the spirits or fayries which you call 3 times on every sticke, being made flatt on one side. Then bury them under some hill, whereas you suppose fayres haunt, the Wednesday before you call her, and the Friday following, take them up and call her at 8, 3, and 10 of the clock which be good planets and hours, but when you call, be of cleane life and turn thy face towards the east, and when you have her, bind her to that stone or glasse."

The conception of fairies apparently differed according to the character of people and country. They seized on the poet's fancy, and in Shakespeare's time we have a reflection of the common belief in fairies in several of his plays.

Above all, they captured the imagination of children

and have survived in story and the drama to the present day.

The good fairy and the bad fairy of the old-fashioned pantomime are the perpetuation, for children, of the fairies of olden times, and as long as the plays of Shakespeare live, the mischievous Puck, Robin Goodfellow and their kind will delight the hearts of everyone.

The elf was another small spirit that was supposed to inhabit the hills and mountains, and was believed to have some approach to human wisdom, being skilled in the mechanical arts. Elves appear to have had their origin in Scandinavian mythology in the form of the Bergelfen.

To them Olaus Magnus attributes the " fairy rings " we now know to be due to a species of fungus. In Scotland, triangular flints are called " elf arrows," from the belief that the elves shoot them at cattle which, although their skin remains unbroken, at once fall down and die, or recover from their convulsion by being touched with the " elf arrow " by which they have been hit, or by drinking the water in which it has been dipped.

The term " elf-locks," applied to matted hair, comes from the idea that the elves might bring misfortune. Shakespeare alludes to it in " Romeo and Juliet " in the lines :

> " This is that very Mab
> That plats the manes of horses in the night ;
> And bakes the elf-locks in foul sluttish hairs,
> Which once entangled much misfortune bodes."

Among other freakish acts attributed to elves is that of changing children in their cradles and substituting beings of their own kind instead, called elfin children. The knights of Spenser's " Court of Faerie " were all thus

13

born. Stories of this kind are common in Scotland, Ireland and in the Isle of Man.

Waldron, in his "Description of the Isle of Man," thus describes an elfin changeling whom he visited. He says : "Nothing under heaven could have a more beautiful face, but although between 5 and 6 years old and seemingly healthy, he was so far from being able to walk or stand, that he could not so much as move any one joint. His limbs were vastly long for his age but smaller than an infant of six months, his complexion was perfectly delicate and he had the finest hair in the world ; he never spoke nor cried, ate scarcely anything, and was very seldom seen to smile, but if any one called him Fairy-Elf, he would frown and fix his eyes so earnestly on those who said it, as if he would look them through."

One method of procuring the restoration of the stolen child was to roast the suppositious infant on live embers.

The elf home, according to the prose "Edda," is in the celestial regions and is the abode of the elves of light, while the elves of darkness live under the earth.

All the Teutonic nations held these beliefs and the romances of chivalry abound with them. In some parts of Germany the peasants believe that elves come and lie on those they find sleeping on their backs and thus produce nightmare. Nightmare has long been thought to have been produced by malevolent spirits like the incubi, hence the custom of hanging a horseshoe over the bed to drive them away.

"Familiar spirits," says Le Loyer, "were those who came at stated times and could not only converse but were visible in various forms they assumed. The Greeks called them Paredrii."

14

Socrates is said to have had an attendant spirit of this kind, and Sertorius claimed to have trained to obey his call, a white fawn which he said was the gift of Diana, who thus conveyed to him her revelations.

The story of Mohammed's pigeon—which was said to represent the angel Gabriel—that appeared to whisper in his ear was a similar myth.

Scott considered the Scottish brownie to be a descendant of the " familiars " of the ancients and it was typical of the brownie, that whatever work he performed, he would take no reward.

The black dog of Cornelius Agrippa, which always accompanied him, is a later story of this kind.

It was believed that " familiars " could be bound or imprisoned in magical figures and rings, in which the magicians of the school of Salamanca and Toledo and those of Italy made traffic.

Heywood says : " Every magician and witch have a familiar spirit given to attend them which are sometimes visible in the form of a dog or cat. . . . These kinds of familiar spirits are suche as are kept in rings hallowed, viols, boxes and caskets."

Philostratus states : " Apollonius Tyaneus was never without one, and Johannes Jodocus Rosa a citizen of Cortacensia, every fifth day, had conference with the spirit enclosed in his ring, who he looked upon as a counseller and director of his affairs. . . . It learnt him the cure and remedy of all griefs and diseases, insomuch that he had the reputation of a learned and excellent physician. At length being accused of sorcery at Arnhem in Guelderland, he was proscribed, and in the year 1548 the Chancellor caused his ring to be layd on an

15

anvil in the public market, and with an iron hammer beaten to pieces."

Paracelsus was believed to carry a "familiar in a stone set in the hilt of his sword, and he never laid the weapon down but placed it by his side in bed. He would often get up in the night and strike it violently against the floor."

The witch's "familiar" usually took the shape of a black cat or toad that followed her about, sat on her chair and with which she had converse.

Butler thus alludes to the stories of "familiars" that were supposed to reside in stones, in the following lines in "Hudibras":

> "Bombastus kept a devil's bird
> Shut in the pummel of his sword,
> That taught him all the cunning pranks
> Of past and future mountebanks.
> Kelly did all his feats upon
> The Devil's looking-glass, a stone,
> Where, playing with him at bo-peep,
> He solv'd all problems ne'er so deep.
> Agrippa kept a Stygian pug,
> I' th' garb and habit of a dog,
> That was his tutor, and the cur
> Read to th' occult philosopher."

The banshee, the supernatural being so common in the legends and stories of the Celtic races, was the warning spirit that attached itself to certain families and clans.

It was generally believed to be the spirit of a woman whose destinies had become linked, by some accident, with those of the family she followed. She was sometimes young, but usually very old with long, ragged locks flowing over her shoulders. She is described as

16

being attired in loose, white garments, and her duty was to warn the family she attended of approaching death or misfortune, by a peculiarly mournful wail at night, " resembling the melancholy sough of the wind but having the sound of a human voice, which could be heard at a great distance. She was rarely visible and only to those whom she attended."

The banshee is mentioned in several of the old Irish ballads, as in the following :

> " 'Twas the banshee's lonely wailing,
> Well I knew the voice of death,
> In the night wind slowly sailing
> O'er the bleak and gloomy heath."

Many of the ancient families of Ireland had their banshee and, to some, the phantom is still said to appear before the death of any near relative.

The warning spirit is not confined to Ireland, and similar apparitions are said to appear to families in Italy and Germany.

Scott records several instances in Scotland, and says that the family of Tullochgorm was haunted by a female whose left arm and hand were covered with hair.

An apparition is supposed to haunt Spedlins Castle near Loch Maben, which is said to be the ghost of a prisoner once confined in a dungeon who was starved to death. Its visits became so frequent that a clergyman was called in to exorcize it. He used an ancient Bible as the medium, and after twenty-four hours, according to the story, he was able to confine it to a part of the castle, but its shrieks and groans were still heard. Some years afterwards, the Bible was taken away to be rebound

17

and at once the spectre renewed its manifestations, which did not cease until the volume had been returned to its place in the castle.

The genius or jinn is supposed to be the spirit who attends an individual from the time of his birth, but is more frequently to be met with in the legends of the East than in those of Western races.

They were spirits of an inferior kind, and were the companions or guardians of men, who prompted them to good actions or otherwise, for the jinns of the East were both good and evil spirits. Those acknowledged by the Arabs differed from those of the Persians. The genii of " The Arabian Nights " were the divs of Indian legends adapted by the Persians to their romances.

The jinns appear to have been the descendants of the divs or dévatés of Hindu mythology, and were considered as spiritual agents or superhuman beings. They were represented by the Arabs as corporeal beings, hairy and sometimes of animal shape. They could assume human form, and had the power of disappearing and then appearing in another place. They were believed to live underground, and could therefore affect the earth with evil. On this account the husbandman would sprinkle new ploughland with the blood of a peace-offering to appease them.

The Persian div was more of the character and conception of a devil of the Middle Ages and might be either male or female.

The males, according to Persian tradition, were entrusted with the ruling of the world for 7000 years anterior to the creation of Adam. They were believed to be able to assume various forms, especially that of a serpent, and are often thus represented in drawings illustrating the early Persian romances.

The divs or daivers of the Hindus were supposed to inhabit a world called Daiver—Logum—and are usually represented in the Hindu romances as engaged in combating the giants. They formed a numerous host and are divided into many classes.

The word " devil " is supposed to have been derived from the Persian " div." The Hebrew word translated in the Old Testament means " hairy ones " applied to goats.

Parkhurst says : " It is not unlikely that the Christians borrowed their goat-like conception of the devil with tail, horns and cloven feet from the representations of Pan."

Sir Thomas Browne remarks, that the Rabbins believed the devil to appear most frequently in the form of a goat, as that animal was the emblem of the sin offering and is the emblem of sinful men at the last judgment.

The Eastern races represented their devil with horns and a tail, and often with deformed heads and faces on certain parts of the body, such as are depicted in many pictures of the Middle Ages. In colour, he is painted a blackish-red or brown and black, while Satan was painted green. At a later period he is sometimes depicted as a black cat, but in witchcraft ceremonial he is generally described as a great he-goat or ram.

The incubus was the spirit to which nightmare was attributed and was supposed to impose itself on the sleeper in the dead of night, and give rise to terrible dreams until the victim could shake it off. Keysler

States, that Nachmar is derived from Mair, an old woman, because the spirit appears to press upon the breast and impede the action of the lungs. The English and Dutch words coincide with the German, but the Swedes use Mara alone. There is a tradition in some countries, that " nightmare is associated with the weird women who were not only in the habit of riding on men but also on horses, and to keep them out of the stables the peasants used to write the pentalpha on the stable doors in consecrated chalk on Walpurgis Night." The horseshoe was employed for the same purpose, and at the present day in some parts of the country, a decorated horseshoe is hung over the bed to prevent a visitation of nightmare.

" Incubi and Succubi," says an old writer, " are devils taking often times to that end the shape and likeness sometimes of men, and sometimes women and commit the greatest abominations. St Augustine said that the satyrs and fauns were incubi."

The word " incubus " is perpetuated and used to-day to describe a burden it is difficult to throw off.

Vampires have fired the imagination of humanity for centuries, and the fact that certain animals are capable of sucking human blood gave some credence to their existence. They are described by ancient writers as, " persons who rise from their graves in the night and suck the blood of the living and then return to their graves."

The fact that after the death of certain persons, their relatives were often observed to grow pale and thin, gave some colour to this belief.

Hungary, in particular, has been the origin of many stories of vampirism and various theories have been suggested to account for the curious and weird tales that have been told of their exploits. In case of a suspected vampire, the body was disinterred, and if it was found to be fresh and full of blood the accusation was declared to be true. To put an end to its activities a sharp stake was driven through the heart and the body was then burnt.

In some places, judiciary proceedings were taken against the gruesome spectres, and the exhumed bodies were examined for the marks of depravity, which consisted chiefly in the flexibility of the limbs and fluidity of the blood.

At length it began to dawn on the minds of the more intelligent that the so-called vampires were persons who had probably been buried alive. Of the many stories related of vampires, one recorded in the " Lettres Juives," 1738, which is attested by two officers of the Emperor's troops at Graditz who were eye-witnesses, may be taken as an example.

" In the beginning of September 1738, a man aged 62, died at the village of Kisilova near Graditz. Three days after he was buried, he appeared at night to his son and demanded food, which the son gave him and he disappeared. The next day the son told the neighbours what had happened. The following night but one, the father appeared again with the same request. The next night the son was found dead in his bed, and five or six persons took ill and died in the village in a few days. A report was made to the tribunal at Belgrade and two officers and an executioner were sent to investigate the matter.

" They opened the graves of those who had been dead

six weeks, and when they came to the body of the old man they found his eyes open and of good colour, and with natural respiration, from which they concluded that he was a vampire. The executioner then drove a stake into his heart and the body was burnt to ashes."

In the account of another case in the village of Liebaea, it is said that the vampire was caught by a peasant who watched from the top of the church tower. He felled the vampire with a blow on his head and then decapitated him with a hatchet.

Such were the stories of vampires that were believed as late as the eighteenth century.

Tournefort states, in 1717, that, in the Archipelago, the people of the islands firmly believe that those excommunicated by the Greek Church preserved their bodies entire and from putrefaction after death. He was present at the exhumation, impalement and burning of a supposed vampire in the island of Mycone, who was said to have broken the bones and drained the veins of half the inhabitants of the island.

The goblin, or Robin Goodfellow, was said to be a freakish spirit who although he frightened people was not an enemy of mankind. Though Shakespeare includes him among the fairy followers of Oberon, he was more of the phantom type.

" Hobgoblins or these kind of spirits," says a writer of the seventeenth century, " are more familiar and domestical than the others, and abide in one place more than another, so that some never depart from some particular house, making sundry noises, rumours, mockeries, gawds and jests, without doing any harm, and some have heard them play on gitterns and Jew's harps, and ring bells and make answer to those that call them, and speak with certain signs, laughters and merry gestures so that they be feared not at all."

The Scottish bogle was a similar frolicsome spirit who delighted more in playing tricks than doing harm.

Drayton alludes to Puck whom he says " most men call hobgoblin." The antics attributed to the goblins are similar to the manifestations of the poltergeist through whose agency objects were said to be hurled across a room, crockery smashed, jugs lifted from the table and the contents poured on the floor, and knives, forks and spoons projected through space as if by unseen hands.

CHAPTER III

THE CULT OF MAGIC—THE MAGI AND THEIR MYSTERIES

MAGIC was intimately connected with the origin of all mythology and also with the ancient creeds of philosophy.

Zoroaster or Zarathustra, the founder of what is called the Magian religion, is supposed to have lived about 1500 B.C., but according to the Zend-Avesta—in which his name is mentioned—he probably flourished at a much earlier period.

The fundamental principles of the religion he founded, the doctrines of which are described in the Zend-Avesta, teach that the world is the centre of the conflict between two great powers, good and evil, and that the good principle is eternal and will finally prevail over the bad.

Zoroaster is said to have been the originator of the Magi, but the religion he founded eventually degenerated into an idolatrous form of fire worship.

The Magi, who are believed to have been a distinct caste of the Medians, can be traced back to about 591 B.C., and were known as the magicians or wise men. They were the disseminators of the wisdom of Zoroaster, and were flourishing at the period when Cyrus founded the new Persian Empire. They appear to have been an order divided into various classes, and became renowned for their skill in divining dreams, closely linked with which was the study of astrology—in which they excelled.

They professed a profound knowledge of the mysteries of Divination, and for that purpose met and consulted in their temples. They claimed to be searchers after Truth, for that alone, they claimed, " could make man like God, whose body resembled light and whose soul or spirit resembled Truth." They condemned all images and worshipped the sky as representative of the Deity. According to Herodotus, they addressed the heavenly bodies and elements and sacrificed to the Sun, Moon, Earth, Fire, Water and the Winds.

Both in Egypt and in Greece, it is stated that the sacerdotal fraternity, or association of the initiated formed by the mysteries, had generally an important influence on State affairs, and in Persia they are said to have acquired a complete political ascendancy. The sacred religious philosophy and science were in their hands and they were healers of the sick in body and in mind. About 500 B.C. they were fiercely persecuted and many emigrated to Cappadocia and to India. It is probable that the migration of the Magi towards the West was the cause of the spread of the influence of magic to Greece and Arabia. The Biblical references to the Wise Men of the East, and their study and knowledge of the stars, are well known and corroborate these statements.

The worship of the mysterious Cabiri has been traced to the Phœnicians and goes back to a remote period.

The mysteries of Eleusis and of Bacchus are of a comparatively recent date compared with these ancient prehistoric rites.

Some thought that the Cabiri were descended from Thoth and Hermes Trismegistus, but Herodotus calls them the " Sons of Vulcan, and Jupiter is often named as their father." Other early writers consider that they were the ministers of the gods who were deified at their deaths.

It is stated that the worship of the Cabiri originated in Egypt and that the Temple of Memphis was consecrated to them. In ancient Rome they were apparently regarded as the household gods of the people.

The island of Lemnos was notable for the worship of the Cabiri, and Vulcan, as represented by fire; and, there, mystical rites were performed over which they presided. The coins of the island sometimes bore the head of Vulcan, or a Cabirus with the pireus, hammer and tongs.

The mysteries of the Cabiric worship were celebrated also at Thebes and especially at the Isle of Samothrace.

They are said to have taken place at night. The candidate for initiation was crowned with a garland of olives, and wore a purple band round the loins. He was prepared by sacred ceremonies, probably hypnotic, and was seated on a brilliantly lighted throne, around which the other initiates danced in a mystic measure. The general idea represented in these ceremonies, was the passage through death to a higher life ; and, while the outer senses were held in the thrall of hypnotism, it is supposed that revelations were made to the priests.

In the mysterious art of foretelling and the beginnings of prophecy, the Oracles played an important part, and among these the Oracle of Delphi was celebrated.

According to tradition, it originated with fumes that

were found issuing from a cave discovered by Coretas, a shepherd. There is no evidence to show whether these were of natural origin or not; but the story continues that, on approaching it, the shepherd was seized with ecstasy and uttered words which were deemed to be inspired.

A tripod was erected over the source, and a girl was chosen to become the medium of the responses, which were believed to be oracular. A bower of laurel branches was built over it, and later came the marble temple and priesthood of Delphi where the Pythoness was seated on her throne. The Oracle is said to have prepared herself by drinking from the sacred fountain— the water from which was reserved for her only—by chewing a laurel leaf and encircling her brow with a laurel crown.

The person who wished to consult the Oracle had first to offer a victim, and then, having written a question, to hand it to the Pythoness before she ascended the golden tripod.

The Oracle of Delphi is said to have spoken only during one month in the year and, at first, only on the seventh day of that month—which was deemed the birthday of Apollo.

The Oracle of Jupiter Ammon and the locality in which it was situated are alike disputed. The temple is described by Lucan and other classical writers. The image of the god was carried abroad by the priests, and is said to have responded not by speech but by nodding. The priests themselves often expressed ignorance of their deity's meaning, and the replies therefore generally left the questioner in considerable uncertainty.

The Oracle of Jupiter Dodona is said to have issued from a tree, recorded by some as an oak and by others as a beech. Bells and copper basins were suspended from the branches, and clanged and tinkled at the slightest breath of wind. A fountain of strange and mysterious virtue issued near the grove, and was said to have the power of relighting a glowing torch after it had been extinguished.

The Oracle of Jupiter Trophonius is described by Pausanias. Trophonius was regarded as the most skilful architect of his day, and tradition states that he was swallowed up by an earthquake in the cave which afterwards became prophetic. According to Pausanias, a deputation from a neighbouring district, where famine was rampant, went to consult the Oracle, which they could not find until they followed the flight of a swarm of bees. The inquirer was obliged to descend into a cave, where he remained for a certain number of days while he made the propitiatory offerings to the Oracle. An intricate ceremonial followed and the entrails of the victims were inspected in order to learn whether Trophonius was in a fit humour to be consulted or not. The responses were said to be given sometimes in a vision, and at others by words. There was only a single instance of anyone who descended to the cave failing to return, and that one deserved his fate, for his object was to discover treasure, and not to consult the Oracle. " I write," says Pausanias, " not only from hearsay but from what I have seen occur to others, and which I myself experienced when I went to consult Trophonius."

The Oracles of Delos and Branchis also had a high reputation. The responses were given by a priestess, three days after consultation, and who then sat on an axle or bar with a charming-rod in her hand, inhaling the steam from a hot spring. Offerings and ceremonies were necessary to render the inspiration effectual, including baths, fasting and solitude.

At Clarus, near Colophon, was the Oracle of the Clarian Apollo, which was delivered by a priest selected for the most part from a Milesian family, who prophesied after drinking the water which gushed forth from a spring and was believed to give insight into futurity. The water was only allowed to be drunk after arduous spiritual exercises.

The Egyptian Oracles were also famous, and that at Amphiaraus, near Thebes, was perhaps the most renowned. Oracular dreams were supposed to visit those who slept on the skins of rams that had been sacrificed and the priests were the interpreters. No rite was performed in the fountain belonging to this establishment, nor was it used for lustrations, but its waters were an unfailing source of profit. All who were satisfied with the Oracle's prescription threw a piece of gold into the consecrated spring before their departure.

Auguries exercised a powerful influence on the minds of communities in early times. The Augurs are thought by some to have originated in Etruria (though it is possible that they go back to a much earlier period), and were four in number.

Although originally of the patrician class, at a later period the plebeians had representatives in the College, and the number of Augurs was increased to nine. On their first institution they were probably chosen from the College of Priests, but their election underwent several modifications. Cicero states that, in the early days of the Republic, it was customary to send six sons of the most eminent patricians to Etruria to be educated in the discipline of Augury, by means of which they were able to penetrate the mysteries of the future. It was a priesthood that continued for life, and so great was its dignity that no crime, however atrocious and however clearly proved, could lead to deprivation. The chief Augur was called the *magister collegii*, and the duties of the priesthood enjoined the public interpretation of the sovereign will of Jove, to attend to signs and auspices and to anticipate the anger of the gods. Among other duties, they had to superintend sacrifices and to declare what victims, rites and prayers were necessary for expiation. The ceremonies at magisterial elections were referred to their judgment, and they could invalidate or confirm the appointments not only of minor officials, but also of prætors, consuls and even dictators. Peace or war was resolved upon, according to their responses, and they exercised a control over the public mind which was without appeal.

The costume of an Augur consisted of a robe striped with purple or scarlet, or a double cloak and a cap of conical shape. He carried a smooth staff, the head of which was curved like an episcopal crosier. This staff was his special badge. Its use was to mark out and distribute the several parts of the visible heaven into different houses, and to assign precise imaginary limits to the quarters which he referred to right and left.

So arrayed, the Augur would proceed to some elevated spot, and, having sacrificed, he either himself uttered a prayer or repeated the prescribed formulary. According to some authors, he turned his face to the east so that the south was on his right and the north on his left. He then divided the heavens into four parts, named the West Antica, the East Postica, the North Sinistra and the South Dextra. With eyes intent upon the sky, and amid the solemn silence of the crowd that surrounded him, he waited until some bird appeared, carefully noting down the spot from which it rose, the course it took, its upward or downward flight and the point at which it disappeared. It was not enough that a single augury should be seen, it was necessary to confirm it. If on passing from the hill or elevated spot, after the reception of an augury, the priest came to any water, he would stoop down and take some in the palm of his hand, and pray that the augury might continue firm, as water was supposed to interfere with its efficacy.

Such appears to have been the earliest form of augury, as practised by the Romans. The procedure differed among other peoples. The Persians and Greeks appear to have made auguries from thunder and lightning; others judged from the flight of birds. Thus, if an eagle were seen on outstretched wings, it predicted prosperity; cranes, if they were diverted from their flight and turned backward by a storm, were regarded as a sign of woe to mariners; swallows were regarded as precursors of misfortune. Auguries were also derived from animals, and even swarms of bees and locusts were regarded for this purpose.

Omens for good and ill, when once believed in, had a strong effect on the mind. Birds played an important part in the auguries, and crows in particular; they were sometimes a good omen, but when seen plucking their own feathers they portended ill.

The Greeks regarded a sneeze in the morning as an omen that the business of the day would be bad; if it occurred at noon, the omen was a fortunate one; if a person were to sneeze after dinner, a dish had to be brought back and tasted to avert misfortune that otherwise was believed to be certain.

CHAPTER IV

BABYLONIAN AND ASSYRIAN MAGIC

WE owe our knowledge of the magical practices and demonology of the Assyrians and Babylonians to the clay tablets inscribed in cuneiform of the time of Assurbanipal which have been translated by R. Campbell Thompson and others. They are believed to be copies of others of a much earlier period, and which probably dated back six or seven thousand years.

These ancient records show the general belief in magic and the part it played in the life of the people.

From the story of Gilgamish which has come down to us, it is evident that they practised sorcery and prognostication. Gilgamish appealed to the god Nergal to restore his friend Ea-bani to him, and the god opened the earth and the *utakku* or spectre of Ea-bani rose up. As they believed that disease was caused by the entrance of demons into the body, it is natural that magic should enter into their treatment of the sick.

The object of the magical texts was to enable the priest-magician to control or exorcize the demons, or to counteract their malign influence. To do this it was important that the evil spirit which affected the sick person should be mentioned by name, so that we find in the tablets long lists of the names of demons or evil

33

spirits, such as the ghosts of the dead who wandered over the earth.

To heal his suffering, the sick man had recourse to the magician who by his knowledge of magical words, incantations and prayers could invoke the aid of the great gods to gain control of the demon. Frequent mention is made in the incantations of the fumigation, which shows the importance attached to this rite, as for example:

" Come, my sorceress or enchantress,
Over a nulukhkha-plant shalt thou recite,
Upon the fumigation bowl which is at the head of the bed shalt thou place it, and with an upper garment shalt thou envelop the bed."

This was accompanied by offerings of various kinds, mention being made of honey, butter, dates, garlic, corn-flowers, plants, pieces of wood, palm spathes, sheep-skin, wool and fragments of gold and precious stones. These were generally destroyed by fire, indicating the sympathetic connexion between the destruction of the ban and that of the object.

In the magical ceremonial of the Babylonians the recital of the incantation was generally accompanied by the burning of incense. Thus :

" A censer of incense before the god —— shalt thou set,"

which is the formula usually employed.

After the formula, in which the suppliant stated his name, mention is often made of " Prayers of the lifting of the hand " which accompanied the performance of certain rites and ceremonies, when a prayer was delivered after an eclipse of the moon.

The rite of the " knotted cord " frequently accompanied the " Prayers of the lifting of the hand," and when the priest-magician loosened the knot certain words were to be uttered. The god or goddess must then be propitiated by gifts, before the suppliant made his appeal, the altar being loaded with the offerings and the censers lighted before the words of the incantation could take effect.

The following text of a prayer to Tăsmîtu is an instance of the formula employed :

" I —— son of —— whose god is —— whose goddess is ——
In the evil of an eclipse of the moon ——
May the sickness of my body be torn away ; may groaning of my
    flesh be consumed !
May the consumption of my muscles be removed !
May the poisons that are upon me be loosened ! "

In the practice of magic three things were essential in exorcism. First, the " word of power " by means of which the magician invoked divine or supernatural aid ; secondly, the name or description of the person or demon he was working against ; thirdly, charms, amulets or figures of wax or clay to help him, and sometimes hair or nail parings were employed. At a later period magical names were used as the " words of power." [1]

The Assyrians had a special demonology and believed that the soul could return to earth after the death of the body. They recognized several distinct classes of spirits, including the disembodied human soul which wandered over the face of the earth ; those which were regarded as partly human and partly demon, and the demons or devils.

The sorcerer was called the " Raiser of the departed

[1] " The Devils and Evil Spirits of Babylonia," by R. Campbell Thompson, M.A. London, 1903.

spirit," while the magician's art appears to have been chiefly practised in the form of sympathetic magic or the transferring of a spiritual power into some object under his control.

The most primitive form employed was the wax or clay figure previously mentioned. After this had been modelled in the likeness of an enemy with incantations, nails or thorns were stuck into it, or it was allowed to melt before a fire so that the human counterpart might suffer similar torment.

The prevalence of this practice in antiquity is remarkable.

The Egyptians employed it at a very early period and the Jews probably adopted it from them. An allusion to it occurs in the following text :

" If thou wishest to cause anyone to perish, take clay from two river banks and make an image therewith, write upon it the man's name, then take 7 stalks from 7 date trees and make a bow with horse hair ; set up the image in a convenient place, stretch thy bow, shoot the stalks at it and with every one say the prescribed words, adding ' Destroyed be —— son of ——.' "

The image or figure was also used in the inverse way and was employed by a sick man to drive out a disease-demon that possessed him. A figure of the ailing one was made in wax, clay or dough, and with the proper charms the magician tried to induce the demon to leave the body of the sick man and enter his counterpart.

When an Assyrian thought himself bewitched or laid under a spell, he would seek a magician and beseech him for counter charms and incantations against the person who had bewitched him.

If a man was attacked by a ghost, he had to be anointed with various substances so that the "hand of the ghost" should be removed. There are several methods recorded in the texts for "laying a ghost," and the following is one for "the ghost that walks at night and comes to the bedside."

"When a dead man appeareth unto a living man—thou shalt make a figure of clay and write his name on the left side with a stylus; thou shalt put it into a gazelle's horn and its face—and in the shade of a caper bush or in the shade of a thorn bush, thou shalt dig a hole and bury it."

The demons or spirits of evil were those generally dealt with by the magician, and many incantations are recorded that were to be employed to counteract their power.

One of these, called Alû, was believed to hide in caverns and ruins and deserted buildings, which even at that early period appear to have been regarded as the haunt of ghosts. He is described as being "horrible in appearance, half human and sometimes without mouth, ears or limbs."

Another was Lilû, Lîlitu or Ardat Lilî, who is thought to be the Lilith of Hebrew traditions, and whose name is frequently mentioned in the Rabbinical legends. She appears to have been the restless spirit of a woman, half human, who wandered over the earth.

The association of ruined and deserted buildings with ghosts and spectres appears to have been universal and is met with in legends and stories from the earliest times.

It is thus referred to in an Assyrian text :

"O thou that dwelleth in ruins, get thee to thy ruins."

During the ceremonial, the Babylonian magician sometimes sprinkled water over a person who was believed to be possessed by an evil spirit, thus symbolizing the cleansing of the man from the spell. Meteoric iron, which was regarded as a gift from the gods, was used as a charm or amulet.

> " Take thou the potent meteorite of heaven,
> Which by the roar of its awful might removeth all evils.
> Place the tamarisk
> The mighty weapon."

A branch of tamarisk was carried by the magician in his hand during the exorcism, probably because it was believed to contain the emanation of the tree-spirit which was supposed to live in the sacred tamarisk tree. It was thought to be all-powerful over the evil demons that inhabited the trees, as the following text shows :

> " These evil ones will be put to flight,
> The tamarisk the powerful weapon of Anu
> In my hands I hold."

The tamarisk was cut with certain ceremonies with a golden axe and silver knife according to a Babylonian incantation :

> " Let a wise and cunning coppersmith
> Take an axe of gold (?) and a silver pruning knife
> Unto a grove undefiled ;
> (Let him carve) a hulduppi of tamarisk,
> Touch it with the axe."

Water was employed in exorcism, as instanced in the text :

> " I am the sorcerer, priest of (Ea),
> I am the magician of Eridu.
> When I sprinkle the water of Ea on the sick man,
> When I subdue the sick man . . . "

Further allusions to the use of fire and water are made in another text as follows :

> " Perform the incantation of Eridu,
> Bring unto him a censer and a torch,
> With the purest water wash him
> And cleanse and purify the king, the son of his god.
> Evil spirit, evil demon, evil ghost, evil devil,
> Evil god, evil fiend,
> Into the (house) may they not enter."

The use of the mystical number seven had both a good and evil significance, and there are many references to it in the Assyrian magical texts : thus, in an incantation :

> " By the seven gates of the earth mayst thou be exorcized,
> By the seven bolts of the earth mayst thou be exorcized."

Then there were the " seven evil spirits " that wrought mischief on the earth :

> " Those seven evil gods, death dealing without fear,
> Those seven evil gods rushing on like a flood."

Against them this incantation was to be said :

> " Seven gods of the broad earth,
> Seven robber gods are they,
> Seven gods of night, Seven evil gods, Seven evil demons,
> Seven evil demons of oppression, Seven in heaven and seven on earth."

They apparently belonged to the class of inhuman spirits and are thus described in another Assyrian text :

> " They creep like a snake on their bellies,
> They make the chamber to stink like mice,
> They give tongue like a pack of hounds."

It was they who rode on the storm clouds bringing

39

devastation in their train, and they brought tempests, hurricanes, unrest and disorder into the world.

> " These seven are the messengers of Anu the king,
> Bearing gloom from city to city ;
> Tempests that furiously scour the heavens,
> Dense clouds that over the sky bring gloom."

In the book of the Revelation it is Beliar who sends seven spirits against man and the seven angels who brought the seven plagues. A further allusion to this number occurs in an Assyrian poem :

> " Seven gods of might,
> Seven evil gods,
> Seven evil demons,
> Seven evil demons of oppression,
> Seven in earth and seven in heaven—
> Seven are they, Seven are they !
> In the ocean deep, Seven are they ! "

At a later period the seven spirits are again mentioned in Syriac magic thus :

> " Evil are they, Evil are they,
> Seven are they, Seven are they,
> Twice Seven are they."

Namtaru, the plague god of the Assyrians, seems to have been of the half-human and half-supernatural type, and there was also Ura, another demon that brought plague and pestilence. In an incantation addressed to the god, the priest-magician is directed to make a figure of the person suffering, in dough, so that the plague god may be induced to leave the man he is tormenting and enter the image. It begins :

" O Plague god that devoureth the land like fire,
Plague god that attacketh the man like fever,
Plague god that roameth like the wind over the desert,
Plague god that seizeth on the man like an evil thing."

Another method of expelling the plague demon is thus directed :

" Lay a sprig of mashtakal on his heart,
With the water perform the incantation of Eridu,
Bring unto him a censer, a torch,
That the plague demon that resteth in the body of man,
Like the water, may trickle away.

.   .   .   .   .   .

Pull off a piece of clay from the deep,
Fashion a figure of his bodily form and
Place it on the loins of the sick man by night ;
At dawn make the atonement for his body,
Perform the incantation of Eridu,
Turn his face to the west,
That the evil plague demon which hath seized upon him
    may vanish away from him."

The Assyrians hung clay amulets over the doors of their dwellings to protect them from spirits that worked evil and harm, and in the British Museum there are two tablets inscribed with the legend of Ura the plague demon, which were probably used to prevent his entrance into the house.

The " evil eye " was a source of terror to the Assyrians, and frequent references are made to it in the incantations.

One of these reads :

" The roving evil eye hath looked on the neighbourhood and
    vanished afar."

And another:

> " Thou man, son of his god,
>   The eye which hath looked upon thee for harm,
>   The eye which hath looked upon thee for evil."

The belief still persists in Palestine that the " evil eye " can throw down a house, break a plough, cause sickness and even destroy a person, an animal or a plant. Charms in the shape of an eye are carried on the person, camels are protected by hanging a holed-stone around their necks, and horses by fastening blue beads on their manes and tails.

The use of a knotted cord as a charm woven by a " wise woman " is thus alluded to :

> " Hath seated the wise woman on a couch,
>   That she may spin white and black wool into a double cord,
>   A strong cord, a mighty cord, a twi-coloured cord on a spindle,
>   A cord to overcome the Ban."

After performing the incantation of Eridu, a " threefold cord on which twice seven knots were tied " and fastened round the head, was believed to cure headache. For persons suffering from ophthalmia, a black-and-white cord on which " twice seven knots were tied," while repeating the incantation, was said to relieve them of their trouble. The idea of the magician was thus to compel the demon to leave the body and enter into something which would give him control over it and which he could destroy.

Certain odours were believed to have an attraction for demons and the smell of newly-shed blood delighted devils or the odour of burnt fat attracted evil spirits. Devils could be expelled by a repulsive odour, while good spirits were propitiated by sweet-smelling perfumes.

A general incantation, potent against evil spirits that afflict man and cause disease, reads as follows :

" Sickness of the head, of the teeth, of the heart, heartache,
Sickness of the eye, fever, poison,
Evil spirit, evil demon, evil ghost, evil devil, evil god, evil fiend,
Hag demon, ghoul, robber sprite,
Phantom of night, night wraith, handmaiden of the phantom,
Evil pestilence, noisome fever, baneful sickness,
Pain, sorcery or any evil,
Headache, shivering,

. . . .

Evil spell, witchcraft, sorcery,
Enchantment and all evil,
From the house go forth
Unto the man, the son of his god come not into,
Get thee hence ! "

Love charms were sometimes made from the brain of the hoopoe mixed into a cake, or a magic wick was formed inscribed with invocations and burnt in a lamp. The bones of a frog if buried for seven days and then exhumed would when thrown into water indicate love or hate. If they sank it indicated hate ; if they floated they were believed to signify love.

The demons were believed to dwell in the underworld of the god Bel, whence they came forth to seize on man or work evil in his house if they could gain entrance. The following charm hung over the door was supposed to drive them away :

" Fleabane (pyrethrum) on the lintel of the door I have hung,
St John's wort, caper and wheat ears,
On the latch I have hung
With a halter as a roving ass."

The peasants in the district of the Landes in France still hang crosses of St John's wort over the doors of their cottages to keep away evil spirits.

The custom of taboo which is still believed in and practised by barbaric races exercised a powerful influence in ancient times.

The idea had a twofold action, first in the primary danger to the person who originally incurs the taboo by his action ; and secondly, the contagious ban to which anyone may become liable from communication with a tabooed person or thing belonging to them.

The penalty for the violation of a taboo was either civil or religious. The religious penalty inflicted by the offended spirits usually took the form of some disease, and the offender died owing to the emissary having entered into him and devoured his vitals.

There were taboos on the dead, on women in certain conditions and other prohibited things. Among the Israelites all who were unclean through the dead were put outside the camp.

There was a special taboo on kings and certain acts from which the king must abstain. Thus, on certain days of the month, he must not change his raiment, neither ride forth in his chariot nor lay his hand on the sick.

From these ancient records of the Babylonians and Assyrians we know that the belief in the " evil eye " existed among them, and that the wax figure or image was employed in their magical ceremonies over five thousand years ago.

From a stamp or seal recently excavated at Ur of the Chaldees, we now have evidence that there was a cultural connexion between Mesopotamia and India in the early Sumerian period before 3000 B.C.

Thus many of the magical practices of these ancient peoples were carried to the Far East; they survived among the Jews and in Syria, and later became part of the magic practised in Europe.

CHAPTER V

MAGIC IN ANCIENT EGYPT

THE earliest records of magic among the ancient Egyptians show that it was recognized and practised as far back as the fourth dynasty. With them, as among the Babylonians, magic began with the gods, the great workers of wonders. Thus some of their greatest deities were associated with magic, like Thoth who endowed men with wisdom and learning, and Isis who worked enchantments and spells.

"From the Egyptian point of view," says Gardiner, "there was no such thing as religion, there was only *hīke*, the nearest English equivalent of which is magical power."

They believed that magic emanated from the gods. Thoth was considered the most powerful magician and from him arose the fame of Hermes Trismegistus. Horus was credited with magical powers, and Isis was regarded as a great enchantress, as evidenced in the following incantation :

"O Isis great enchantress, free me, release me from all evil red things, from the fever of the god and the fever of the goddess. From death, and death from pain, and the pain that comes over me ; as thou hast freed, as thou hast released thy son Horus, whilst I enter into the fire and go forth from the water."

46

In the story of the healing of a child who had been bitten by a scorpion, by Isis, the goddess cries :

" Come to me, Come to me ! for my word is a talisman which beareth life.   I will do away the evil by means of the word of my mouth which my father hath taught me."

In order to bring back the spirit of the child to its body, she lays her hands upon him and says :

" Come Tefen, appear upon the ground, depart hence, come not nigh ! "
Come poison of Befen, appear upon the ground.
I am Isis, the goddess, the lady of words of power, who doeth deeds of magic, the words of whose voice are charms.
Obey me, O every reptile that stingeth and fall down headlong !
O poison of (Mestet) Mestetef, mount not upwards !
O poison of Petet and Thetet, draw up nigh,
O Metet, fall down headlong."

Isis then uttered certain words of the charm which had been given to her by the god Sebin in order to keep poison away from her, and said, " Turn away, get away, retreat, O poison ! "

According to a papyrus written in the time of Amenophis III over 1000 years after the reign of Cheops, " some rites were found at nightfall in the forecourt of the Temple of Coptos as a secret of this goddess (Isis) by a lector of that fane ; the earth was in darkness, but the moon shone upon this book illuminating it on every side."

The pyramid texts of Unas state, that a book with words of magical power was buried with him, about 3500 B.C.

The Egyptians aimed at being able to command their

deities to work for them and to appear at desire. These results were to be obtained by the use of certain words or formulæ uttered by a trained man who practised magic, or the words were inscribed on papyrus or precious stones and carried on the person. This practice became so general, that it is little wonder the Egyptians at a very early period came to be regarded as a nation of magicians.

Moses apparently acquired his knowledge of magical practices from the Egyptians, as it is recorded in the Old Testament that he was " learned in all the wisdom of the Egyptians and mighty in words and in deeds." The story of the brazen serpent, and the power to control and direct the movements of such venomous reptiles, are acts that were doubtless known to the Egyptians in those days. Lane mentions, that the native magicians he met with had a method of hypnotizing a viper by compressing its head and making it appear like a rod.

A papyrus of the Ptolemaic period records the story of a prince called Setnau Khā-em-uast, who was learned in magic and the powers of amulets and talismans and had a library of magical books. One day when he was talking, one of the king's wise men laughed at his remarks, and Setnau said, " If thou wouldst read a book possessed of magical powers, come with me and I will show it to thee. The book was written by Thoth himself, and in it there are two formulas. The recital of the first will enchant (bewitch) heaven, earth, hell, sea and mountains, and by it thou shalt see all the birds, reptiles and fish, for its power will bring the fish to the top of the water. The second will enable a man, if he be in the tomb, to take the form which he had upon earth."

Later on, Setnau set out with his brother to seek the book, which was said to be in the tomb of Ptah-nefer-ka at Memphis.

On their arrival, Setnau recited some words over the tomb and the earth opened, and they went down to the place and found the book.

The tomb was brilliantly illuminated by the light from the book, and they saw Ptah-nefer-ka and his wife and their son. Setnau said he had come to take away the book, but Ahura the wife, begged him not to do so, and related the terrible misfortunes that had happened since it had been in their possession. On Setnau pressing his request, Ptah-nefer-ka proposed that they should play a game of draughts and the winner should have the book. Setnau won, and by means of his talismans flew up to heaven with the book in his grasp. These ancient legends

A MAGICAL FIGURE
(From a Græco-Egyptian papyrus *ca.* 200 B.C., at Leyden.)

are interesting, as they point to the assumption that there were books on magic, now unknown, written at a period of remote antiquity.

Like the Egyptian magicians, both Moses and Aaron employed a rod to perform their wonders, as it is recorded that when Moses stretched out his rod, there was " hail and fire mingled with the hail, very grievous," and also when the locusts came at his command.

The Egyptians had an all-prevailing faith in magic.

49

It exerted a powerful influence over the life of the people, and was invoked in all questions of life, death, love, hatred, health and disease. It was closely interwoven with both religion and medicine and was so practised by the priests in the temples.

Disease was believed to be caused by evil spirits that entered the body, and to effect a cure they had to be expelled. Thus magic formed part of their medical treatment, and the sick came or were brought to the temples to be healed either by incantations, drugs or incubation.

The priest-magician had first to discover the nature of the disease and the name of the possessing demon, after which, he exercised his magic functions to rid the patient of the intruder.

" He who treats the sick must be expert in magic, learned in the proper incantations and know how to make amulets to control disease." He used physical as well as psychical therapeutics. There were invocations and impressive ritual, all of which would probably have their effects in cases of psycho-neurosis.

Incubation sleep in the temples was resorted to in some diseases, suggestive intimations being given by the deity during natural or drug-produced dreams, and interpreted by the priest-magician. Suggestions received during dreams were found to have achieved their purpose, when the sufferer woke and declared himself healed by the deity.

Magical rites could apparently be performed at any time, but certain rules had to be observed and the magician was enjoined always to stand with his " face to the east." In one spell it is mentioned that it had to be recited "at eventide, when the sun was setting," and in another, seven knots were to be tied, one in the morning, another in the evening, and so on, until the seven knots were complete.

It was regarded as essential that the priest-magician should be pure in life, and secrecy in his practices was imperative. There are warnings in connexion with them, that " certain things were not to be looked at."

The Egyptian medical papyri abound with incantations, but a difference is made between the incantation and the remedy, and apparently the physician might be a layman while the magician was a priest.

The drugs themselves were supposed to possess magical power, as evidenced in the following from the Papyrus Ebers :

"The magic of Horus is victorious in the remedy."

" The physician practised his art by the book, mechanically, while the priest acted through religious feeling," says Maspero.

There does not appear to have been any common word for magician, but the " lector priest " is specially mentioned as being empowered to perform cures, as having discovered incantations, and as one endowed with prophecy.

The employment of images and figures played an important part in Egyptian magic. These figures were not immediately potent in themselves, but had to be charged with magical power, and so the oral rite was first recited over them to ensure their efficacy. Sometimes drawings on papyrus or other material were similarly treated, or the figures of the gods invoked were inscribed on the patient's hand and licked off. Magical charms or amulets were generally attached to the person, as contact was considered necessary in order to make them effective. Spells were sometimes fastened to the left foot, but the neck was usually chosen for the amulets, and the string on which they were suspended was generally tied with seven magical knots.

The idea that drawings of deities, after " words of power " had been recited over them, would have magical effects is instanced in the " Book of the Dead," which was to be said after the deceased person had been cleansed and purified. The text reads : " When he is arrayed in apparel and is shod with white leather sandals, and his eyes have been painted with antimony, and his body has been anointed with ANTI unguent, and when he hath made offerings of oxen and birds and incense, and cakes and ale, and garden herbs. And behold thou shalt paint a picture of what shall happen in the Hall of Maati upon a new tile, moulded from earth upon which neither a pig nor any other animal hath trodden, and if thou writest upon it this chapter, the deceased shall flourish and his children shall flourish, and his name shall never fall into oblivion."

The Egyptians believed that it was possible to transfer to a wax or clay figure of a man, woman or animal the soul of the being it represented, together with its qualities and attributes ; and this form of magic was practised from the fourth to the twentieth dynasty.

One of the earliest records of the practice is related in the Westcar papyrus of an event which happened in the time of Neb-ka, who reigned about 3830 B.C.

While this king was visiting one of his high officials

named Abā-āner, the wife of the latter fell desperately in love with one of the king's soldiers. Abā-āner, on being informed of his wife's infatuation, took a quantity of wax and made a model of a crocodile seven spans long; then reciting magical words over it said, "When the man cometh down to bathe in my waters thou shalt seize him." He then told his servant, when the soldier came to bathe, to cast the crocodile into the water after him. This was done and the wax crocodile straightway turned into a living crocodile seven cubits long (about 12 feet) and seized upon the man and dragged him down under the water. For seven days, according to the story, the man remained in the depth of the water.

On the seventh day Abā-āner went out to walk with the king, and invited him to come and see a wonderful thing that had happened to a man. On coming to the water, Abā-āner adjured the crocodile saying, "Bring hither the man," and the crocodile came out of the water bringing the man with him. Abā-āner took it up and it at once became a wax crocodile again. Then he told the king of the unfaithfulness of his wife with the soldier whom the crocodile had brought out of the water, whereupon the king said, "Take that which is thine and begone," and immediately the crocodile seized the man and sprang into the water and disappeared.

This curious story is interesting, as it shows that wax figures were used for magical purposes in Egypt at least 5000 years ago, and probably even before that early period.

Another allusion to this method of working magic occurs in an account of a conspiracy against Rameses III, King of Egypt, *ca.* 1200 B.C. Not content with fomenting a revolt among the soldiers and a revolution among the people, a high official called Hui went to some person who had access to the Royal library, and got from him a book on magic with recipes for working magic, from which he is said to have obtained "Divine Power," and through it was able to cast spells. He made figures of men in wax, and amulets inscribed with "words of power" to provoke love, and introduced them into the Royal Palace. Hui is said to have found means of carrying out "horrible things and all the wickedness which his heart could imagine by his magic." He made gods of wax and figures of men, which would cause the persons whom they represented to become paralysed and helpless. From this narrative it would appear that books on magic existed in the Royal Library of Rameses III.

More than one of the Kings of Egypt practised magic and, among them, the most famous according to tradition was Nectanebus, the last native king of Egypt, who reigned about 358 B.C.

He is said to have been profoundly learned in astrology, in the interpretation of omens, in casting horoscopes and in magical practices. It is recorded that he was able "to rule all kings by his magical powers," and by means of a bowl of water, in which he placed wax models of the ships and men of his enemies, he destroyed their power. Having put the models of his own ships and men on the water, he would place those representing his enemies opposite to them; then, having robed himself in an Egyptian prophet's cloak, he would take an ebony wand, and pronounce "words of power" and invoke the gods to come to his aid.

After this, we are told, "the figures of the men in

wax would come to life, and the ships begin to engage in battle. He contrived that the models representing his own navy should vanquish the enemy and sink their ships to the bottom of the bowl, as did his real ships sink the enemy's vessels on the sea. Thus Nectanebus fought his battles by aid of magical art."

He is also credited with the knowledge of being able to cause dreams, by extracting the juice of certain herbs, which he poured over the wax figure of the person who was to dream.

According to Abu-Shâker, an Arab of the thirteenth century, Aristotle presented Alexander the Great with several wax figures nailed down in a box that was fastened by a chain, which was never to leave his hand. He was to take the box wherever he went and recite certain formulæ over it, when he took it up or put it down. The figures were intended to represent the enemies likely to be opposed to him. Some of them had lead swords and others spears or bows, and were laid face downwards in the box.

This curious story of a military talisman is interesting, especially in connexion with that related of Nectanebus.

The image or figure also plays a part in many Egyptian charms, and the following, to enable a person to receive an oracular revelation in a dream, is thus recorded in an early papyrus :

" Take of the inner leaves of laurel 28, and virgin earth and wormwood seeds, flour, and the herb cynocephalium ; and I have heard from a certain Heracleopolite that he takes of the leaves of an olive tree lately sprouted 28. It is carried by a chaste boy and ground up with the materials and mixed with the white of an ibis's egg. And take the image of the cloaked Hermes and let Hermes hold the herald's wand, and write the spell upon a sheet of hieratic paper or on the windpipe of a goose, and insert it into the figure for the purpose of inflation. When you wish for an oracular response, take the paper and write the spell upon it, and having cut off a hair from your head, wrap it up in the paper and tie it with a Phœnician knot, and place it outside an olive branch and put it at the feet of the image. Let the figure lie in a shrine of lime-wood, and when you wish for an oracular response, place the shrine with the god at your head and invoke, offering frankincense upon an altar, and some earth from a place where corn grows, and one lump of sal ammoniac. Let it lie at your head and lie down to sleep."

In the magical papyri translated by Chabas there are several formulæ recorded for preservation from attacks of sea and river monsters, of which the following is an example :

" Hail, Lord of the gods ! Drive away from me the lions of the country of Meru [Meröe ?] and the crocodiles which come forth from the river, and the bite of all poisonous reptiles which crawl forth from their holes. Get thee back O crocodile Māk, thou son of Set. Move not by means of thy tail ! Work not thy legs and feet ! Open not thy mouth ! Let the water which is before thee turn into a consuming fire, O thou whom the 37 gods did make, and whom the serpent Rā did put in chains. O thou who wast fettered with links of iron before the boat of Rā. Get thee back O crocodile Māk, thou son of Set."

This charm was to be pronounced over the figure

of the god Amen painted on clay. The god was to have four rams' heads upon one neck, under his feet was to be a figure of the crocodile Māk, and on the right and left were to be the dog-headed apes.

The Gnostics and other sects probably adopted their magical names from the Egyptians, from the time of the Ptolemies to the end of the Roman period between 150 B.C. to A.D. 200.

Perfumes and incense played an important part in the ritual and embalmment and were employed by the Egyptians in their magical ceremonies. According to an address to the deceased, translated by Maspero, " The perfume of Arabia hath been brought to thee, to make perfect thy smell through the scent of the god. Here are brought to thee liquids which have come forth from Rā to make perfect —— thy smell in the Hall [of judgment].

"O sweet-smelling soul of the great god, thou dost contain such a sweet odour that thy face shall neither change nor perish. Thy members shall become young in Arabia, and thy soul shall appear over thy body in Ta-neter [the Divine land]."

The priest or embalmer was then to take a vase of liquid which contained ten perfumes, and smear the body with it from head to foot, taking care to anoint the head thoroughly.

The perfume was believed to have the power to make the members of the body perfect.

The deceased is then told that the liquid is secret, and that it is an emanation from the gods Shu and Seb, and that the resin of Phœnicia and the bitumen of Bybeos will make his burial perfect.

Among the objects presented to the deceased, perfumes and unguents played a prominent part, and to certain oils, magical properties have been attributed by the Egyptians from very early times. Oils were and are still largely used to soften the skin, to heal wounds and to relieve pain in the limbs.

Many of the charms employed in the Middle Ages can be traced to Egyptian sources, such as the following, " to see visions and cause dreams," which is given in a manuscript of the sixteenth century.

" Make a drawing of Besa (Bes) on your left hand, and envelop your hand in a strip of black cloth that has been consecrated to Isis, and lie down to sleep without speaking a word, even to answer a question. Wind the remainder of the cloth round your neck.

" The ink with which you write must be composed of the blood of a cow, the blood of a white dove (fresh), frankincense, myrrh, black ink, cinnabar, mulberry juice, rain water, and the juices of wormwood and vetch. With this write your petition before the setting sun (saying), ' Send the truthful seer out of the holy shrine, I beseech thee, Lampsuer, Sumarta, Baribas, Dardalam, Iorlex. O Lord, send the sacred deity Anuth Anuth, Salbana, Chambré, Breïth, now, now, quickly, quickly. Come in this very night.' "

The Egyptians practised the art of casting nativities and drawing horoscopes. Budge assigns to Egypt the birthplace of the horoscope, and in a Greek papyrus in the British Museum there is an allusion made to the art of astrology, which " the ancient Egyptians with their laborious devotion to the art had discovered and handed down to posterity."

Nectanebus used a tablet made of gold and silver and acacia-wood, to which was fitted three belts.   Upon

THE METTERNICH STELE

the outer one was Zeus with the 36 decans, on the second the 12 signs of the Zodiac, and on the third the sun and the moon.   He placed the tablet on a tripod,

59

and then from a small box emptied on it models of 7 stars that were in the belts, and put into the middle 8 precious stones.

" These he arranged in the places wherein he supposed the planets which they represented would be at the time of the birth of Olympias, and then told her fortune from them."

Amulets and talismans may be said to have had their home in ancient Egypt and were extensively employed by the Egyptians both by the living and for the dead. One of their most remarkable magical stones, known as the Metternich stele, was excavated at Alexandria in 1828 and dates from about the fourth century B.C.

It is thought to have been used as a talisman or amulet for a building. On it are representations of some of the great gods of Egypt, demons, monsters and texts of magical formulæ and magical names. In the centre is a figure of Horus standing upon two crocodiles. Above is the head of Bes and on either side figures of Horus Rā standing on a serpent, Osiris in the form of a hawk, Isis on a serpent and Nekhebet in the form of a vulture.

Thoth is also represented standing upon a coiled serpent, and Uatchet in the form of a serpent is standing on a papyrus sceptre.

It is further interesting to note that the name of Nectanebus the magician-king is also inscribed on this stone.

CHAPTER VI

ANCIENT JEWISH MAGIC—THE KABBALA

THE Jewish traditions connected with magic are of historical importance, as it has been found that many of the rites practised down to the Middle Ages had their origin in these sources.

In the Pentateuch, the references concerning magic, sorcery and witchcraft are chiefly connected with Egypt, from which it may be assumed that the knowledge of the Jews was acquired from that country during the captivity.

According to a Samaritan legend, the two Egyptian magicians who unsuccessfully withstood Moses were named Jannes and Jambres, and the sorcerer who predicted his birth was called Palti. It further attributes the origin of witchcraft and sorcery to the " Book of Signs " which was given to Adam before he left Paradise, but which in Jewish tradition is called the " Book of Adam " or the " Book of Rāziēl," a title that survives in a book of the Kabbala.

A story in the " Book of Enoch " says, " The art of witchcraft was communicated to man by two angels who had forfeited all rights to the happiness of heaven, and their names were Uzza and Azael. It was the latter who taught women the art of witchcraft and the use of cosmetics." There is also an ancient Egyptian tradition, ascribing the origin of the magical arts to the teaching of an angel who had fallen in love with a woman.

In the "Book of Tobit," the story is related of how the angel Raphael sought, by means of fumigation, to counteract the work of a demon who had fallen in love with Sarah. The spirit thus exorcized, called Ashmodæus, afterwards became recognized as "the king of the powers of evil."

Many of these names survived and are mentioned in the books of magic that have come down in manuscript form to the present day.

To obtain the assistance of spirits, the Jewish magicians employed fumigations, gifts and sacrifices. Maimonides says, " The gift most acceptable to the evil spirits was blood, and the magician must partake of the blood, thus sharing the food of the evil spirits, so as to become their associate. The perfume of the fumigation was very acceptable to these spirits." Then there was the lighting of candles, the use of a knife with a black handle, philtres served in glass bowls and other ceremonies employed in propitiation.

The magician possessed the secret of the mysterious names given to the evil spirits, without which he could not gain their help. These were among the secrets that at first were not committed to writing. It was through the names of the spirits that Balaam was able to work his magic. He was considered a great magician, and is said to have taught the daughters of Moab to practise sorcery and witchcraft.

The practice of magic was enveloped in the greatest mystery, and the books of the magicians were regarded as inviolable secrets and were only accessible to adepts.

62

The magician often used bowls with conjurations written upon them for the purpose of making his incantations, which made them more effective. These conjurations often consisted of the names of demons and spirits in his service.

Although the Jews were strictly forbidden to practise magic, and the Rabbis decreed that the penalty was stoning to death, operations were performed in the Holy Name, and were sanctioned when carried out by angelic and not by evil powers. This imaginary division in the magical arts continued throughout the Middle Ages; for, while the so-called black magic was prohibited, what was termed white or good magic, performed through the agencies of good spirits, was regarded as legitimate.

Early Hebrew records of conjuration are rare, but the following is one translated by Gaster:

" Take bdellium [crystal] and write upon it with olive oil, *Aungil*, and take a boy seven years old and anoint his hand from the top of the thumb to the end of the finger, and put the bdellium into his hand in the anointed place, and seize his hand, and you shall sit upon a three-legged stool, and put the boy between your loins so that his ear shall be against your mouth, and you shall turn your face towards the sun and say in his ear, '*Aungil*, I adjure thee in the name of Lord God, God of Truth, God keeper of the hosts, *Alpha*, AIDU, that thou shalt send from the three angels.' Then the boy will see a (figure) like (that of) a man and say (the charm) twice more and he will see two (figures) and the boy shall say unto them, ' Your coming be in peace,' and then tell the boy to ask of them that which you wish. If they will not answer him, the boy shall adjure them and say, ' *Kaspar, Kelei,* ' *Emar* (or) *Bleiteisar*, the master and I adjure (you) with a second adjuration, that you tell me that thing or who has committed that theft."

Similar conjurations are to be found in the manuscripts of the " Key of Solomon," and this method of

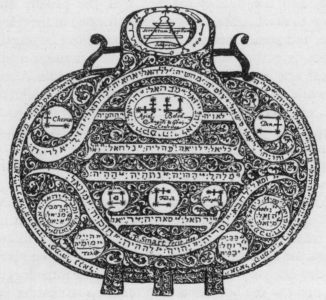

JEWISH MAGICAL DIAGRAM, SHOWING THE SECRET SEAL OF SOLOMON
(Drawn by P. Smart, 1699.)

employing a boy as a medium was used by Cagliostro as late as the eighteenth century.

The magical powers attributed to King Solomon appear to have arisen about the time of his building of the Temple.

Tradition assigns to him the authorship of certain works which, written in manuscript under various titles about the sixteenth century, are still extant. They are known as " The Clavicle or Key of Solomon," " The Worke of Solomon the Wise," or " The Key of Solomon the King," and will be dealt with more fully later on.

The introductions to these books vary, and some which are undoubtedly apochryphal are very curious. One states, that " Solomon possessed knowledge inspired by the wise teachings of an angel, and when he was near the end of his days he left to his son Roboam a testament, containing all the wisdom he had possessed. The Rabbins called this testament the ' Clavicle or Key of Solomon,' which they caused to be engraved on (pieces of) the bark of trees, while the Pentacles were inscribed in Hebrew characters on copper, so that they might be carefully preserved in the Temple.

" This Testament was in ancient times translated from Hebrew into Latin by Rabbi Abognazar (probably Aben Ezra), who transported it with him into the town of Arles in Provence, where the ancient Hebrew Clavicle fell into the hands of the Archbishop of Arles, after the destruction of the Jews in that city, who from the Latin translated it into the vulgar tongue."

Another states, " The book was sent to Solomon by a Prince of Babylon by name Sameton, while the two wise men who brought it were Kamazan and Zazant. It was the first book after Adam written in Chaldean and afterwards translated into Hebrew."

The prologue of another manuscript begins, " Secret of all Secrets of all crafts magicall of Nigromancy, as Ptolomei the most wisest philosopher in Greece doth testify."

It is said to have been revealed to Solomon by an "Angell of God" in a dream. "The angel Raziell appeared to him in his sleep and he inscribed a secret work." He adjures his son Roboam to have a casket of ivory made for it, and when he shall depart to cast it into his sepulchre so it may not come into the handling of fools.

"When the sepulchre had stood a long time, certain philosophers of Babylon that were his scholars, when restoring the tomb, removed the casket. They could not understand its words, but Ptolemy, a Grecian, prayed that he should be able to interpret the secrets, and an angel appeared and gave him light to read the clavicle, and he rejoiced with gladness, and read Solomon's works and made clear the profound and obscure secrets of this art."

The story of the ivory casket is repeated in another codex, with the addition of the statement that "a Babylonian philosopher called Iohe Grevis deciphered it and revealed it through an angel."

Josephus mentions that Solomon left some works on Magic, and in the Talmud, reference is made to "the princes or rulers over all shining objects and crystal," which probably indicates the use of the latter in magical practices.

Authorities are somewhat vague, and vary in their definitions of the meaning of the mysterious Kabbala or Qabalah.

It is stated, by one, to be the secret traditional knowledge handed down from generation to generation by word of mouth.

Another says, it was "the esoteric Jewish doctrine

66

which was handed down by oral transmission and is nearly allied to tradition."

The Kabbala was apparently divided into many parts, a great portion being a mystical doctrine giving the inner occult meaning of the Jewish sacred writings.

It is contended that all faiths and beliefs are but the echoes conveyed, in an allegorical and symbolical form, of some original race concerning which all traces are lost. The secrets known to the priests of Egypt which were regarded as sacred were not committed to writing and so have been lost.

Mathers states, that "the Kabbala was first taught by God himself to a select company of angels, who after the fall communicated the doctrine to man.

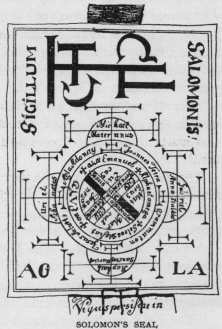

SOLOMON'S SEAL
(From a drawing in an MS. of the XVI century.)

From Adam it passed to Noah, then to Abraham who took it to Egypt, and so the Egyptians and some races of the East obtained a knowledge of it. Moses, who was learned in all the wisdom of Egypt, was first initiated in the land of his birth, and became proficient in it during his wanderings in the wilderness, and received

67

instruction in it from one of the angels. By the aid of this mysterious science, he was enabled to solve the difficulties which arose with the Israelites. He initiated the seventy elders, and they again transmitted it down to David and Solomon, who were the most deeply learned in the Kabbala. No one, however, dared to write it down, till Schimeon Ben Jochai, who lived at the time of the destruction of the second Temple. After his death, his son Rabbi Eleazar and Rabbi Abba collated Simon Ben Jochai's treatises, and out of these composed the work called ZHR, Zohar (splendour) which is the great storehouse of Kabbalism."

" The term 'unwritten Kabbala' is applied to certain knowledge which is never entrusted to writing, while the practical Kabbala deals with talismanic and ceremonial magic."

Josephus records how he saw Eleazar draw out an evil demon by holding a ring under the nose of a possessed man, under the seal of which was one of the roots recommended by Solomon.

Another writer says, "The Kabbala was a system of religious philosophy which has exercised a great influence on the Jews and many philosophers from the fourteenth to the seventeenth century.

" The ZHR or Zohar contains several books including the ' Siphra Dtzenioutha ' or ' Concealed Book of Mystery,' a treatise called the ' House of Elohim,' the book of the Revolutions of souls, ' Asch Metzareph,' or Purifying Fire, is chiefly alchemical, while the ' House of Elohim ' treats of angels, demons and spirits."

These three books are said to have been originally written in Chaldean and Hebrew text. " The name of the deity, Jehovah," says Mathers, "is in Hebrew IHVH, and the true pronunciation of it is known to very few. It is a most secret arcanum and is a secret of secrets. Therefore, when a devout Jew comes to

The Tenn Names of God with their Ideas Orbs & Hyerarchs largely Explained

(Drawn by P. Smart, 1699.)

it when reading the scripture, he makes a short pause or substitutes for it the name Adonai, Adni Lord.

"The prince of the demons is Samael Smal, who is the angel of poison and death. IHVH, the Tetragrammaton, is the greatest trinity, and Adni is the Queen whose Christian assumption is the Virgin."

69

" The Jewish idea of a mystical name of God," says another writer, " rests upon the interpretation of the Tetragrammaton or the word IHVH that stands for God in the Hebrew text which from ancient times the priests first, and then the people, refrained from pronouncing in the way it was written." A substitute was found for it so as to avoid a possible profanation of the sacred name.

The names Adonai, Elōai, found frequently in magical formulæ, are also derived through the Hebrew. The IAŌ, the three vowels also met with, were intended to represent JAH, one of the Hebrew names for God.

The frequent allusions to magic and its practitioners in the Bible show how widely its influence extended among Eastern races. In the Old and New Testaments there are mention of magicians, sorcerers, astrologers, soothsayers, seers or interpreters of dreams, diviners, observers of the times (monthly prognosticators), enchanters, witches, charmers, consulters with familiar spirits, wizards and necromancers. Besides these there were the Chaldeans, who were called before the King of Babylon, and the Magi or Wise Men.

Sorcery in the time of Moses was forbidden, as stated in Deuteronomy xviii. 10–11 : " These things are an abomination unto the Lord and are forbidden."

Wizards or witches and those who had a familiar spirit, are mentioned in Leviticus xx. 27 : "A man or woman that hath a familiar spirit or that is a wizard shall be stoned to death."

Manasseh is stated to have been one who " observed times, used enchantments and witchcraft and dealt with a familiar spirit and with wizards " (2 Chron. xxxiii. 6).

MAGICIAN CALLING UP A DEVIL.
From an MS. of the XV century. British Museum.

THE WITCH OF ENDOR
From an MS. of the XV century. British Museum.

Isaiah refers to wizards that " peep and mutter." " Thy voice shall be as one that has a familiar spirit out of the ground," and " thy speech shall whisper out of the dust." One must infer from these allusions that the spirit was supposed to speak out of the earth.

In the account of Saul's visit to the witch of Endor, there is corroboration of this suggestion. " Seek me a woman that hath a familiar spirit," and he said to the woman of Endor, " Divine unto me by the familiar spirit." The woman knew that the practice was forbidden and thought it was a trap.

Saul apparently saw nothing himself, as he asked her for a description of what she saw. That the voice *came from the ground* is evident from the text, as " he stooped with his face to the ground," and eventually collapsed from fright (Sam. xxviii. 7–19).

There is mention of a " mistress of witchcrafts " in Nahum iii. 4, and divining with rods, for which the Moabites and Medes were famed, is thus alluded to by Hosea iv. 12 :

" My people ask counsel at their stocks, and their staff (rod) declareth unto them."

" They sacrifice and burn incense upon the hills under oaks and poplars and elms because the shadow is good."

That the offering of incense was believed to give pleasure to the deity is evidenced from the Lord's command to Moses, where among the penalties of transgression are found the words, " I will not smell the savour of your sweet odours."

In the New Testament there are references to three sorcerers, first of whom was Simon, who had bewitched the people of Samaria and continued with Philip after

71

he became a Christian and believed, " wondering and beholding the miracles he wrought." Then there was Elymas, and Bar-jesus, " a certain sorcerer, a Jew of the Isle of Paphos."

From the account of the damsel from whom Paul cast out an evil spirit, she was probably a medium, for " she brought her master much gain through her divination " (Acts xvi. 16).

The acts of the Apostles were imitated by vagabond or travelling Exorcists who professed to cast out evil spirits, such as the seven sons of one Scera, a Jewish chief of the priests, who attempted to expel a demon, that " leaped upon them and overcame them " (Acts xix. 1–6).

Ephesus at the time of the Apostles appears to have been a centre for magical practitioners, who abounded in the city.

That there must have been large libraries of works on magic in the city is evident from the statement, that many who practised curious arts brought their books, some of which even at that time were thought to be valuable, being worth 50,000 pieces of silver, and they were publicly burnt (Acts xix. 19).

A loss to posterity which it is impossible to estimate.

Jewish magic was held in high esteem by both the Greeks and the Romans, and the Arabs absorbed their teaching.

During the Middle Ages, the belief that many Jews possessed occult powers persisted, and in the East invocations and prayers often accompanied the administrations of medicine as practised by the " Gabbetes," elderly men who sometimes attended the sick.

The phylacteries still worn by Jews at certain parts of their ritual are believed to act as a protection against evil influences. The amuletic ligatures with magical

בְּלִגִּיג

צָמְרְבָה

THIS HEBREW LIGATURE WORN ROUND THE ARM "PRESERVETH FROM ALL MISCHIEF OF AFFRIGHTMENT OF ENEMIES AND EVIL SPIRITS AND ALL OTHER DANGERS IN ARMS OR CONTESTS."

From an MS. of the XV century. The symbols are to be written on the ligature. Top row, on the fore part, and bottom row, on the hinder part.

inscriptions probably had their origin in the same custom. The Jews, in Syria to-day, still practise some of their ancient magical ceremonies with fumigations, offerings and lighted candles.

CHAPTER VII

GREEK AND ROMAN MAGIC

WHAT little is known of the practice of magic in early Greece may be said to begin with Homer, in whose mythological stories frequent mention is made of magicians. The Telchines, Dactyli and Korybantes in their semi-divine power had a knowledge of the magical arts. The Telchines knew all the secrets of Nature, the Dactyli were masters of music and the art of healing, and imparted their knowledge to Orpheus, Pythagoras and others, while Prometheus, Melampus, Agamedes, Circe and Medea were all accounted great magicians.

The story of Circe, who lived in the mysterious sea and enticed wandering seamen by her charms, and brewed magic philtres to turn men into swine, is well known.

Medea appears to have been more inclined to sorcery ; and terror and fascination were inspired by her very presence and look.

She was mistress of magic herbs and could bestow youth and invulnerability, calm storms and even " call down the moon," a famous love-charm that is said to have emanated from Thessaly, which at the time of Aristophanes was the country of magicians and witches. The magic herbs of Thessaly were supposed to have

74

sprung from the spot where Medea lost her box of charms, as she flew over the land with her winged dragons.

The potions and salves attributed to these magicians appear to have been used as the media for exercising their powers. Thus Circe's salve brought her victims back to human form, while that given by Medea would render its user invulnerable to his foes.

Aphrodite gave Phaon a salve which procured him youth and beauty, and Pamphila a box filled with little caskets each containing a special salve for producing magical effects of transformation. The use of philtres to provoke love is very often mentioned and appears to have been a common practice in early Greece.

The story of the magic wand employed by Athene and Hermes shows that some knowledge of the magic of the Babylonians and Egyptians had penetrated into Greece.

The influence of Chaldean and Persian magic becomes apparent about the fourth century before the Christian era, when Osthanes, who recorded all the secrets of magic of his time, was said to have initiated Democritus, the Greek alchemist, in the art. To him is also attributed the first book on medical magic.

The Greek magician was believed to derive his powers from a close acquaintance with the forces of Nature, although magic was regarded as a gift and attributed to some accident of birth or special privilege. It was associated with anything abnormal: thus a person with the "evil eye" was accounted a magician; the ventriloquist and hump-backed people, and those born with a caul, were believed to have the gift of prophecy.

Demons and spirits were regarded as the cause of evil,

as among other races, and it was with them the magician had to deal.

Like the Babylonians, the Greeks believed that the spirits of the dead who wandered over the earth were the cause of trouble to mankind. The gods were invoked for aid, and Hecate, the mighty goddess of magic, was called upon for help and believed to have universal powers.

The magician had to observe certain special rules and to know how to perform the necessary rites and ceremonies, of which some record has survived.

To prepare himself, it was essential that he should first be pure and clean, bathing at stated intervals and be anointed at certain times with oil. He had to avoid certain foods, especially fish, and practise chastity and fasting.

" His robes must be flowing, without knots or fastening of any kind, and be made of linen, either all white or white with purple streamers. Above all he must have faith in the accomplishment of his rites."

The time at which the rites were to be performed was important and depended on the god to be invoked ; thus for Hecate, the hour of sunset or a few minutes before sunrise were regarded as most favourable, and the best time was just at the new or full moon.

The position of the planets and stars did not become important until a later period, when astrology began to exercise its influence on the Greek magical practices.

Graveyards or cross-roads were regarded as the most suitable places for carrying out the rites.

Hubert thus describes the ceremonial and apparatus employed by the Greek magician.

The most important implement was the wand, without which no magician was completely equipped. Lamps, basins of water, keys for symbolic use, cymbals, threads of various colours, portions of a dead person, the rhombus or witch's-wheel—by the spinning of which the individual over whom one wished to gain ascendancy was influenced—were all necessary in carrying out the magical rites and formed part of the magician's equipment.

When casting spells, it was not necessary for the persons on whom they were imposed to be near. His or her place could be taken by a symbolical substitute in the form of a figure, into which needles were stuck according to the extent of the spell.

These figures, which were modelled in clay or wax, were sometimes made hollow so that written incantations could be placed within the bodies. Eusebius mentions an image of Hecate composed of powdered lizards and the root of rue, but the body of a bird and a sprig of rue or myrtle might also be used in the same way. It was necessary, however, to inscribe the figure with the name of the person whom it was intended to represent, and to specify every part in which the victim was to suffer.

Magical hymns and litanies were sometimes chanted to ensure the presence of an appropriate spirit.

The power of incantations was supposed to be increased by frequent repetition, and so in the course of time the words themselves became to be thought magical. By the arrangement and grouping of letters, especially when formed into certain shapes, they were believed to be made more effective ; while magical alphabets and certain sacred inks were said to enhance the power of written spells and charms. In like manner, certain numbers became associated with magic. Odd numbers were considered significant, such as three, and multiples of that number were regarded as sacred to Hecate.

Sacrificial offerings were sometimes made during the rites, the offering chosen being that most acceptable to the god invoked.

Wine, honey, milk, perfumes, meal, certain cakes, a cock to Hermes and a white dove to Aphrodite, were usually employed.

The remains of the sacrifice or offerings had to be disposed of ceremonially, and were generally deposited on some prescribed spot sacred to the deity to whom they had been offered.

They were sometimes laid at the cross-roads with the object of placating Hecate, the terrible goddess of the underworld. These offerings were called " Hecate's suppers," and were intended to appease the wrath of the goddess, and the ghosts of those in the underworld who were unable to rest and compassed evil on earth.

In one of the Græco-Egyptian papyri on magic found at Thebes and now preserved at Leyden, formulæ are recorded " to provoke love," " to produce dreams " and for " consulting a divinity." A recipe is also given for making a ring having the property of causing every enterprise to succeed. In another in the British Museum, the following method is recorded of finding a thief :

" Take a crysolite vessell and put water in it and the herb cynocephalium and dipping in it a branch of laurel sprinkle each person with the water. Take a tripod and place it on an altar of earth. Offer myrrh and frankincense and frog's tongue, and taking some unsalted wheat meal and goat's cheese, give to each one 8 drachms of meal and 8 drachms of cheese, pronouncing the spell, and write this name and place it beneath the tripod, 'LORD IAO, Light bearer, give up the thief whom I seek.' If any of these swallow not what is given him—he is the thief."

In another Greek papyrus, directions are given for

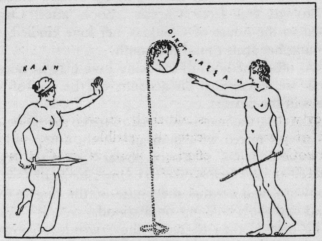

"DRAWING DOWN THE MOON"
(From a Greek vase, *ca*. 200 B.C.)

driving out a demon from a man by pronouncing "the name" and fumigating his nostrils with bitumen and sulphur, no doubt with the idea that the obnoxious odour would cause the evil spirit to depart.

Of the many love charms used by the Greeks that known as "Drawing down the Moon" is perhaps the most interesting. It is mentioned in Aristophanes and by several later writers, and is said to be practised in some parts of Greece at the present day.

It is described in Lucian in the story of the love-sick youth Glaukias. The condition of Glaukias, owing to his love for Chrysis, became so serious that the services of the great Hypoborean magician were sought, who decided that it was necessary to " Draw down the Moon," a never-failing charm for unrequited love. Hecate and her attendant ghosts were invoked, and the moon came down, and the magician made a figure of clay which he told to go and fetch Chrysis. Soon after, Chrysis rushed to the house of Glaukias, her love kindled, and she flung her arms round the youth.

Two other methods of inducing love may be quoted, which are interesting on account of the use of wax figures in the charms.

In the first, the man is directed to make the figure of a dog in wax mixed with gum and pitch, 8 fingers long, and write certain " words of power " over the region of the ribs. A tablet is then to be inscribed with " words of power " and on this the figure of the dog is to be placed and the whole put on a tripod.

The man is then to recite the " words of power " written on the dog's side and the names on the tablet. Should the dog then snarl or snap, the lover will not gain the object of his affections, but if he barks she will come to him.

In the second method the lover is to make two wax figures, one in the form of Ares and the other of the woman. The latter is to be in a kneeling position with her hands tied behind her, and the male figure placed standing over her with a sword at her throat. On the limbs of the woman are to be written the names of demons and then thirteen bronze needles are to be stuck into her limbs, the man reciting the words, " I pierce (mentioning the limb) that she may think of me." Certain words must then be written on a metal plate and tied to the wax figures with a string containing 365 knots, and then both of them are to be buried in the grave of someone who has died young, or one who has met with a violent death. An incantation must then be recited to the infernal gods, and when all is carried out the lover will obtain his desire.

The Greeks sometimes practised divination by water and a mirror, when the image of what was to happen was said to be reflected on the water. They also had a method of divining by filling certain round vessels with water about which were placed lighted torches. They then invoked a demon, praying in a low voice and asked the question they wished to solve.

The magical practices of the Romans were chiefly derived from Greek sources, which will be gathered from descriptions of the magicians and sorcerers that have come down to us.

The first mention of Roman magic is in the law of the " Twelve Tables," which forbids the transference by magic of the crops growing in one field to the land of another. The Etruscans and Sabines in particular were famed for their magical powers, and the former are said to have been able to call up the dead, cause rain to fall and to be able to discover hidden springs.

The simplest form of malefic magic deeply rooted in the Romans and which survives in Italy to the present day was the " evil eye," which was believed to be equally powerful in working evil on persons, health and property.

To combat this influence, charms of various kinds were universally employed, a favourite one being a model of the phallus, which took many forms, fashioned in gold, silver or bronze. These were worn by men, women and children.

Many of the Roman writers allude to the practice of magic and sorcery, and Virgil has left a detailed description of a sorceress and her assistant in his eighth eclogue, as well as her method of working a love-charm.

The assistant is directed to burn vervain and frankincense, which is followed by a solemn chant, said to possess great powers, and to be capable of " Calling down the Moon," or making the cold-blooded snake burst in the field. An image of the one whose love is sought is then ordered to be thrice bound round with fillets of three colours, while the words, " Thus I bind the fillets of Venus," are recited, and the figure is then carried round the altar.

An image of clay and one of wax are placed before the same fire, and, as the figure of clay hardens, so the heart of the one whose love is sought hardens likewise, or, as the image of wax softens, so the heart is made tender. A sacred cake is then to be broken over the image and crackling laurels burnt before it.

The sorceress bruises poisonous herbs of resistless power gathered in the kingdom of Pontus ; herbs which enabled him who took them to turn himself into a hungry wolf prowling amidst the forests, to call up ghosts from the grave, and to translate the ripened harvest from the field where it grew to the lands of another. The ashes of these herbs were to be cast over her head into the running stream, while she must not look behind her.

Horace tells us of a witch's incantation where Canidia and three assistants are assembled in order to work a charm, by means of which a youth named Varus, for whom Canidia had conceived a passion, may be compelled to reciprocate her affections.

Canidia, with the locks of her dishevelled hair twined round with venomous and deadly serpents, orders the wild fig tree and the funeral cypress to be rooted up from the sepulchres on which they grow, and these together with the eggs of a toad smeared with blood, feathers of a screech-owl, various herbs gathered in Thessaly and bones torn from the jaws of a famished dog, to be burnt in flames fed with perfumes from Colchis.

One assistant, whose hair stands stiff and erect like the quills of the sea-hedgehog or the bristles of a hunted boar, sprinkles the ground with drops from the Avernus, while another who is reputed to have the power of conjuring the stars and moon down from heaven assists her. The third digs a hole with a spade into which Varus is to be plunged naked up to his chin, so the charm may be completed.

Lucian gives an account of a journey he took with the magician Mithrobarzanes, and says, " Passing over the Euphrates we came to a wild-wooded sunless place, the magician going first. We then dug a pit and slaughtered a sheep and sprinkled the blood all about the pit. In the meantime, the magician, holding a lighted torch, cried out loudly, invoking all kinds of demons, the avengers, the furies, nocturnal Hecate and the lofty Proserpine, mixing up with his invocations certain barbarous and unintelligible polysyllables."

83

Love-philtres were sold in Rome chiefly by the old women and others who dealt in abortifacients, and the *poculum amatorium* appears to have been in great and constant demand. In the time of the first Emperors they became used to such an extent, that a decree was promulgated under the Roman criminal law, whereby love-philtres were deemed as poison, and the punishment inflicted on those discovered using them was very severe.

Judging from the substances employed in compounding them, it is not to be wondered at that they were deemed poisonous. Hairs from a wolf's tail, the bones from the left side of a toad which had been eaten by ants, pigeon's blood, skeletons of snakes, hippomanes, or a piece of flesh found in the head of a newly-foaled colt, and the entrails of various animals were among some of the least disgusting of the ingredients used for this purpose.

Pliny states : " If a nest of young swallows is placed in a box and buried, on being dug up after a few days, it will be found that some of the birds have died with their beaks closed, while others have died as if gasping for breath." The latter were used for exciting love and the former for producing the opposite effect.

CHAPTER VIII

CELTIC, ARAB, SLAV AND TEUTONIC MAGIC

ALTHOUGH the early Celtic deities were said to exercise the magical arts, the Druids appear to have been the first adepts to practise it among the Celts. They were the magician-priests and healers, and had a considerable knowledge of the properties of plants.

The men were accounted the greatest magicians, but women also played an important part in their mysterious rites, and the " spells of women " were dreaded by the people.

The Druids claimed extraordinary magical powers by means of which they were able to rule the elements, cause the sea to cover the land, change day into night and create storms. They lived in strict abstinence, preserved profound secrecy concerning their mysteries, and only admitted novices after prolonged initiation. They built no temples, but performed the rites and ceremonies of their religion on dolmens, or in the glades of woods and forests. They taught that the souls of ancestors watched over children and that protecting genii overshadowed trees and stones.

They held the moon in great veneration, arranging all their festivals to follow the day dedicated to it, and sought its presence at their ceremonies, so that its rays

85

might be invoked. They also consulted its phases on all important occasions.

They generally accompanied the armies in time of war and claimed to be able to heal the wounded by magical power on the battlefield. They were said to be able to make themselves invisible at will and assume any shape.

The priestesses of Sena took the form of birds, and the "Children of Ler" became swans through the arts of their stepmother, the daughter of the god Bodb Derg. They appear to have practised hypnotism, as it is said they could "make persons motionless, and cause them to reveal secrets" when in that state.

They also claimed to be able to induce a magical sleep by means of music from Dagdas' harp, which first caused mirth, then tears and afterwards sleep. They also produced sleep by means of a draught they concocted called the "drink of oblivion," which they probably made from some narcotic herbs with which they were doubtless familiar.

To cause a man or woman to waste away and die, they modelled a figure of the person and stuck pins or thorns into it or placed it in running water. The practice of making an image called the "corp creadh," for this purpose, survived in Ireland for centuries afterwards. Stones took a prominent part in the rites of the Druids, and their magical stones were believed to have the power of producing wind or rain ; while certain pebbles when dipped in water were supposed to have curative properties in the case of men and animals.

All the details of ritual, the chanting of Runes, the prayers and the offering of sacrifices, were carried out by the Druids as the mediators between the gods and men. They practised divination by examining the entrails of the sacrificial offerings, and by the manner in which the blood flowed from wounds in the limbs after death. Their aid was sought to foresee the future, and they sometimes predicted from the streams and wells.

Among the signs found on their sacred stones is the pentagon, which shows they must have had some communication with the East, probably through the Phœnicians.

The Druids used a magic wand and carried a branch of mountain-ash in their hands to ward off evil spirits.

They were renowned for their medical skill and their knowledge of the virtues of herbs, many of which they gathered with solemn ritual. Thus, when cutting the mistletoe, which they regarded as sacred, it was necessary that the Druid should be clothed in white, that his feet should be bare, and that he should offer a sacrifice at a special time, and in a special way, and cut the bough with a golden sickle.

Verbena they regarded with great reverence and gathered it with a peculiar ritual, and it formed one of the ingredients in the mystical cauldron of Ceridwen.

The fact that their rites were carried on in secluded forest glades and consecrated groves—where their sacrifices were also made—no doubt added much to their mystery.

Although Christianity destroyed the Druids, the Celtic saints continued to perform magical or miraculous acts and many of the Druidic superstitions remained.

According to an Arab tradition, magic or *sihr*, which

means " to produce illusion on the eyes," was revealed by two angels in Babel, named Hārūt and Mārūt, who instructed mankind in the art.

The *sihr* showed how to separate a man from his wife, and, on the other hand, directed how love could be provoked.

When a miracle was deemed a *sihr*, it was regarded as an optical delusion or due to an illicit dealing with demons.

The practice of magic was forbidden by the Arabs under the penalty of death, and it was held that one convicted of sorcery should not even be allowed to repent.

Jinns were, however, recognized, and their conception appears to have influenced the imagination of the poets and writers of romance. They are to be met with in most of the old traditional stories, many of which are embodied in " The Arabian Nights."

In the latter, the magician is often described as a Moor, which gives colour to the suggestion that the magical arts were to a great extent communicated to the Arabs by other races, and were probably introduced by Moors and Jews from other countries.

In the life of Mohammed, an instance is recorded in which magic played a part. He was at one time attacked with a sickness which was said to have been caused by a malevolent Jew, who obtained some hair from the prophet's comb, which he hid with another object in a well, the article hidden being said to be a string in which was tied several knots, by means of which he worked his magic to Mohammed's ill.

The Prophet apparently sanctioned the use of magical

prayers to counteract the "evil eye" and snake poison, also in the treatment of disease, as verses from the Koran were and are still believed to be effective in relieving various bodily ills.

The Arabs practised crystal-gazing, and to foretell future events divination was made from the entrails of slaughtered animals. Sortilege was carried out with pebbles or nuts, auguries from the movements of birds and animals, geomancy with sand and divination with letters. The inspection of the shoulder-blade of a dead animal, together with the lines on it caused by the formation of the bone, were said by the Arabs to foretell if the year would be a good or a bad one.

In Turkestan, to-day, live coals are placed on the shoulder-blade of a sheep, and from the cracks, colour and the parts that fall away, good or bad luck is foretold. Insome cases the jinns also were supposed to inspire divination.

The use of the magic mirror—which was made of metal or glass with a polished surface—for seeing spirits, was known to the Arabs at an early period. The image was said to appear in a cloud or vapour floating between the medium used and the gazer's eye, and not in the mirror itself. Khalīf Mansūr possessed a mirror which was said to rust in the event of meeting an enemy. Ink and water were also employed for a similar purpose.

According to an Arab writer on auguries, "when mountain beasts and birds leave their places it presages a severe winter, loud croaking of frogs foretells plague, loud hooting of an owl near a house where there is sickness presages the person's recovery and loud breathing presages loss of money."

89

The Arabs believed that certain names were endowed with magic power, and if written on a piece of parchment, then steeped in water and the water drunk, they would cure various ailments.

To cause love, a maiden is directed to put certain written seals in a vessel of water from which the desired youth is to drink, and, says the writer, " he will love thee with a strong love."

Small pieces of cornelian shaped as arrow-heads were worn as charms in the form of necklaces as a protection from danger, an ancient custom adopted from the Assyrians, who threaded three cornelians on a hair of a dog and a lion for the same purpose.

Another early belief common among the Arabs, which was probably derived from the Assyrians, was, that the soul of a murdered man must be nailed down; if not, it would rise from the ground where his blood was shed. A new nail which has never been used before was therefore driven into the ground at the spot where the murder was committed, a custom described as " nailing down the ghost."

Egyptians suffering from headache will drive a nail into a wall to-day, or into the old south gate, in Cairo, with the idea of nailing down the demon that causes the pain.

In a book on sorcery called " The Goal of the Sage," written by Maslamah in Madrid, in 1008, astrology is an important factor. Mars is said, by the author, to have the power of attraction for natural science, surgery, toothdrawing, the gall, heat, hatred, bitter tastes and divers other things. To the sign of the Ram belonged the face, the ear, yellow and red, and animals with cloven hooves. The days of the week besides their planetary assignation were associated with certain angels : Monday with Gabriel, Thursday with Isrāfīl, Saturday with 'Azrā'īl, and Wednesday with Michael, which gives the idea of a Jewish origin. " Those who desire the services of the planets should bow down to them and address them by their names in Arabic, Greek, Indian or Yunani."

The magical beliefs of the Slav races have survived in the folk-lore of the northern countries of Europe.

In Russia, the sorcerer lived in solitude. He had learnt his magical formulæ from the fairies, the wood-spirits or the goblins. He handed down his secrets to his youngest child.

He was said to have physical marks through which he could be known, and these included " a troubled eye, a grey face and a husky voice." The incantations were pronounced facing the east on Midsummer Day. Spoken charms were often employed, and believed to have great power. One to keep a man from strong drink, was to take a worm from an empty wine cask, dry it and steep it in wine, then recite the following : " Lord of the sea depths, carry the mettlesome heart of thy servant out of the shifting sands, the burning stones ; breed in him a winged brood."

Some of the magical practices of the northern Teutons may be traced to the Finns who acquired fame in magic.

The magic utterance and the magic rune were used to cure disease, as a defence from enemies, a protection from storm and tempest, and to inspire love. Amulets and ligatures were also frequently used; and to protect the dead, belemites, amber rings and stone arrow-heads were often placed in the graves. Ligatures of medicinal herbs were tied round the head or limbs for healing purposes.

Among the Slavs, the practice of magic for evil purposes was forbidden. Later, in the sixteenth century the penalties for practising magic and soothsaying were certain fines, yet in the Hamburg criminal code the punishment for malefic magic was death by fire, and the persecution of witches began about this period.

Among the Germans the gods were consulted by means of the lot, and the priest-magician carried a magic wand engraved with symbols while pronouncing the incantations.

The magic spells of the Teutons consisted chiefly of formulæ uttered to ensure protection and bring good fortune. They believed that magical effects could be directly produced by the spoken word, hence the frequent use of the spell or utterance in their practices.

Many of these became Christianized during the Middle Ages, and the names of Christ, Mary and the Apostles were introduced in place of the pagan deities. Adjurations against disease were numerous and these survived in monastic times in the form of exorcisms.

CHAPTER IX

HINDU, CHINESE AND JAPANESE MAGIC

IN India, magic has been practised from a very early period, especially by certain castes. The Yogīs, in particular, claim to hold the material world in fee by the magical powers they have acquired, and even profess to have discovered the secret of the transmutation of metals, which according to one of their traditions they knew in the thirteenth century. This is embodied in the story of Yogī Dīna Nāth, who, when passing a money-changer's shop one day, noticed a boy with a pile of copper coins. He asked for alms, but the lad said the coins belonged to his father, and offered the Yogī some of his own food. The Yogī, impressed by his honesty and generosity, prayed to Vishnu for power to reward the boy, and telling him to gather all the copper he could find, proceeded to melt it down, at the same time reciting some charms and sprinkling it with magic powder, which changed the copper into gold. The Brahmins also have considerable lore in which magic plays a prominent part and are said to possess secret books of figures and mystic symbols. Magical rites form part of most of their ceremonies from birth to death. Thus, to ensure safe and easy delivery of a child and to determine the sex, the Cheruman in Madras employ devil-drivers who seat the woman

93

in front of a tent with a coco-nut palm flower on her knees. When cut open the fruits are supposed to predict the child's sex, the birth of twins, and the expectation of the life or death of the infant.

In the marriage ceremonies, at the beginning of the wedding, the Bedar scatter rice and grain (*dhal*) on some white ant earth near five pots filled with water. By the time all the ceremonies are concluded, the seeds have sprouted, and are cut by the bride and bridegroom and thrown into the village well to ensure fertility. Seeds and grain enter largely into the charms connected with marriage, and an Idaiyan man and woman will sow nine kinds of grain in seven trays and watch the result, the symbolism of the seed and its fertility being regarded as an assurance of the future of their married life.

A magical rite of resuscitation of the dead is practised by the Dasaris, a class of priests who minister to Sūdras in Madras.

When a Dasari is offended, he will sometimes revenge himself by self-mutilation or by cutting off his own hand. The news is carried to his caste fellows, and they get together and display their magical powers by frying fish, which come to life again on being put into water, by joining limes together that have been sliced in half, and by bringing the suicide to life.

The use of charms to avert evil and harm is very common in most parts of India. They are usually composed of natural substances, such as a piece of some tree which is supposed to be inhabited by a jinn.

The Bark Har (*Celtis caucasia*) is believed to possess magical properties, and the one who cuts it down becomes ill and loses all his hair. Its juice causes blisters and it is thought to be dangerous even to sit under its branches.

In order to drive out demons from women, the Hindus take three different-coloured threads of silk or cotton and form *gunda*, which means to tie twenty-one or twenty-two knots on it. The Moollas in making each knot read an incantation and blow upon it. When finished, it is fastened to the neck or the upper part of the arm of the person possessed, with the idea that the demon may be transferred by the power of the magician to the knotted thread, which is then cut off and thrown away.

Magical squares of figures are used for various purposes. One, which totals 90 lengthways, is used as a charm to cure quartan fever ; another, totalling 100 every way, is believed to increase milk in cows ; while a third, that totals 130 every way, when worn round the neck is said to give one power over any person, and a square totalling 15 each way will bring good luck to the wearer.

An ancient formula for conjuring a Bīr or demon was to " Fast the whole of a ninth lunar day falling on a Friday, and in the evening take sweet rice milk. At 8 p.m. don red clothes, perfumed, and make a circle of red lead on the ground. Sit in its centre with 4 cardamoms, some catechu, betel nuts and 8 cloves. Light a lamp fed with clarified butter and say, ' Incantation can break down the stars,' 5000 times, and a demon will be at your service."

The Muslims are believers in magic but condemn that which depends on the aid of Satan or evil jinns. Enchantment is regarded as a branch of magic and is permissible if practised with the help of a good jinn, although the results may be disastrous, and it may even cause death or paralysis and other terrible afflictions.

As a protection against such enchantments, talismans written in mysterious characters in the form of seals are engraved on metal and carried on the person.

Among the followers of the various religions, there appears to be a universal belief in the existence of spirits which are believed to throng the air, the earth, the sky, the trees, and the magical practices so common in India probably had their inception in this belief.

Witchcraft appears to be intimately blended with the Vedic rites in which religion and magic are closely combined. In the Rigveda, the hymns, the earliest writings of which it consists, are chiefly addressed to various gods ; but, in the Atharvaveda, magic is the essential feature, and the work is mainly a collection of spells and ceremonies aiming at the welfare of the magician or the injury of his enemies.

The Vedic literature is important, as it represents aspects of magic practised 3000 years ago. From it we learn that the sacrificial priest was also a magician, but alliance with evil spirits or the use of magic for malevolent purposes or injury was not approved. Asceticism, fasting, abstinence and silence were practised, as they were believed to confer power. Magical rites were largely associated with sacrificial ceremonies which were carried out in lonely places. The locations that were generally selected for the purpose, viz. a burial ground, cross-roads, a solitary house or hut in a forest, were adopted later by Western races.

The magician had to face the south, which was

supposed to be the abode of the demons, or in other rites to move from left to right following the course of the sun, but occasionally the direction was reversed. The demons were said to appear sometimes in human shape, generally deformed, but they might also appear in the form of animals or birds. Even the magician might assume an animal form if he wished to injure his enemies, and the Rigveda alludes to certain magicians who flew about like birds at night. Evil spirits were most active at night, especially during a new moon, and sought to attack the magician who had undergone consecration. They were said to frequent places where four roads met, and entered a man generally by his mouth. They would devour his flesh, suck his marrow, drink his blood, and cause disease, madness and loss of speech.

Evil spirits were especially dangerous at the time of birth, marriage and death. They could do harm to a man's property, his cattle and his crops, hence the importance placed upon casting spells as preventive measures.

Contagious magic is evidenced in the belief that the power of lightning remained in a splinter of wood from a tree that had been struck. The skins of animals were believed to be able to communicate the power of the animal to man, and he who seated himself on the skin of a he-goat was said to acquire abundance, on the hide of a bull, fertility ; on that of a tiger, courage and invincible power.

Abstention from food was practised to prevent hostile demons from attacking the body. A special kind of fasting was the avoidance of a particular variety of

97

food; thus a newly married pair were enjoined to avoid all salted and pungent dishes during the first three days after their marriage.

Charms and amulets composed of various kinds of wood and other substances were carried for preventing evil influences, or to bring good fortune, and were called god-born or the gift of god to man. A spell on the Kustha plant was invoked to abate fever and another operation on a herb to destroy snake poison.

An ointment is mentioned in one hymn, which is associated with the following spell:

" From him over whose every limb and every joint thou passest, O Salve, thou dost as a mighty interpreter drive away disease."

The curative properties of water are thus referred to in another spell:

" The waters verily are healing, the waters chase away disease, the waters cure all ailments, may they prepare a remedy for thee."

Fire was regarded as being one of the most effective methods of driving away demons and the effects of sorcery. The god of fire was thus invoked:

" Burn, O Agni, against the sorcerers and the allies of the demons."

In the birth-chamber, a " Lying-in fire " was lighted with small grains mixed with mustard seed, as a fumigation to drive off evil spirits. A brand lighted at both ends was borne by the priest round the funeral offering; and, during the ritual, another brand was taken from the southern fire and laid down pointing south, so as to drive away all demons.

Lead was believed to possess magical power and it

was used to counteract the evil influences of demons and sorcerers.

Injurious substances were removed by " wiping them off with lead," and the passing of a piece of lead over the face after an evil dream was said to prevent any after-effects that otherwise might occur. At a Royal inauguration, the King was anointed with a mixture of butter, honey, rain-water and other substances to which magic was attributed, with the idea that they would communicate their power to him.

Of the magical powers attributed to various woods from which amulets were made, a piece of liquorice root, tied to the little finger with thread coloured with lac, was used by a bridegroom to secure the love of his bride, and a charm fashioned from the Parna tree was worn to strengthen Royal power.

In Vedic magic we again come across the use of the clay or wax figure in various operations. Thus, to destroy an enemy, a figure of clay was made and the spot over the heart was pierced with an arrow ; or his death might be caused by making an image of wax and melting it over a fire, or by burning a chameleon representing him.

Soldiers, elephants and horses were modelled in dough and sacrificed piece by piece in order to destroy an enemy's army.

To exterminate worms, twenty-one roots of the Usīra plant were burnt, while the words, " I split with the stone the head of all worms male and female ; I burn their faces with fire," were pronounced by the magician.

Divination was practised from the flight or cry of

99

animals and birds, especially those of the wolf, hyena, the owl, crow and vulture. In one of the Sūtras the owl is thus addressed :

" Flying round the village from left to right, portend to us luck, O owl ! "

Spells were accompanied with rites, or spoken alone, and curses were placed or cast on individuals by invoking the gods, and spells could also be used to counteract the effect of the latter.

The following is a spell of this kind from the Atharvaveda :

" Avoid us, O curse, as a burning fire, a lake,
  Strike him that curses us as the lightning of Heaven the tree."

It will be noticed that many of the practices instanced in Vedic magic were similar to those employed in Europe at a later period.

The practice and belief in magic by the Chinese goes back to a period of unknown antiquity and it still forms a powerful factor in the life of the people.

The cleverness of the Chinese in legerdemain or sleight-of-hand shows a natural instinct for what is now called conjuring. Their literature on magic is enormous, and one can only mention briefly some of their practices connected with the art which appear to be of native origin.

The sorcerer or wizard, as far as can be gathered, was originally known as Wu, a name which was applied both to male and female practitioners. They apparently held recognized positions as diviners or exorcists and were entrusted with certain court and public ceremonials. They professed to be able to conjure spirits of the dead, chanted magical formulæ and foretold the future.

As Confucian culture advanced they were succeeded by the Taoists, who according to tradition date from centuries before the Christian era.

The dancing of witches formed part of the ritual observed on the occasion of the official rain-making sacrifices, and as early as 947 B.C. there is a tradition that King Mu used magic music on his flute to put an end to a great drought.

The aid of the magician or wizard was sought to bring about the fulfilment of wishes and desires as early as the fourth century. The " Pao Po-tzu," a book on magic, said to have been written by the wizard Ko Hung, contains a description of how to use the magic mirror to detect the presence of evil spirits.

A feature of Chinese magic is the large number of trees, plants and herbs believed to possess occult properties and which are employed in their magical practices. The willow is used as a rain charm during periods of drought in Shansi, and at such times willow wreaths are worn by the people on their brows. Peach twigs and blossoms are credited with magical powers, and a wand cut from a peach tree is used by the professional Wu when exorcizing spirits.

Taoism claims to be of native origin and is said to be founded on the " Tao-Teh King," a book ascribed by tradition to Lao-tse, an early contemporary of Confucius, who flourished about 604 B.C. Tao was believed to be the principle of all existence, and " the heart of all knowledge." The founder of the Taoism of the present day is said to have been Chang Tao-ling, who lived about A.D. 34. It is apparently chiefly a mass of magic and superstition in which divination plays the leading part. For this purpose the dried stalks of a grass called Shih-ts'ao which grows on the grave of Confucius is highly valued. It is carefully gathered and made into packets, and is believed to have absorbed some of the spiritual efficacy from the sacred soil in which it has grown.

Divination by means of tortoiseshell and the dried stalks of plants is of great antiquity in China, and it is said it was by these methods " the early sage kings made the people believe in seasons and days, revere spiritual beings and stand in awe of their laws and orders." Astrology, cheiromancy, automatic-writing and clairvoyance were all known and have been practised by the Chinese from an early period.

They placed certain plants over their doors to prevent the entrance of evil spirits and bring good luck, just as the peasants in some parts of Europe do to-day.

They entwine red threads in their children's hair to protect them from the demons that bring disease, and stitch buttons, bearing representations of certain deities and sages, as charms on their clothing. From ancient times they have also practised the method of making a figure of wax or clay in the image of a person, and sticking pins into it should they wish to work evil upon him.

An illustration of this occurs in a romantic story told of the great artist Ku K'ai-chih, who flourished in the fourth century and was a believer in the power of magic. Finding that the girl he loved spurned his attentions, he drew a portrait of her, and when it was finished, stuck a thorn into the picture over the region of the heart. The girl, who had no knowledge of what he had done, was at the same time stricken with a pain in the same spot, and when Ku K'ai-chih went to visit her afterwards, she did not turn him away. When he returned to his house he at once withdrew the thorn from the picture, and the pain in the damsel's heart is said to have immediately disappeared, but her love for him remained.

The magical rituals of the Japanese are believed to date from about the eighth century, although many of their traditions have probably come down from a much earlier period. They are gathered in their " Engishiki," which was written about the tenth century.

It is stated in these records, that the priest-magician accompanied his incantations and formulæ by mysterious rites which were supposed to make them more powerful and effective. The earliest rites appear to have been connected with the harvest, and were carried out every year at seed time. Offerings were made of a white horse, a white pig or a white cock. Thus in a record of the ninth century, Mi-toshi No Kami, the god of the August harvest, had cast his curse on the rice fields, but the divinities obtained from him by the gift of these white animals the secret of a magical process, which enabled them to save the imperilled crops.

From the VIIIth ritual called the " Luck-bringer of the Great Palace," it appears that the celestial, magical, protective words to ward off all calamities from the Palace were a kind of spoken charm. In the IXth ritual a description is given of a company of priests and vestals who go through the Palace in all directions, from the great Hall of Audience to the bathing rooms, the vestals sprinkling rice and *sake*, while the priests hang precious stones on the four corners of the rooms. The rice was to ward off evil spirits, being a custom that was frequently practised in Japanese magic.

Rice was scattered inside the room in which a child was about to be born, and, in the divination performed at the cross-roads, a boundary line was sometimes strewn with rice, so that the words spoken by the first person who passed by and crossed it might be taken as an oracle. The precious stones were believed to protect the occupants of the rooms from evil influences.

Throughout Japanese magic, jewels and sparkling stones played an important part. Those of a red colour, in particular, " caused the dark threats of the invisible everywhere to retire before their brightness."

In the Xth ritual, called the " Ritual of the Great Purification," many rites are included. It begins by stating, that it is the Emperor who deigns to purify and wash away the offences committed.

The Emperor was regarded as superior to the gods invoked and the right of absolution was invested in him.

One of the offences condemned was the practice of witchcraft against a neighbour's animals. It is further stated that, " when the high priest recites the Celestial ritual, it is so powerful that the gods of heaven and earth approach to listen and all offences will disappear." A number of magical formulæ are included in the XXVIIth ritual, and mention is made of a descendant of Ame-No-Hoho, one of the celestial ambassadors to earth, " who brings to the Emperor divine treasures consisting of sixty jewels, white, red and green."

They are thus described : " The white are the great august white hairs to which your majesty will reach. The red jewels are the august healthful ruddy countenance. The green are the harmonious fitness which the august Emperor will establish far and wide. Each jewel conferring a power corresponding to its colour."

Ancient Shinto is said to be a religion in which the magical element still prevails over the religious sentiment, and its rituals are addressed to magician-gods by magician-priests and encircled in magical rites. "Therefore," says M. Revon, "magic is at the base of the natural cult of the Japanese."

An interesting tradition in which native sorcery plays a part is given in the "Kojiki." " The deity of the Idzushi, the country of the sacred stones, had a daughter, whose name was the Deity Maiden of Idzushi, whom eighty deities wished to marry but none could do so. Among her suitors were two brothers, the elder of whom was called ' Youth-of-the-glow-on-the-autumn-mountains ' and the younger named ' Youth-of-the-haze-on-the-spring-mountains.'

" The elder said to his brother, ' Though I beg for the Maiden of Idzushi, I cannot obtain her in marriage ; wilt thou be able to obtain her ? '

" He replied, ' I will easily obtain her.'

" Then the elder brother said, ' If thou shalt obtain this maiden, I will take off my upper and lower garments and distil liquor in a jar of my own height, and prepare all the things of the mountains and of the rivers in payment of the wager.'

" Then the younger brother told his mother every-thing. Forthwith the mother took wistaria fibre, and wove and sewed in one night an upper and a lower garment, and made a bow and arrows and clothed him in these garments, and made him take the bow and arrows to the maiden's house, where both his apparel and the bows and arrows were turned into wistaria blossoms, and he hung them up in the maiden's private bower. When the Maiden of Idzushi, thinking the blossoms strange, brought them forth, he followed behind her into the house and forthwith wedded her. So she gave him birth to one child. Then he spoke to the elder brother saying, ' I have obtained the Maiden of Idzushi,' and the elder brother was vexed that he should have wedded her and would not pay his wager. When the younger brother complained to his mother, in her anger with her elder child, she took a one-jointed bamboo from an island in the River Idzushi, and made a basket with eight holes, and took stones from the river, and mixing them with brine, wrapped them in the leaves of the bamboo and caused this curse to be spoken, ' Like unto the becoming green of these bamboo leaves do thou become green and wither.' Again, ' Like unto the flowing and ebbing of this brine do thou flow and ebb.' Again, ' Like unto the sinking of these stones do thou sink and be prostrate.'

" Then she placed the basket over the smoke. There-fore the elder brother dried up and withered and sickened, and lay prostrate for the space of eight years."

There is a widespread belief among the Japanese that a mysterious connexion exists between the life of man and the flowing and ebbing of the sea. So, according to the legend, the fate of the elder brother was connected with the ebbing of the tide, for it is said, " When the sea is flowing in, one is born and becomes strong ; and, when it is ebbing, one loses energy, falls ill and dies."

CHAPTER X

NECROMANCY—SORCERY—PACTS WITH THE DEVIL

NECROMANCY, negromancy, or necyomancy, as it was originally termed, was that branch of the magical arts which professed to reveal future events by means of communication with the dead.

Although it belonged to the class called evil or black magic, its practice was apparently tolerated if good angels and not devils were invoked for the purpose.

In ancient times it was understood to mean a descent into Hades to consult the dead concerning the living.

There are many references to this practice in the mythological stories of the Greeks and it is mentioned by Homer and Virgil. Lucian relates a legend of the hero Menippus, who had recourse to a Magus, who was a disciple and successor of Zoroaster, having heard that he possessed spells and incantations by which the portals of Hades could be unlocked. He was also said to be able to invoke and afterwards dismiss the spirit of any dead person whom he pleased to summon, and by his aid therefore the opinion of Teiresias might be obtained. With this object Menippus undertook an expedition to Babylon, and lodged under the roof of this Chaldean, " a man of notable wisdom and profound skill, a diviner, venerable for his hoary locks and flowing beard." His name, Mithrobarzanes, avouched his necromantic pretensions, and after much solicitation and promises of lavish reward, Menippus is said to have obtained his object.

In the Talmud, magic is divided into three classes. The first includes all evil enchantments, magical cures, the citation of evil spirits and the calling forth of the dead through the aid of demons, for all of which, like idolatry, the punishment was death.

The second includes those magical practices which are carried on by the aid of evil spirits, and the third includes astrology and all intercourse with the lower spirits.

In attempting to define the meaning of the names applied to the various branches of magic, it is interesting first to consider the explanations given by writers who lived in the Middle Ages.

In the thirteenth century necromancers were called jugulors, from which we may assume they were often regarded with suspicion and the practice of necromancy was forbidden by the Church.

According to an account written in a fifteenth-century manuscript the Papal Conclave came to the following conclusions :

" The help which the Lord hath given his people is now through magic and negromancy turned into the damnation of all people, for even the magicians themselves being intoxicated and blinded by the devil and contrary to the order of Christ's Church, transgress the commandant of God which doth say, thou shalt not tempt the Lord thy God but him only shalt thou serve. Negromancers denying the sacrifice due unto

God, and in tempting him, hath done sacrifice unto
devils and abused his name in calling of them contrary
to the profession made at their baptism. Hath also
brought all people through these marvellous illusions
and drawing the ignorant into damnation of soul and
body.

"Pluck up and utterly destroy this deadly root and
all the followers of this art."

Another writer of the same period states :

"Necromancy was used in old times by faithful and
unfaithful. It constrains the devils and makes them
perform, obey and accomplish their commands.

"It may be exercised in two ways :

"First, the natural, which may be wrought through
things whose virtue and property is natural to do them,
as herbs, plants and stones, the planets and heavenly
influences. This art is lawful.

"Secondly, the other kind of necromancy is that
which is practised through the help and favour of the
devil, which hath been long exercised in the world. Of
this the Holy Scriptures testify, speaking of the magicians
of Pharaoh who contended with Moses and Aaron, and
in the New Testament making mention of Simon Magus
rebuked by St Peter. The devils may be forced and
constrained by the good angels, and this is because of
the grace which the one lost and the other yet retains.

"None can use or exercise the art of necromancy
unless he first make an agreement or expressed covenant
with the devil. . . . Some devils are preferred as prin-
cipals to command the rest and the inferior devils are
subject unto these which are of mighty force to execute
that wickedness.

POWERS OF EVIL
THEUTUS, ASMODEUS AND INCUBUS
From Barrett's 'Magus'

" Wicked demons are divided into nine degrees or orders, as the good angels are divided into nine orders or hierarchies.

" The first are called Psoudothei or false gods who would be worshipped as gods, as that demon who said to Christ, if thou wilt fall down and worship me. The prince of these is Beelzebub.

" The second are the Mendariorum or spirits of lying. Their prince is that spirit Python. This kind of spirit deceive by their oracles, divinations and predictions.

" The third are the Iniquitatis or the vessels of anger, and are the inventors of all wicked arts. The prince of them is Belial.

" The fourth are the Revengers of wickedness and their prince is Asmodeus.

" The fifth are the Prestigiators who imitate miracles and serve the magic and maleficks and seduce people in their miracles.

" Their prince is Satan.

" Sixth are the Arial powers who mix themselves with thunders and lightnings, corrupting the air, bringing pestilence and other evils. Their prince is Merizim, a south demon, raging and furious, whom Paul calls, in the Ephesians, ‘ a prince of the power of the air.’

" The seventh are the Furies, the sowers of mischief and discords, wars and destruction. Their prince is called Apollyon, in Hebrew Abaddon, who destroys and lays waste.

" The eighth are the Criminators, whose prince is Astaroth. He is the calumniator.

"Ninth are the Temptors, and all bad genii. Their prince is Mammon, interpreted covetousness."

There are many traditions concerning the covenants or pacts made with the devil in exchange for certain powers, renewed youth and other desired attainments, many of which are no doubt fabulous, but there are some transcripts to be found in manuscripts purporting to be copies of these curious documents.

Pacts with the devil were said to be always signed by the executor with his blood as being the most sacred seal.

In a pact recorded in the seventeenth century, the signatory agrees, " To deny God being the Creator of all things. To blaspheme the three Saints and the Holy Trinity. To trample underfoot all the mysteries of the redemption, and to spit on the face of the Virgin, and all the saints. To abhor the name of Christian and renounce Christianity, baptism, and the commendations of the Church and the sacraments. To sacrifice to the devil, make a pact for the adoration of him, pay him homage of fidelity, dedicate innocent children to him, and recognize him as Creator."

Another reads :

" Je . . . renonce à tous les biens tant spirituels que corporels qui me pourraient estre conférez de la part de Dieu, de la Vierge Marie et de tous les saincts du Paradis, pareillement de mon patron saint Jean Baptiste, saint Pierre, saint Paul et saint François et de me donner de corps et d' me à Lucifer icy présent avec tous les biens que je feray à jamais ; excepté la valeur du sacrement pour le regard de ceux qui le recevront.

" Et ainsi le signe et atteste."

In the library at Upsala there is preserved a written paƈt made by one Daniel Salthenius who sold himself to the devil.

The methods, rites and ritual employed by necromancers are fully described in the books of ceremonial which will be dealt with later.

A sorcerer was said to be one who praƈtised the arts of magic and witchcraft, and who had acquired a supernatural knowledge by the use of enchantments which gave him command over evil spirits.

The sorcerer made no paƈt with the evil one, which diſtinguished him from the necromancer.

The objeƈt of the sorcerer was therefore to conſtrain some evil spirit to appear, so that he might queſtion him, the evocation being carried on with myſterious rites and ceremonies.

In order to carry this out he had firſt to fix upon a place proper for such a purpose, which might either be a cave or vault draped with black hangings and lighted by a magical torch ; or it might be among the ruins of an ancient caſtle or abbey, a churchyard or any other solemn place, between the hours of twelve and one in the morning, either when the moon shone brightly or when the elements were diſturbed with ſtorms of thunder, lightning, wind and rain. When a proper time and place were seleƈted, a magic circle was to be drawn, within which the sorcerer and his associate were to ſtand. A piece of ground was chosen nine feet square, at the full extent of which parallel lines were drawn, one within the other, containing crosses and triangles, close to which was formed the firſt or outer circle. About six inches within this a second circle was described,

A MAGICIAN OR SORCERER STANDING IN THE MAGIC CIRCLE PERFORMING
A CONJURATION
(From a drawing in an MS., XIV century, in the British Museum.)

A MAGICIAN OR SORCERER STANDING IN THE MAGIC CIRCLE INVOKING
SPIRITS
(From a drawing in an MS., XIV century, in the British Museum.)

having within it another square corresponding to the first, the centre of which was the seat or spot where the master and his associate were to stand.

The ground having thus been prepared and the circle completed, the sorcerer was not, at the peril of his life, to depart until he had completely dismissed the spirit.

Great importance was attached to the discharging of the spirit after the ceremony was finished, and after he had answered all the demands made upon him.

" The magician must wait patiently until he has passed through all the terrible forms which announced his coming, and only when the last shriek has died away, and every trace of fire and brimstone has disappeared, may he leave the circle and depart home in safety," says a writer of the sixteenth century.

A picturesque account of a visit to the house of a sorcerer in Paris, in the seventeenth century, is thus recorded by an old French writer :

" On the ceiling and in the corners were divers unclean animals, which seemed to be still alive, here the serpent crawling and writhing, there the bat with its membraneous wings, there the toad with eyes of brilliant yet sinister beauty ; and there the skeleton of some oddly formed fish. The room still further contained the furnace, the alembics, and all the preparations and the instruments of the sorcerer. On the right, on the left, in every direction lay strangely formed or grotesque phials and vases and books, closed or half open, portraits in wax and some symbolical images ; and amidst this strange collection stood a brazier from whence arose a bluish flame which revealed the figure of the sorcerer.

" A long loose and trailing black robe enveloped his

tall figure; in his left hand he held a book and in his right a divining wand.

" The constellations, the sun and the moon shone upon his broad chest, on his head he wore a sort of turban, and his shoes were long and narrowed off to a slightly curving point.

"His countenance was not destitute of a certain grave dignity; his gaze was fixed and contemplative, and a thick beard descended to his chest.

" Making an imperative gesture he waved me back, and then the flame in the brazier redoubled its intensity; a thick smoke arose in cloudy whirls and speedily filled the whole room. For a moment the magician seemed to be invoking a familiar demon, and then suddenly in the centre of the brazier arose a phantasmagoric apparition."

There was hardly a more terrible accusation one person could bring against another during the Middle Ages, than that of charging him with practising sorcery.

In 1324 Robert Marshall of Leicester and John Notingham were indicted for conspiring to kill the King, the two Despensers, the Prior and two other officials of Coventry, by magic arts. Marshall, who turned King's evidence, said that certain citizens came to John Notingham as a man skilled in " nigromancy," and bargained with him for the death of the persons named, paying a certain sum down, and giving him seven pounds of wax. With the wax, Notingham and Marshall made seven images, six being of the proposed victims and the other of Richard de Sowe, who was selected for experimental purposes. The work was carried out with the closest secrecy in an old, deserted house not far from Coventry, and when the images were ready the sorcerer bade Marshall thrust a leaden bodkin into the head of the figure that represented Richard de Sowe, and the next day sent him to the house of the said Richard, whom he found raving mad ; Master John then removed the bodkin from the head of the image and thrust it into the heart, and within three days Richard died. Notingham died in prison before the case was finished, and Robert Marshall in the end came to the scaffold.

CHAPTER XI

WITCHCRAFT—DEMONOLOGY

THE belief in witchcraft as known in mediæval times was probably derived from the wild mythology of the northern races.

The Hebrew word *mekaseepah* literally means one who makes spells, amulets, poisons and incantations, and corresponds to the Latin *venefica*. It is probable therefore that the name " witch " mentioned in the Bible had a different meaning to that applied to it in later times.

As Scott points out, " There is not a word in scripture of a contract of subjection to a diabolic power, no infernal stamp or sign of such a fatal league, no revellings of Satan and his hags and no infliction of disease or misfortune upon good men."

On the other hand, during the Christian era and through the Middle Ages, the name came to be applied to one (either male or female) who was believed to be able to perform some operation beyond human power by the agency of evil spirits, such as working evil upon the life and fortunes of other people, and casting spells on human beings and cattle.

The witch was said to acquire these powers by making a bond or compact, sealed with her blood, between herself and the devil.

By the terms of the bond it was understood that she renounced the sacraments of the Christian religion, and

118

after a term of years or for the rest of her life devoted her soul to the powers of evil where it was beyond redemption.

"Witches," says Sir Walter Scott, "were generally old, blear-eyed, wrinkled dames, ugly and crippled, frequently papists, and sometimes atheists; of cross-grained tempers and cynical dispositions. They were often poisoners and generally mono-maniacs. Epilepsy and all diseases not understood by the physicians were set down to the influence of witches. They were said to make two covenants with the devil, one public and one private. Then the novices were presented to the devil in person, and instructed to renounce the Christian faith, tread on the Cross, break the fasts, joining hands with Satan, paying him homage and yielding him body and soul. Some witches sold themselves for a term of years, and some for ever; then they kissed the devil, and signed their bond with blood, and a banquet ended the meeting, their dances being accompanied with shouts of ' Ha, ha ! devil, devil ! Dance here, dance here ! Play here, play here ! Sabbath, sabbath.' Before they departed, the devil was said to give them philtres and amulets."

"Concerning witches," says a writer of a manuscript of the sixteenth century, " these haggs are a lineage and kind of people expressly agreed with the devil, holding and obeying him as their sovereign and master, and suffering themselves to be marked by him, which mark they bear on one of their eyes, fashioned like a toad's foot, by which they know one another, for they have among themselves great companies and fraternities, making often general meetings, which they pollute with all filthyness, abominable villainies and infernal ceremonies, and do homage to the devil who moſt commonly appeareth to them in the figure of a great Ram goat."

Although a good deal of nonsense has been written concerning the witches' meetings, there is some evidence to show that these abnormal women did have secret meetings at night in out-of-the-way places, where they performed myſterious rites and ceremonies which probably concluded with an orgy.

ST PATRICK AND THE DEVIL
(From a woodcut, XV century.)

An intereſting description of a witches' Sabbath is recorded by Alonso de Caſtro in a manuscript of the sixteenth century. He was a learned man of Spain and a Franciscan, who had a friend who was a sorcerer, with whom he went to a witches' Sabbath, under the pretence that he wished to make a covenant with the devil.

It was a dark night when the sorcerer took him out of the town into the country, and they walked together through certain valleys and woods, until they reached a plain field enclosed round with mountains. Here they found a great number of people, men and women, who went up and down in great mirth and received him as a novice with gladness, assuring him that there was no greater happiness in the world.

120

THE DEVIL AND EVIL ANGELS PRESIDING AT A SABBATH

Seated on a throne in the centre is the Devil in the form of a goat with five horns. In the foreground a sorceress is represented offering an infant to the evil one. Pierre de Lancre, 1613.

"In the midst of the field a throne was built very sumptuously, on which stood a great and mighty Ram goat to whom at a certain hour of the night they all went to do reverence.

" The reverence and homage which they do unto him, is by turning their shoulders and bowing down their heads as low as they can. He which is newly assumpted into this brotherhood doth first with words wicked and abominable, blaspheme and renounce all the holy points and mysteries, vowing unto the devil his faithful service for ever with many other execrable ceremonies, vows and oaths, which being accomplished, they mingle themselves together and many devils with them in likeness of young gentlemen and beautiful dames without shame or respect."

Castro goes on to say: " There are certain oyles and oyntments with which they anoynt themselves, which deprive them of their right sense, making them imagine they are transformed into birds or beasts, deceiving not only themselves with this error, but oftentimes the eyes of others, for the devil and other enchanters so dazzle and deceive our sight, turning and transforming men into beasts to the seeming of those which behold them, though in truth it was nothing so, but the sorcerers think themselves in their imagination to be transposed. Sometimes they anoynt themselves with other oyntments whose operation maketh them think they are like fowls and can fly in the air."

This account written by a man of intelligence and a seeker after truth in his time, goes to show that the supposed magic worked by witches was largely due to imagination and deception, no doubt aided by certain drugs the properties of which they understood.

De Lancre gives the following description of the devil presiding at a Sabbath or meeting of witches :

" He is seated on a black chair, with a crown of black horns, two horns on the back of his neck, and one on the forehead which sheds light on the assembly ; the

WITCHES IN FLIGHT
(From a woodcut of the XV century, Ulric Molitor.)

hair bristling, the face pale and exhibiting signs of uneasiness, the eyes round, large and fully opened, inflamed and hideous, with a goat's beard. The neck and rest of the body deformed, and in the shape of a goat ; the hands and feet of a human being."

The oath to the demon had to be pronounced in the centre of a circle traced on the ground, accompanied by the offer of some pledge, such as the garment of the novitiate. The edge of the circle was supposed to establish a mark which the demon could not cross. Heavy perfumes, such as vervain, with burning incense and lighted tapers, always formed part of the ceremonial. The smoking brazier, which entered largely into the ritual, was believed to act on the demons, and was constantly fed with all kinds of those vegetable and animal substances that would produce the most smoke.

The presence of toads or familiars, which were sometimes dressed up by the witches in scarlet velvet with little bells, is mentioned in connexion with the Sabbaths.

In the Basque provinces, the toad played an important part in witchcraft, and when a novice was presented at the Sabbath for the first time, a toad was given into the care of her introducer, until she had completed her noviciate and was considered fit to receive it into her keeping. It was dressed in a little sack with a cowl, through which the head passed, and open under the belly, where it was tied with a band that served as a girdle. This dress was generally made of green or black cloth, or velvet. The toad was to be treated with the greatest care and to be fed and caressed by its owner.

The fumes from the narcotic plants used, such as belladonna, stramonium and hemlock, would probably produce a state of semi-stupor and so influence the imagination of the scared spectators that they might easily fancy that they saw the writhing forms of spirits in the air.

One method of casting a spell on a person employed by witches was by means of the wax or clay image. The figure of the intended victim had to be modelled with great secrecy. This having been done, a swallow was killed and the heart placed under the right arm of the image and the liver under the left. The effigy was next pricked all over with new needles, each prick being accompanied by an incantation and terrible imprecations against the victim.

Sometimes the figure was moulded in earth taken from a graveyard mixed with powdered human bones. Certain magical signs were then inscribed upon it which were believed in time to cause the death of the victim.

In the British Museum there is an interesting manuscript entitled " A discourse of Witchcraft, as it was acted in the family of Mr Edward Fairfax of Fuystone, York, 1621."

In the manuscript, Mr Fairfax gives an account of how his two daughters, Helen, aged twenty-one, and Elizabeth, aged seven, and a child called Maude Jeffrey, were bewitched by six witches who are named.

One was " Margaret Waite, a widow, whose familiar was a deformed thing with many feet, black of colour, rough with hair and the bigness of a cat." Another was " Jennit Dible, a very old widow and a reputed witch for many years, whose familiar was a white cat spotted with black." He observes that, " Satan maketh use of ye mass priests, confirming their supposed holiness by conjuring and by casting forth devils where they never entered."

On October 28th, 1621, Helen was found lying on the floor in a deadly trance, and remained unconscious for a considerable time. For several days in succession she had these trances, which could not be accounted for. On November 3rd at break of day, she called out loudly, " Oh, I am poisoned," and told her mother that " a white cat had been long upon her and drawn her breath." They endeavoured to persuade her it was a dream, but on the 14th she again awoke the household and said she had " found a black dog by her bedside."

Her sister Elizabeth had similar seizures and it was concluded they had been bewitched, and suspicion fell on the old women in the village who were believed to

A WITCH AND HER 'FAMILIARS'
From the Fairfax MS. 1621. British Museum.

work witchcraft. They were arrested, and after they had been brought to trial, the girls are said to have recovered

The manuscript is illustrated by many curious drawings, in black and white, of the witches implicated, and a variety of weird and curious animals, birds, and other strange apparitions, said to have been seen by the girls, together with some of the familiars.

The witch's familiar, which was constantly with her, was supposed to take the shape of a cat, dog or a great toad, and so the black cat became associated with magic and witchcraft.

The weasel has also been associated with witchcraft from early times, and Apuleius in " The Golden Ass " mentions a practice of the witches of Thessaly, of cutting or biting off the ears of the dead in order to use them as ingredients in their mysterious compounds.

Thelyphron relates, how he kept watch over a body for about half the night, and then received a visit from a witch in the form of a weasel who stared at him with " a confidence unusual in so small an animal."

A familiar is said to have once been dissected by the famous physician Dr. William Harvey, the discoverer of the circulation of the blood.

The story is related by Notestein thus :

" About 1685, a Justice of the Peace in south-west England wrote a letter, in which he said that he once asked Dr Harvey his opinion of witchcraft.

" Harvey replied, that he believed there was no such thing and recounted a story of a visit he made to a reputed witch, when he was at Newmarket with Charles I."

The woman lived in a lonely house on the borders

of the heath. Harvey told her that he was a wizard and had come to converse with her on the common trade. The woman believed him, because as Harvey said, " You know I have a very magical face." Harvey then asked to see the witch's familiar, whereupon the woman brought out a dish of milk, made a chuckling noise and a toad came out from under a chest and drank some milk.

The witch was persuaded to go out and get some ale half a mile away, and while she was absent Harvey cut up the toad and found the milk inside. He came to the conclusion that " it differed noways from other toades," but that the old woman, having tamed it, had come to believe that it contained the spirit of her familiar.

On her return, the old woman " flew like a tigress " at Harvey, and would not be pacified with money, so that he was obliged to tell her that he was the King's physician sent to discover if she was a witch, and in case she were, to have her apprehended, and so he took his departure.

The beginning of the fifteenth century saw the commencement of an epidemic of witchcraft and persecution throughout Europe which continued until near the close of the seventeenth century. It was not until witchcraft was placed by the Church under the head of heresies, that witches were rigorously prosecuted.

The first Papal Bull against witchcraft was that of Gregory IX in 1233, and in 1484 Pope Innocent VIII promulgated his celebrated Bull against various practices of sorcery and witchcraft, and introduced the terrible Courts Extraordinary, presided over by three Sorcery

A WITCH SURROUNDED BY FAMILIARS AND STRANGE APPARITIONS
From the Fairfax MS., 1621.   British Museum.

Inquisitors, which spread consternation in Germany and other parts of Europe. In this Bull sorcery and heresy were confounded together, while liberty and life itself were no longer safe to anyone under the Tribunal. Pope Alexander VI renewed the Bull against witchcraft, but the number of witches suddenly appeared to increase; spies, informers and exorcists multiplied also, and the rack was in constant use to extort confession, while the fires were kept burning for those whom the torture had driven to confession.

In three months during the year 1515, 500 witches were burnt in Geneva alone; a thousand were condemned in the diocese of Como; a single inquisitor boasted of having condemned 900 in Loraine, and " Trois Echelles " confessed that he knew of 1,200 witches in France and claimed to have passed judgment on at least two thousand of his pretended associates.

In the time of King Athelstan there was a law providing that where witchcraft caused death it should be punished by death, but where the effect was less serious the offender was imprisoned or fined.

A statute against witchcraft in England was passed in the reign of Henry VI, and additional laws were added by Henry VIII, Elizabeth and James I, the last being particularly industrious in his persecution of those accused of witchcraft.

In Scotland, in particular, witchcraft appears to have abounded and persecutions were very frequent.

King James VI, before he became James I of England, took an active part in several witch trials, especially in the inquisitions to discover the practices of one Cunningham. The most horrible tortures were inflicted on the unfortunate people who were accused, some of whom were persons of high rank and position, such as Lady Fowlis and others, whose trials are recorded by Pitcairn.

One method of detecting witches, and at the same time torturing them to make confession, was by means of running pins into their bodies, on pretence of discovering the devil's mark or sign. This practice was actually carried on as a calling in Scotland, and the men who exercised it were known as " prickers."

Scott states that, at the trial of Janet Peaston of Dalkeith, the magistrates and ministers of the town caused John Kincaid of Tranent, the common pricker, to exercise his craft upon her.

He reported, that " he found two marks of what he called the devil's making and which appeared indeed to be so, for she could not feel the pin when it was put into either of the said marks nor did they (the marks) bleed when it was taken out again ; and when she was asked where she thought the pins were put in, she pointed to a part of her body distant from the real place." They were pins of 3 inches in length.

Beside the fact that the bodies of old people, especially, sometimes have spots void of sensibility, there is also reason to believe that the professed prickers used a pin, the point or lower part of which was, on being pressed down, sheathed in the upper part which was hollow for the purpose and which, while appearing to enter the body, did not pierce it at all.

In 1678 the Privy Council received a complaint from a poor woman, who had been abused by a country magistrate and one of the so-called prickers. The members of the Council expressed high displeasure at the presumption of the parties complained against, and treated the pricker as a common cheat.[1]

An Act of Parliament was passed in England in 1664 against witchcraft, and twelve bishops attended the committee when it was discussed in the House of Lords. The Puritans urged that the persecution of all witches should be renewed. The Episcopal party refused to support it, or to take an active part in the persecution. Under the Long Parliament, however, the campaign broke out with fiercer intensity. Zachary Gray states that he had seen a list of three thousand witches executed during that period. Sir Matthew Hale presided when some of the unfortunate creatures accused of the offence were brought to trial, and charged the juries to convict the persons. Even Sir Thomas Browne, the humane author of the " Religio Medici," gave evidence at the trial and asserted the reality of the crime. So general did the charges of witchcraft become, that no class of society was safe from accusation and suspicion, thousands perishing by the faggot and torture.

After several thousands of victims had suffered the penalty, Sir John Holt, by his judicial firmness, stemmed the tide of fury against the unfortunate accused. Among the last victims condemned in England were a woman and her daughter, the latter only nine years of age. They were accused of selling their souls to the devil, and causing a storm " by pulling off their stockings and making a lather of soap."

In the eighteenth century, even men like John Wesley

[1] "Fountainhalls Decisions," Vol. I, p. 15.

and William Blackstone were believers in witchcraft, and it was not until 1735 that Parliament repealed the statute against witchcraft and the fear of witches began to die out.

The Witchcraft Act of 1735 (George II), which is still in force, provides that " no prosecution shall be brought for witchcraft, sorcery, enchantment, or con-

A BISHOP EXORCIZING A DEMON
(From a woodcut, XV century.)

juration ; but it is enacted that if any person *pretend* to exercise any kind of witchcraft, sorcery, enchantment, or conjuration, or undertake to tell fortunes, or *pretend* from skill in any occult science to discover where lost goods may be found, such person shall be imprisoned for a year, and be put in the pillory once in every quarter of such year."

Concerning demoniacal possession there is a considerable difference of opinion and the subject has long been a matter of controversy. There appears to be little doubt that it had its origin in the belief held by primitive peoples that evil spirits or demons could enter the human body and thus cause disease and other ills, until they were driven out by incantations or exorcism by invoking a higher power.

According to Biblical accounts, the demons sometimes made their presence both seen and felt, and in numerous pictures, representing saints in the act of exorcizing in the Middle Ages, the devil or demon is represented with the traditional horns and forked tail.

It is evident, however, from the period from which we have any detailed and accurate accounts of these unfortunate people, that their condition was generally due to some form of insanity, epilepsy, or condition of neurosis that was not understood at the time.

It was not until the fifteenth century, that doubts appear to have arisen in the minds of some thinkers as to the nature of demoniacal possession, and one of the first to comment on it was Nider, a Dominican friar who died at Colmar in 1438. John Wier, who also wrote about 1563 on the power of the devil, limited it to an influence on the imagination. Others then began to notice the resemblance of certain diseases, believed to have been caused by demons, to those known to be from natural causes, and Boquet declared that such maladies could be cured by physicians. Schenck, who studied the cause of nightmare, which at that time was generally believed to be due to an incubus, attributed the cause to " the obstruction of vessels which unite the spleen to the stomach, by the thickening of the gastric juice having become black bile." The principal symptom, he observes, " consists in a sensation of oppression as if the weight of a burden prevented the person from breathing, and horrible dreams accompany this sensation."

As to demoniacs, Schenck says he considers them as sick people. They have been cured even after the prayers of the Church and by the physicians, and he concludes that the same maladies which seem to be caused by the occult forces can be met with in people who are ill from natural causes.

With reference to confessions wrung by torture from those accused of sorcery or witchcraft, it was said that the fear of the torture alone could produce the effects which appeared to confirm their guilt. But even at the end of the sixteenth century, men like Fernelius and Ambroise Paré, who had described epilepsy and hypochondria as diseases, believed that sorcerers were able to cause demons to enter the human body and cause " a madness that resembled mania."

It is now known that neurasthenia is due to a derangement of the nervous system, to which is added an emotional intensity. Every faculty becomes sensitive, even pain is felt, the senses sometimes perverted, and spasms, paroxysms and loss of sensibility may occur, but that these manifestations can be controlled by the will power of another person.

Charcot has shown the effects of hypnotic treatment upon those suffering from acute hysteria, and has proved, that when a person is hypnotized the elastic muscular coating of the arteries constrict to such an extent as to stop the flow of blood, and that when needles are stuck into the flesh no bleeding follows.

Thus the light of modern science has dispelled much that was thought in the past to be due to occult forces.

CHAPTER XII

WITCHES' OINTMENTS

VARIOUS ointments or unguents were made and employed by witches, which were supposed to enable them to fly in the air, to see spirits, and produce other mysterious effects, and there is no doubt that some of these were highly active preparations.

The secret of the composition of these ointments was jealously guarded, but we have been able to gather from various manuscripts several recipes said to have been used in the sixteenth century.

Baptista Porta gives a recipe for an unguent used by the witches in Italy in the sixteenth century. It is composed of aconite, boiled with the leaves of the poplar, then mixed with soot and made into an ointment with *human fat*.

In this, the aconite, or monk's-hood, a common plant in the country, is the active ingredient. It is a powerful poison and contains several alkaloidal principles, the chief of which is aconitine, a minute quantity of which will cause death. Applied externally, aconite produces a tingling sensation, which is succeeded by numbness of the part. The soot was used simply as a colouring agent, and the fat as a vehicle for making the unguent. Another formula, of the same period, consists of *Acorus vulgare*, *Verspertillionis sanguinem* and *Solanum somniferum* boiled together in oil. To this, Indian hemp and stramonium were sometimes added, and the whole made into an ointment with the blood and fat of nightbirds.

In this recipe there are three highly toxic substances. Belladonna is a strong poison and given internally will produce delirium. Its active principle, atropine, has a powerful effect on the eyes. Indian hemp, taken internally, produces a kind of intoxication, attended by exhilaration of spirits and hallucinations, followed by narcotic effects, sleep and stupor. Stramonium, or thorn-apple, yields a principle called daturine, which, like atropine, dilates the pupils of the eyes and will cause delirium. The " blood and fat of nightbirds " were of course innocuous, and were doubtless introduced as elements of mystery.

WITCHES MAKING THEIR
MAGIC UNGUENT

(From a woodcut of the XV century.
Ulric Molitor.)

Another ointment was prepared by mixing " aconite, belladonna, water parsley, cinquefoil and baby's fat."

The water parsley was probably cowbane or water hemlock, a herb of a highly poisonous nature.

Hemlock, given internally, may produce delirium and contains a powerful alkaloid called conine, which causes paralysis of the voluntary muscles.

There is little doubt that both the magician and the

witch knew the properties and effects of many of these plants, from experience gained in their use in the fumigations employed at all their ceremonies.

Besides the drugs mentioned, they also employed hellebore, which contains a powerful principle called veratrine, that has a strong irritating action on the skin; henbane, a narcotic which contains among other poisonous alkaloids hyoscyamin, which dilates the pupils of the eyes; and mandrake, which, owing to its active principle mandragorine, has powerful narcotic properties and was used by the Greeks in ancient times as an anæsthetic, owing to its action in producing deep sleep and stupor. From the poppy they got the soporific effects of opium.

Other formulæ are also found which are quite innocuous, as the following, said to have been used by witches for working magic and seeing visions:

" An oyntment to see spirits.

" Take the gall of a bull, ants eggs and ye fat of a white hen all mixed together and anoynt your eyes to see spirits."

" Anoynt your face with ye fat of a lap-wing, or ye blood of a lap-wing, and of a bat or a goat and make an ointment."

Bull's gall, diluted with water, was used as an application to the eyes by the Anglo-Saxons. It was reputed to have the property of " clearing " and improving the sight, and was a well-known domestic remedy for affections of the eyes.

Another magical eye ointment used by witches to " see visions " is given in a sixteenth-century MS. and is directed to be prepared as follows:

" Take 8 pint Sallet oyle and put it into a real glasse

and at firſt wash it with rose water and marygold flower water the flowers being gathered towards the eaſt. Wash it until the oyle come white then put it into the glasse and then put thereto the budds of holyhocke the flowers of marygold, the flowers or tops of wild thyme and the budds of young hazel.   The thyme muſt be gathered near the side of a hill where the fayries use to be oft and the grasse of a fayre throne there.   All these put into the oyle in the glasse and get it to dissolve 3 days in the Sunne and then keep it for thy use.   Ut Supra.

" Anoynt under the eyelids and upon them morning and evening but especially when you call or finde your sight not perfeƈt."

CHAPTER XIII

THE BLACK MASS—THE MASS OF ST SÉCAIRE— "THE GOATS"

FANTASTIC stories have been written concerning the so-called Black Mass associated with the practices of sorcery and witchcraft in the sixteenth century; and, although many of these are but fables, there can be no doubt, from historical records still extant, that certain infamous and blasphemous rites were carried on long after that period.

The men who officiated at these profane ceremonies appear to have been renegade or degraded priests who had given themselves over to the service of the devil, and were ready to perform any abomination for gain.

In 1593, the Parliament of Bordeaux condemned to be burnt alive one Pierre Aupetit, curé of Pugeas, after confessing that for twenty years he had worshipped the devil at witches' sabbaths, and performed impious Masses in his honour. Charles IX is said to have employed an apostate monk to celebrate the "Eucharist of Hell" before himself and his intimates, and in 1597 there is record that Jean Belon, a curé of the diocese of Bourges, was burned at the stake for desecrating the sacraments and celebrating abominable ceremonies.

In 1609, several other priests were arrested in the

Bayonne district on similar charges and for celebrating " Satan's Mass."

About the middle of the seventeenth century, Madeleine Bavent, a Franciscan sister attached to the convent of Saints Louis and Elizabeth at Louvilles, by the direction of her confessor wrote a description of the blasphemous ceremonies of this Mass, at which she stated she had defiled the crucifix and trampled on the consecrated wafer. In connexion with this, a priest called Boullé was burnt in 1647.

In the time of Louis XIV, the practice of sorcery was carried on all over France, while in Paris it spread like an epidemic throughout the city, and from the highest to the lowest among the people there was a belief in the occult powers of the magician. Sorcerers abounded, and their services were sought by some of the greatest in the land for poison to rid themselves of undesirable relatives, or love-philtres to attract fresh lovers.

Chief among these evil characters was the notorious La Voisin (Catherine Deshayes), who lived in the Rue Beauregard and who was associated with many of the poison mysteries of the time.

The infamous Abbé Guibourg, who aided her in her crimes, was another of the gang, and in the cellars of the houses where they carried on their nefarious practices the " Black Mass " was probably celebrated.

It was stated, and possibly with some truth, that young children were killed during these rites, and there is an account that Lemeignan, vicar of St. Eustache, was convicted of having thus sacrificed infants to Satan.

These evil ceremonies were carried on into the

eighteenth century, and on the night after the murder of Louis XVI, in 1793, a number of these Satanists, as they came to be called, assembled and performed their Mass.

Various accounts have been recorded of the blasphemous ritual that was carried out at these meetings. According to one description, the altar was covered with three linen cloths and upon it was set six black candles and in the centre an inverted crucifix or a figure of the devil. The missal was bound in the skin of an unbaptized baby. The vestments are variously described as sometimes being all black, with a cope of white silk embroidered with fir cones, or a chasuble of a violet colour.

The celebrant sprinkled his followers with filthy water by means of a black brush, or used consecrated wine for the purpose.

The ritual began with an invocation to the devil, which was followed by a mock general confession, the celebrant making an inverse sign of the cross with his left hand.

The Host was then borne to the altar, and at the Elevation those present made hideous screams and frenzied yells.

The wafers are said to have been sometimes dark and round, stamped with horrible designs, or coloured red with blood, or were black and triangular in shape.

The Host was first stabbed with a knife by the celebrant, then thrown on the ground and trampled on, while the contents of the chalice were poured over it with abominable execrations.

At the close of the celebration, those present gave

themselves up to wild dancing with every kind of obscenity.

A similar ritual, but for a different purpose, was that called in Gascony the Mass of St Sécaire, by means of which priests were believed by the Gascon peasants to revenge themselves on evil men who were their enemies. It is thus described by Bladé.[1] It was to be said in a ruined or deserted church, the abode of hooting owls and bats and where toads squat under the deserted altar.

" Thither the priest comes by night and at the first stroke of eleven begins the Mass backward and ends at midnight. The Host he blesses is black and has three points. He consecrates no wine, but drinks of the water of a well into which the body of an unbaptized infant has been flung. He makes the sign of the cross, but it is on the ground with his left foot, and many other things he does which no good Christian could look upon without being struck blind, deaf and dumb for the rest of his life.

" Meanwhile the man for whom the Mass is said is believed to be withering away, little by little, and no one can say what is the matter with him. They do not know that he is slowly dying of the Mass of St Sécaire."

Towards the end of the eighteenth century, a mysterious society called " The Goats " was brought to light in Limberg. The members met at night in a secret chapel, and after infernal orgies at which they paid divine honours and homage to Satan, put on masks like goats'

[1] " Quatorze superstitions populaires de la Gascogne," J. F. Bladé, 1883.

heads. After enveloping themselves in long mantles, they went forth in bands to plunder, rob, and destroy all they met with.

It is stated, that between 1772 and 1774, the Tribunal of Foquemont condemned four hundred of these people to be hanged, but the whole society was not stamped out until 1780.

CHAPTER XIV

DIVINATION

DIVINATION for foretelling the future has been employed since the time of primitive man. It was performed in various ways, which may be classified as natural and artificial.

Rawlinson says that the custom of divining by means of a number of rods was purely Magian, and Herodotus describes the method employed and states that it was practised by the Scythians in Europe.

" Scythia," he observes, " has a band of soothsayers who foretell the future by means of a number of willow wands. A large bundle of these rods is brought and laid on the ground ; the soothsayer unties the bundle and places each wand by itself, at the same time uttering his prophecy.

" While still speaking, he gathers the rods together again and makes them up once more into a bundle."

A divine or magical power appears to have been believed to rest in the wands, and they were supposed to be consulted on the matter in hand both severally and collectively. The bundle of rods thus believed to be endowed with supernatural wisdom became part of the recognized priestly vestment, and was carried by the Magi on all occasions of ceremonial.

Twigs of tamarisk were sometimes used instead of

willow, and the number of the wands varied from 3 to 5, or 7 or 9.

Hosea the prophet, referring to the practice of divination, says : " My chiefs ask counsel with their sticks, and their staffs declare it unto them."

It was probably practised by the people of Western Asia as early as 700 B.C.

Another form of divination is mentioned in Ezekiel xxi. 21 called the mingling of arrows. Thus when " the King of Babylon stood at the head of the two ways to use divination, he made his arrows bright, he consulted with images and he looked into the liver." The latter form of divination, called extispicy, was practised by the Babylonians about 1500 B.C. and was also applied to the inspection of entrails.

Both the Etruscans and the Romans employed this method of divination, which they carried out by the examination of the internal organs and entrails of animals, and also of the drink offerings.

The Roman Aruspices, or officers appointed for this purpose, had four distinct duties : to examine the victims before they were opened, to examine the entrails, to observe the flame as the sacrifice was burnt, and to examine the meat and drink offering which accompanied it.

It was regarded as a fatal sign if the heart was wanting, and this is said to have been the case with two oxen that were sacrificed on the day that Cæsar was killed.

If the priest should let the entrails fall, or they were charged with blood, or if they were livid in colour, it was believed to be a portent of immediate disaster.

The origin of extispicy is said to be due to the custom of primitive, nomadic tribes examining the viscera of animals before settling on a place for encampment, to ascertain if the neighbourhood was healthy. A similar method of divination to foretell the future, which is said to be still practised in Turkestan, was to draw conclusions from the lines and dots found on the shoulder blade of a sheep after it had been dried in the sun.

Seven divining arrows were at one time kept in the great mosque at Mecca, but the Arabs are said to have only made use of three when divining. On one was inscribed " My Lord hath commanded me," on another " My Lord hath forbidden me," and the third was blank. If the first was drawn, it was looked upon as divine approbation of the enterprise; if the second, they made a contrary conclusion; but if the third happened to be drawn, they mixed them and drew them over again until a decisive answer was given by one of the others.

The method of divination by casting lots called Sortilege has been employed from early times by Eastern races for detecting a guilty person.

An instance of its use is to be found in the story of Jonah, when the sailors on the ship cast lots and judged him to be the cause of the tempest.

It was carried out by various methods, but usually by means of pebbles or counters engraved with certain characters, which were placed in an urn, and the first withdrawn was believed to give the correct indication. Another way was to place pieces of wood or parchment on which letters were written in a box, and after duly shaking them, to throw them on the ground, when any words thus accidentally formed were regarded as omens.

Divination by opening a book, and accepting a portion of the text that first appears, was another method employed in foretelling. The early Christians used the Bible for this purpose and the Muslims the Koran.

It is said that Charles I and Lord Falkland made a trial of this method shortly before the outbreak of the Civil War. " The former opened at that passage in the fourth book of the Æneid, where Dido predicts the violent death of her faithless lover ; while the latter opened it at the lamentation of Evander over his son in the eleventh book."

As instances of divination for judicial purposes there are records of two cases that occurred in London in 1382. One refers to Simon Gardiner, who lost his mazer bowl and employed Henry Pot, a German, to trace it. Pot made 32 balls of white clay, and after appropriate incantations declared that one Nicolas Freman and Cristine his wife were the thieves.

In another case, " Maud of Eye had her mazer bowl stolen, and Robert Berewolf was consulted to find the thief. Robert took a loaf, and fixed in the top of it a round peg of wood, and four knives at four sides of the same, in the shape of a cross. He then performed some operations called ' art magic,' and named Joan Wolsey as the thief," but apparently this fraud was discovered, for we find that Robert Berewolf was placed in the pillory with a loaf hanging round his neck.

There is another interesting record in 1382 of Mistress Alice Trig, who lost her Paris kerchief, and suspected Alice Byntham of having stolen it. The two women seem to have been fairly intimate, and Alice Byntham went to a cobbler, William Norhamptone, and told him certain private matters concerning Mistress Trig. William then saw Mistress Trig, and posing as a Wise Man, and skilled in magic, revealed to her his knowledge of her private affairs. Impressed by this, she asked him who stole her kerchief, to which he replied that, whoever it was it certainly was not Alice Byntham, and told her that she would be drowned within a month. Although terrified at his prophecy, she lived to see William standing in the pillory for misdemeanour.

Crystallomancy, or divination by means of a transparent body, such as a crystal ball, precious stone or mirror, was practised from early times. A beryl was generally preferred for this purpose. The crystal gazer, or "skryer" as he was called, would look for a prolonged period into the globe and profess to see a future event, spirit or writing, foretelling certain things. The methods employed will be further described in the chapter following. Aubrey says, there were prescribed prayers to be said before the speculation could be made, which the soothsayers termed a "call." Simon Forman relates in a manuscript, in 1585, that the Earl of Denbigh, then Ambassador at Venice, "did assure him that one did show him three several times in a glass, things past and to come." When Sir Marmaduke Langdale was in Italy, he went to one of these Magi, "who did show him a glass where he saw himself kneeling before a crucifix. He was then a Protestant, and afterwards became a Catholic."

He gives an interesting account of a "consecrated berill, in the possession of Sir Edward Harley of Bath, which he kept in a closet at Brampton Bryan, Herefordshire. It came first from Norfolk. A minister had it there, and a caul was to be used with it; afterwards a miller had it, and both did work great cures with it.

In the berill they did either see a receipt in writing, or else a herb. The berill is a perfect sphere, with a diameter I guess to be something more than an inch. It is set in a ring of silver resembling a globe ; the stem is about 10 inches high, all gilt. At the four corners of it are the names of four angels, Uriel, Raphael, Michael and Gabriel. On the top is a cross patee."

Crystallomancy has still its believers, and yet forms a prominent part of the stock-in-trade of the fortune-teller of to-day.

Hydromancy was a similar form of divination carried out on the edge of a silent pool or by means of a mirror. Dark lakes and rocky pools are frequently referred to in stories of witchcraft, and were often associated with this practice.

The operator knelt and gazed into the surface for a considerable time, to compose his mind for the revelations that might come to him from the water.

The Hindus and Arabs use a little ink, poured into the palm of the hand, or into a shallow bowl marked with cabalistic characters, for this purpose.

A black mirror was another medium favoured by some adepts for practising this form of divination.

Geomancy was a form of divination intimately connected with astrology. The earliest method of practising it was by casting pebbles on the ground, from which conjectures were formed, much the same as from chance lines and dots on paper. The Arabs, however, at a later period based the practice on the supposed effect of motion under the crust of the earth, or, what is more probable, surface cracks on the ground caused by the heat of the sun. The geomantic figures obtained by

147

inspecting the chance lines were supposed to represent a certain situation of the stars, and the diviner then proceeded on astronomical principles.

Lithomancy was a method of divining by using particular stones. These stones, which are described as " rough, hard, black and graven everywhere with veins or wrinkles," were supposed to possess extraordinary properties and were considered to be controlled by a genius or familiar spirit. On placing one close to the eyes, characters were supposed to be read on it.

Dactylomancy was a method of divining by rings. A plain ring or circlet of gold was suspended by a thread or hair within a glass vessel or within reach of it, and by the involuntary movements of the hand, it would strike the glass once for " yes " and twice for " no." Another ancient method of divining with a ring was to hold it suspended over a round table, the edge of which was marked with the letters of the alphabet. When the ring stopped over certain letters, they were joined together and so formed the answer.

Pyromancy was the art of divination by fire. *A* flaming fire was made to consume the sacrifice. The presage was considered good when it was vigorous and the fuel quickly consumed, when it was clear and strong and a transparent red, not dark in colour, and when it did not crackle. If it burnt silently, or was difficult to light, and the wind disturbed it, or it was slow to consume the sacrifice, the presage was evil.

Besides the sacrificial fire, the ancients divined by observing the flames of torches, and even by throwing powdered pitch into a fire ; if it caught quickly, the omen was considered good. The flame of a torch was good if it formed one point, but bad if it was divided; on the contrary, three points were a better omen than one. Sickness or death were foretold by the bending of the flame, and disaster by its sudden extinction.

Cheiromancy, or the method of foretelling from the creases or lines on the palm of the hand, is of great antiquity, and has been practised throughout the ages to the present time.

Scyphomancy, or divination by the cup, was another method of discovering future events by reflection. The divining cup of Joseph shows that its use was known in Egypt at a very early period, and most of the ancient Persian sovereigns and other Eastern rulers kept a cup for this purpose, which was highly valued. The divining cup was probably the primitive drinking cup, and when libations were required it had to be filled to the brim, and whenever a name was mentioned a small quantity of the wine was poured on the ground as a drink offering.

Alectromancy was an ancient form of divination with a cock. A white cock was placed in a circle drawn on the ground, which was equally divided into as many parts as there were letters in the alphabet. A grain of wheat was then placed on every letter, beginning with A, and after the diviner had repeated several incantations the cock was placed within the circle, and it was observed from what letters he pecked the grain. These when placed together were said to reveal the name of the person concerning whom inquiries had been made.

Oneiromancy was a method of divining by interpreting dreams. It was denounced by Pope Gregory as a " detestable practice," but this did not prevent the belief in it for forecasting the future.

Arnauld de Villeneuve, who wrote a work on the subject in the thirteenth century, gives a certain code by which those who practised it worked.

" Whoever dreamt that his hair was thick and carefully curled would soon become wealthy. If anything was wrong with the hair, evil was betokened. It also foreshadowed harm if a wreath was worn composed of flowers that were not in season." Other codes signified that to dream of the eyes related to children ; the head, to a father ; the arms, to brothers ; the feet, to servants ; the right hand, to the mother, to sons and to friends ; the left hand, to the wife and daughter. Another method was founded on the theory that, whatever was dreamt of, the antithesis or opposite would happen in life. Thus to dream of a wedding was said to presage a funeral. According to many old writers, there was scarcely any important event in the Middle Ages which was not announced by a dream.

The day before Henry II of France was struck by the blow of a lance during a tournament, Catherine de Medici dreamt that she saw him lose one of his eyes. Three days before he fell by the knife of Jacques Clément, Henry III dreamt that " he saw the royal insignia stained with blood and trodden under foot by monks and people of the lower orders."

Henry IV also, before he was murdered by Ravaillac, it is said, heard during the night his wife, Marie de Medici, say to herself as she woke, " Dreams are but falsehoods ! " and, when he asked her what she had dreamt, she replied, " That you were stabbed upon the steps of the little Louvre ! " " Thank God, it is but a dream," rejoined the King.

CHAPTER XV

THE practice of foretelling by looking into a reflecting surface probably began by gazing into the depths of a silent lake or pool. Mirrors of highly polished metal were employed in China for this purpose from a very early period, and the Greeks used bronze mirrors in order to foresee into the future.

The use of a crystal ball or stone came at a later date and was in general employment about the fifteenth century, when it was believed that spirits could be invoked and become visible in the stone. Various methods are described in the manuscripts on magic for " conjuring with the stone," and the ceremonies that had to be performed before so doing.

The ritual is thus described in a manuscript of the sixteenth century : " First have a glass or stone, fair, clean and sound without crack or blemish and thou must have Olive oil to anoint the stone withall, then you must confess yourself to God Almighty, read some good prayers and Psalms, and then consecrate your book and your stone together with the oil, and your instruments necessary for your work.

" First say one Pater Noster, one Ave Maria, one Creed, then say Dominus vobiscum Spiritu, God of Abram, God of Isaac, God of Jacob, God of Elias, God of Tobit, God of Angels, God of Prophets, God of Martyrs,

God of Confessors, God of Virgins, God of all good livers who hast given virtues to stones, woods and herbs, I am emboldened through thy great and manifold mercies, consecrate this book and stone."

According to a later description written by one Peter Smart, M.A., of London,

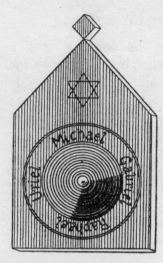

" THE TRUE SIZE AND FORM OF THE CRYSTAL, WHICH MUST BE SET IN PURE GOLD."

(Barrett's "Magus.")

" The crystal stone in which celestial powers have visible appearance should be of a round globic form, or ball of clear and solid glass or thick hollow of glass, with a little hole on the top of like form of any convenient bigness, and the same to be set in a frame, and also the glass to be made with a stalk or shank thereto and so to be put in a socket, with a foot or pedestal to stand upright. The stone being called a Show Stone and the glass by the name of a glass receptacle.

" For invocation for spiritual appearance, there shall either be a wax candle on each side or a lamp behind burning and set on a table. The sign of appearance most seemeth like a veil or curtain, or some beautiful colour hanging in or about the stone or glass, as a bright cloud or other pretty kind of hyeroglyphical show, both strange and very delightful to behold.

" Either good or bad angels may appear and they will be known by their appearance.

" The good angels are dignified powers of light and in countenance very fair, beautiful, affable, youthful, smilling, amiable and usually flaxenish or gold coloured hair, without any of the least deformity either of hairyness in the face or body or any crooked nose or ill-shaped members. Their garments or vestures without spot or blemish and always embrace the word mercy.

" When they appear the gazer must say :

" ' Welcome to the light of the highest and welcome to the messengers of Divine grace and mercy, unto us the true servants and worshippers of ye same God, whose name be glorified both now and for ever more. Amen.'

" The gazer then demands : ' Are ye the same whom we have moved and called forth visible appearance now before us by the name —— or what are ye and of what order among the blessed angels ? '

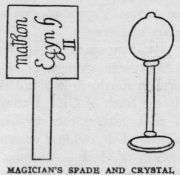

MAGICIAN'S SPADE AND CRYSTAL
(From an MS., XVI century.)

" If it make no answer repeat the words. Then it will show forth and tell its name and thou shalt say :

" ' If you be as you say, In the name of Jesus, say that all wicked angels are justly condemned and by the mercy of God in the merits of Christ mankind elect is to be saved.'

" Whereupon it will return a satisfactory answer and depart.

" If unsatisfactory or if there be silence, then make

humble request for answer to such desires and proposals, as in a certain writing is contained which ought to be in readiness with you.

"Failing these, there are nine great Celestial Keys or Angelical Invocations that could be used for calling forth to visible appearance the governing angels. These are METHRATTON, RAZIEL, CASSIEL, SACHIEL, SAMAEL, MICHAEL, ANAEL, RAPHAEL, AND GABRIEL."

It was apparently sometimes necessary for the magician to compel a spirit to speak, and to do this it had to be thus addressed:

"'Thou spirit, thou knowest that God doth live + Christ doth overcome + Christ doth rule in Heaven and in Earth, in Air and in ye Water and in all places. By ye truth of God, I conjure thee by the will of God. I do constrain thee by ye power and potency of our Lord. I do bid and command thee and by all the Holy names of God . . . Jesus ye Son of ye Virgin Mary, which shall come to judge both ye quick and ye dead and ye word of fire. Amen.

"'I do commit thee into ye hands of ye infernal spirits Lucifer, Deucaleus, Sathan, to be tormented in fire and brimstone, until thou hast done my will.'

"Then let the conjurer make a cross upon the ground with Holy Oil, then kneel, kiss the cross, rise up, take the sword in his right hand, command his fellow which shall bear thy work to kneel down and lay the bare sword upon his head."

In order to bind or fasten down a spirit who had appeared in the stone so that it could not depart until licensed, the conjurer had to say: "I bind thee spirit

that art appeared in this stone of crystal, that thou do
not disobey my commandments but do all things for
me that to thy office appertaineth and more too. I
bind thee not to go thy way from me till I release thee.
Here to remain until thou hast fulfilled all my command-

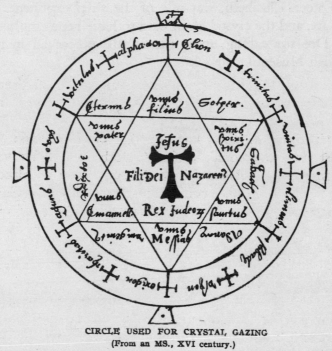

CIRCLE USED FOR CRYSTAL GAZING
(From an MS., XVI century.)

ments, for I will use art towards thee and nothing but
art, and thou spirit therefor here stand, I charge thee
in this crystal stone."

The writer concludes with " a general curse for all
spirits, both for ye stone, glass or circle. This is to be
carried out by making a fire of dry cow turds, brimstone
and suchlike stinking stuff and writing the spirit's name

on virgin parchment, burning it and saying the curse."

The professional conjurer with the crystal was known as a "skryer" in the sixteenth century. Edward Kelly, who was associated with Dr Dee in the time of Queen Elizabeth, was one of the chief exponents of the art, and the crystal globe said to have been employed by Dee for calling up spirits is still preserved in the British Museum.

CHAPTER XVI

HOW THE MAGIC CIRCLES AND PENTACLES WERE MADE

ONE of the most important parts of magical ceremonial was the drawing of the magic circle which formed the spiritual barrier, protecting the magician from evil and wicked spirits that he might invoke. Without a magic circle traced for defence, says a writer of the sixteenth century, " the invocation to visible appearance of such fearful potencies as Amaymon, Egyn and Beelzebub would probably result in the death of the exorcist on the spot, such death presenting the symptoms of one arising from epilepsy, apoplexy or strangulation. The circle once formed, let the evocator guard carefully against either passing or stooping or leaning beyond its limits during the progress of exorcism or before the licence to depart has been given."

The magic circle can be traced back for a period of over 5000 years and was probably employed at a much earlier date. Its origin is unknown, but it has been suggested that it arose from the ancient symbol of the serpent with its tail in its mouth.

The Assyrian sorcerer sprinkled lime around him and set seven little winged figures before the god, as described in the following early text :

" I have completed the usurtu (magic circle), with a sprinkling of lime I have surrounded them.

" The flour of Nisaba (the corn god), the ban of the great gods I have set around them.

" At the head of those seven with fearful wings have I set a figure of Nergal."

The ancient Hindu magician made a circle of red lead or black pebbles to ward off the approach of demons, and it was customary to encircle the bed of a woman at childbirth with black pebbles for the same purpose.

Henry found traces in early Hindu magic of the double pentacle or seal of Solomon, and suggested that the points of the star may have been intended to pierce or ward off invisible foes. This is only conjecture, but the use of the pentacle shows a connexion with Semitic magic.

Psellus alludes to Hecate's circle as " a golden sphere enclosing a sapphire in the centre, turned by a thong of bull's hide and having characters through the whole of it. Conjurations were made by turning it."

The primitive circle used by the magicians in early times developed during the Middle Ages and assumed a variety of forms according to the kind of spirits that the conjurer wished to evoke.

The circle was usually marked or drawn with the magic sword or knife and was generally nine feet in diameter, but sometimes it was made portable by being drawn on parchment and marked with metal amulets and talismans.

The blood of doves was often employed for writing the names and formulæ on the parchment.

The power of the circle as a ban or " castle," as it was sometimes called, was shown by leaving a gate or opening

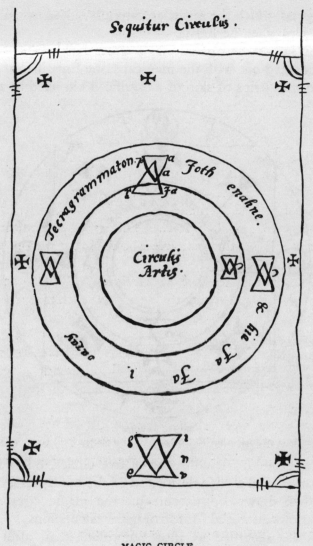

MAGIC CIRCLE.
(Drawn by a magician in the XVI century.)

for egress, which the magician carefully closed by making pentacles when he left it.

For important operations, a great Kabbalistic circle was marked out with the magical ſtone Ematille, or was made with ſtrips of skin of a sacrificed kid fixed by nails

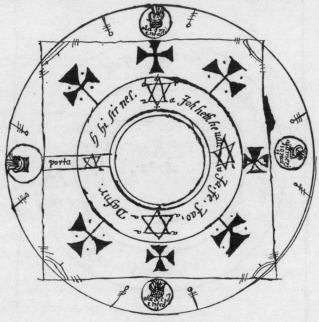

MAGIC CIRCLE

(Drawn by a magician in the XVI century, showing places for the fumigation pots.)

to the ground. It consiſted of five circles, one within the other, and a triangle inſtead of the pentagram.

When drawn on parchment, the magic circle was sometimes also used for aſtrological calculations.

It was regarded as moſt important that, after the operation had concluded, the magician should obliterate the circle so that no trace of it should remain, a practice

160

which survived from the early primitive magical rites. The licence to depart was also of great importance, as if omitted it was believed that the death of the conjurer might result.

Peter de Abano, writing " of the Circle and its composition " in the fifteenth century, says : " There is not one and the self same manner of circles used for the calling of spirits, but places, times, and hours are to be observed and the circle to be altered accordingly.

" It behoveth therefor, a man to consider in the making of his circle in what time of the year, in what hour, what spirits he would call forth, what star and region they govern and what functions they have. Therefor make three circles, in breadth nine feet and which stand distant one from the other a handsbreadth, and write in the middle of the first the name of the hour in which thou shalt make thy work. In the second place, the names of the angell of the hour ; third, the seal of that angell ; fourth, the name of the angell that governeth that day and his ministers ; fifth, the name of the present time ; sixth, the names of the spirits governing and ruling in that part of the time ; seventh, the name of the head of the signe ; eighth, the name of the earth according to that part of time, and the ninth, write the names of the sun and moon according to the season of the time. In the outward circle, in the four corners, the names of the angells governing the air that day to wit, the King and Three of his ministers. Without the circle, in the four corners, place pentagons. In the inward circle, write the four deume names placing crosses between them. In the middle of the circle, to wit the

East, write Alpha, and at the West, Omega, and let a
cross divide the middle of the circle."

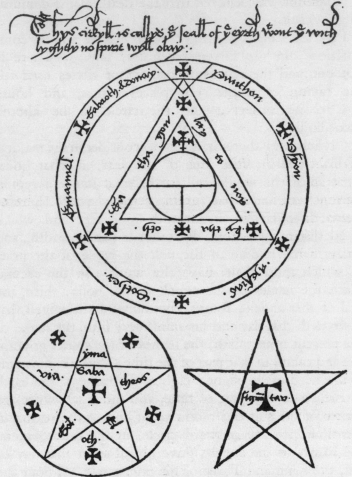

MAGIC CIRCLE AND PENTACLES FOR THE CRYSTAL
(From an MS., XVI century.)

The next important ceremony was the blessing and
consecration of the circle, which, after it was perfected,

was sprinkled with Holy Water, the magician repeating the following formula :

" Sprinkle me, O Lord, with hyssop and I shall be clean. Thou shalt wash me and I shall be whiter than snow."

The pentacle also formed a very important part of the magician's equipment and on it the science of magic was believed to depend.

The origin of the five-cornered figure, and how it came to be used as a symbol in magic, is unknown, but it undoubtedly goes back to a very early period and probably before the time of Solomon to whom it is generally attributed. In the early manuscripts it is variously called a pentagram, pentangle, pentalpha or pentagon of Euclid.

It is formed by two interlaced triangles, and can be drawn without a break in the drawing. Moxon defines it as, " a geometrical figure having 5 angles used as a symbol in magic."

It has been found engraved on Druidic remains and also on some ancient stones in India. A writer in a manuscript of the thirteenth century alludes to it as " the pentangel of pure gold, the sign that Solomon set."

It formed an integral part of the magic circle, as well as part of the vestment of the magician, and its power consisted not only in the diagram itself, but in the characters drawn upon it. Thus Agrippa observes, " The pentacles consist of the characters and names of the good spirits of the superior order, preserving us from evil events and helping us to bind and exterminate the evil spirits, and reconciling the good ones to us."

They were sometimes drawn on parchment or paper and affixed to the magician's vestment, or drawn on the robe itself, with the idea of protecting the wearer from the attacks or influence of devils or obnoxious spirits that might appear.

There are various directions given in the early manuscripts on magic as to how the pentacles are to be made, and the following may be taken as an example:

" They must be made upon a Wednesday, the day of

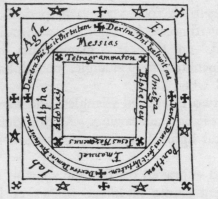

A MAGIC CIRCLE AND PENTACLE TO BE WORN WHEN USING IT
(From an MS., XVI century.)

Mercury, at the increase of the Moon. After making a fumigation in a secret chamber and sprinkling it with water, have your virgin paper and begin to write a pentacle of noble colour following the pen and ink. Let them be writ and other things to be exorcized. Then take some noble cloth of silk, wherein ye may hold the pentacle and have there a great earthen pot full of coals, and let there be mastic and Aloes wood, and let the conjurer be clean, as it is meet, and prepare juice

164

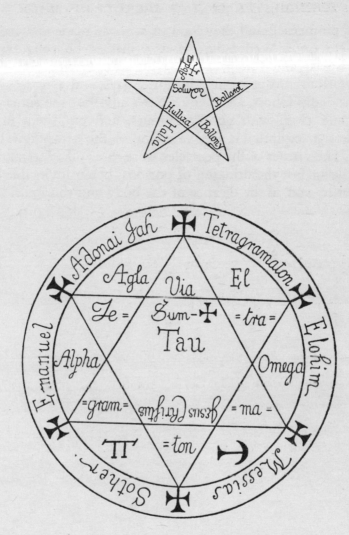

A MAGIC CIRCLE AND PENTACLE "FOR ALL EXPERIMENTS"
(From an MS., XVI century.)

of pimpernell and the blood of a goose made and complete on a Wednesday. Let 3 masses be sung with gospels, and fumigate it, saying the Psalms and the Oration. After saying this for 3 days, and 3 masses of the Holy Ghost, and one of our Lady, put the signs in a silk cloth with goodly savours, and put them in a clean place until it is need ye may work the Arts Magical."

The virtues of the pentacles were said to be " remarkable against the drinking of poisons, being invincible in battle, and in the defence of the body and the soul."

CHAPTER XVII

PERFUMES USED IN MAGIC

IN most of the ceremonies connected with the practice of the magical arts, perfumes or fumigations played an important part, and they appear to have been employed in mystic rites from the earliest times of which we have record.

Their use probably originated in the same idea as that of incense, viz. to give pleasure to the deity in order that an appeal might be more favourably received, but, as magic developed, it will be seen that the perfume or fumigation served other purposes.

A pleasing and fragrant odour was favourable to the angels and good spirits, while an evil one was used to drive the wicked spirits away. The same idea is common among barbaric races to-day, and to drive off a demon, the burning of substances that give off a repulsive smell is commonly resorted to.

In magical formulæ, certain fumigations were credited with the power of raising and causing spirits to appear, and to lay and bind them. As will be shown later, many of the substances employed possessed narcotic properties, and when burnt in a confined space and inhaled would doubtless produce somnolence, and sometimes hallucinations. The magicians were well aware of their effects, as one writes, " There are some

167

perfumes or suffumigations and unctions which make men speak in their sleep, walk, and do those things that are done by men that are awake, and often what, when awake, they cannot do or dare do. Others again make men hear horrid or delightful sounds, noises and the like."

In a manuscript on magic of the sixteenth century, the writer relates a curious tradition of how the knowledge of herbs came to be handed down. He states that, " Abel the son of Adam made a book of all the virtues and properties of plants, which knowing that the world should perish through the general flood, enclosed it so cunningly in a stone that the waters could not come to corrupt it, whereby it might be preserved and known for all people. This stone was found by Hermes Trismegistus, who breaking it, and finding the book therein, profited wonderfully by applying the contents to his use, which book afterwards came to the hand of St Thomas."

An examination of manuscripts on magic written in the fifteenth and sixteenth centuries throws an interesting light not only on the substances used for fumigations but also on the reasons for which they were employed.

" Of perfumes," says a writer of the sixteenth century : " A perfume made of hempseede and of the seeds of fleawort, violett roots, and parsley (smallage) maketh to see things to come and is available for prophesie. A perfume made with coriander, saffron, henbane and parsley (smallage) and white poppie all bruised and pounded together. If any shall dig gold or silver or any precious thing, the moon being joyned to the sun in the lower heaven, let him perfume the place with this suffumigation."

Certain perfumes were dedicated to the planets specifically, or were sometimes offered to the whole constellations. Thus a general perfume for the planets was composed of " myrrh, costus, mastic, camphor, frankincense, sanders (sandalwood), opoponax, aloes wood, asam euphorbium, storax and thyme of each 1 ounce, mixed together."

" For the Sun, yellow amber ½ oz., musk 12 grains, aloes wood 36 grains, liquid balsam and the berries of lawrell of each 34 grains, of gilliflowers, myrrh and frankincense of each 1 oz., with the blood of a white cock make pills in the quantity of half a drachm.

" Perfumes for the Moon. Take white poppie seeds 1 oz., frankincense ½ oz., camphor 1 oz., with the blood of a goose make into balls.

" Also mirtle or aloes, ye first of these have appointed to every place is according to Hermes Trismegistus who sayeth they are very powerful.

" A perfume for Saturn. Take seeds of black poppies and the seeds of hyoscyamus (henbanc) of each 2 ozs. Root of mandragora 1 oz., the stone lapis lazuli ½ oz., myrrh 3 grains, mixed with the brains or blood of a batt to balance the quantity of 1 oz.

" Also pepperwort, olibanum, gum Arabick or sandarach may be employed.

" A perfume for Jupiter. Take seeds of ash 2 ozs., aloes wood 2 ozs., storax, bengamin of each 1 oz., lapis lazuli 1 oz. Of the very tipps of the feathers of the peacock, let these be incorporated with the blood of a stork or of a swallow or the brain of a hart. Let

169

these be made in trochisk (lozenges) in the quantity of a groat.

"A perfume for Mars. Take euphorbium, bdellium of each 1 oz., ammonick roots, of both sorts of hellibore, lode stone 2 drachms, brimstone 1 drachm. Lett them be incorporated with the brain of a catt. Make trochiskis (lozenges) of 1 drachm.

"A perfume for Venus. Take musk 18 grains, amber 9 grains, aloes wood 1 oz., red roses 2 ozs., red corral 2 ozs. Mingle them with the brain of a sparrow and the blood of a dove. Make trochisk (lozenges) in quantitie half a drachm.

"A perfume for Mercury. Take mastich 1 oz., frankincense 2 ozs., gilliflowers 2 ozs. Incorporate with the brain of a fox or weasel and with the blood of a magpie. Make trochisk (lozenges) in quantitie half a drachm."

There were also combinations of perfumes for each day of the week. Thus for Saturday, "All good things and well-smelling roots as costus and herb thuris.

"For Sunday, mastich, musk, and suchlike gums of good odour as benjamin, storax, labdanum, amber, and ammoniacum.

"For Monday, leaves of myrtle and laurel and leaves of good odour and sweet flowers.

"For Tuesday, sandal, red, white and black, and all sweet woods as aloes wood, cyprus, balsam and suchlike.

"For Wednesday, the rinds of all sweet woods as cinnamon, cassia, laurel bark, mace and all sweet seeds.

"For Thursday, all sweet fruits as nutmegs, cloves, the rinds of oranges and citrons, dried and powdered, with suchlike of good odour.

" For Friday, roses, violets and all other fruits of flowers of good odour, as crocus and suchlike.

" Hermes said, that thimiamate of the moon is cinnamon, aloes wood and mastich while crocus, costus, mace and myrtle each planet hath a part in it."

The writer goes on to state, that, " Solomon makes distinction upon the days and planets of the spices which a man ought to make thimiamate, and saith, that Saturn is each good root in good and evil, of Jupiter all fruits of good and each rind of same, each flower and odoriferous herb, of the Moon each leaf and berry, and cardamoms was put with these things.

" There is no such fumigation to call spirits as amber, aloes wood, costus, musk, crocus and blood of a lapwing."

A marvellous efficacious fumigation, " to cause a man to see visions in the air and elsewhere, was made with coriander and henbane, and the skin that is within the poundgarnet (pomegranate) and the fumigation made is finished as you desire."

Another to cause visions of the earth to appear :

" Take root of cane reed and the root of fennell, with the skin of the pomegranate, henbane and red saunders, and black poppy."

" According to Hermes," says another writer, " there is nothing like unto Sperm-a-ceti to raise spirits suddenly, being compounded of sperm oil, aloes wood, pepperwort, musk, saffron, red storax mixed with blood of a lapwing. If it be fumigated about tombs and graves of ye dead it causeth spirits and ghosts together."

There were certain herbs and substances called " the herbs of the spirits," which included " coriander, sorcellage, henbane, and hemlock, made up with sweet gums, as of storax or benzoin or frankincense and myrrh, and these are called ' herbs of spirits,' because they cause them to come presently together."

Other formulæ which are said to have been taken from an ancient manuscript are as follows :

" Take mastick, sanders (red) and of musthalaperate and amber all mixed together, and fumigated quickly, quickly brings them in place.

" Anise and camphire mixed (it is an herb of chastity) cause to see secret things ye clepe spirits. Fumigate with cardamoms and eat thereof. It causeth gladness and gathers spirits together. Artemesia (wormwood) which in these things is called a ' Crown for a King,' for its virtue and power, put in all other fumigations."

The way to see spirits in a metal mirror is thus described :

" Take canabis viz. hemp, and artemesia and stand thee before a steele glasse and ye shall be able through God's help to see and bind and loose spirits, but if ye anoynt ye glasse with juice of artemesia it is better.

" A steele glasse well polished and must be anoynted with the juice."

" To cause apparitions to be visible to ye sight, you must take, artemesia, hemp, flax, cardamoms, anise, camphire, coriander, hypericon, aloes wood, apia mortegon (chicory)."

Of the substances of animal origin used for this purpose, the following are mentioned: " Ye lapwing, ye haysouke, ye lion's gall, ye bull's gall. Fat of a white hen, ye eyes of a black cat and antes eggs. Of fish, ye balena, and cancer (crab). Of aromatics, musk, amber-grise, myrrh, frankincense, red storax, mastick, olibanum, bdellium, red sanders, saffron, benzoin and labdanum."

" To have friendship or wouldst have of a prince of Spirits of ye ayre ; take juice of hypericon, saffron, artemesia and root of valerian and of these make a fumigation. To make spirits glory in themselves, take of ye powder of withy coales mixed with oil of nard and light it with a candle.

" To see future events, fumigate yourself with linseed and seed of psellium, or with violet roots and wild parsley."

To drive away evil spirits or devils, it was necessary to make a noxious fumigation with sulphur, black myrrh, red sandal, putrid apples, vinegar, wine galls, and arsenic mixed with dregs of wine, or a mixture of calamus, peony, mint and palma christi.

Before the perfumes or fumigations were used, the following benediction was to be said over them :

" ' O God of Abraham, God of Isaac, God of Jacob, bless here the creatures of these kinds, that they may fill up the power and virtuc of their odours, so that neither enemy nor any false imagination may be able to enter into them through our Lord, Jesus Christ. Amen.' Then let them be sprinkled with Holy Water. The fire which we use in fumigations, let it be put in a new copper, iron or earthen vessel, and exorcize it as follows : ' I exorcize thee O thou Creator of fire, by him by whom all things are made, that it shall not be able to do hurt to anything, but bless O Lord this creature of fire and sanctify it.' "

There were certain perfumes or fumigations associated with the Seven Angels, and the substances employed

175

in making these consisted of nutmeg, aloes wood, mastick, saffron, cinnamon, myrtle, mixed with rose-water, cloves, olibanum, frankincense and myrrh, amber, bdellium, red storax (called styrax), and a little ambergris and musk. "All these made into a body with the said gums, of which make little balls of the bigness of peas and cast into a clear charcoale fire, set in a new earthen pot, in ye middle of a room."

Among the drugs employed in these fumigations there are at least five powerful narcotics the fumes of which if inhaled would affect those in their vicinity. Cannabis Indica produces strange hallucinations, and the effects of opium from the poppies, henbane, hellebore and mandrake (which was employed by the Greeks as an anæsthetic), no doubt contributed to the belief in the visibility of spiritual beings invoked by the magician.

Certain herbs had to be gathered with great ceremony ; thus the magic herb valerian to be effectual had to be approached with the following solemn rites :

"First kneel down on both your knees, your face to the East, and make a cross over the herb, and say, 'In the name of the Father, and of the Son, and of the Holy Ghost. Amen.'

"Then say a Pater Noster, Ave Maria and Creed, also St John's gospel. This must be done secretly, alone on the Friday or Thursday, the Moon being at the full and before you speak a word to any creature. Also you must say before you take him out of the ground, 'I conjure thee herb that are called valerian, for thou art worthy for all things in the world. In pleasance, in Court before Kings, Rulers, and Judges thou makest friendship so great that they that bare thee his will, for thou doest

174

great miracles. The ghosts of Hell do bow to thee and obey thee. For whosoever hath thee, whatsoever he desireth, he shall have in the name of the Father, of the Son and of the Holy Ghost. Amen.'

" Keep it cleane in a faire cloth."

The ceremony is thus described by another writer :

" Go to the place where it grows on the 2nd day of May and kneel down before the shrub and say a Pater Noster and an Ave Maria, then dig with an instrument that has no iron about it until the roots appear, then let it lie until tomorrow and the first thing in the morning say the prayer.

" Then take the shrub out of the ground and wash it clean in woman's milk and wrap it in a new linen cloth, and set it upon the altar and say masses sublime to the Blessed Virgin, and keep it cleanly for it is of great value."

CHAPTER XVIII

MAGICAL NUMBERS

THE belief that certain numbers possessed magical properties has persisted from early times. The mystical number 7, so frequently mentioned in the Old Testament in connexion with Jewish ceremonial, is still retained, and the superstitions connected with the number 13 are believed by some people at the present day.

" A wonderfull efficacious virtue lies in certain numbers," says a writer of the sixteenth century. " The number 7 works wonderful things, thus the 7th son can heale distempers and could foresee into the future."

Pythagoras preferred number 4 as the root and foundation of all other numbers. " 4 angels govern the cardinal points of heaven, viz. : Michael, Raphael, Gabriel and Uriol. There are also 4 elements, Air, Earth, Fire and Water, and the 4 seasons, Spring, Summer, Autumn and Winter."

" Number 5 has great force in Holy things. It drives out bad demons and expels poisons. There are the 5 senses, viz. : Tasting, Hearing, Seeing, Touching and Smelling.

" Number 7 is full of majesty." The Pythagorians called it the vehicle of human life. " It is venerated in religion and is called the number of blessedness and rest. Thus there are 7 days, 7 planets, 7 colours and 7 metals, and the 7 ages of man. It is called the number

176

of an oath by the Hebrews and so Abraham when he made a league with Abimilech appointed 7 ewe lambs.

" In the whole context of numbers 6 is the most perfect number in nature. In 6 days the world was made, and it is called the number of man because on the sixth day he was created. In the law it was ordained 6 days to work, 6 days to gather manna, 6 years to sow the earth. A cherub had 6 wings, there are 6 circles in the firmament, viz. : the Arctic, the Antarctic, two Tropical, the Equinoctial, and Errliptick.

" Number 8 is called the number of Justice and of safety.

" Number 9 was sacred to the Muses. On the 9th hour Christ expired and after 9 days the ancients buried their dead.

" Number 10, a decade. It was the custom with the Egyptians whoever was initiated in the sacred mysteries of Isis must fast for ten days.

" This number is a unity.

" Number 12 is a Divine number wherein heavenly things are measured. There are 12 signs of the Zodiac, 12 months in the year, 12 orders of spirits, 12 tribes of Israel, 12 prophets, 12 Apostles, 12 Stones in Aaron's breastplate and 12 principal members of man's body.

" The ancients revered number 40 and held it in great veneration.

" For 40 days lasted the Deluge, 40 days the children of Israel lived in the desert, after 40 weeks Christ was born, 40 days from the nativity before he was offered in the Temple, for 40 months he preached publicly, for 40 hours he lay in the sepulchre and forty days after his resurrection he ascended into heaven.

" This," concludes the sage, " was the beginning of the wonders of numbers."

Another early writer gives the following symbolism and lore connected with magical numbers :

" No. 1 is regarded as the father of numbers and signifies harmony. It is a fortunate and prosperous number.

" No. 2 is the number of intellect and the mother of numbers. It is generally held to be an evil number bringing trouble and unhappiness. It has been an evil number to Kings.

" No. 3 is a holy number, the number of the Trinity. It signifies plenty, fruitfulness and exertion.

" No. 4 was the sacred number of the Pythagoreans and over it they swore their most solemn oaths. It is the square number, and in astrology the square was evil. It is the number of endurance, immutability, firmness of purpose and will.

" No. 5 was a peculiar and a magical number used by the ancient Greeks and Romans as an amulet to protect the wearer from evil spirits. The pentacle, with its five points, was regarded as a powerful talisman of protection and health. In India it is the emblem of Siva and Brahma. It is the symbol and number of fire, justice and faith.

" No. 6 was regarded as the perfection of numbers. It was sacred to Venus and regarded as the ideal number of love. To some it signifies trouble and strife, entanglement and uncertainties in marriage.

" No. 7 is the sacred number and in religion was highly esteemed by the ancients. It is the number of Royalty, triumph, fame and honour.

"No. 8 was regarded as a great power by the ancient Greeks, who held that 'all things are eight.' Pythagoras called it the number of justice and fullness. It is a number of attraction and also repulsion, of life and terrors and all kinds of strife and menace.

"No. 9 was the crooked number of the Pythagoreans and is connected with intellectual and spiritual knowledge. Numbers 9 and 7 are peculiar to the lives of men. Nine is a number of wisdom, mystery, rulership and protection.

"No. 10 is a holy and divine number and is the number of Karma in the philosophy of India.

"No. 11 is a number of evil reputation and signifies violence and power.

"No. 12 was esteemed as the number of grace and perfection. It is the number of time, experience and knowledge.

"No. 13 is a number of change and sometimes misfortune. It signifies death and destruction. In love it is not evil, and is a number of harmony. It was accounted a sacred number by the ancient Mexicans. The Romans considered it unlucky and an evil omen for thirteen to sit down in a room together, which probably accounts for its evil repute, and the Hindus have the same tradition.

"No. 14 is a number of ignorance and forgetfulness, trials and dangers.

"No. 15 was generally regarded as evil in magic, and was associated with the witch's sabbath which was sometimes held on the 15th day of a month.

"No. 16 is associated with weakness, accidents, defeat and danger.

"No. 17 is a good number. In ancient Eygpt it was considered unholy. It symbolizes immortality and intuition.

"No. 18 is a bad number, signifying treachery and deception.

"No. 19 is a good number and was considered one of happiness, good fortune and success.

"No. 20 is a good number, and signifies life and good impulses.

"No. 21 is a good number and is associated with truth, honour, elevation and success.

"No. 22 is a number of error and folly and cannot be trusted.

"No. 23 is a favourable number and means success and gain.

"Nos. 26 and 28 are associated with evil, disaster, greed and struggle in life.

"No. 37 is a good number and portends good fortune and success.

"No. 43 is a very unlucky number, and is associated with death, failure and destruction.

"No. 65 was the holy number of Adonay, and was good in all things. Pythagoras held that numbers were the principles of all things, and odd numbers were accounted by the ancients more fortunate than even ones, as they associated the odd with their greater and more powerful gods."

CHAPTER XIX

MAGICAL TALISMANS

MAGICAL talismans, usually consisting of certain symbols or characters in various combinations, written on parchment or engraved on metal, were carried and worn to prevent the owner from danger and the attacks of evil spirits.

According to a manuscript on figures of geomancy written in the sixteenth century, the ten names of the deity were regarded as being specially potent and effective for this purpose.

" The talisman, called in Hebrew a scutcheon, or shield in Chaldean, signified a figure or image written or drawn on a piece of paper or parchment marked with certain characters drawn from the Tetragrammaton, made under certain constellations. They are a buckler or shield of defence against disease, lightnings and tempests."

The same writer states, " The Arab, Haly Rhodoam, had the image of a scorpion engraved on a bezoar stone, by which he cured those bitten by venomous beasts. Apollonius by making a talisman of a stork, kept those troublesome birds from Constantinople, and by another he drove away all the gnats out of Antioch."

" Talismans, made under the sign of Pisces, were placed in the prow of their ships by the early Latins, to preserve them from shipwrecks and tempests, and the Greeks set up the same. These figures were not in

181

any human form but of some celestial figure. Mariners also had statues of some deities, as of Mars, Apollo or Mercury, which they placed on the poop or hinder parts of their ships.

" The custom of mariners setting up these figures is very ancient against shipwreck. The ship of Alexandria that Paul sailed in, had the images of Castor and Pollux or, according to the Arabs, the Gemini, and that which carried Hippocrates, when he took his journey to Abdera

I   2   3

MAGICAL SEALS TO BE USED AS TALISMANS AGAINST CERTAIN
DISEASES

1. For pains in the head.
2. Against flux and catarrhs.
3. Against trembling of the heart.
" Make these signs on a lead plate with the brain of a hog."
(From an MS., XV century, in the Bodleian Library.)

for the curing of Democritus, bare the figure of the Sun."

All these talismans were not so much for the avoiding of shipwreck as for the turning away of some disaster or accident, and the procuring of good fortune.

"From this practice of the ancients the Christians have taken example by setting up images of saints in their vessels."

The founders of ancient cities and castles first brought astrologers to find out a lucky position of the heavens under which the first stone might be laid.

182

The influence of astrology on magic in the Middle Ages is shown in the description of how the talismans were to be made.

Each planet had a table or square consisting of an arrangement of names, figures or numbers, which were supposed to both give and receive power. This table, or certain symbols written or engraved, formed the talisman.

Thus, Saturn's table consisted of a square containing

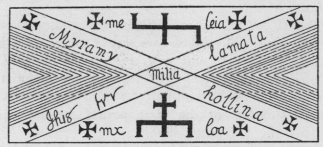

"THIS TALISMAN ENGRAVED ON BRASS WILL WIN THE WEARER HEALTH"

(From an MS., XVI century.)

nine divisions in each of which the following numbers were written, 4, 9, 2, 3, 5, 7, 8, 1, 6. These when engraved on a plate of lead and worn on the person were believed to bring good fortune, "to help child-birth and make a man powerful."

Jupiter's table engraved on a silver plate was said to bring favour and love to him who wears it. "It will dissolve witchcraft, engraven on coral."

"Mars engraven on iron or swords makes him that bears it valiant in wars and terrible to his adversaries. Cut in carnelian, it stops bleeding."

183

" The Sun engraven on gold, makes the bearer fortunate and beloved, and to be a companion of Kings.

" Venus engraven on silver, brings good fortune and love of women. It makes the wearer powerful and dissolves witchcraft, also generates peace between man and wife.

" Mercury engraven on silver, tin or brass, or written on virgin parchment, will make him that wears it obtain what he desires. It brings gain, gives memory and understanding, and knowledge of occult things by dreams.

" The Moon engraven on silver, brings cheerfulness, takes away ill will, makes him secure when travelling and expels enemies and evil things. Made in lead and buried, it shall bring misfortune to the inhabitants of a city, also ships and mills."

Another writer of the same period, in describing how to make talismans, states,

" An image whose figure was the head of a man with a bloody neck, bestoweth success to petitions and maketh him who carrieth it bold and magnanimous and

helpeth against witchcraft. The sign is

" Done under the greater Dog star, the image of a hound and a little virgin, bestoweth honour and favour

of men. The sign is

" Under the heart of Leo they made the image of a lion or cat which rendereth a man temperate, appeaseth wrath and giveth favour. The sign is

184

SOL .

MICHAEL, THE ANGEL OF THE SUN
(From an MS., XV century, in the British Museum.)

185

" Under the heart of Scorpio, they made the image of a man armed with a coat of mail or the figure of a scorpion. It giveth understanding and memory and aideth against evil spirits. The sign is 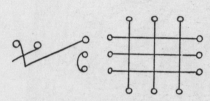 "

The association of angels with the planets, the months of the year and the four winds was probably due to the influence of astrology. Four angels were said to serve Saturn, 4 under Jupiter, 4 under Mars called Martyans, 4 under the Sun, 3 under Venus, 3 under Mercury and 4 under the Moon.

"To expel and drive away flies from any place, write these signs on a plate of tin."

(From an MS., XVI century.)

The angels of the four winds were Michael for the east wind, Gabriel for the north wind, Raphael for the west and Uriol for the south.

The colours associated with the planets were black with Saturn, red or saffron with Mars, violet with Venus, yellow with Mercury, saffron or orange with the Sun and white with the Moon.

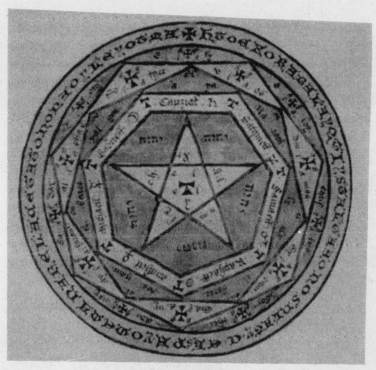

THE DIVINE SEAL

From an MS. XVI century. British Museum.

CHAPTER XX

MAGICAL RINGS

THE connexion of rings with magic goes back to a very early period and, like the circle, their origin is lost in the mists of time. It is probable that their use arose from the same idea. The circle and the ring symbolized protection, and if the latter was set with certain stones, or engraved with signs or inscriptions of power, it was believed to be endowed with magical virtues.

According to an ancient Hebrew manuscript, a ring of copper and iron engraved with certain magical signs, when worn, would enable the wearer to become invisible at will.

The Greeks in ancient times wore rings set with stones, sometimes engraved with representations of the deities whom they believed had the power of warding off evil. Plutus alludes to the practice in the Scholiast of Aristophanes, in which the Just Man remarks, " Here's a charmed ring I am wearing that I bought for a drachma from Eudemos."

Rings were also used for healing purposes from the first century, and were recommended by Marcellus for relieving pain in the side, also by Alexander of Tralles for various ailments.

From the time of Edward the Confessor rings have been employed for curing certain diseases in Great

187

Britain, and in the Middle Ages " cramp rings," believed to have the property of relieving pain, after being " blessed " by the reigning monarch, were much sought after.

The magician's ring usually formed part of his equipment and was made of copper or lead. It had to be three inches in breadth, and have the word Tetragrammaton well-engraved on it. A hole was made through the middle of it, so that it could be secured to the finger.

Before being used, it was necessary to consecrate it in the following manner :

" O thou creature of God, thou ring, I conjure thee which was blessed and anointed of King Solomon with Olive Oil, so blessed, I adjure thee still to be blessed through Jesus Christ, the Son of the living God, that thou mayst have the form, the figure, the virtue and power for that purpose that thou art ordained, for and like as the Ark of God in the Old Testament, the golden ring was borne, so be thou to this servant of God a token of knowledge unto this faithful servant of the true science of calling of spirits, that when thou art held up he may have help of thee, and through thy virtue he may subdue the power of evil spirits.

" Then anoint the ring with Holy Oil, sprinkle it with Holy Water and put it on the finger of the left hand kneeling."

In a manuscript of the sixteenth century, a formula is given for making a ring for receiving an oracle, to be made of lead, the metal of Saturn. When made, " write or grave thereon ye name of ye angell Cassiel, then fumigate it. Then being so prepared, put it on thy finger as thou art entering into thy bed and speak no word to any person, but meditate thereon. If thou wilt complete the ring, truly, ye shall put a piece of ye roote of some especial herb governed by Saturn and put it under ye stone of a signet, as for

SEALS OF THE PLANETS
(From an MS., XVI century.)

example a little root of dragon or dragon-wort, or of black hellebore or hemp, upon which put some little onyx stone or sapphire, or lapis lazuli, but onyx is best, but let it first be made and engraved, and make ye mould to cast it, and all finished in due time with name of ye angel of Saturn."

189

Another method of making a magical ring was to " cast a ring of pure gold and engrave on it the name of an angel and the character of ye Sun. Then being made, fumigate it with masticke, red storax, benjamin and musk, or new sweet wine and rose water, all mixed with saffron. Forget not to first put a piece of root or yellow flower of marygold or some bay leaf, especially of angelica or root of bay tree. Then place either a carbuncle, hiacinth, chrysolite, or ye stone etites which is found in ye eagle's nest, over it."

There was believed to be a close connexion between the stars and certain metals dedicated to them, also with various precious stones and herbs. John Gower in " Confessione Amantis," dedicated to Henry VIII, gives a list of these from which the following is extracted :

" Aldebaran is appropriated to the stone carbuncle and the herb anabulla.

" Asgol to the diamond and black hellebore.

" Clota or the pleiades to the crystal or fennell.

" Ashaiot to the sapphire or horehound.

" Canis major to the beryl or sauma.

" Asmareth to the jasper or plantago.

" Aspheta to the topaz or rosemary.

" Scorpionis to the sardonix or aristolochia.

" The 15 stars called scorpio to the calcedony or majoram.

" Rings made of lead should be set with black onyx, and have a piece of root of yew, cypress, willow or black hellebore. Of tin, set with sapphire, amethyst or emerald, hiacinth or topaz, and root of oak, cherry tree, almond, chestnut, clove, mulberry or barberry tree. When made of copper, they should be set with jasper with the root of olive, sycamore trees, or with silver set with sardis or crystal and root of the linden tree."

Rings to cure gout and rheumatism were highly esteemed in the sixteenth century, and the " rheumatic ring " composed of zinc and copper was in vogue in this country until a few years ago.

There is an interesting letter among the Historical MSS. in the British Museum addressed to the Earl of Lauderdale, requesting him to send the Duke of Hamilton a " gout ring." It is partly written in cipher, signed " M.L." and dated " 8 of Feby 15 . . .

" This is only to demonstrate I doe not willingly neglect occasion of writing, when I shall only say none knew you were in Scotland. Lord save my Lady Duchess, for my Lord Duke is gone away to-day. . . . Speaking of the Duke puts me in mind to bid you send him such a gout ring as you gave me to send to my father when you were last at home, for the Duke hath that wearing now, and your old servant Kenedy hath got a loan of it from my father, and he wanted it, for he is undone with the gout which was a means to keep him from any trouble of it while he wore it. My Lady I hope will be well."

A love charm, in which cramp rings play a part, is thus recorded in a manuscript of the sixteenth century.

" Take 2 cramp rings of gold or silver and lay them both in a swallow's nest that buildeth in the summer. Let them lie there 9 days, then take them and deliver the one to thy love and keep the other thyself."

There are several ancient traditions regarding the famous ring of King Solomon. One avers, it had the mystic word SCHEMHAMPHORASCH engraved upon it, which gave him the command of spirits and procured for him the wonderful SHAMIR, which enabled him to build the temple. "Every day at noon it transported him into the firmament, where he heard the secrets of the universe. This continued until he was persuaded by the devil to grant him his liberty and to take the ring from his finger; the demon then assumed his shape as King of Israel and reigned three years, while Solomon became a wanderer in foreign lands."

Another story states, that "when he looked on his ring he beheld whatsoever he desired to know in heaven or upon earth. One day he took it off when about to enter his bath, and it was snatched up by a fury and thrown into the sea. Greatly disturbed by the loss of the ring, that gave him power over the spirits of air, earth and sea, and which also deprived him of the wisdom to rule, he resolved never to reseat himself on his throne until he had recovered it.

"At the end of forty days he miraculously found his ring in the belly of a fish brought to his table."

Pope Innocent is said to have sent to King John four rings set with mystical stones, the virtues of which are set forth in the following letter which accompanied the gift.

"Pope Innocent to King John of England.

"Though we are persuaded that your Royal Excellence has no want of such things, we have thought proper to send you as a mark of our goodwill, four rings set with stones. We beg the favour you would consider the mystery contained in their form, their matter and their colour rather than their value. Their roundness denotes eternity, the number four, which is a square, signifies firmness of mind, not to be shaken by adversity nor elevated by prosperity. This is a perfection to which yours will not fail to arrive, when it shall be adorned with the four cardinal virtues, justice, fortitude, prudence and temperance.

"By the gold is signified wisdom, as gold is the most precious of metals, wisdom is of all endowments the most excellent. Accordingly Solomon, that pacific

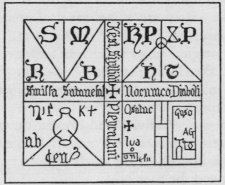

"SEALS OF THE DEVIL," DESCRIBED AS VERY POTENT
(From an MS., XIV century, in the Bodleian Library.)

king, only asked God for wisdom to make him to well govern his people.

"The green colour of the emerald denotes faith; the clearness of the sapphire hope; the redness of the ruby charity; and the colour of the opal good works. In the emerald, therefore, you have what you are to believe; in the sapphire what you are to hope; in the ruby what you are to love; and in the opal what you are to practise."

The use of magical inscriptions and characters on

rings appears to have originated with the magic seal or talisman that was first written on parchment and carried on the person. As this could easily be obliterated or destroyed, the seal was sometimes transferred to metal and worn as a ring.

The Earl of Peterborough possessed a magical seal engraved with symbols on silver, with an iron handle, a wax impression of which is still in existence. The centre is a square in which is enclosed a diamond-shaped diagram surrounded by stars and crosses. Outside the circle are three rows of magical names. To the impression the date " 2 Dec 1671 " is attached.

Another magical ring of which an impression remains, and also a sketch, is that of Dr Simon Forman, the notorious magician, astrologer and alchemist of the sixteenth century.

The ring was of silver, and on the outside edge of the signet were engraved the words ARIEL and ANAEL, while on the outside of the circle were the words DIE ET HORA and the date 1598.

Simon Forman was born in 1552 and entered Magdalen College, Oxford, as a poor scholar. In 1579 he was sent to prison for sixty weeks for practising magic, after which he travelled the country for some years as a quack doctor and eventually settled in New Street, London, in 1583.

Five years later, we find he began publicly to practise necromancy and professed to call up spirits. In 1593 he was summoned by the College of Physicians for practising medicine without a licence and fined. Gaining notoriety, he attracted several aristocratic patrons, including Lord Hertford. He was prosecuted many

This is the Impression of a Sigill, graved on a Silver plate, & fixed to an Iron handle: being in the Earle of Peterborough's hands 2 Dec: 1671.

1   ✠ AGLA ✠ BARACHIEL ✠ ON ✠ ASTASIEEL
    ✠ ALPMAETO ✠✠✠ →✠→ ✠ RAPHAEL ✠✠✠
    ALGAR ✠ VRIEL.

2.   ✠ MICHAEL ✠ IEHOVA ✠ GABRIEL.
    ✠ ADONAI ✠ HAKA ✠ IAN ✠ TETRAGRAMATON

3.   ✠ VVSIO ✠ VALACTRA ✠ IENIFRA ✠ MENA
    ✠ IANA ✠ IBAM ✠ FEMIFRA.

    MEDCHAET ✠ MELRHAM ✠

THE EARL OF PETERBOROUGH'S MAGIC SEAL

times for illegally practising medicine, but in the end received a degree as doctor of medicine from Cambridge University.

He was associated with the murder of Sir Thomas Overbury in 1615, and, according to a letter produced in Court, the Countess of Essex had asked him to give her a philtre to alienate her husband, and also one to

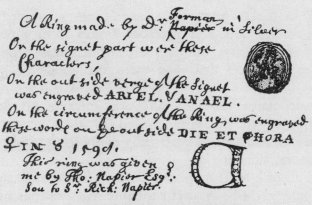

SIMON FORMAN'S MAGIC RING
(From an MS., XVI century, in the British Museum.)

gain the love of the Earl of Somerset. During the trial, wax images of the persons concerned, made for working magic, were produced in Court.

Forman left a mass of manuscripts to Richard Napier, who bequeathed them to Sir Richard Napier, his nephew. Thomas, his son, gave them to Elias Ashmole, who left them to the Bodleian Library, where they are still preserved.

CHAPTER XXI

MAGIC IN JEWELS

MAGICAL properties have been attributed to certain rare and precious stones from a period of antiquity, the origin of which was probably due to the belief that they were the abode of good spirits.

Their association also with the planets no doubt contributed to the faith placed in their mysterious virtues, which covered practically every form of physical and moral ailment.

As disease was supposed to be due to evil spirits that entered the body, it is probable that precious stones were originally worn as amulets to protect the wearer from sickness and ill, or that the beneficent spirits that dwelt in them might drive the evil ones away.

The diamond, pre-eminent in brilliancy and beauty, was believed to be most powerful in spiritual magic and potent in its effects.

It was the one unchangeable substance in Nature against which even fire was powerless. It was consecrated to all that was celestial, and was regarded as a protection against sorcery, enchantments, evil spirits and nightmare. It was said to endow the wearer with courage and strength of mind, while it calmed anger and was regarded as the stone of reconciliation.

Anselm de Boot, physician to Rodolph II, in a work written in the seventeenth century on the " Virtues of precious stones," argues, " whether the power of discrimination between right and wrong, legal or illegal affection be a natural quality of the stone, or belongs to a spirit residing in it."   He inclined to the opinion that, " the evil spirit taking the semblance of an Angel of Light, taketh up its abode in precious stones and enacts by them prodigies, in order that, instead of having recourse to God, we may rest our faith on the said stones and consult them when we would compass some object."

According to an Eastern tradition, Abraham wore a precious stone around his neck, which possessed the property of curing disease when gazed upon. When the patriarch died, the Almighty placed this stone in the Sun, from which originated the Hebrew proverb, " When the Sun rises the disease will abate."

MAGICAL JEWEL
(XVI century, said to have been designed by Holbein.)

The Egyptian king Nechepsus (630 B.C.) is said to have worn a green jasper cut in the shape of a dragon surrounded with rays, which, " when applied to the region of the digestive organs strengthened that part wonderfully."

The ruby, or carbuncle as it was called in early times, was believed to protect the wearer from plague, and was said to have the power of " banishing sadness, averting evil thoughts, dispelling terrible dreams and repressing sensuality."

On the other hand, the ruby was supposed to disturb

the circulation of the blood and incline the wearer to anger.

Their is a curious tradition that, if misfortune threatened anyone who carried a ruby, it became darker in colour and when the peril had passed it resumed its original bright hue.

Gabelschoverus commenting on this legend says, " On the 5th day of December 1600 I was going with my beloved wife Catherina from Stuttgardt to Caluna, I observed by the way that a very fine ruby which I wore mounted in a gold ring which she had given to me, lost repeatedly and each time almost completely its splendid colour, and that it assumed a sombre blackish hue which lasted several days ; so much so, that being greatly astonished, I drew it from my finger and put it in a casket. I also warned my wife that some evil followed her or me. And truly I was not deceived, for within a few days she was taken mortally sick. After her death the ruby resumed its pristine colour and brilliancy." Madame de Pompadour wore a large ruby cut in the form of a pig, as a charm to bring good-luck, which is still preserved in the Louvre Museum.

The sapphire was believed to possess many virtues. To gaze long into it was said to preserve the eyesight, and if worn over the region of the heart it reduced fever and gave strength and energy.

" It had the magical power of inspiring chaste thoughts," says an early writer, " which caused it to be recommended to be worn by ecclesiastics." St Jerome asserts in his comments on Isaiah, chapter xix, that " the sapphire conciliates to the wearer the favour of princes, calms the fury of enemies, dispels enchantments, delivers from prison and softens the ire of God."

As an amulet, the emerald was said to drive off evil spirits, give knowledge of secrets, of future events, and bestow eloquence on its owner. It was supposed to betray inconstancy by splintering into fragments when it could not prevent the evil, a superstition which Miss Landon embodies in the lines :

> " It is a gem which hath the power to show,
> If plighted lovers keep their faith or no ;
> If faithful, it is like the leaves of spring ;
> If faithless, like those leaves when withering."

There is a tradition connected with the emerald, that it foretells an evil event should it fall from its setting. At the coronation of George III, a large emerald is said to have fallen from his crown, which believers in the omen say presaged the loss of America.

Placed round the neck of a child, it was said to protect it from attacks of epilepsy, dispel terrors and stop hæmorrhage.

The topaz when worn on the left hand was believed to calm anger, banish melancholy, brighten the wit and give courage to the wearer. As a talisman, if bound round the left arm, it was said to dispel enchantments, while it was also credited with the properties of healing affections of the mind, preventing sleep walking and curing hæmorrhoids.

The amethyst had the reputation of keeping the wearer from intemperance and was used as a cure for inebriety. Camillus Leonardus, referring to this, states, " Bound on the navel it prevents drunkenness. It was also held to sharpen the wit, turn away evil thoughts and give a knowlege of the future in dreams. It was frequently engraven with the head of Bacchus, and was a favourite with the Roman ladies."

The opal has long been a much-maligned jewel and was generally believed to bring the wearer ill-luck, but according to early writers it by no means deserves this reputation. On the contrary, they attributed to it all good qualities, moral and healing, that pertained to other precious stones, as it radiated their many colours. It was reputed to be helpful to the eyesight, to be able to dispel sadness and melancholy, and to preserve the wearer from contagion.

The opal was highly esteemed by the Romans, and Pliny says that " the Senator Monius was exiled by Mark Antony for the sake of the magnificent opal he wore that was the size of a hazel-nut."

The turquoise was another gem that was supposed to lose its colour when evil threatened its wearer. Thus writes Donne :

> " As a compassionate turkois that doth tell,
> By looking pale, the wearer is not well."

It was supposed to have the properties of preventing headache, placating hatred and reconciling lovers.

The beryl is said to possess many healing virtues and was efficacious in relieving hysteria, jaundice, liver troubles and ailments of the mouth and throat. As a charm, there was an ancient belief that it made the idle industrious and quickened the intellect of those who were dull. Its most important property, however, was its use as a medium for magical vision, and, for gazing, no stone was believed to be so effective and valuable as the beryl.

The onyx was also a stone associated with magic. When worn on the neck it was said to stimulate the spleen, dispel melancholy and other mental disturbances. It was applied to the bites of venomous animals and was suspended round the neck to allay pain.

The carnelian, probably on account of its colour and coldness, was used to stop hæmorrhage, and the sardonyx was believed to protect the wearer from the bites of scorpions.

Coral has been highly esteemed for its properties from early times, both on account of its occult power and its medicinal virtues. Pliny says, " Formerly it was deemed excellent as an antidote to poisons." A later writer states, " Witches tell, that this stone withstandeth lightning, and putteth it, as well as whirlewindes, tempestes and storms, from shippes and houses that it is in."

Like the turquoise it was believed to alter in colour according to the health of the wearer, and if worn by one who is ill or in danger of death it would become livid and pale. This property is alluded to in the following lines in the " Three Ladies of London " written in 1594 :

" You may say jet will take up straw, amber will make one fat, coral will look pale when you be sick, and crystal will staunch blood."

As an amulet or charm it was used as a protection against witchcraft, enchantments, epilepsy, " assaults of the devil," storms at sea and perils by land.

The superstition has survived in the custom of placing coral necklaces round the neck of an infant soon after birth, while the coral and bells were supposed to drive away evil spirits and protect the child from ill. An early writer observes, " It stops bleeding, preserves houses from thunder (?) and children from goblins and sorceresses." Taken internally it was said to relieve indigestion and prevent attacks of epilepsy.

Amber has long had a reputation as a curative charm, especially in connexion with the throat. Worn round the neck it was believed to relieve chest troubles, sore throats and whooping-cough. In the form of oil of amber it is still employed to rub on the chest and neck for these ailments.

Many other stones were associated with magic and believed to possess occult properties of which only brief mention may be made. These include chalcedony, which was said to bring good fortune and prevent illusions of evil spirits ; chrysoletus carried in the left hand to drive away night-hags, illusions and witches ; jasper against nightmare and epilepsy ; jacinth against plague and lightning ; and jet, concerning which Pliny observes, " Magicians use this jet stone much in their sorceries which they practise by the means of red hot axes, for they affirm that being cast thereon it will burne and consume, if that we desire and wish shall happen accordingly."

CHAPTER XXII

LOVE AND MAGIC

IT seems natural to suppose that the aid of the practitioner of magic should be sought in connexion with the " malady " of love common to mankind from the time of the Creation.

His help was sought by both sexes who desired to obtain the object of their affections, or assistance in the pursuit of their amours. In mythology, the media employed usually consisted of philtres or potions of magical herbs and plants, charms to be worked, or rites to be performed, in order to obtain the desired end.

Many of these employed by the ancient Egyptians, Greeks and Romans have already been described ; but, judging from an examination of the secret books of the magicians of the Middle Ages, the demand for love-charms must have considerably increased, and some of them are of an extraordinary character.

In a Syriac manuscript, written about the eleventh century, there is a story of an Egyptian who fell in love with another man's wife, but whose advances were repulsed by the object of his affections. He thereupon sought a magician, and asked him to make the woman love him and her husband hate her. The wizard transformed her into a mare, but finally she was restored to her former shape by the holy man, Macarius, who took some water and blessed it and threw it over her head.

The love-charms of the Middle Ages sometimes took the form of seals of magical power, letters or words written on parchment, an image of wax, the use of magical herbs, or potions to be swallowed.

In an ancient Hebrew manuscript found at Mossoul, there are a number of curious charms for love, and among them are the following :

" For love when thou wishest that a woman should come after thee, and thou shouldst please her father and mother. Write in starch (?) and saffron and touch whomsoever thou lovest and she will come to thee."

Another method was to " Write and put into the fire, Alp, Sulb, Nin, W'Alkom, Apksa, Bal in the heart of ―― daughter of ―― for love of ―― son of ―― like the love of Sarah in the eyes of Abraham.

" Or thou shalt fashion parchment after the fashion of male and female and on the picture of the female write, Bla Bla Lhb Lhb Lhb Hbl Hbl Hbl, and on the other write Zkr Zkr Zkr Rhz Rhz Rkz Rkz Krz, and then shalt put them together, front and back, and thou shalt put them in the fire."

Another written charm to be cast into the fire runs, " In the name of Whil Ykidta Bliba, I invoke you to put love for ―― son of ―― in the heart of ―― daughter of ―― that he sleeps not neither by day or night, nor shall he speak with any man either in the street or in the house, except with relation to love for ――"

" To bring a disdainful woman, Let him write on one of her garments and make a wick of it and burn it in a pottery lamp, this, Halosin Halosin Alosin Alosin Alosin Sru'in Sru'in that ye come and assemble in the body of ―― daughter of ―― and harass her that she

204

eat not, drink not, or sleep not, until she come near me and do the pleasure of me —— of ——."

A charm for a girl " that is not sought in marriage " is given as follows : " Let him write these Seals and hang them up on the door of her house, and immediately they shall take her in marriage."

The charms for love are varied by one to cause hatred :

" To do this, you must take the egg of a black hen and boil it in urine and give half of it to a dog and half of it to a cat and say, As these hate one another so may hatred fall between —— son of —— and —— son of ——"

Love-charms in the sixteenth century were sometimes written on the person ; thus one directs, that these letters must be written on the left hand of the lover, H.L.D.P.N.A.G.U., " carry them in the morning before sun rising and touch whom thou wilt and she will follow thee." The writer naïvely remarks, "*you may try it upon a dog.*"

Another combination of letters, to be written on the left hand before sunrise, was H.L.N.P.M.Q.U.M. This is for a woman, who is directed to " touch his neck secretly and he shall love thee."

A charm to provoke love was to write "N.A.P.A.R.A.B.O.C.L.P.E.A. in small squares on the right hand with thine own blood, before the sun rising, or after the sun setting, and touch the parties flesh and say, ' Ei signere me et stat in vaniet tibi.' "

A more complicated charm was worked as follows : " Take 3 hairs of his head and a thread spun on a Friday by a virgin, and make a candle therewith of virgin wax four square, and write with the blood of a cock sparrow the name of the woman, and light the candle, whereas it may not drop upon the earth and she shall love thee."

A still more powerful charm was to " take the navel string of a boy, new born, dry and powder it and give him or her to drink.

" *There is none such,*" declares the writer.

The Seal of Venus, another love-charm, was to be " graven on thin copper or brass when the planets were favourable and in good position, Venus being near the moon."

" To get the love of any woman," says a writer of the sixteenth century, " first make it known to her it is her love you desire, and in the day and hour of Venus, give her to drink of the powder of the Seal in the place where she may be, and she shall love thee marvellously."

" The powder of the Seal secretly placed in the garments or about the breast is equally effective."

A curious charm was to " take the tongue of a sparrow and close it in virgin wax under thy clothes for the space of IV days, then take it and keep it in thy mouth under the tongue and kiss the woman thou lovest."

The use of a wax image or figure was apparently common in the sixteenth century in magic and enchantments connected with love.

The charm was worked thus :

" Make an image of her you love in virgin wax, sprinkle it with holy water, and write the name of the woman on the forehead of the image and thy name on her breast.

" Then take four new needles and prick one of them in the back of the image, and the others in the right and left sides. Then say the conjuration. Then make

206

a fire in her name, and write on the ashes of the coals her name, and a little mustard seed and a little salt upon the image, then lay up the coals again, and as they leapeth and swelleth so shall her heart be kindled in thy love."

Sympathetic magic is indicated as the basis of the next charm, which reads : " Take the hairs of the woman whose love thou desirest, and keep them until the Friday following, and that day before sun rising. Then with thine own blood, write thine own name and her name in virgin wax or parchment, and burn the hair and letters together to dust on a red hot fire, and give it to her in meat and drink, and she shall be so much taken with thee that she shall take no rest."

A love-charm of the sixteenth century, which has survived until recent times, is to " take a spider within his web, whole, and see it breaks not and shut it inside 2 shells of a nut. After this, boil it in oil in a silver spoon called cochlearia and give part of the webbe to drink. It makes the party who drinkes to love him so long as the spider be shut up in the nutshell."

Another method used " to gain the love of a woman," was to " take a piece of virgin parchment as broad as your hand, and make on it 2 images, the one of thyself and the other of the woman ; then with the blood of the little finger of thy left hand, write on thine own image thine own name, and on the other her name. Betwixt the image write Sathan, Lucifer, Donskton. You must make it so that when you close the parchment the images may be right over one another. Make thine own image on Friday, the first hour that Venus governs, and the other the Friday following, in the same hour.

This done, put the images under your foote three times a day, and then removing it to the other foot. In the morning, the first hour of the day after 12 o'clock at noon, and at night before it be dark, say the conjuration, beginning Sathan, Lucifer, and Donskton, which are princes which expelled Adam and Eve out of Paradise. I charge you to go to her named, and suffer her not to sleepe, nor to take any reste, nor to drinke nor to stand nor to sit, nor to lie quiet, until she hath accomplished and done my will whatsoever I request her to doe.

" Then you must have 5 pieces of golde, to be sent her in the time you begin your work before it be ended, and she will love you as long as you live."

The association of apples with love enchantments goes back to an early period. The following are five taken from manuscripts of the fifteenth and sixteenth centuries :

" Write on an apple, Guel + Bsatirell + Gliaell +, and give it her to eat."

" Write on an apple, Raguell, Lucifer, Sathanus, and say, I conjure thee apple by these three names written on thee, that whosoever shall eat thee may burn in my love."

" Write on an apple before it fall from the tree, Aleo + Deleo + Delato +, and say, I conjure thee apple by these three names which are written on thee, that what woman or virgin toucheth and tasteth thee, may love me and burn in my love as fire melteth wax."

" Write on an apple your names and these three names, Cosmer + Synady + Heupide, and give it to eat to any man that thou wouldst have and he shall do as thou wilt."

" Cutt an apple in IV parts, and on every part write, Sathiel + Sathiel + Obing + Siagestard, and say, I conjure thee apple by the Holy God, by the IV Evangelists and gospels, and by Samuel and by Mary, that thou shall not stand still until I have the love of the woman which shall eat of thee."

Several herbs and plants were employed in love-

KING SOLOMON'S APPLE, WITH MAGICAL CHARACTERS
(From an MS., XVI century.)

charms and among them verbena or vervain played a prominent part, probably owing to its association with witchcraft.

" To gain the love of man or woman," says a writer of the sixteenth century, " go to the herb Vervain when it is flowered near the full of the moon and say to it the Lord's Prayer. Then say, in the name of the Father, Son and Holy Ghost, I have sought thee + I have found thee + I charge thee Vervain by the Holy names of God, Helion, Heloy, + Adonay, when I carry thee in my mouth, that whosoever I shall love or touch, that thou make them obedient unto me and to do my will in all things. FIAT + FIAT + FIAT + AMEN."

In another, the lover is directed to take more aggressive methods :

" Place Vervain in thy mouth, and kiss any maid saying these words, ' Pax tibi sum sensum conterit in amore me,' and she shall love thee."

Verbena was used to bring quarrels to an end, and was placed in the shoes when travelling so the wearer should not grow weary.

It was also employed as a charm to catch fish and to hive bees.

To become invisible, says the same writer, " Let 4 masses be said over Vervain and bear it about thee. It should be gathered on the Monday night before Holy rood days."

The plant valerian had also a reputation as a charm for love. The lover was enjoined to gather it when the moon is in the south, saying these words, " Misere mei Beatus Vix qui intilligex," and also 3 Paternosters, 3 Aves, and 3 Creeds. " Put it under thy tongue and kiss hers and she will love thee."

Valerian was also sometimes burnt, or reduced to powder, and given to the desired one to drink to provoke love.

Another love-charm was to " goe into a garden where selueyne growes on a Thursday by the rising of the sun, and kneeling on thy knees say thus, ' In nomine patrie, I sought thee, In nomine filii, I have found thee. I conjure thee that thou man or woman love me that I touch with thee,' and so gather it and keep it for thy use."

The plant St John's wort, was reputed to possess magical properties, and among others that of compelling love. A lace or girdle anointed with the oil of the plant and given to a maiden to wear, was said to make her love the giver. A charm in which a nutmeg forms part is directed to be worked as follows : " Take a nutmeg and prick it full of holes and you shall see it wear a dew upon it. Put it in your arm-pit 2 days, then dry it on a tilestone and so it will fall to powder the which put in a woman's portion of potage and drink not of it yourself. She shall love thee without doubt."

A love-charm into which toads enter appears to have had its origin in the Assyrian charm previously mentioned. It begins : " In March when toads do engender, kill two, and put them in a box full of holes and put it in a pissmire bank. When all is consumed but the bones, take them and cast them into running water and you shall see that one of the bones will go against the stream. Another will stand upright and another will sink. These three keep. Put that which swimmeth against the stream in a ring, and she that taketh it at your hands shall love thee. Put that that stood upright in a ring and give it to a woman, and she shall obey thy wish. Grate that to powder that sinketh, and she that drinketh thereof shall hate thee."

In the Egyptian magical texts it is recorded that hair, feathers, snake's skin, and " the blood of the mystic eye " were employed as love-charms and had both protective and destroying powers. The " blood of the mystic eye " is thought to indicate dragon's blood, which for centuries has been believed to be an effective ingredient in charms for provoking love. The Greeks called dragon's blood cinnabaris, and apparently did not know whether it was of mineral or vegetable origin. Coles states, that " Pliny, Solinus and Monardus have set it down for truth, that it was the blood of a dragon or serpent crushed to death by the weight of a dying elephant falling upon him," but he thinks it was certainly so called from " the bloody colour that it is of, being nothing else but a mere gum."

The substance known as dragon's blood is a gum-resin obtained from the *Pterocarpus indicus*, a tree indigenous to the East Indies. In early times it had some repute in medicine for its astringent properties and also as an emmenagogue, but it has gone out of use and is now employed as a colouring agent for varnishes and stains. Three hundred years ago, it is said to have been used by goldsmiths and painters on glass, by the former as a base for enamel and by the latter to strike a crimson for stained windows.

Its use, however, as a magical charm has survived to the present day, and it is still employed as a love-charm in some parts of London and in the North of England. A great deal of mystery surrounds its employment for this purpose, and it is only with difficulty some details have been obtained. There seem to be several methods of working charms of a romantic nature with this otherwise ordinary article of commerce. The most common of these is practised by girls on All Hallowe'en, who are jealous of their lovers and desire to win back their affection. To do this a small quantity of dragon's blood is procured, wrapped in paper, and thrown on the fire whilst the following couplet or incantation is repeated :

"May he no pleasure or profit see
Till he comes back again to me."

Another method employed by women of a certain class, and used by them to attract the opposite sex, is to mix dragon's blood, quicksilver, saltpetre and sulphur and throw them on the fire while repeating a similar incantation.

A chemist in the North of England, giving his experience on the sale of dragon's blood, says : " I have had great difficulty in finding out for what purpose it was used. It was not for medicine, but for a kind of witchcraft. The women burn it upon a bright fire, while wishing for their affection to be returned by someone of the opposite sex ; also those who have quarrelled with their husbands and desire to be friends again ; girls who have fallen out with their young men and want to win them back, as well as young women wanting sweethearts. A working-man recently came to me for a small quantity, and I inquired for what purpose it was required. He was very reluctant to mention anything about it, but at length said a man had made him lose three sovereigns, and he wished as he had been swindled out of the money to have his revenge, and make him suffer for it. He was going to burn the dragon's blood on a clear fire, and he believed that the ill wishes of the person thus burning it would have a dire effect on the individual thought of."

Some love-charms in the sixteenth and seventeenth centuries were worked by writing certain mystic characters on parchment or paper, of which the following may be taken as an example :

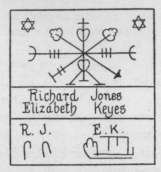

"A CHARACTER FOR LOVE"
(From an MS., XVII century.)

" Write these characters on virgin parchment with the blood of batts and hold it in the left hand and show it to her and without doubt she will come to thee. But take heed that thou showest to none but she who thou desirest for if thou do she will go mad and die."

Another charm of this kind in the form of a magical square was to be written on parchment and carried by the lover.

S	I	C	C	F	E	T
I						
C	E	N	A	L	I	F
O	R	A	M	A	R	O
F						
E						
T						

"FOR A MAIDEN IN PARTICULAR"

CHAPTER XXIII

RECORDS OF MAGIC FROM THE FOURTH TO THE FIFTEENTH CENTURY

THERE are but few manuscripts on magic extant that were written between the first and the fourteenth century, but some light has been thrown on the subject by the translation of certain ancient Hebrew texts in the British Museum, and at Oxford and Munich by Gaster. One of these, called " The Sword of Moses," is believed to date from the first four centuries of the Christian era, and serves as a connecting link between the Greek papyri and the early Middle Ages.

It is especially interesting, as it includes names that are mentioned in manuscripts many centuries later, and deals with magic and medicine. It begins :

" In the name of the Mighty and Holy God." Four angels are appointed to the sword given by the Lord, the Master of Mysteries.

Their names are SKD HUZI, MRGIOIAL, VHDR-ZIOLO, and TOTRISI.

The man who utters conjurations over this " Sword," its mysteries and hidden powers, its glory and might, they will not refuse, as it is the command of God.

" If thou wishest to use this ' Sword ' and to transmit it to the following generations (then know) that the man who decides to use it must free himself three days from accidental pollution and from every thing unclean, eat and drink once every evening, and must eat from a pure man, or wash his hands first in salt, and drink only water. The mysteries are to be practised only in secret."

Then follows a prayer to the " Lord our God, King of the Universe, and a conjuration to Azliel, Arel, Tafel, Yofiel, Mittron and other angels."

After some long and explicit directions in which there are names not transliterated, we come to the " Sword," which consists of a number of mysterious names of God or angels with which are connected various recipes. Only a few of the more interesting need be recapitulated. They are chiefly in the form of charms which are to be written on bowls, or the saucer of a cup, amulets to be hung round the neck, to be written on a plate, or charms to be whispered in the ear, some being accompanied by the use of oils.

Charms for various diseases are numerous, thus, " for hæmorrhoids, take tow and put salt on it and mix it with oil, saying over it a charm and sit on it."

" To heal leprosy, take the patient to the side of a river and say to him, ' I conjure thee leprosy, in the name of —— to disappear and to vanish and to pass away from —— Amen, Amen—Selah,' and he is to go down and dip seven times in the river and when he comes out write an amulet with the words, ' I conjure— Selah,' and hang it round his neck." This is reminiscent of the Assyrian charm given in a previous chapter, and is also similar to the story of Naaman, who to cleanse himself from the disease was told to bathe seven times in the Jordan.

A man who is bald is directed to say a charm over " nut oil " and anoint his head with it. " To remove a rich man from his riches, say a charm upon the dust of an ant-hill and throw it in his face."

"To know if a sick person will live or die, say before him charm ——. If he turns his face towards you he will live. If away, he will die."

"To subdue a woman, write with the blood of thy hand thy name upon thy gate, and write thy name upon a scroll of leather of a hart with the blood of thy finger and say, this 'Sword' and she will come to thee."

To put a spell upon an enemy, say, "I call thee, evil spirit, cruel spirit, merciless spirit. I call thee, bad spirit, who sittest in the cemetery and takest away healing from man. Go and place a knot in —— head, in his eyes, in his mouth, in his tongue, in his throat, in his windpipe; put poisonous water in his belly. If you do not go and put water in his belly I will send against you the evil angels Puziel, Guziel, Psdiel, Prziel. I call thee and those 6 knots that you go quickly to —— and put poisonous water in his belly and kill —— whom I mean. Amen. Amen. Selah."

The manuscript concludes:

"Verily, this is the 'Sword of Moses' with which he accomplished his miracles and mighty deeds and destroyed all kinds of witchcraft.

"It had been revealed to Moses in the bush when the great and glorious name was given to him. Take care of it and it will take care of thee. If thou approachest fire it will not burn thee, and it will preserve thee from every evil in the world.

"If thou wishest to try it, take a thicl (green) branch and utter this word 'Sword' over it five times at sunrise and it will dry up."

There is a good deal of similarity between the Hebrew " Sword " and some of the Greek papyri, in one of which Moses is mentioned as " one who keeps divine mysteries."

Another early Hebrew manuscript has been translated by Gaster called the " Secretum Secretorum," a mediæval treatise ascribed to Aristotle and written for King Alexander.

It begins, " O men of knowledge and who understand riddles, who search by means thereof for precious objects, lift up your eyes on high and read the book that is called the ' Privy of Privies.' Therein is contained the direction in the governance of the kingdom which Aristotle wrote for the great King Alexander."

The book is said to have been discovered in the Temple of the worshippers of the Sun, which the great Hermes built for himself. It was written in gold, and was translated from Greek into Syriac, and from Syriac into Arabic.

It contains thirteen treatises which deal mainly with advice on governance, but the last treats of " natural secrets and talismans, on the good of bodies, on the properties of precious stones and plants and living beings, and wonderful things of the mysteries of leechcraft."

Among the stones mentioned is the bezoar, famous throughout the Middle Ages as a remedy for plague and other diseases. It was a biliary concretion found in the stomachs of small animals, like the deer, and mysterious occult properties were attached to it. "If hung round the neck of a child," says the writer, " it becomes proof against epilepsy and saves from bad accidents."

218

" The pearl called Iakut in Arabia ; there are three kinds : red, yellow, and black. The red prevents illness, gives courage and brings honour. The emerald in a ring appeases stomach ache and dissolved and drunk is good for leprosy. The stone Firzag is highly prized by great kings and its great property is that no man can slay him who wears it. The stone Alkahat saves from hot fevers. Fire has no power over it and cannot burn it. He who goes to war with one, no man can fight against him."

" If thou make a ring of silver and gold with a red jacinth set in it, and engrave on it the image of a naked girl, tall and strong, riding on a lion, and six men worshipping her, and it is made in the morning of Sunday at the hour of the sun, at the conjunction of Leo and Sol and the sun is in it, and the moon is in the tenth degree at the height which is called Shrf in Arabic ; whosoever wears such a ring shall be reverenced by the people. They will listen to his voice and fulfil all his wishes in the world and no man shall be able to withstay him."

"One of the greatest poisons is Bish, but it is not recognizable through taste or colour, for when people taste it, it has no bitterness. And the gold lime (orpiment or yellow sulphide of arsenic) which is called Klas, is also one of these poisons which are indispensable to thee. It is *one of the secret instruments of war* by means of which misfortune in war can be averted."

It should be remembered, that this letter is said to have been addressed to a great military commander and shows that poisons were apparently used in time of war at this early period. It was probably employed for poisoning wells.

There is an interesting manuscript originally written in Hebrew in the Bibliothèque de l'Arsenal, Paris, which has been translated from French into English by Mathers. It is written in red and black inks, and is said to date from the middle of the fifteenth century.

It is entitled " The Book of Sacred Magic of Abramelin the Mage, as delivered by Abraham the Jew unto his son Lamech A.D. 1458."

The story told by Abraham the Jew of how he acquired his secrets, his journey to Egypt, and his meeting with magicians of the time, forms an interesting narrative.

It begins with " The first book of the Holy Magic, which God gave unto Moses, David, Solomon, and other saints, patriarchs and prophets, which teacheth the true divine wisdom."

Abraham the son of Simon says, that he learnt it in part from his father, and in part from other wise and faithful men.

He goes on to state :

" I have written this with mine own hand and placed it in this casket and locked it up as a precious treasure.

" My father Simon shortly before his death, gave me certain signs and instructions concerning the way in which it is necessary to acquire the Holy Kabbala. After his death finding myself twenty years of age, I had a very great passion to understand the true mysteries of the Lord.

" I learnt that at Mayence there was a Rabbi called Moses who was a notable sage, and the report went, that he possessed in full the Divine wisdom. I was induced to go and seek him in order to leatn from him, but I found, that in his magic, he did not make use of his wisdom of the Lord, but instead availed himself of certain arts and superstitions of infidel and idolatrous nations in part derived from Egyptians, together with images of the Medes and of the Persians, with herbs of the Arabians, together with the power of the stars and constellations and even from the Christians, some diabolic art.

" For ten years I remained buried in so great an error, until I arrived in Egypt at the house of an ancient sage called Abra-melin, who put me in the true path and to understand the Sacred Mystery, and how to command and dominate the evil spirits."

Abraham says, that he began his journey to Egypt on February 13th, 1397, and stayed in Constantinople for two years.

During his sojourn with Abra-melin, he received from him two books in manuscript containing the secrets, which he told him to copy for himself with care. He avers he did so exactly and it is these books he records in this text.

He then left Egypt and travelled back to his own country, and on his journey evidently sought out all the practitioners of magic in the cities that he passed through, and thus relates his adventures. At Argentine he found a Christian called James, " but his art was the art of the Juggler or cup-and-balls player, and not that of the magician." In the town of Prague, he states, " I found a wicked man named Antony, who in truth showed me wonderful and supernatural things, but the infamous wretch avowed to me, that he had made a pact with the demon, and had given himself over to him in body and in soul, while the deceitful Leviathan had promised him forty years of life to do his pleasure. Unto this day do they sing in the streets of the terrible end which befel him, for his body was found dragged through the streets and his head without any tongue therein, lying in a drain."

After passing through Hungary, where he " found but persons knowing neither God nor devil and who were worse than the beasts," he came to Greece where he found many wise and prudent men. Among them were three who " principally dwelt in desert places, and who showed me great things. . . . In Epipha near Constantinople, there was a certain man who made use of certain numbers which he wrote upon the earth, and so caused terrifying visions to appear."

At Lintz he met with a young woman who gave him an unguent with which he was to rub the principal pulses of his feet and hands.

He then felt as if he was flying in the air where he seemed to remain a long while, and then recovered his senses and " found the young woman seated by his side." " I concluded," he sagely remarks, " it was a simple dream and that this unguent was the cause of phantastic sleep, whereupon she confessed to me that this unguent had been given to her by the devil."

Of the wonderful things performed by Abra-melin, how he healed 8413 persons bewitched unto death, how he delivered the Duke Frederick Elector of Saxony by means of 2000 artificial cavalry, " which I did by mine own art cause to appear, and other marvels are they not written in this book."

In the second part of the manuscript he describes certain operations which he carried out by means of a child of 6, 7 or 8 years of age whom he used as a clairvoyant, a method not unusual at that time.

" The choice of a child of tender years for this purpose is said to be on account of his innocency and freedom from contamination with outside influences. He is to be clothed in white and upon his forehead is to be placed a veil of white silk, very fine, to cover even the eyes, on which must be written the word Uriel. He who operateth shall do the same thing, but upon a veil of black silk with the name ' Adam ' written thereon. Thou shalt make the child enter into the oratory and place the fire and the perfume in the censer, and then kneel before the altar, as so soon as the child shall have seen the angel, thou shalt command him to tell thee, and to look upon the altar and take the lamen or plate of silver which thou shalt have placed there for that purpose, and whatever the angel shall have written thereon."

Then follows an account of the training and initiation of the magician. " In age he should not be less than 25, nor more than 50."

Among women, only virgins are suitable, but it is strongly advised that no important matter should be communicated to them, because of the accidents that they might cause by their curiosity and love of talk.

" Let each one speak his own language. The magician's bed chamber must be near the oratory and the sheets and all linen changed every Sabbath eve. No dog, cat or other animal shall enter, and eating, drinking and sleeping should be in moderation and never superfluous. Especially shun drunkenness and flee public dinners."

The following instructions are given as regards clothing :

" Flee all vanity. You shall have two dresses and you shall change them on the eve of each Sabbath, brushing and perfuming them always beforehand."

The preparations of the adept are to last six moons, and then the place is selected. " If a dwelling place in a town be used, an apartment should be chosen with a window adjoining an uncovered terrace or balcony on which a covered lodge or hut is to be erected. The floor of the terrace should be covered with river sand to the depth of two fingers at least, and the day after the ceremonies are said, the sand must be cast into a secret place but not thrown into a river or the sea.

" A small wood is, however, to be preferred to a house, in the midst of which the altar should be set and covered with a hut of fine branches. The altar should be of wood and hollow like a cupboard, wherein shall be kept the two robes, the crown or mitre, the wand, the holy oil, the girdle or belt and the perfume."

A description of the robes worn by the magician for full ceremonial is then given. It is to consist of a shirt or tunic of linen, large and white, with sleeves. Another robe will be of crimson or scarlet silk with gold, and should not be longer than just to the knees, with sleeves of similar stuff. The girdle is to be of silk, the same colour as the tunic, and the beautiful crown for the head is to be a woven fillet of silk and gold.

The following formula is given for the preparation of the sacred oil :

" Myrrh (in tears) 1 part, fine cinnamon 2 parts, galingal ½ part, and the half of the total weight of these drugs of the best olive oil." It is to be kept in a glass vial.

The perfume is to be made thus :

" Take of incense (olibanum) in tears 1 part, stacte (storax) ½ part, lign. aloes ¼ part or cedar, rose, citron or any odoriferous wood." Reduce to powder and mix well together. This is to be kept in a box. The magician must also have a wand of almond-tree wood, smooth and straight, of about half an ell to six feet long.

All being thus prepared, the magician so clad, without shoes, enters the oratory and begins the ceremonial with the orison, after which he anoints himself with the sacred oil, and also the vestments and all instruments.

Then he is to put on the white tunic, and proceed, and await the angel to write with the sign on the silver plate on the altar as described, with the child.

These ceremonies are to be performed seven days, and on the period of the sixth moon be put to the test. This begins with the conjurations to evoke the spirits in visible form, and in " a little while they will appear and will swear to their symbols."

Three different kind of demands can be made on three successive days.

" If during the invocation the spirits should appear with tumult and insolence, fear nothing, neither give way to anger.

" Only show them the consecrated wand and if they continue to make a disturbance, smite upon the altar twice or thrice and all will be still."

Abraham records the names of the spirits that may be summoned, which include the four princes and superior spirits, Lucifer, Leviatan, Satan, and Belial, also the sub-princes and servient spirits which number in all over three hundred.

He firmly believed in guardian angels, and advises that one should never take from such any symbol wherewith to operate for an evil end. Should the magician wish to perform his operations in a city, he adjures him to take a house which is not overlooked by anyone, " seeing," he states, " that in this present day (1458) curiosity is so strong, that you ought to be upon your guard."

The magician's fee (for him who shall receive it) was ten golden florins or their value, which he should distribute to the poor.

He further remarks, that the angel will write on the plate of silver as it were in drops of dew, the symbol as you ought to make it, together with the name of the spirit who would serve you.

To use it, " first take the symbol in your hand, place it upon the top of your head under your hat, and either you will be secretly warned by the spirit, or he will execute that which you have the intention of commanding him to do."

This magician was apparently a pioneer in aviation, for he gives a formula, " To fly in the air and travel anywhere," that is to be carried out as follows : " Name the place whither unto you wish to travel and place the symbol upon your head under the bonnet or hat, but take well heed less the symbol fall from you through negligence or want of caution. Do not journey at night

226

time unless necessity or some pressing reason thereto compelleth you, but select the day time and that serene and calm."

In the 3rd book of the Sacred Magic, Abra-melin gives all the symbols by means of which he says he worked his wonders. They cover a wide range and include, " Things to happen in war," " How to know all things past and future," " To cause any spirit to

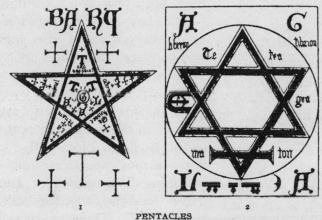

PENTACLES

1. For all secrets of knowledge.   2. For calling the angels.
(From an MS. of the XIV century in the Bodleian Library.)
(See page 228.)

appear," " To heal any disease," " For mirrors of glass or crystal," " To make all metals," " To transform men into asses," and " To cause a dead body to revive and perform all the functions which a living person would do, during a space of seven years, by means of the spirits." With reference to books of magic, Abraham says : " Many ancient books have been lost. By these symbols you can have many supposed extinct works brought to you, but I could never copy them, because

227

the writing disappeared as fast as I wrote them, but I was permitted to read some of them." His magical symbols consist chiefly of squares of letters arranged as a double acrostic, some being irregular in disposition and others void. The user is warned, that unless he is animated by the best and purest motives he will find them react terribly against him.

MAGICAL SEALS FOR IN-
VOKING FIVE SPIRITS
(XV century.)

The key of the operation to enjoy the vision of the angels, was to place the symbols upon the brow of the child and of him who performed the operation.

In a manuscript on magic written in the fourteenth century, in the Bodleian Library, there are two curious pentacles, one for obtaining " all secrets of know-ledge " and the other for " calling the angels." These are probably the earliest of their kind known.

In another fragment on magic in the same library written about 1450, there are three magical seals for invoking five spirits who are called Fategan + Gagagan + Bigan + Deigan + Usagan.

CHAPTER XXIV

THE "CLAVICLE OR KEY OF SOLOMON"—RITES, CERE-MONIES AND MYSTERIES OF CONJURATION

AMONG the existing works on magic, there is probably none better known than the "Clavicle or Key of Solomon," numerous copies of which in manuscript are to be found in various great libraries of Europe. They are written in English, French, German and Italian. The texts vary, and the earliest date from about the sixteenth century. There are seven codices in the British Museum, most of which were written between the sixteenth and seventeenth centuries, and there are several others in the Bibliothèque Nationale and the Bibliothèque de l'Arsenal in Paris, of a later period.

Although Josephus mentions that, Solomon was the author of magical works in which he recorded his secrets that Hezekiah is supposed to have suppressed because they were leading the people astray, there is no real evidence of his connexion with the Clavicle associated with his name. It is more probable that the treatise was compiled by Rabbinical writers about the fourteenth century from ancient records, as there are certain details of the ritual that appear to have come down from an earlier period.

In the introductions to several of the codices, it is

ſtated that they were compiled from an ancient Hebrew text which is now loſt, but there is no record of such a manuscript ever having been in exiſtence. On account of the early traditions it embodies, and the detail of the rites and ceremonies of magic, it is undoubtedly intereſting, as the following epitome taken from a copy of the work written by " H. G. on April 8, 1572," now in the British Museum,[1] will show.

It is entitled, " The worke of Salomon the Wise, called his Clavicle revealed by King Ptolomeus ye Grecian."

It consiſts of ten parts which are headed as follows :

1. Of ye hours and points necessary in experiments and arts mathematical and magical.

2. Of all arts magical or of nigromancy or of certain spirits how they shall be ordered.

3. How and what manner the pentacles be made.

4. How experiments of these should be ordered.

5. Of experiments of invisibility.

6. Of experiments of love.

7. Of experiments of grace and favour.

8. Of experiments of hatred and deſtruction.

9. Of experiments of mockes and direction.

10. Of experiments extraordinary that be forbidden of good men.

" The beginning of our Clavicle is to fear God and to honour him with contrition of heart with great devotion and to worship him.

" To practise the right day, and time, is very essential if you will find anything of the sciences. You muſt have a sure order of days, the changing of the moon and of

[1] MS. Sl. 3847.

MAGIC CIRCLE WITH A MAGICIAN EVOKING SPIRITS

From a MS. XVI century.   British Museum.

hours.   Next the position of the planets muſt be considered and all this muſt be prepared.

" Then take the sword that you make the circle, and make a cross in the air, and put your right hand with the sword upon the pentacles being on your breaſt, and say with a low voice the oration with the exorsyzation, but before so doing, fumigate yourself and your fellows in the circle and sprinkle yourself with water.

" Let the conjurer sit down in his place and comfort his fellows in the circle and say the oration and conjuration, then the devils will fear and by the virtue of the pentacles will come to do your will."

The pentacles have innumerable virtues, and for a description of how they were made see page 163.

The ceremony began with prayers which were said in Latin, firſt kneeling and then uprising.   They were followed by the conjuration, which was first said facing the Eaſt, and South, and then in the North and Weſt, and the spirit which you wished to call was then named. " If the spirits do not then appear, looking up into the air, making upon your forehead the sign of ye Holy Cross saying, ' In nomine patris et filii et spiritus Sanĉti. Amen.'   Then bless the place with the sign of the cross, beating the air with your hand, make a hissinge and repeat the prayer toward the Weſt and the North. Then if they (the spirits) be bound in chains of iron they will come, except they be in some greevous place or holden, or else they will send some certain messenger whereby you shall know what they will do.   If they do not appear, let the conjurer rise up boldly and ſtrongly and comfort his fellows, and let him beat the air toward the four parts of ye world and ſtanding in the middle of the circle go up on his knees, and his fellows with him kneeling and holding the book let him say the prayer. Then if they will appear, show them the pentacle and they will talk with thee and grant thy petition."

Of experiments of love :

" Whoever will make or prepare anything upon any woman, he may make an image of wax. Then say over the wax when it is prepared, the charms, ' Venus est Astroposuastro." When that is done you shall form your image and if it be necessary to write any other thing up on the image with a needle or a pen and if it be necessary to fumigate the image, let a fume be made and hold the image over it and say, ' O tu Orions, etc.'

" If ye woman come in that hour it is well, if she come not, then put that image under thy bed's head and ye shall see before the third day great marvels.

" The same can be done with an apple. Prepare that day and hour and have an apple fair in thy hand in some secret place, and before you take it from the tree sprinkle it with water, and fumigate it, afterwards say unto the fruit, ' Deus qui fecisti Adam et Eve, etc.' "

Then follow directions how the conjurer should prepare himself :

" He shall go into his secret chamber and strip himself, and have a bath prepared, and let him take the water and put it on the top of his head so that it may run down unto his feet, saying, ' Domine Jesu.' Afterwards wash wholly in that water and put on linen gear next your body, and abstain for three days from all uncleanness and say the oration. The novice must abstain from great eating and drinking for the space of nine days before his inception."

The following is a description of the vestments or garments to be worn by the magician :

" Upon the white vestments, woollen garments on which the pentacles be sown with a needle.

" Let them have white hosen, and upon those hosen written the following signs :

" Let your shoes be of white leather, whereon write the same signs, and the hose and shoes must be made within the time of custody within nine days.

" The Master should have a crown of virgin paper on the which crown let there be four names written : AGLA. AGLAY. AGLATHA. AHLAOTH. with ink or some other colour in capital letters and these characters :

" After that, fumigate all the garments and sprinkle with water.

" All the vestments must be linen and if these were priest's garments they were better.

" The places where the arts mayst be done.

" The places must be hid and secret or desert, far from the habitations of men. *Let no woman come there in any case.*

" Let the first scholar bear the censer and incense, making fragrant savours. Let the second bear paper and books, pen and inks and spices of fumigation.

The third bear the knife. The fourth bear the pots, wherein they put fire of the coles in which the fumigation of the spice must be put.

"Then the master shall take the knife or the instrument wherein he maketh the circle best. Let him make the circle as he should fumigate it, and cross it with water before he begin any invocation. The Master shall have a bell, and toll four times towards the four parts of the world, with four paternosters. On that bell should be written 'A' 'V' 'O' 'B' 'Y' and these characters:

"Of knives and swords.

"It is necessary in operations of artes to have swords and knives and other instruments of which circles may be made and other necessary operations. The knife should have a white haft of ivory, tempered in the blood of a goose and the juice of pimpernell, and let it be made on a certain day and hour. Write on the haft with a pen:

and fumigate it and sprinkle it with water and say the conjuration and put him in a silk cloth.

234

"If there be staves or roddes they ought to be virginal and treated likewise.

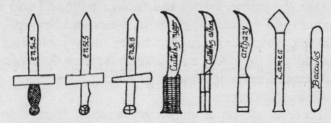

CHARACTERS FOR STAVES AND RODS

"If swords be necessary let them be scoured and clean, and clean from the first hour. Let them be fumigated and put in a fair place in silk cloth.

"The form and fashion of them is :

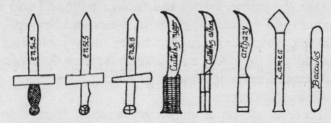

"Let them be of virgin iron and never occupied in any work."

How the circles are to be made :

"When you be in the place, take the knife in your hand and fasten him in the earth in the middle of the place where ye would make your circle. Then take a cord of length of 9 feet, both parts from the East, from the west, from the south and ye north and put a sign and in this sign make a circle, and beyond the circle of the art make another circle a foot wide, always leaving one gate before another, and beyond the circle of art make pentacles with the names of our Saviour, and about the circle that is beyond, make crosses and beyond that circle make a square. In the summit of every

235

corner let a little roundle be made wherein the pot of coles and spices shall be put, and let one sword be fastened in the ground a foot behind.   Let the Master of the art then take his followers and bring them through the outer into the inner circle.   Let them follow towards the east.   Let each one of them have a clean sword in his hand by the pommel.   Let the Master then go out of the circle and kindle the pots and put in the spice of fumigations.   Let him have a grosse candle in his hand and let him light it and put it in a lanthorn.   Then let him reform the circle again and close the outer ring, and take the bell as before and fumigate himself and his followers and sprinkle them with water and hyssop.

" After that, let the Master begin to say, standing in the middle of the circle with a knife fastened at his foot, and there toll the bell toward the east.

" Of Fumigations.

" There be divers fumigations in artes, some odoriferous, some stinkinge.   If it be odoriferous take incense, Lign, Aloes, Saffron, Mirre, and Muske, and say over it, 'Deus Abraham, Deus Issaak, Deus Jacob.'

" After that, sprinkle them with Holy Water and put it in a new silk cloth until the work with it be done, when you will put it in the fire of new coles and in new pots, vitreous both within and without, and say over it ye conjuration of ye fire.   That being done put the pot on ye fire and you will make sweet smelling savour.

" If it needeth a stinckinge fumigation, as brimstone, hazar, eazay and other foul spices, say over it, ' Adonay-dalmay salmay saday' invocation, sprinkle it with water and put it in a pipe, and put that in new cloth of silk and there let it be until ye work.

236

" Then make a dassell of vervain, fennel, valerian, sage, mint, marjoram, basil and bind all these herbs in a rod of hazel that must be cut off at one cut with Arthana (the knife), and cause to be sung over it St John's gospel, then write upon the rod of hazel with a needle point of iron."

The magician's pen, ink and colours :
" When ye should write any scripture necessary for artes, take a live gander and plucke off a feather of the right winge, and say in the taking of, Arbog, Narbog, Nazay, Tamaray.

" Afterwards mark the pen with Arthana and fumigate and sprinkle with water, put him in a silk cloth and write on it with a needle ' Joth, Heth IIe, Van, Anosbias, Ja, Ja, Ja Antroneton, Sabaoth.' If you will, write with saffron or azure. You may write with the blood of a Becke or Dormouse taken alive and pricked with a needle.

" Ye penne for writing with the blood must be of ye right feathers of a swallow, the first feather that is strongest."

" Of virgin paper (skin) :
" Take the paper unborn of any beast."

" Virgin wax or earth for making images or candles :
" Take virgin wax of bees that never made fruit.

237

Virgin earth is that under the earth near the water like clay."

" Sacrifices :

" Some sacrifice black beasts or white, some black birds or white, some of the blood of them, some sacrifice meat and drink, but such must be pure and virginall. The sacrifice of meats and drink must be made on a table without the circle, ready with a tablecloth, with bread, wine and water and cock's meat roasted. They must be fumigated and sprinkled with Holy Water."

" Of the silk cloth :

" If any thing be consecrated by any occasion it must be put in a silk cloth or white linen. Write on it :

These briefly were the ritual, prayers and implements employed by the practitioner of magic of the sixteenth century, according to the " Clavicle of Solomon."

It is a curious blending of magic and religion, and it can well be believed that many of those who practised it were men who, if they did not deceive themselves, succeeded in duping others. To some of the codices several formulæ and experiments are added. Thus in a manuscript in the Lansdowne collection there is a formula, " How to make the Magic Garters," which would undoubtedly be desirable articles at the present day.

They were to be made by taking " the skin of a stag sufficient to make two hollow tubular garters, and before sticking them up, mark them with certain characters with the blood of a hare killed on the 25th of June, and having filled the garters with green mugwort gathered on the same day before sunrise, thou shalt put in the two ends of each the eye of a barbel.

" Before using get up before sunrise and wash them in a brook and place one on each leg above the knee. Then take a short rod of holm-oak cut on the 25th of June, turn in the direction thou wishest to go, write upon the ground the name of the place, and commence the journey and thou wilt accomplish it in a few days without fatigue.

"When thou wishest to stop, thou hast only to say ' Amech ' and beat the ground with the wand, and incontinently thou shalt be on firm ground."

The Magic Carpet of Arabian Nights fame is also mentioned in this manuscript, and is recommended " to transport one to any appointed spot for discovering treasure." It had to be woven of white and new wool.

Further instruments mentioned include a short lance, a scimitar, a sickle, a dagger and poniard, a knife called Andamco, with a curved blade, staves of elderwood, cane, or rosewood, wands of hazel or nut tree and the Burin or graver.

There is also a formula for making the " cleansing hyssop water " by filling a vessel of brass or lead with clear spring water and adding salt.

" A bunch of vervain, fennell, lavender, sage, valerian, mint, garden basil, rosemary and hyssop gathered in the day and hour of Mercury, bound together with a thread, spun by a young maiden, when dipped in water and sprinkled, will chase away all phantoms that shall hinder or annoy."

There are several manuscripts of the seventeenth

century called " Lemegeton or the Lesser Key of Solomon " which are also said to have been translated from the Hebrew, and which deal with all kinds of spirits, both good and evil.   One includes the rites of Lucifer, Bel and other bad spirits, and conjurations of 72 chief devils and their ministers, and the latter part called the " Pauline Art " deals with the " angels of the Hours " of the day and night, and other " choirs of spirits."

The use of the name of Jesus and Mary in some of the prayers of the ritual show that they were introduced in Christian times.

It has been asserted that the inclusion of the Divine names of the Almighty in the ceremonial of the magician, was in the hope of securing power and virtue from heaven, to control the evil spirits, their utterance being supposed to make the devils tremble and place them at the will of the magician.

CHAPTER XXV

"THE NINE TOMES OF MAGIC"—"THE BOOKE OF HIDDEN
PHILOSOPHY"—"THE BOOKE OF THE SEVEN IMAGES"

THERE is an interesting manuscript, written in
the early part of the seventeenth century, by an
unknown author, who makes an attempt to classify
magic into what he calls "Nine Tomes," which he
divides as follows:

"The first is called Hagoge or a book of the in-
stitutions of Magic.

"The second is microcosmicall Magic, that is, what
is effected by spiritual wisdom and how.

"The third is Olympicall Magic. How a man worketh
and suffers by Olympicall spirits.

"Fourth, Hesiode's and Homer's Magic which
teacheth works by the spirits called Casodivills as if
they were not enemies to mankind.

"Fifth, Romane or Sibbiline Magic, which worketh
with defending spirits. This is the doctrine of the
Druids.

"Sixth, Pythagoras, his Magic, which only works
with spirits to whom the doctrine of Arts is given, as
natural philosophy. The art of physick, mathematics,
alchemy and the like arts.

"Seventh, the Magic of Apollonius and the like,
joining with Romane which hath power over the spirits
which are enemies to mankind.

" Eighth, the Magic of Hermes which is the Egyptian Magick, and is not far from Divine Magick. This produceth gods of every kinde which dwell in the Temples.

" Nineth, Wisdom which dependeth on the word of God alone, and is called propheticall magick or wisdom."

The writer declares, that " man is ordained a magician from the wombe of his mother that would be a true magician. Others that have taken upon them this office are unhappy."

He goes on to reveal the " Seven chief secrets of Magic," which he states are : " 1. The curing of all diseases in seven days, either by characters or natural things, or by the superior spirits with the help of God. 2. To know how to be able to produce life at pleasure unto what age soever, to wit a corporal life and natural. 3. To know how to have obedience of the creatures in the elements which are in form of personal spirits. Also in form of pigmies, of satirs, of the nymphs, of the driads. 4. To confer with the intelligence of all things visible and invisible. 5. To know how to govern oneself until the end perfixed by God. 6. To know God and Christ and His Holy Spirit. This is the perfection of our microcosm. 7. To be regenerated that he may be king of Henoch the inferior of the world."

This apparently epitomizes the dreams of the philosopher who was a believer in magic.

The " Seal of the Secrets " is to be made thus :

" Make a circle. Place A. in the centre. B.C. in the East. G.B. in the North. D.E. in the West. E.B. in the South. Divide each quarter into seven parts which maketh 28 parts. Then divide again every part by four being 112 parts in all, and so many true secrets there are to be revealed. This circle so divided is the SEALE OF THE SECRETS of all the world."

"The study of all wisdom is in the East. The West is for force and strength. The South for culture and husbandry. The North for a rugged and hard life.

"Magic is twofold. In the first division thereof, the one sort is of God which he giveth to the creatures of Light. The other is like unto it but it is the gift of the creatures of Darkness. And this magic is twofold, the one tending to a good end, as when the Prince of Darkness endeavours to do well to the creature (God helping forward). The other a bad end, as when God permitted such to be deceived magically unto the punishing of the bad and unto their hurt."

The writer believed in the use of the crystal for communicating with spirits, and next describes how " To call the good angells into a cristall stone or looking glasse in thine own sight. Doe as follows :

" First bless thyself in the name of the Father + Son + Holy Ghost. Then repeat a prayer to be followed by the invocation. ' O you good Angells of God, only and only, come hastyly and tarry not, make your personal appearance visible to my sight in this Cristall Stone.' This is to be repeated three times. Then when they have appeared make your demands.

" Thou mayst call them through a little child, thus :

" After the prayer, make a cross on the forehead of the child with the thumb of the right hand, saying a Pater-noster. Then with a new pen write in the midst of the

243

ſtone or glass with oylle ollive this name, Hermes. Then set the child between thy legs, thou sitting in a chair, and lett him say the Lord's Prayer.

" Then pray, ' Send unto us three of thy goode angells from thy right hand of glory into the midſt of this Criſtall Stone or Glasse. To the visible sight of this child, maide and virgin.

" Let them make true answers, true judgement and true appearance, revealing unto us all things." REPEAT THE PRAYER THREE TIMES.

" Then shall three bright angells with crowns of gold on their heads appear to the child, who will answer and show thee by the child anything thou shall require. The angells being once appeared, will not depart the glasse or ſtone untill the Sunne be sett except you license them."

The following is the license to be said " For Spirits to depart " : " In his name that you came goe againe. The Father with me, the Sonne with me and the Holy Ghoſt betwixt us and be for ever. Amen."

The writer then gives a number of curious formulæ and conjurations for various operations, the firſt being, " How to know if a sick person shall recover or die, and if medicine is to be adminiſtered."

To ascertain this, " the angels are besought, naming the person, town, parish, and ſtreet in which he lives and his trade or profession, thus : Name —— is dangerously ill, he complains of extreme pain in his side, his back, his belly, or he was taken lame in his leggs. ' Tell us O angells of God whether this man will live or dye.' If they say he shall recover, ask whether you shall do it, or whether it must be done by physick or not. If they

244

say for physick, first ask of what disease and what disease they think it is ?

" Then ask, whether such a medicine wilt recover him or not ? "

Should the magician be called upon to remove a spell cast upon a person by a witch, he is directed to begin with the following conjuration :

" Say ' You angels of God, there is a man or woman called —— in the county of —— upon such a day was suddenly taken in such a manner. Tell us ye angels of God what was the cause of this sickness or infirmity. Was it witchcraft ? or no ? ' If they say witchcraft, you shall say, ' I charge you to call us the witch or witches with their assistants which doth molest or trouble— call them I say in this glasse.'

" They having appeared say :

" ' O thou cursed and damned witch, and thou spirit of witchcraft and sorcery, assistant to this hellish and cursed creature which doth hale, pull, terrific and torment the body or carcase of —— of —— in the county of —— open your ears and hear, and be obedient and do my will faithfully and instantly. I do bind and charge you and command you upon paine and perill of your present and everlasting damnation, that you, neither any other wicked witch, spirit or fairie do at any time hereafter to the end of the world, meddle or make any more, but you let be this christian man in peace and quiet.' "

The operation given for discovering a thief is reminiscent of the charm still practised in some parts of the country on All Hallow-e'en. The conjurer is directed to write the names of all the suspected on paper generally, and put every name written in a piece of clay and put

them into a basin of fair water. " Then say a Pater-
noster and a conjuration. The name of the man or
woman which have stolen these things may rise up out
of the water. Then say Psalm 58, Psalm 43 and Psalm
77 concluding each with ' Glory be to the Father.' "

That the writer of this manuscript had been or was a
priest, is evident from the portions of Christian liturgy
introduced into the conjurations, and from his description
of the vestments to be worn by the operator. He states :
" Let it be a priest's garment, if not of cleane linnen.
On it have a pentacle made on the day and hour of
Mercury, the Moon increasing, made on parchment of
a kidd's skin, but first say a mass and sprinkle it with
baptism water."

The following prayer is to be said when the vesture
is put on :

" Alncor, Almacor, Amides, Theodomas, Almitor. O
Lord by the merits of the Holy Angells I will put on the
vestments of Health. That this which I desire I may
bring to effect through thee, O most holy Adonay,
whose kingdom endureth through all ages for ever.
Amen.

" All the prayers, conjurations and exorcisms having
been rightly performed there will appear infinite visions
and phantasmes playing on organs and all kinds of
musical instruments.

" After these things thou shalt see infinite bowmen,
with infinite number of horrible beasts, which seem as
if they would devour our fellows, but notwithstanding,
fear nothing. The priest or the Master holding his hand
on the pentacle adjures them to depart.

" These things being finished, there will be a hissing

noise in the four corners and thou shalt see immediately

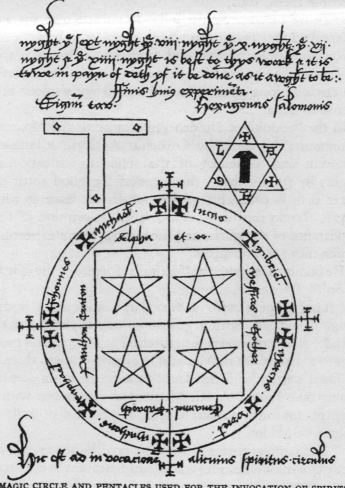

MAGIC CIRCLE AND PENTACLES USED FOR THE INVOCATION OF SPIRITS
(From an MS., XVI century, in British Museum.)

great motions. Then immediately they will come in their proper forms and thou shalt see them nigh the circle. Show them the pentacle and uncover it, then welcome them, thus,

" 'Ye are welcome Spirits and moﬅ noble Kings, for we have called you by him to whom every knee boweth of things in Heaven, Earth and Hell, for as much as we bind you that you remain affable and visible here before the circle as long as my pleasure is, and not without my license to depart.' "

In the " Booke of Hidden Philosophy or the Magical Ceremonies," written by Cornelius Agrippa, a famous magician and alchemiﬅ of the sixteenth century, he begins by ﬅating that " the name of the good spirit of every man is called his genius, which we have to find out." To do this he gives a detailed description of the appearance of the spirits and the various planets through which they are influenced.

He commences with the " Familiar formes of the spirits of Sol."

" They appear with a very large and great body, sanguin and fatt, with a golden colour about the dyed cloud. Their motion is the glittering of Heaven and their sign is to trouble or move sweat in him that calleth them."

Their particular forms are, " A king having a sceptre riding on a Lion. A King wounded. A queen with a sceptre. A bird, a lion, a cock, a garment of saffron colour or golden.

" The familiar forms for the spirits of Venus are a faire body of a middle feature, amiable and pleasant in countenance, of white or green colour, gilt from above. Their motion is like to a clear ﬅar.

" For their signe, maides will be seen playing without the circle.

248

" Their particular formes are, a maide fairly apparelled, a naked maid, a shee goat, a camel, a shee doe or a white or green garment.

" The invocation of the holy and Divine names," says Agrippa, " with the signing of the holy seals, which tend unto sanctification to God, these, added to a religious life, are necessary to the magician. Therefor thou shalt take out that prayer of Solomon in the dedication of the Temple, as thou art about to consecrate any place or circle.

" Thou shalt bless the place with blessed waters and fumigation, remembering in blessing the mysteries what they are, the sanctification of the throne of God, the mountain of Sinai, the ark of the covenant and the Holy of Holies.

" In consecrating the sword we remember that of the gospell. He which hath two coats in the II book of Machabees."

Agrippa's directions for " the setting out of the Place for the performance of magical ceremonies," are as follows :

" The first is that a clean place be chosen, fast shut, quiet and remote from noise. In this place sett a table or altar covered with a clean white linen cloth placed towards the East, and upon it put the two consecrated wax candles set burning. In the middle of the Altar sett the plates of metal or holy paper covered with fine linnen. Also thou shalt have the precious fumigation provided and ready, and the pure oyle of anoynting, both being consecrated. Also the censer being placed at the head of the altar, which being kindled and the fire blessed thou shalt perfume every day as long as thou prayest.

" Thou shalt have a long garment of white linnen, shut before and behind, which may cover the whole body and shall bind it with a like girdle."

He gives us a striking picture of the magician thus robed, standing with a " headpiece like a mitre made of fine linnen on his head," on which a plate of metal was fastened, being gold or gilded with the inscription, Tetragrammaton. " Then they must go in barefooted and when they are entered into the Holy Place, sprinkle it with Holy Water, then thou shalt perfume upon the altar, afterwards on bended knees thou shalt worship before the altar. At the sunrising thou mayest enter the Holy Place, after the rite sprinkle thyself, then perfuming thou shalt sign thyself on the forehead with Holy Oil, anoynt the eyes, doing all these consecrated things with some prayer."

1. MAGICIAN'S PENTACLE OF GREAT POWER FOR INVOKING SPIRITS.
2. MAGICIAN'S KNIFE.
(From an MS., XVI century.)

The discovery of hidden treasure appears to have been a frequent question brought to the magician to solve, and certain spirits were invoked for this purpose. Among them was one called Beasphaves, who was said to appear in the likeness of " a faire man or faire woman who will come at all times." "He will tell thee," says Agrippa, "of hidden treasures. He will bring thee gold or silver. He will transport thee from one country to another without any harm of body or soule."

To conjure this desirable spirit the ceremonies lasted three days, and on the third day, "when it is dark and when the starres shine he will appear." The magician must, however, prepare himself by first "bathing in a clear well-spring and be clothed in clean white clothes, and bear with him ink and penne, and in a secret place write + Agla + and he must have a thong of lion's or hart's skin, and make thereof a girdle and write the holy names of God all about, and in the ends certain signs."

The secret of certain images or figures made to represent each day of the week, and used for special magical purposes, are revealed in a manuscript called "The Booke of the Seven Images of the dayes, that Philosophers that were blessed knew and understood whereby to have their desires. But these should not be showed nor taught but to good men and secret, therefor take heed. BEWARE AND PRONE."

For Sunday, the image was made of gold 1 part, copper and yellow wax. When finished it was inscribed with the sign of the angels. It must be made when the moon was increasing in August or April. For Mondays, the image was composed of silver and white wax. For Tuesdays, of red brass (copper) and red wax. For Wednesdays, of lead. For Thursdays, of brass, the colour of saffron and yellow wax. For Fridays, of white wax; and for Saturdays, of clean pitch.

These images were employed in conjurations, or as charms for love and also to breed discord between man and wife. For the last purpose the name of the man was engraved on the heart of the image, also the name of the woman, and it was then hung before the stars and smote with a twig of olive tree while the conjuration was said. It was then burnt before the gate of the house where they passed by each day.

This book also contains an account of " the Roman Secret, touching the spirit called Sathan by which the Romans did understand of things present, past and to come." This invocation is interesting as it appears to have come down to the sixteenth century from Roman times, although it is obvious that it has been adapted to Christian ideas. The operation is thus described :

" The spirit of this invocation doth appear in a basin, and to be wrought every day except the Lord's Day and the double feast days.

" First beware that thou be not defiled with luxury nor wrapped in any deadly sin, and be thou fasting and have a fair chamber, and take with thee a fair and bright well-furnished basin and have there IV wax candles, and make them fast on the brim of the basin and upon every candle write these names, Moses + Aaron + Jacob + Vsion + Tetragrammaton + Moriaton +. Then take the sword and write opposite these words, Jesus Nazarus Rex in deorum + Jesus of Nazareth, King of the Jews, have mercy upon us, and make the circle with the sword and sitting in the midst of the circle, turning thee first towards the South putting the basin out of the circle once against thee, and perfuming the basin with mastik and lig. aloes, say the gospel and 4 conjurations. Then put out the candles after the fourth conjuration and fumigate the basin as before. Then say, ' I conjure thee to appear to me in the form or figure of a monk in white without any hurt or without any fear or astonishment to me and that thou shall tell me the whole truth I shall demand. By the virtue of all these and by the virtue of all the names of God. FIAT + FIAT + FIAT. Amen.'

" Then the spirit will appear to thee and let him declare the truth of everything thou shalt enquire of him."

The manuscript concludes with some charms, such as the following :

" If any be in danger of witchcraft let them carry about them stitch-wort or pimpernel."

" To goe invisible. Sow beans. Take a bean and put it into the heart of a black cat being reddy roasted, then bury it in a dunghill and when they be ripe carry one about, and thou shalt be invisible. Or take a piece of lead and write thereon, Athatos, Stivos, Thern Pantocraton and put it under thy left foot."

" To have conferance with a fayre, you must stroll underneath an elder tree when the sun is at the highest, and stand near the tree and say Magram, Magrano, three times, and you shall see a flower spring like yellow gold, and when you have it you shall want nothing. There will also appear a faire woman. Demand of her what thou wilt have and thou shalt have it."

A curious recipe for making a very deadly poison shows the knowledge possessed by the practitioner of magic, of mineral as well as animal toxic substances in the sixteenth century. It is as follows :

" Take ye venom of a toad 2 ozs.

" Arsenicke 1 oz. 1 drachm.

" Teeth of a lizard or as many as you can get.

" Ye shavings of Mule's hoof 3 drachms that has been beaten to death.

" Put these in a crucible, calcine them, then project upon copper. "

The use that was to be made of this compound is not mentioned, but it is evident, from the quantity of arsenic it contained, that a very minute quantity would cause death.

Another method of discovering hidden treasure is described in a manuscript of the fourteenth century. This experiment is to " disclose if there be any treasure hid in any place where it is thought to be or not." " Take several hazel rods of one year growing and write on them this name ELOY, and put them in the place where the treasure is thought to be late in the evening, and take them away in the morning. Then take that rod which be broken or otherwise than it was before, and under that rod in the ground where it stood is the treasure or else near that place."

A useful charm which was no doubt frequently employed was :

" To make money spent to return."

To do this, " make a purse of mole's skin and write in it Belzebub, Zetus Caiphas, with the blood of a batt and lay a good penny in the high way for the space of three days and three nights and after put in the purse and when you will give it say, Vade et Vine."

The following rules as to " what a magician must know " are given in a manuscript of the sixteenth century. They are stated to have been laid down by Cyprian, Bishop of Antioch, who, according to tradition, was a practitioner of magic.

254

" 1. The Master must have faith and doubt not in his work.

" 2. He must be secret and betray not the secrets of his art but to his fellows and to them of his counsel.

" 3. He must be strong minded, severe and not fearful.

" 4. He must be clean in conscience, penetent for his

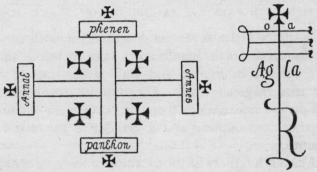

A very powerful charm to be worn as a protection against devils and all their work. To be written in ink on virgin parchment. XV century.

He that beareth this sign about him shall be holy in every need and necessity. XV century.

sins, never willing to return to them again so far forth as God shall give him grace.

" 5. He must know the reigning of the planets and the times meet to work.

" 6. He must lack none of his instruments, and must speak all things plainly and distinctly. He must make his circle in a clean air and due time.

" Whoso observes these rules, by God's grace shall not miss but obtain his purpose."

CHAPTER XXVI

THE GRIMOIRES OR HANDBOOKS OF BLACK MAGIC

DURING the seventeenth and eighteenth centuries, several small handbooks were printed and circulated in France and Italy professing to record the true magical ritual. They consist mainly of a collection of nonsensical formulæ, and were written for popular consumption and to pander to the tastes of the curious.

Although largely fictitious, some of them bear evidence of having been founded on portions of earlier works, thus the " Grimorium Verum " or book of Black Magic, printed in French, is a quaint mixture of " The Clavicle of Solomon " and some fantastic jargon written about the middle of the eighteenth century.

According to the title page, its author was " Alibeck the Egyptian," and it was printed in " Memphis in 1517 " ! Another little book of the same character is entitled " True Black Magic," while the " Grand Grimoire " which is inscribed, " printed from an MS. in 1522, signed Antinio Venitiana del Rabbina," appears to be of Italian origin.

All these little treatises are badly printed on poor paper and evidently written by men who had but little knowledge of the subject.

The " Book of True Black Magic " observes, that the

bath is most necessary to magical art. It must be taken on the final day of the fast, and the magician must bathe himself from the crown of his head to the soles of his feet with warm exorcized water, a measure probably very necessary at the time.

With reference to vestments, Peter de Abano is quoted and recommends a priest's garment or alb, but, according to the Jewish rites, all the robes were to be of linen cloth, the thread of which must be spun by a young maid. Shoes and hat were to be of white leather, with the magical characters written thereon in cinnabar mixed with gum water, and with the pen of the art.

According to these treatises, the material of which the magic wand was composed varied. One states that the staff should be of cane, and the wand of hazel, both virgin, while another declares the wands should be of wood from trees that have never borne fruit, the first being cut from an elder tree and the second from a hazel. It should be 19½ inches long, and on the ends two pointed steel caps should be placed, made from the steel blade of the sacrificial knife, and the steel ends when fixed must be magnetized with a loadstone. This wand is described as a " Most priceless Treasure of the Light."

For the sacrifice, the victim should be a kid, dog, cat or hen or whatsoever was necessary to invoke the devil.

The signature to a pact must be written with the blood of the operator, but the ink for writing should be prepared as follows :

" Take gall nuts 10 ozs., Green copperas 3 ozs., Rock Alum or Gum Arabic 3 ozs. Reduce to fine powder and place in a new glazed earthen pot with river water. Then take sprigs of fern, gathered on St John's Eve, and vine twigs cut in the full moon of March. Then make a fire of virgin paper, and when the water boils the ink will be made."

The silken cloth to preserve the instruments clean and pure could be of any colour, except brown or black, the characters to be inscribed upon it being written "with pigeon's blood and a male goose quill."

The forms in which the infernal spirits were said to appear is fully described and somewhat amusing.

" Lucifer manifests himself in the shape of a comely boy. When angered he has a ruddy countenance, but there is nothing monstrous in his appearance."

Beelzebub occasionally appears in repulsive shapes, such as " a misshapen calf, or a goat with a long tail or a gigantic fly. He howls like a wolf."

" Astaroth is sometimes of black and white colour, usually as a human figure and occasionally in the likeness of an Ass ! His breath is foul, and the magician must defend his face with his ring."

" Belial appears in the shape of a beautiful angel, seated in a chariot of fire, and speaks in a pleasant voice."

" Beleth, a terrible and mighty king, appears riding on a pale horse preceded by all manner of musicians. He is very furious when first summoned, a silver ring must be worn on the middle finger of the left hand, which must be held against the face."

The "Grand Grimoire" says that the magician, or Karcist as he is sometimes called, must purchase a bloodstone, which he must carry on him as a protection from accident and the machinations of the spirits. Then he must buy a virgin kid which must be decapitated on the third day of the moon. Before the sacrifice, a garland of

POWERS OF EVIL
OPHIS AND SPIRIT OF ANTICHRIST
From Barrett's 'Magus.'

vervain must be placed round its neck below the head and tied with a green ribbon. The sacrifice must be offered on the place of evocation, a desolate spot free from interruption.

With the right arm bare to the shoulder, and with a blade of fine steel, and having made a fire of wood, the operator makes his offering, burning the body of the animal, but preserving the skin to form the round or grand Kabbalistic circle in which he must stand later.

On the great night, he must take his rod, goatskin, the bloodstone (ematille), two crowns of vervain, two candlesticks, two candles of virgin wax made by a virgin girl and daily blessed.

He must also take a new steel and two flints and sufficient tinder to kindle a fire, also half a bottle of brandy (*this is to feed the flames*), some blessed incense and camphor, and four nails from the coffin of a dead child. Then the grand Kabbalistic circle is to be drawn and the evocation begun.

In the " Grimoire of Honorius," which exists in manuscript, there is a further description of certain rites said to be connected with the practice of the Black Arts ; they are mostly too absurd for repetition, but they are interesting as showing the tendency at this period to form a perverted ritual similar to those used in the descriptions of the " Black Mass."

" The slaughter of a black cock, and the extraction of the eyes and tongue and heart," are part of one ceremony. The Holy Elements are introduced and a " Mass of Angels " is to be said, writing is to be made with consecrated sacramental wine as the " Blood of Christ."

As an instance of the ridiculous character of the conjurations, the following may be taken as an example:

" How to cause the appearance of three ladies or three gentlemen in one's room after supper.

MYSTERIOUS CHARACTERS AND SECRET ALPHABETS
(From Barrett's "Magus.")

" After 3 days preparation, cleanse your chamber as soon as it is morning immediately after dressing, the while fasting. There must be no hangings nor anything set crosswise, no tapestries, no hanging clothes, hats, bird-cages or bed-curtains, and all appointments must be clean in every respect.

"After supper, kindle a good fire, place a white cloth on the table round which set 3 chairs, and before each chair a wheaten loaf and a glass of fresh clear water, then return to rest.

"After uttering the conjuration, the 3 persons having arrived, they will rest themselves near the fire drinking and eating.

"They will then draw lots as to who shall remain, and the one who wins will come and be seated in the arm chair you have set by your bed. So long as she remains, you may question her upon any art or science, and she will immediately give you a positive answer. You may also inquire if she is aware of any hidden treasure, and she will tell you as to its locality and how to remove it.

"At parting she will give you a ring which worn on the finger will render you lucky at play. Observe, that you must leave your window open in order that they may enter."

CHAPTER XXVII

SOME REMARKABLE MAGICAL MANUSCRIPTS—SPELLS AND CURSES

THERE are several remarkable codices dealing with the magical arts in the Rawlinson and Ashmolean collections in Oxford. One consists of a long scroll, which is said to have been written with human blood in the sixteenth century.[1]

It has been in the Bodleian Library since 1680, but is believed to date from about 1525. It is 32 feet long and an inch and a half wide, and is written on fifteen strips of parchment stitched together. A single line of text runs along the centre of its entire length, with a border above and below of magical signs, consisting of crosses of various forms and pentagons, arranged alternately.

The text begins with an incantation and the names of God, followed by fourteen verses from the first chapter of St John's gospel, a chapter which formed part of magical ritual at a later period.

It concludes with the Lord's Prayer in Greek, written in Latin characters. The object of such a document can only be conjectured, but it was probably regarded as a powerful charm, to invoke the aid of good spirits and to protect its owner from evil influences.

The association of the Gospel of St John with magic goes back to an early period of the Christian era.

[1] MS. 3115.

PORTION OF A MAGICAL SCROLL WRITTEN WITH HUMAN
BLOOD

XVI century. Bodleian Library.

FIGURE OF THE GREEN DRAGON EMPLOYED WHEN EVOKING
THE SPIRIT BIRTO

From an MS. XVI century. British Museum.

(See page 269)

In the time of St Augustin, it was customary to place the Gospel of St John on the heads of sick people for the purpose of inducing supernatural cures.

In 1022, a Council held at Seligstadt, near Maintz, by its tenth canon prohibited the laity and matrons especially from hearing daily the Gospel commencing " In Principio," from which it has been assumed, that it had been read, and masses such as the Holy Trinity had been said for magical purposes.

Gifford writing in 1593 states, that " some hang a piece of St John's gospel about their necks," and in Ireland until recent times, the reading of this portion of scripture was regarded as an infallible cure for sore throat.

Reciting the first fourteen verses called " In Principio," was believed to be of singular and extraordinary power in exorcizing demons.

Durandus declares, that " the gospel will expel a devil, because devils hate nothing so much as a gospel."

In the early part of the seventeenth century, Pope Paul V, in his Rituale, orders the clergy when visiting the sick, to place the hand on the head while reading the gospel of St John. The powers attributed to it above all others were probably due to the indulgence granted by Pope John XXII of a year and forty days, on its recital.

Catalini commenting on the use of the beginning of St John's gospel in exorcism says, that " as the devil is greatly afraid of the gospels, this particular one is read to show forth the ineffable Being of God." Thiers records, that even dogs were led to church to be cured of sickness by having the gospel read over their heads.

An ancient Manx charm against all diseases was to

wear around the neck the first fourteen verses of St John's gospel written on paper.

Another curious manuscript of the sixteenth century is called " The Magic of Arbatel." [1] It begins with a description of the " Olimpick spirits which inhabit the firmament and in the stars beneath, whose office is to declare the fate and destiny of mortals."

It states that, " in the sixtyth year before the nativity of Christ was the beginning of the administration of the spiritual Prince Bethor whose government continued until A.D. 430. Then succeeded Phaleg whose government lasted until 920. Then began Och who governed until 1410 and Hagith who ruled afterwards."

Each of these spirits had his seal and planet, and was able to perform certain marvels and could be called to appear in the crystal. The writer states that a true and divine magician may use all the creations of God and offices of the governors of the world at his own will. But they heed not the false magician. He that is a true magician is brought forth a magician from his mother's womb. A manuscript on magic, written in 1515, claims to describe the principal operations in the " sacred art of invocation." [2]

It commences, " Here beginneth the first treatise of the most noble art of Solomon and Apollonius termed the ' Golden Flowers,' made from antiquity of Solomon, Manicheus and Enduchius.

" The following works are out of the most ancient books of the Hebrews which are unknown in man's language, reputed for a miracle to be given from the Lord God."

[1] MS. Rawlinson, 1363.   [2] Ashmole MS. 1515.

The first chapter consists of " this most Holy Art from Chaldean, Hebrew and Arabic. This oration Solomon appointed, first knowing it to be described by Chaldean, Hebrews and Arabs."

This is followed by " The Glasse of Apollonius : Called Ars Notoria or Ars Memoratina, revealed by an angel Phanphilus, on golden tablets in the Temple of Solomon."

In the Rawlinson collection at the Bodleian Library, there is a manuscript written on vellum in red and black inks inscribed " Moses Long, the conjurer." It is entitled,[1] " The Secrets of Secrets " and begins with " Aphorisms of directions " for conjuring the angels, followed by a prayer, that the " Holy angells may help thee in thine occasions " and the injunction " First pray to God dayly."

Then follow directions for making a pentacle of kid's skin or parchment to be covered with fine silk " until ye open it for use."

It is to be held in the hand or pinned to the breast until, if they visit and will not obey, open it saying, " ' Behold your conclusion and be not disobedient.' It ought to be borne about thee in all good experiments and business. It may be made in gold, silver, virgin parchment or in virgin wax, silk or clean parchment. Perfume it with sweet perfume. Ink may be made of smoke of frankincense and mirrh, taken in a basin mixt with rose water, a little sweet-smelling wine and gum arabic."

The seven angels and the planets dedicated to them are thus enumerated :

Cassiel to the planet Saturn, Sachiel to Jupiter,

[1] Rawlinson MS. 253.

Samael to Mars, Michael to the Sun, Anael to Venus, Raphael to Mercury and Gabriel to the Moon.

The manuscript concludes with an account of some experiments of which the following are the most interesting :

" A true experiment proved in Cambridge Anno 1557 of 3 spirits, to be done in a chamber, whose names are Durus, Artus and Æbedel.

"Rise early on the first Monday after ye new moon, Cut 3 rods stock or body of a Palme tree and not on ye top, with a new sharpe knife never used on which let it be written on ye blade + Alpha + on ye one side and + Omega + on the other side and with this knife in thy hand say ye name of God ye Father, I have sought these rods, so taking hold of them saying in ye name of God and Son, I have found you rods, saying in ye name of ye Holy Ghost, I cut you all 3 (so cutting all three at once). Then take fine parchment and cut 3 pieces and on ye first write Durus and on ye second write Artus and on ye third write Æbedel. Then take the first and wrap it about one of ye rods and so on do the others in order. Then take the first rod in thy hand and say, ' Through ye blessed power and mercie of God I command thee rod and by the virtue of the rod wherewith ye prophet Elias raised up the waters between him and Eliseus, ye spirit whose name is written and wrapped about, be obedient to me allways whenever I shall call him.' Then set down ye rod in the east part of ye chamber.

" The same is to be done with the second rod and the spirit is commanded by the virtue of ye rod wherewith Moses turned ye water of Egypt into blood. This is to be put in the west part of ye chamber. The third rod when consecrated in like manner is to be put in the south part of ye chamber. Then say ' I require and command you spirits 3 in the name of God, the Father, Son and Holy Ghost you dread and owe obedience. Come gently and peaceably in ye form and shape of three beautiful ladies and truly to answer all my will and desire.'

" This must be done 3 nights and the third night ye spirits will appear.

" Then say ' Welcome ye faire and gentle spirits which God hath created.' "

There is also " Ye experiment for ye spirit Birto," said to be made by Roger Bacon or Fryer Bacon. " To be done in a wood or secret place." This is described in some detail in a later manuscript.

Finally there is an experiment of " Askariell in a glasse or Cristall," and to call up this angel you must " have a cleane consecrated Cristall or glasse stone wrapt over ye middle with a thong of Hart's skin. Ye cristall may be in ye middle when ye wrappest the thong about it."

Among the historical papers of the sixteenth century in the British Museum are some leaves from a torn book said to have been found among the secret writings of Dr Caius, Master and founder of Caius College, Cambridge.

John Caius was born in 1510 and became one of the most famous physicians of the sixteenth century. He was nine times President of the College of Physicians of London and for nearly twenty years lectured on anatomy at the Barber-Surgeons' Hall.

He was reputed to have been one of the most skilful and enlightened physicians of his time, but judging from

CHARACTERS OF EVIL SPIRITS
(From an MS., XVII century.)

the leaves of this manuscript found among his writings he was also well versed in magic.

The papers consist of tables showing the signs of the planets and the names of the angels under those signs, also notes on familiars, formulæ for exorcism, an invocation to have " a spirit in a glass to tell all things " ; two drawings of magic circles and a pentagon. The most interesting of the leaves consists of drawings of the secret signs used for calling the spirits, similar to those to be found in manuscripts on the magical arts about that period.

Several English monarchs appear to have been interested in magic, and among them King Edward IV is mentioned, as having requested a magician of his time to put him in communication with a spirit called Birto.

The story is recounted in a manuscript of the sixteenth century, of how Birto was invoked and the part a " green dragon " played in it, of which a picture is given.

Birto seems to have been a spirit of considerable power, and after he had been conjured to appear, he comes to the circle prepared for him " in fair and human shape in the form of a man and noways horrible or hurtful." He was then to be questioned and to tell truly of all such things as the Master should ask.

The Master is directed to receive him courteously and gently, to bind him with the bond of spirits, and " he will freely and faithfully declare and make answer, to whatsoever shall be demanded, and will surely obey and fulfil all commands."

But to obtain the presence of Birto, it was necessary that the circle of the invocant should have the "effigy or character of a dragon fairly drawn or painted, and the circle in which the spirit is to appear should be made on a calve's skin parchment."

According to the writer of this manuscript, King Charles I is said to have carried a charm against danger and poison that was written for him by Pope Leo IX. It was inscribed as follows :

" Who that beareth it upon him shall not dread his enemies, to be overcome, nor with no manner of poison be hurt, nor in no need misfortune, nor with no thunder he shall not be smitten nor lightning, nor in no fire be burnt soddainly, nor in no water be drowned. Nor he shall not die without shrift, nor with theeves to be taken. Also he shall have no wrong neuther of Lord or Lady. This be in the names of God and Christ. + Messias + Sother + Emannell + Sabaoth +."

A powerful conjuration to call up a spirit is thus recorded in a manuscript of the fifteenth century :

" I conjure and constrayne thee —— by all virtues and powers, and by the Holy Names of God + Tetragrammaton + Adonay + Agla + Saday + Saboth + Planaboth + Panthon + Craton + Neupmaton + Deus + Homo + Omnipotens + Sempiternus + Yssus + Terra + Unigenitis + Saluator + Via + Vita + Virtues and powers, I conjure and constrayne thee to fulfil my will in everything faithfully, without hurt of my body or soul, and so be ready at my call as often as I shall call thee, by the virtue of one Lord + Jesus + Christ of Nasareth."

Both the magician and the witch were credited with the power of casting spells on human beings and cattle, and this appears to have been attempted through the medium of evil spirits.

Few of such spells or maledictions are recorded, but the following extracted from manuscripts of the fifteenth and sixteenth centuries will serve to show their nature.

"Curse thee, and Almighty make thee so that thou shalt never have rest day or night, tyd nor time, till thou hast performed my will and commandments, and if thou wilt not, all the curses of the great maledictions of God with all the paynes and torments of all the devells in hell be multiplied upon thee, so plentifully as the starrs be in the firmament, and as the sands be in the sea."

Another is to "Cast sickness on a man."

"Make an image of wax in the man's name and write on the side these characters as appointed:

Head them with the name of the man and then with 'Usher' (a knife), cut this image from the back to the head saying, Haade, Mikaded, Rakcben, Rika, Rita lica, Tasarith, Modeca, Rabert, Tuth, Tumch. Then hang this image over the fire with great smoke and he shall be sick."

There were several methods of slaying an enemy, and in one the wax image is again used as a medium.

"To slay an enemy:

"Make an image of wax and write the characters with a needle of brass upon the image, and dry it by a soft fire near chimney, and when it is dry cast the image down from some house, that the image may be broken, saying

271

these words, Haade, Mikaded, Rakeben, Rika, Rita lica, Tasarith, Modeca, Rabert, Tuth, Tumch. Here with this image I will slay the sick man soon. Name him, then take the pieces of the image and bury them, and he shall be dead and no man shall know but the worker."

Another method, which was apparently to be accompanied more by violence than magic, was to cut a stout bough from a tree and while doing so say, " I cutt this bough of this summer's growth in the name of (here name the person) whom I mean to beat and kill. Then cover the table and say in the name of the Father + Son + Holy Ghost + striking thereon, punish him that hath wrought this mischief, and take it away by thy great justice. Eson + Elion + Emares."

CHAPTER XXVIII

SOME ELIZABETHAN MAGICIANS—DR JOHN DEE—EDWARD KELLY—" THE BOOK OF MYSTERY "

OF the practitioners of magic in England in Tudor times, perhaps the best known was John Dee, who reached the height of his fame during the reign of Queen Elizabeth.

His life, compiled from his journals, and his extraordinary career have been fully described, but the following episodes in which magic played a part are perhaps not so well known.

He was born in 1527 and educated at the Chantry School at Chelmsford, whence he proceeded to Cambridge and entered at St John's College, but later on became a Fellow of Trinity.

He excelled in mathematics, which led him to the study of astronomy, of which he undoubtedly acquired a considerable knowledge.

At the age of twenty, in 1547, he made his first journey to the Continent to confer with learned men of the Dutch Universities, and here he came in contact with Mercator. Returning to England for a time, the following year he travelled to Louvain in order to study at the University, and there he is said to have graduated and obtained his degree as doctor.

In 1551 he obtained an introduction to the Court of

King Edward VI, to whom he had already dedicated two books.

When Mary Tudor succeeded to the throne in 1553, Dee—who had by this time achieved some notoriety as an astrologer—was invited to calculate her nativity, and he also cast the horoscope of the Princess Elizabeth who at that time was living at Woodstock.

It was probably shortly after this that he began to practise magic, for he soon got into trouble and was arrested at the instance of a man named George Ferrys, who alleged that one of his children had been struck blind and another killed by Dee's magic. In addition to this charge, it was rumoured that he was directing enchantments against the life of the Queen.

While in prison, his lodgings were searched and sealed up, and he was afterwards examined before the Secretary of State and brought to the Star Chamber for trial, but here fortune favoured him, for he was cleared of all suspicion of treason and eventually liberated.

Astrology at this time had taken a firm hold on the minds of the people, and the belief in the controlling power of the stars over human destinies was common to all classes.

The caster of horoscopes was in constant demand by persons of high and low degree, and Dee, who had already acquired a reputation for his prognostications, now became more famous. He became well known at Court and, when Elizabeth came to the throne, his first commission, commanded by Robert Dudley, was to name an auspicious day for her coronation. The Queen sent for him soon after her accession and invited him to enter her service at Whitehall, and is said to have promised him a Mastership at St Catherine's Hospital.

One morning, the whole Court and Privy Council became greatly excited when the news was spread abroad that, " a wax image of the Queen had been found lying in Lincoln's Inn Fields, with a great pin struck through its breast, which was believed to portend the wasting away and death of Her Majesty."

Messengers were despatched in hot haste to summon Dee, to ask his advice on this momentous matter.

He professed to regard it as a hoax, but at once went with the Secretary Wilson to Hampton Court to assure the Queen.

From the narrator's account, one can picture the scene on their arrival. Elizabeth was seated in that part of her garden that sloped down to the river, near the steps of the Royal landing-place at Hampton Court. Around her, stood the Earl of Leicester, in attendance, together with the Lords of the Privy Council who had also been summoned.

Dee, who wore a long beard and was of dignified presence, slowly approached the Queen and, after making her a deep obeisance, solemnly assured the assembly that the wax image " in no way menaced Her Majesty's well-being," which it is added, " pleased Elizabeth well."

The Queen afterwards proved a good friend to Dee, for about this time strong popular feeling began to be roused against him, and it was commonly said that he was a magician of doubtful reputation who had dealings with the devil.

He certainly practised divination openly, and held séances at which he professed to raise spirits.

For the former purpose he made use of a black mirror which he describes in the following words :

" A man may be curſtly afraid of his own shadow, yea, so much to feare, that you being alone nere a certain glasse, and proffer with dagger or sword to foyne at the glasse, you shall suddenly be moved to give back (in maner) by reason of an image appearing in the ayre betweene you and the glasse, with like hand, sword or dagger, and with like quickness foyning at your very eye, like as you do at the glasse. Strange this is to heare of, but more mervailous to behold than these my wordes can signifie, nevertheless by demonſtration opticall the order and cause thereof is certified, even so the effeĉt is consequent."

Dee's famous magic mirror is described as a polished oval slab of black ſtone or cannel coal. It was formerly in the Museum of Horace Walpole at Strawberry Hill, and he attached to it a ſtatement of its hiſtory in his own handwriting.

It is said to have been for a long time in the possession of the Mordaunts, Earls of Peterborough. In this colleĉtion it was described as " the black ſtone in which Dr Dee used to call his spirits." It passed from them to Lady Elizabeth Germaine, from whom it went to John Campbell, Duke of Argyll, whose son, Lord Frederick Campbell, presented to it Walpole. This intereſting relic was bought at the Strawberry Hill Sale by Mr Pigott, and from thence it passed into the hands of Lord Londesborough, and later became part of the colleĉtion of Mr Geoffrey Whitehead of Eaſt Grinſtead, which was sold by auĉtion in London on Auguſt 7th, 1915.

It is to this mirror that Butler alludes in his well-known lines :

> " Kelly did all his feats upon
> The Devil's looking-glass, a stone,
> Where, playing with him at bo-peep,
> He solv'd all problems ne'er so deep."
> > "Hudibras," Part II, Canto 3.

About 1570 Dee went to live at Mortlake near the river, and to this house he removed his library and laboratory. The Queen, when riding out in Richmond Park with her lords and ladies, would sometimes pass through the East Sheen gate and stop at Dee's dwelling between Mortlake Church and the Thames, to see his latest invention. It was here at the church wall that he is said to have once shown the Queen the black mirror.

To most of the European Courts of this period an astrologer was attached, and both the Queen and Lord Burleigh appeared anxious that Dee should occupy that position at Whitehall.

It is probable that the story of his search for the Philosopher's Stone may have had something to do with this desire to secure his services, as there is an account of an interview he had with the Queen in the gallery at Westminster, when there was a talk between them " of the great secret for my sake to be disclosed unto Her Majesty by Nicolas Grudius, one of the secretaries of the Emperor Charles V," which is supposed to have referred to the transmutation of metals.

Of his operations with the crystal, he records in his diary in 1581 his first séance, when the " skryer " (medium) was bidden to look into the great crystalline globe, and a message was transmitted by the " angel

277

Annael through the percipient " to the effect, that many things should be declared to Dee, " not by the present worker but by him that is assigned to the stone."

A little later he writes, " I had a sight in Chrystallo offered me and I saw," but he evidently thought that he himself was not a good medium, for he set out to search for another.

In 1582 he came across one in the person of Edward Kelly, a plausible and clever rogue, whom he engaged as a skryer to operate the crystal in his laboratory.

Kelly is said to have begun life as an apothecary's apprentice and had an extraordinary career. He declared that when wandering in Wales—probably when hiding from justice—he accidentally stumbled on an old manuscript on alchemy, and two phials or caskets containing a mysterious red and white powder, which he regarded as being of priceless value, for when properly manipulated they were capable of transmuting base metals into gold.

He apparently deceived Dee, who seems to have believed in the story, for he records in his diary :

" E. K. (Kelly) made projection with his powder in the proportion of one minim (upon an ounce and a quarter of mercury) and produced nearly an ounce of best gold ; which gold we afterwards distributed from the crucible, and gave one to Edward." How Kelly worked the trick there is no evidence to show.

The story of Kelly's alleged claim soon became known, and frequent séances took place at Mortlake where he worked in Dee's laboratory, and the transmuting operations were carried on.

The news reached the ears of Lord Burleigh, who

DR. DEE'S 'SHEW STONE' OR GAZING CRYSTAL.
British Museum.

apparently also became a believer in his operations, for he wrote for " a specimen of his marvellous art," and it was reported that the Queen was actually the recipient of a warming-pan, from the copper or brass lid of which a piece had been cut, transmuted into gold and replaced.

Even such an astute person as Elias Ashmole was deceived by Kelly's tricks, as he writes :

" Without Sir Edward's touching or handling it or melting the metal, only warming it in the fire, the elixir being put thereon it was transmuted into pure gold." He adds " from a very credible person (who had seen them) that Kelly made rings of gold wire twisted twice round the finger, which he gave away to the value of £1,000."

Bacon relates an interesting story of a dinner given by Sir Edward Dyer, at which Sir Thomas Browne, the author of " Religio Medici," was present. He says, " Sir Edward Dyer, a grave and wise gentleman, did much believe in Kelly the alchemist, that he did indeed the work and made gold, insomuch as he went himself into Germany, where Kelly then was, to inform himself fully thereto.

" After his return he dined with my Lord of Canterbury, wherat that time was at the table Dr Browne the physician. They fell in talk of Kelly. Sir Edward Dyer turning to the archbishop said, ' I do assure your grace that I shall tell the truth. I am an eyewitness thereof and if I had not seen it, I should not have believed it. I saw Master Kelly put of the base metal into the crucible and after it was set upon the fire and a very small quantity of the medicine put in and stirred with a stick of wood, it came forth in great proportion, perfect gold, to the touch, to the hammer, to the test.'

" Said the bishop, ' You had need take heed what you say Sir Edward, here is an infidel at the board.'

" Sir Edward Dyer said again pleasantly, ' I would have looked for an infidel sooner in any place than at your Grace's table.'

" ' What say you Dr Browne ? ' saith the Bishop.

" Dr Browne answered after his blunt and huddling manner, ' The gentleman hath spoken enough for me.'

" ' Why ? ' saith the Bishop.

" ' Marry,' saith Dr Browne, ' he said he would not have believed it except he had seen it, AND NO MORE WILL I.' "

Kelly's next exploit was the announcement that a mysterious book had been revealed to him by an angel, which he claimed to have written down and produced in manuscript form.

There are two copies of this extraordinary production in existence. One is among the Ashmolean MSS. in the Bodleian Library (Ashm. 422) and the other in the British Museum (Sl. 3189).

The former is entitled " The Book of Mystery." " Liber Mysteriorum Sextus et Sanctus."

A note by Ashmole in this copy states that he " copied it from the original borrowed off Sir John Cotton out of his library written by the hand of Edward Kelly, which he copied from the view of it exhibited to him by the angel in 1583."

It begins with an account by Kelly of his interview with the angel, as follows :

" He plucked out a book, all ye leaves are as though

they were pure gold and it seemed to be written in blood not dry.

"Behold! Behold! yea let heaven and earth behold, for with this they were created and it is the voice and speech of him which proceeded from ye first and is ye last.

"Loe this it is—(E. K., he showeth a book as he did before, all gold).

"And it is truth therefor shall endure for ever. (E. K. The leaves of the book are all lined and full of square places and those squares have characters in them, some more than other, and all written in the colour of blood and not yet dry. 49 square spaces everyway in every leaf which make in all 2401 square places.

"He wiped his finger on the top of the table and there came out above ye table certain characters enclosed in lines, but standing by themselves, and pointed between them written from the right to the left hand.)

"The 49 parts of this booke—49 voices whereunto so many powers with the inferiors and subjects have been and shall be obedient.

"Every element in his mystery is a world of understanding.

"Everyone knoweth here, what is his due obedience, and God shall differ in speech from a mortal creature.

"Every element have 49 manner of understandings.

"Therein is compounded many languages.

"They are all spoken at once and generally by yourselves by distinction may be spoken.

"In 40 daies must the booke of the secrete and key of this world be written. Begin to practise in August. Serve God before from March 29 (Good Friday) to April were 30 tables of this book written.

" The letters of the Adamicall alphabet. This book and Holy Key which unlocks the secret of God concerning ye beginning.

" So excellent are the mysteries contained, it is above the capacity of man.

" In 40 days more must this booke be perfect.

" Herein shall be decyphered and truly from imperfect falsehood, true religion from false and damnable errors. May 1583."

The contents of the book are then stated :

" This book containeth 3 kinds of knowledge :

" 1. The knowledge of God truly.

" 2. The number and doing of the angels.

" 3. The beginning and ending of Nature substantially.

" This book is written in the Holy language.

" The book shall be called "Logaeth," which signifieth ' Speech from God.' "

This manuscript begins with a transcript of the book called " Logaeth " in common characters, followed by 22 pages written in small squares, 72 similar pages and 4 pages written vertically.

The codex in the British Museum is called " The Book of Enoch, revealed to Dr John Dee by the Angels."

It contains a note stating, " This is the original MS. in Edward Kelly's handwriting. It formerly belonged to the Cottonian Collection as appears from a note by Ashmole."

There is also a manuscript partly in Dee's handwriting, with his autograph (Sl. 3188) entitled " Dr John Dee's conference with angels from Dec. 22, 1581 to May 30, 1583, being what precedes ye other conferences." This MS., which has an introduction by Elias Ashmole in 1672, stating how it came into his hands, was printed in London in 1659 under the title, " A true and faithful relation of Dr Dee and some spirits." It purports to contain a conversation held between certain spirits by Dee and Kelly respecting the " Logaeth " and a key to decipher its mysterious pages.

The angel begins by saying, " Touching the book. It shall be called Logah, which in your language signifieth Speech from God. Write it Logaeth. It is to be sounded Logah.

" The first leaf (as you call it) is the last of the book."

The angel then proceeds to say how it is to be written in the Holy characters and explains that the last leaf " is a hotch potch of the wicked in the world and damned in hell."

Elaborate instructions are given how to read the tables, from which it appears that sometimes the words are ascending, sometimes descending, sometimes at an angle, on the left or right.

Groups of letters form words, thus M R E means with, B A C with a rod, E R N O Z delivered you, R I P the Holy ones, M A S R G with admiration, I D L A of gathering, E G R P with the fire and so on.

The numbers from 1 to 80 also signified words thus :

1 Signified Behold, 2 Faith, 3 Your God, 4 I am, 5 A circle and so on.

Kelly then artfully asks the angel, " If Moses and Daniel were skilful in the arts of the Egyptian magicians, why may not I deal with these without hindrance to the will of God ? "

To which the angel gives the cryptic reply, " For the doings of the Egyptians seem and are not so."

It is difficult to conceive what Dee and Kelly expected to gain from this elaborate effusion, the writing of which alone must have taken considerable time and labour.

Kelly next went off to Prague, apparently to find the highest bidder for his discovery of a method of obtaining gold.

While he was there, we find Lord Burleigh writing to the Queen's agent in Germany, asking him to urge every means in his power to entice Kelly to come back to his native country, and requesting him, in case Kelly will not return, to send a very small portion of his powder to make a demonstration in the Queen's own sight.

But Kelly was too cunning to be caught. In Prague he felt secure, and he did not feel inclined to carry out the test that he knew would be put to him if he returned to London.

Eventually he got into trouble with the Emperor Rudolph, and was imprisoned in one of his castles, and it is said that while attempting to escape from a turret window, he fell from a great height and received fatal injuries.

Dee, who had meanwhile been living at Bremen, resolved to return to England after an absence of six years, but during his stay abroad his popularity had waned and we find him making repeated applications to his old influential friends at Court for money.

Although his house began again to be visited by such notable people as the Countess of Cumberland, the Countess of Kent and Lord Willoughby, who occasionally sent him money, he fell into poverty and ill-health.

Queen Elizabeth sent for him to come and see her in the Privy Garden at Greenwich in 1584, where she received him with Lord Warwick. Dee presented her with an effusion in writing, which he called the "Heavenly Admonition," and took the opportunity of pleading his cause. His supplications apparently prevailed with the Queen, for he was soon after appointed warden of the Collegiate Church at Manchester, where he took up his abode in 1586.

Some years afterwards accusations were again brought against him, that he was a conjurer of spirits and had dealings with the devil, and on June 5th, 1604, he presented a petition to the King at Greenwich, in which he prayed, " to be tried and cleared of that horrible and damnable and to him most grievous and dammageable slaunder, generally and for many years past in this kingdom raised and continued by report and print against him ; that he is or hath been a CONJURER or CALLER or INVOCATOR of DEVILS.

He prays " that a speedy order be taken to be tryed in the premises to the punishment of death (yea eyther be stoned to death or to be buried quicke or to be burned unmercifully) if by any due, true and just meanes the said name of CONJURER or CALLER or INVOCATOR of DEVILS or DAMNED SPIRITES can be proved to have beene or to be tru duely or justly reported of him or attributed unto him."

A copy of this petition is still preserved in the Bodleian Library. Dee died in 1608, and was buried in the chancel of Mortlake Church, near the house where he lived so long.

A study of his works shows that he was a man of considerable intelligence and by no means altogether a charlatan. He had a real devotion to science, and muſt have been grossly deceived by Kelly, and their association no doubt did much to damage Dee's reputation.

A cryſtal ball or " Shew ſtone " said to have belonged to Dee, together with three large wax discs engraved with magical figures and names, are preserved in the British Museum. The latter are said to have been used by him when consulting his " Shew ſtone " or magic mirror.

WAX DISCS ENGRAVED WITH MAGICAL FIGURES AND NAMES, SAID
TO HAVE BEEN EMPLOYED BY DR. DEE WHEN USING HIS 'SHEW
STONE' OR MAGIC CRYSTAL

British Museum.

CHAPTER XXIX

MAGIC IN SHAKESPEARE'S PLAYS

THE influence of magic, and the part it played in social life in the sixteenth century, are reflected in several of Shakespeare's plays. Ghosts, fairies, spirits, conjurers, witches, soothsayers, apparitions and supernatural beings form part of his *dramatis personæ* and flit across his stage in comedy and tragedy.

In eleven of his plays he introduces the supernatural in one form or another, or refers to magical practices.

In " The Tempest " there is the sprightly Ariel and his attendant spirits, who at the bidding of Prospero, himself a practitioner of magic, raised terrible tempests which apparently wrecked the ships of the King and the usurping Duke of Milan.

The misshapen and uncouth Caliban, " a freckled whelp, hag-born," is a true son of the foul witch Sycorax.

Prospero has also goblins, naiads and nymphs at his command to wreak his vengeance, and divers spirits in the shape of hounds :

> " Go, charge my goblins that they grind their joints
> With dry convulsions ; shorten up their sinews
> With aged cramps."

Later on we see him arrayed in his wizard's robes and drawing his magic circle he declaims :

" Graves, at my command,
   Have wak'd their sleepers, op'd, and let them forth
   By my so potent art."

Alonso, Sebastian and Antonio then enter the magic circle and there stand charmed.

In " The Comedy of Errors " we are introduced to Pinch, who combines the professions of schoolmaster and conjurer in the city of Ephesus, which, according to Antipholus of Syracuse, at that time bore an unenviable reputation as a centre for practitioners of the magical arts :

" They say this town is full of cozenage ;
   As, nimble jugglers that deceive the eye,
   Dark-working sorcerers that change the mind,
   Soul-killing witches that deform the body,
   Disguised cheaters, prating mountebanks,
   And many such-like liberties of sin."

Pinch is called in by the wife of Antipholus of Ephesus, to exorcize the supposed demon that has taken possession of him and caused all the trouble, and she thus addresses him :

" Good Doctor Pinch, you are a conjurer ;
   Establish him in his true sense again,
   And I will please you what you will demand."

Pinch approaches Antipholus and says :

" Give me your hand, and let me feel your pulse."

To which he replies :

" There is my hand, and let it feel your ear."

Then Pinch utters his conjuration :

> " I charge thee, Satan, hous'd within this man,
> To yield possession to my holy prayers,
> And to thy state of darkness hie thee straight ;
> I conjure thee by all the saints in heaven."

Antipholus afterwards describes Pinch in terms that are far from flattering :

> " They brought one Pinch, a hungry lean fac'd villain,
> A mere anatomy, a mountebank,
> A threadbare juggler, and a fortune-teller,
> A needy, hollow-cy'd, sharp-looking wretch,
> A living-dead man.   This pernicious slave,
> Forsooth, took on him as a conjurer,
> And, gazing in mine eyes, feeling my pulse,
> And with no face, as 'twere, out-facing me,
> Cries out, I was possess'd."

In " A Midsummer-night's Dream " we enter fairy realm, ruled by Oberon, the King, and his Queen Titania.

In Puck we have a picture of a " knavish sprite call'd Robin Good-fellow " :

> " That frights the maidens of the villagery ;
> Skim milk, and sometimes labour in the quern,
> And bootless make the breathless housewife churn ;
> And sometime make the drink to bear no barm ;
> Mislead night-wanderers, laughing at their harm."

In truth a mischievous hobgoblin.

The touching of Titania's eyes with a magic herb, to change her once more into a fairy, is evidence of Shakespeare's knowledge of herb-lore, and it is probable that he had the little plant " Eye Bright " in mind.

The most complete description of a magician's conjuration, in the plays, is that given in " The Second Part of King Henry VI," when Bolingbroke, at the instance of the Duchess, raises the spirit in the Duke of Gloucester's garden in London. Bolingbroke, the magician and conjurer, enters, accompanied by Margery Jourdain, a witch, together with Hume and Southwell, who are described as priests.

Hume leaves to inform the Duchess, and Bolingbroke addressing the witch thus begins the séance :

> " Mother Jourdain, be you prostrate and grovel
> on the earth ; John Southwell, read you ; and
> let us to our work."

The Duchess now enters, and presently Hume.

Duchess.   Well said, my masters, and welcome all.
   To this gear the sooner the better.
Bolingbroke.   Patience, good lady ; wizards know their times.
   Deep night, dark night, the silent of the night,
   The time of night when Troy was set on fire ;
   The time when screech-owls cry, and ban-dogs howl,
   And spirits walk, and ghosts break up their graves,
   That time best fits the work we have in hand.
   Madam, sit you, and fear not : whom we raise,
   We will make fast within a hallow'd verge.

Here they begin to perform the ceremonies appertaining, and after making the magic circle Bolingbroke reads the conjuration.

Accompanied by terrible thunder and lightning the spirit riseth.

Spirit. Adsum.
Margery Jourdain.   Asmath !
  By the eternal God, whose name and power
  Thou tremblest at, answer that I shall ask ;
  For till thou speak, thou shalt not pass from hence.
Spirit.   Ask what thou wilt.   That I had said and done !

Bolingbroke puts the questions and the spirit answers, after which he gives the licence to depart :

  " Descend to darkness and the burning lake !
  False fiend, avoid ! "

It is evident from his description of the conjuration that Shakespeare, with his remarkable versatility, had an intimate knowledge of magical ceremonial. Several famous practitioners of magic flourished about his time, including Dr Dee, Edward Kelly and Simon Forman ; but, as the rites and ceremonials of magic probably only existed in the form of manuscripts at this period, he must have had access to them. This is evident later in the play when Smith introduces the Clerk of Chatham to Cade.

Smith.   Has a book in his pocket with red letters in't.
Cade.   Nay, then he is a conjurer.

The manuscripts on magical ceremonial are generally written in red and black inks. The conjurer was usually accompanied by a reader, who carried the book of the ceremonies and pronounced the conjuration and prayers.

There is a brief account of the trial of the Duchess of Gloucester, Margery Jourdain, Southwell, Hume and Bolingbroke for sorcery and witchcraft, in which Jourdain was condemned to be burnt in Smithfield as a witch and the three men to be strangled on the gallows, while the Duchess, after doing three days' public penance, was banished to the Isle of Man.

According to the historical facts of the case, the accusation against the Duchess was of compassing the death of the King with Marie Gardimain and Bolingbroke, by having made a figure of him in wax and melting it before a fire.

Marie Gardimain was the original of Shakespeare's Margery Jourdain, and was burnt at the stake, Bolingbroke was hanged and the Duchess was condemned to imprisonment for life.

In "Richard III," the ghosts of Prince Edward, King Henry VI, Clarence, Rivers, Grey, Vaughan, Hastings, the two young Princes, Queen Anne, and Buckingham, appear to him while sleeping in his tent on Bosworth Field. These apparitions are evidently intended to represent his dream and are not spirit manifestations. The vision described in "King Henry VIII" in Act II, where the six personages clad in white robes, wearing garlands, appear to Queen Katherine in her illness is shown in a similar manner.

The Soothsayer is introduced in "Julius Cæsar" to warn him to "beware the ides of March"; and in "Antony and Cleopatra" the Soothsayer who tells Charmian's fortune is evidently also an adept in Cheiromancy.

> *Charmian.* Is't you, sir, that know things?
> *Soothsayer.* In nature's infinite book of secrecy
>   A little I can read.
> *Alexas.* Show him your hand.
> *Charmian.* Good sir, give me good fortune.
> *Soothsayer.* I make not, but foresee.

Later, a Soothsayer is brought from Egypt by Antony and taken to Cæsar's house.

Antony.   Say to me, whose fortunes shall rise higher, Cæsar's or
        mine ?
Soothsayer.   Cæsar's.
        Therefore, O Antony ! stay not by his side ;
        Thy demon (that thy spirit which keeps thee) is
        Noble, courageous, high, unmatchable,
        Where Cæsar's is not ; but near him thy angel
        Becomes a fear, as being o'erpower'd, therefore
        Make space enough between you.

Yet another Soothsayer is introduced in " Cymbeline " who tells Lucius of his vision.

Soothsayer.   Last night the very gods show'd me a vision
        (I fast and pray'd for their intelligence) thus :
        I saw Jove's bird, the Roman eagle, wing'd
        From the spungy south to this part of the west,
        There vanish'd in the sunbeams ; which portends,
        (Unless my sins abuse my divination)
        Success to the Roman host.

Later in the play, Posthumus, a prisoner in his cell, has a vision in which his father, Sicilius Leonatus, his wife and his two young brothers appear, who circle round him and eventually invoke the aid of Jupiter, who descends amidst thunder and lightning, sitting upon an eagle. He throws a thunderbolt and the Ghosts fall on their knees and he thus addresses them :

    " No more, you petty spirits of region low,
        Offend our hearing ; hush ! How dare you ghosts
        Accuse the Thunderer, whose bolt, you know,
        Sky-planted, batters all rebelling coasts ?

293

Posthumus awakes and finds a book, and in the last act the Soothsayer interprets the parable and thus ends the play in the promise of peace and plenty to Britain.

The witches introduced into " Macbeth " form a prominent feature in two acts of the play. In the scene on the Heath, they encounter Macbeth and Banquo, and the latter thus describes them :

" What are these
  So wither'd and so wild in their attire,
  That look not like th' inhabitants o' the earth,
  And yet are on't ?   Live you ? or are you aught
  That man may question ?   You seem to understand me
  By each at once her choppy finger laying
  Upon her skinny lips : you should be women
  And yet your beards forbid me to interpret
  That you are so."

After they vanish he remarks :

" Were such things here as we do speak about,
  Or have we eaten on the insane root,
  That takes the reason prisoner ?

The mandrake or " insane root " alluded to is frequently mentioned by Shakespeare. It was a plant around which clustered many superstitions, and its root not only possessed powerful narcotic properties, but produced hallucinations, hence was sometimes known as insane root.

It was credited with other mysterious powers, and on account of the resemblance of the root to the human form it was used by witches to injure their enemies.

In Hecate's speech to the witches, there is a beautiful

allusion made to an ancient tradition of the magical effect of the moon mist :

> " Upon the corner of the moon
> There hangs a vaporous drop profound ;
> I'll catch it ere it comes to ground :
> And that distill'd by magic sleights
> Shall raise such artificial sprites."

In the account Shakespeare gives of the ingredients used by the witches in making their hell-broth, he enumerates some of the weird and mysterious articles that formed part of their stock-in-trade. Their incantation is also interesting from other points of view, as they chant round the boiling cauldron :

> " Round about the cauldron go ;
> In the poison'd entrails throw.
> Toad, that under cold stone,
> Days and nights, hast thirty-one
> Swelter'd venom sleeping got,
> Boil thou first i' the charmed pot.
>   Double, double, toil and trouble ;
>   Fire burn and cauldron bubble."

The method here used by the witches to measure the time that the cauldron should boil, by singing their incantation, is an ancient mode of calculating time still employed in some parts of the country. By thus repeating several verses they could regulate the time of boiling fairly well. Centuries ago, the apothecaries used the moon as a method of calculating the time that certain processes should take, and the word menstruum, still commonly used, was employed, because certain drugs were allowed to macerate a month in the liquid to extract their active constituents.

The idea of using a toad that had lain dormant for a month, was probably due to the knowledge that its venom would be then most active, besides the advantage of catching him napping, when he would have no opportunity of getting rid of the poisonous principle secreted in his skin.

Some toads secrete an active poison called phrynin, which resembles digitalis in its action on the heart.

In the allusion to

" Root of hemlock, digg'd i' the dark,"

there is reference to another ancient custom of gathering herbs at night, in the belief that their properties after dark were more potent than in the daytime. That there was some reason for this old supposition has been proved by the researches of Sachs and Brown, who found from their investigations, that starch is formed in the leaves of plants during the night, and so the ancient belief of the increased activity of the midnight-gathered herb was not entirely mythical.

The failure of Hamlet to recognize the ghost of his father is perhaps not to be wondered at :

" Be thou a spirit of health or goblin damn'd,
   Bring with thee airs from heaven or blasts from hell,
   Be thy intents wicked, or charitable,
   Thou com'st in such a questionable shape."

The Ghost's reply :

" I am thy father's spirit ;
   Doom'd for a certain term to walk the night,
   And for the day confin'd to fast in fires,
   Till the foul crimes, done in my days of nature,
   Are burnt and purg'd away."

This embodies an early tradition, that certain spirits were kept in purgatory during the day and allowed to wander the earth at night, and the belief that disembodied spirits thus haunted ruined buildings was held by the Assyrians over three thousand years ago.

CHAPTER XXX

HERBS OF MYSTERY AND THE DEVIL—THE WITCH'S BROOM

IN ancient times certain trees and herbs of evil omen were deemed plants of the Devil. They included those dedicated to Hecate, who presided over magic and enchantments, as well as those made use of by her daughters, Medea and Circe, in their sorceries. Circe especially was supposed to have been distinguished for her knowledge of venomous herbs, and in later times the plants said to have been used by her were universally employed by witches and sorcerers in their incantations.

The evil reputations of certain herbs are often indicated by their popular names. Thus asafœtida is known as "Devil's Dung" in some countries; the fruit of the belladonna or "Deadly Nightshade" as the "Devil's Berry," and the plant itself as "Death's Herb."

The mandrake was known as the "Devil's Candle" on account of the supposed lurid glare emitted by the leaves at night.

Some plants were supposed to exercise a baleful influence on human life by their emanations.

The tradition connected with the "Deadly Upas Tree" may be taken as an instance of this. It was said to blight all vegetation that grew near it, and to cause even the birds that approached it in their flight to drop down lifeless. It was believed that no animal could live where

298

its evil influence extended, and no man dare approach its pestilential shade.

The noxious exudations of the manchineel tree were said to cause death to those who slept beneath its branches.

Linnæus mentions a case in which the odour of the oleander proved fatal. In India this shrub is called " Horse Killer," and in Italy " Ass Bane," as the foliage and flowers are believed to exercise a deadly influence on many animals.

Hemlock, from which a powerful poisonous alkaloid called conine is extracted, has had an evil reputation from a period of great antiquity. Pliny states that " serpents flee from its leaves " and in Russia it is regarded as a Satanic herb. In England, it has always been associated with witches, potions and hell-broths.

Henbane is another plant of ill-omen which was used at funerals and scattered on tombs. The Piedmontese have a tradition that, if a hare be sprinkled with henbane juice, all the hares in the district will decamp. They have also a saying that, " when a mad dog dies he has tasted henbane." This plant is known amongst the German peasants as " Devil's Eye."

Of verbena or vervain, a plant much used in witchcraft, Gerard says that " the Devil did reveal it as a secret and divine medicine." In some parts of Germany a species of ground moss is called " Devil's Claws," the plantain is known as " Devil's Head," and a certain variety of orchid is styled " Satan's Hand."

Clematis bears the name of " Devil's Thread," the yellow toadflax is termed " Devil's Ribbon," and the scandix is known as the " Devil's Darning Needles."

299

In Sweden, a species of fungus is termed the " Devil's Butter," while the spurge bears the name of the " Devil's Milk." In Ireland the nettle is called the " Devil's Apron," and the convolvulus is known as the " Devil's Garter." Hair parsley is designated the " Devil's Oatmeal," and the puff-balls of the lycopodium are termed the " Devil's Snuffbox." In some localities, the common houseleek is known as " Devil's Beard," while the tritoma with its bright red blossoms is called the " Devil's Poker."

The *Jatropha urens*, a plant indigenous to Brazil, is said to possess powerful poisonous properties. A prick from one of its fine spines causes numbness, swelling of the lips and, finally, stoppage of the heart's action. Its effects are said to be those of a powerful arterial poison which has not yet been investigated.

Pouchkine describes an Indian plant called autchar, thought to be a variety of *Aconitum ferox*, which grows in a wild, sterile desert. The roots and leaves exude a sticky substance which, melted by the midday sun, falls in drops and congeals like a transparent gum in the cool of the evening. This exudation is of an extremely poisonous nature. Birds avoid the neighbourhood of the plant and even the tiger turns aside from it. It is used as an arrow poison by certain of the Frontier tribes.

Another plant of ill-omen is the Flor de Pesadilla or "Nightmare Flower," which grows in the neighbourhood of Buenos Aires. It is a small shrub with dark green leaves of lanceolate shape, and clusters of greenish-white flowers which emit a powerful narcotizing smell.

According to tradition, from the acrid, milky juice

expressed from the stem of this plant, witches obtain a drug which, administered to their victims, gives them terrible dreams. They awake with a dull, throbbing sensation in the brain, while a peculiar odour pervades the room, causing the air to appear heavy and stifling.

There is a tradition among the peasants of Friesland that no woman is to be found at home on a Friday, because on that day the witches hold their meetings and have dances on a barren heath.

The Neapolitan witches held their gatherings under a walnut tree near Benevento, and the peasants near Bologna say their witches hold their midnight meetings beneath the walnut trees on St John's Eve.

" Eastern as well as European witches are said to practise their spells at midnight and the principal implement they use is a broom," says a writer on Indo-European folklore.

The association of brooms with witches is very curious and probably arose from the tradition that they used them for riding through the air. But, although connected with witches, a broom was sometimes used to drive them off, and in some parts of Germany it was customary to lay a broom inside the threshold of a house to keep them from entering the dwelling.

The large ragwort is known in Ireland as the " Fairies' Horse," as it was said to be used by the witches when making their midnight journeys. Burns alludes to witches who " skim the muirs and dizzy crags on rag-bred nags."

Foxgloves in some parts of the country are called " Witches' Bells," as they are said to decorate their fingers with the cap-like flower, and in certain localities the hare-bell is known as the "Witches' Thimble." The St John's wort, which is supposed to have the property of driving witches away, is known in Italy as the "Devil-chaser" on that account, and the elder was said to possess the same power.

The sea or horned poppy was reputed to be a favourite plant with witches and to be used by them in their incantations; so too was the magical moonwort, that was believed to open locks. The mullein, or "hag-taper," and the honesty were said to be equally "excelled in sorceries." Among the trees and plants especially obnoxious to witches there was none they feared more than the mountain-ash or rowan tree. Probably on account of its connexion with Druidical ceremonies, it was accounted as the greatest protection against witchcraft; hence the lines:

> "Rowan-tree and red thread
> Put the witches to their speed."

Even a small twig carried in the pocket was believed to ensure immunity from their evil charms—so says the old ballad:

> "Witches have no power,
> Where there is row'n-tree wood."

Throughout Europe the mountain-ash is in equal repute, and in Norway, Denmark and Germany it is customary to place branches over stable doors to keep the witches from entering.

Many plants are credited with the property of protecting from the " evil eye " : thus in Russia the stem of the birch tree, tied with a piece of red ribbon, is carried, in Italy the herb rue is employed, in the Highlands of Scotland groundsel is used, and in Germany the radish ; while the Chinese believe garlic affords the most effective protection.

CHAPTER XXXI

SURVIVALS OF WITCHCRAFT AND MAGIC IN MODERN TIMES

THE belief in magic and witchcraft has by no means died out, and beside the pursuit of fortune-telling, crystal-gazing, cheiromancy and other methods of divination still carried on and believed in by many people to-day, cases of the survival of the practices of the Middle Ages occasionally come to light in our police courts. Thus on April 1st, 1895, a man called Michael Cleary was charged at Clonmel with having, on March 14th, burnt his wife Bridget, a woman of 27 years of age, for being a witch and thus causing her death at Ballyvadhen, County Tipperary.

Johanna Burke swore that boiling herbs out of a sauce-pan on the fire were forced down the woman's throat, while her husband asked her, in the name of the " Father, Son and Holy Ghost," if she was his wife. He then stripped her clothes off and threw her on the floor, and, pouring paraffin oil over her, set her on fire. Cleary, assisted by three other persons, next took her to the fire and forced her to sit upon it, in order " to drive out the witch " that possessed her.

She was then laid upon the bed and shaken, while her husband recited the words, " Away with you " (meaning the evil spirit) and, at six o'clock in the morning, the priest was sent for to exorcize the spirits with which the house was thought to be filled. The prisoners were found guilty, and sentenced to various periods of imprisonment.

Among other practitioners of magic, the gipsy still enjoys a reputation among a certain class of people, and the Romany, who is said to have inherited his occult knowledge from early ancestors, is sought and believed in by many countryfolk to-day.

An instance of this came to light in the Police Court at Higham Ferrers in Northamptonshire on November 15th, 1926, when a gipsy of the historic name of Smith was charged with obtaining money from a widow. It was stated that she had sold her " charms to burn, wear and put under her pillow." If those to be burnt, burned brightly, it meant that £400 was coming to her, but if the fire was dull some enemy was holding the money back. The fortune-teller received a month's hard labour for her charms from an unsympathetic bench. A police superintendent in charge of the case sagely remarked, that the widow was only one of many simple folk who were easily gulled by " gipsy magic," and added, " These fortune-tellers are becoming a danger to the countryside."

Another curious story was related before the magistrates at Batley in 1925, when a widow of 73 was summoned for doing damage to a pair of trousers and a curtain belonging to a lodger, who was a miner.

The landlady declared that he never went to bed, but " sits up all night burning vitriol and cayenne pepper.

" I call him a wizard. He can do any mortal thing," she exclaimed to the Bench.

Her daughter in giving evidence against the alleged wizard said :

" He does something that makes mother ill. We can smell cayenne and things he uses. It is something you don't understand, and he has brought my mother to the brink of the grave. Twice I have taken her out of his way, but wherever we go we can feel his devilish work going on."

It is evident in this case that both women were under the firm conviction that the man was trying to cast some spell upon one of them.

It is not often that a man accuses his wife of being a witch, but recently a husband applied for a separation order, alleging that his wife practised witchcraft. He declared that she told him that she was working on her son and herself, " by throwing something on a rug " when the former was ill, and by " placing one of his possessions near her photograph." He also stated that " she placed pokers in the fire and made rings of salt around his chair to drive away evil spirits."

An amusing case came before the Glastonbury magistrates in January 1926, when a man applied for a summons against a neighbour for bewitching his clock, which, he said, " ticked three times as loud as usual and stopped every night although it was wound up."

He further alleged that the accused man " came to him as a witch when he sat by the fire, but only his head and beard appeared. He spat at him twice and he disappeared as a ball of smoke."

He accused another neighbour of poisoning the cabbages in his garden so that they made him ill when he ate them. The Court regarded the charges as not proved and the case was dismissed.

The peasantry in some parts of France are still highly

superstitious. In the country districts of the south-west the belief in charms and the " evil eye" is almost as general as it was centuries ago. This is shown in a curious case that came to light in January 1926 when an Abbé of the small village of Bombon, near Melun, was accused by a number of people in the neighbourhood, of being a sorcerer, and of casting wicked spells over a woman.

Feeling in the village became so strong against him that he was ill-treated and beaten by some of his parishioners, and at length he took proceedings against his accusers.

The chief evidence was given by a municipal employee of Bordeaux who declared in Court, with great solemnity, that he struck the Abbé with a whip " to drive the devil out of him."

" Once," he said, " he sent, over our Oratory in Bordeaux, birds which traced in the air the letters of his name. That was an evil omen and from that moment we suffered.

" By similar diabolical practices he made mushrooms of an unknown and venomous kind grow suddenly in the garden of our chapel. I found that all my physical and intellectual force had gone and I became a mere log."

A woman also testified, that she had suffered less from the spells, because she kept reading a tract on exorcisms against Satan, which she invited the Judge to read, and she further declared, that the " evil spirit " made her " bump about in bed like a parcel."

A case in which a modern " magician " who specialized in restoring recalcitrant husbands to their wives, and in settling marital differences, came before the magistrates in Berlin a short time ago. The complainant, a shopkeeper, stated that his suspicions were aroused by hearing his wife apparently talking to herself in her bedroom late one night.

Listening at the closed door, he heard her repeating the words, " He will be true.   He will be true."

His conscience smote him as he listened, and he went into the room with the intention of vowing that his wife's prayer should be fulfilled, but he changed his mind when to his astonishment he saw that she was feeding the flames of the stove with one of his waistcoats. Upon his expostulating, she confessed that she was following out the instructions of a fortune-teller named Kuhn whom she had consulted, and who had assured her that she could secure her husband's fidelity by burning one of his garments while repeating the incantation.

The husband failed to be convinced, but let the matter pass until a few weeks later he caught her *burning his trousers*.

That decided him to put an end to the magician's practices, and he hailed Kuhn before the tribunal and charged her with fortune-telling.

Another woman charged with practising the " Black Art " was sent to prison for four months recently by the magistrates at Liége in Belgium.

One of her victims was a young woman who, suffering from pains in the head and body, consulted her twice a week for several months, and eventually, in order to pay her fees, stole money and was sent to prison.   Here the woman, who was known as Victorine, visited her and told her to " Invoke my name in a loud voice and you will not know you are in prison."   The fee for this advice was charged in her bill, but prison life remained unaltered.

Another victim was a married man whose wife had left him. He consulted Victorine and paid her fee, and she told him that in order to get his wife back, he must go to Gouvy (a place fifty miles from Liége) and back, in the company of three professors.

He found the necessary three companions and made the journey, and, lo, his wife returned. But unfortunately she soon ran off again, and none of Victorine's magic processes could induce her to return, hence the prosecution which ended so unhappily for Victorine.

In Devonshire, a few years ago, an old woman was found sticking pins into a sheep's heart while muttering imprecations, and after a while hung it in the chimney, with the object, she explained, of working ill on a neighbour to whom she had taken a dislike.

In some parts of East Anglia belief in witchcraft and the power of the " evil eye " still survives. The rector of Merton, in Norfolk, a short time ago stated that his people round about that district had an ingrained belief in " good and evil spells."

" The charge of witchcraft is usually whispered against old women of dominant personality, Roman-nosed women." There is a common belief that " if I offend 'un (the old woman) then she'll do me a mischief." He related the following account of how he laid a local curse known as " the curse of Sturston."

" This story dates back to the time of Queen Elizabeth. Sir Miles Yare—an Elizabethan vicar of Bray—was then the rector. For the country folk he held a Protestant service in the church on Sunday morning and then recited Mass in his parlour for the Popish gentry.

" An old Protestant lady, as she lay dying, solemnly

cursed this very accommodating parson-priest, his church, his rectory and the Great Folks' Hall. And the curse seemed to come true.

" When I came upon the scene," says the Rector, " I was asked to lay the curse. For the Old Hall had become a farmhouse surrounded by a few cottages, and the people feared that the curse might still be working itself out.

" I held a public service, using an old altar tomb in the ruined churchyard as a lectern. People flocked to the service from miles around. In the sequel nothing further dreadful happened. I had laid the curse."

An interesting case, which recalls the methods employed by the witch in the Middle Ages, is reported from Cosenza in northern Italy. In a village near that town lived two sisters, on whom a spell is said to have been cast by a woman who was believed to practise witchcraft. She succeeded in convincing them, that only by following her directions could they liberate themselves from the curse.

She prepared special food for them ; administered mysterious philtres and forbade them to leave their house.

In a short time both the sisters began to show signs of wasting away, which so alarmed their friends that they called in the aid of the police.

Accompanied by an officer they forced their way into the house, where they discovered the two sisters in a moribund condition and one of them died soon afterwards.

The so-called witch was at once arrested, and was only with difficulty saved from the anger of the villagers.

There is a curious superstitious custom in connexion with children that still survives in some parts of Wales, which consists of making an incision into a certain part of the cartilage of a child's ear, in order to cure it of backwardness. The operation is usually performed during the waxing of the moon by a woman who is supposed to have inherited the knowledge of performing the operation correctly. It is done repeatedly on the child until it is found to prove effective.

The belief in charms and mascots is still as common in our crowded cities as in remote parts of the country. The countless mascots to be seen on motor-cars in our streets to-day evidence the belief in the occult that lingers in modern times, and yet we smile at the credulity of the people of the East, who hang strings of blue beads about their horses' manes to ward off the " evil eye."

It is hardly credible, but nevertheless true, that tiny glass tubes filled with mercury and enclosed in washleather cases are still sold in a chemist's shop in the heart of the City of London, to people who believe that, by carrying them in their pockets, they will prevent attacks of rheumatism.

A certain scientific man is said to have expressed himself confident that he had checked a tendency to bleed at the nose, by suspending round his neck nine strands of red silk in each of which were tied nine knots. In order to be effective each knot had to be tied by a woman and separately wished over.

A short time ago, a shop was opened in one of the principal streets of the West End of London for the sale of a so-called Egyptian charm or mascot. Numerous letters were exhibited in the window, purporting to have been received from users of it, testifying to its wonderful powers. Tradesmen declared it had increased their business, boxers wrote that it had given them victory over their opponents, dancers asserted that it had found them partners, bookmakers stated it had given them success in betting, other people said it had obtained them situations and motorists declared it had helped them to win races !

These few instances of human credulity, at the present day, serve to show the prevalence of superstition and how little human nature has changed from the early centuries.

The tendency to believe in the supernatural still exists in all communities, and appears to be wrapped-up with the mystery that envelops the future and the fear of the unknown. The desire to pierce the veil that hides the beyond is innate in the human race throughout the world.

The manifestations of the magicians of the Middle Ages appear ridiculous to us to-day, but there are many people who still believe that they can communicate with the spirits of the dead by means of supernatural agencies.

If we look back through the past centuries we shall find that some of the greatest thinkers and intellectual men of their time, such as Roger Bacon, Cornelius Agrippa, Paracelsus and Van Helmont were believers in the occult.

There is no proof, however, that the practitioners of magic ever wrought any phenomena that could not be produced by natural agencies, nor is there any real evidence, in the records of magic, that the spirit of a dead person has ever materialized or been made to appear on earth in human form.

Although many of the rites used in magic were probably derived from those employed in early times as part of religious ceremonial, and founded on principles that lie deep down in the mind of man, it is evident that they formed but part of an elaborate system of imposture, designed to deceive and based on the credulity of humanity and the fear of the unknown.

The more the mystery surrounding the rites and ceremonies carried on, the more they seem to have inspired belief in the ordinary mind, and all tended to create an atmosphere of deception and illusion. The effects of the narcotic drugs employed by the magicians in their fumigations, to impress the imagination, no doubt sometimes produced hallucinations that appeared to be real. It is probable that they had a knowledge of certain powers, such as hypnotism, which they kept secret; for the " wise man," from the earliest times, was generally one who was cunning enough to be able to acquire and hold an influence over his less intelligent fellows by mysteries and secrets.

A knowledge of acoustics formed a natural means of deception in the working of the ancient oracles, and even apparitions may have been produced by the effects of reflection on polished surfaces.

It will be remembered how the illusion known as " Pepper's Ghost " mystified the general public many years ago, until it was explained that the apparitions were produced by the reflections of limelighted figures standing beneath the front of the stage.

" The Cabinet of Proteus," the astonishing " spirit " tricks performed by Anderson the "Wizard of the North," the remarkable feats of legerdemain executed by Houdin at his Temple of Mystery in Paris, also by Dr Lynn and Heller in London, and later the ingenious automata and cabinet tricks invented by Maskelyne and performed at the old Egyptian Hall, are but a few of the natural deceptions that created amazement and wonder in the last generation, and which a few centuries earlier would have been attributed to magic.

The old saying that " seeing is believing " is not always correct, as the sleight-of-hand tricks of the modern conjurer readily prove how the eye can easily be deceived by movements that are quicker than sight.

The extraordinary manifestations performed by Eastern jugglers are further instances of the manner in which vision can be deceived, and of how an erroneous impression may be conveyed to the brain. A person concentrating his thoughts, and constantly thinking of certain persons or things, may conceivably have a waking dream in which an occurrence may be pictured in his imagination, so that he believes that he has actually seen it.

The advance of science and education has done much to dispel the mysteries and reveal the secrets of magic, and the scientist may fitly be called the magician of modern times. His boundary is illimitable.

The discoveries of recent years, such as the production of the perfume of flowers from the refuse of the gasworks, the transference of photographs by electricity, television, the transmission of the human voice and of music through the ether for thousands of miles, are but a few of his achievements.

Surely these alone are more extraordinary than anything ever attributed to magic.

The laboratory is his " magic circle " where he works his wonders without mystery, and his discoveries outvie the greatest secrets that were claimed to be known by the magicians of the past.

314

BIBLIOGRAPHY

Manuscripts, British Museum.
Sloane, 2731, 3648, 3805, 3850, 3851, 1727, 3849, 3821, 389, 1306,
3824, 3189, 3846, 3847, 3822, 2577, 3853, 1306, 3851, 3826,
3653, 521, 647, 3821, 3883, 3884, 2544, 702, 738, 78, 1512,
3188, 3655, 3189, 3655.
Harl. 2267, 6482, 4381, 584, 6483.
Lans. 846, 1202.
Tib. A, VII, 6 E VI, 12 F XVI, 17a XLII, 25311, 32496, 36674,
32496, 35125, Ar 295.
Bodleian, Ashmolean, 187, 182, 421, 1406, 1442, 346, 1388, 1393,
1398, 1406, 1435, 1438, 1442, 1447, 1450, 1453, 1488, 1491,
1494, 1497, 335, 580, 1451, 133, 431, 3115, 961.
Rawlinson, 868, 252, 253, 1067, 1363.
Persian, 1563, 1564.
Bibliothèque Nationale, MSS.
Bibliothèque de l'Arsenal, MSS.

Life in Ancient Egypt.   Maspero.
The Light of Egypt.
Egyptian Magic.   Budge.
Babylonian Magic.   King.
Semetic Magic.   Thompson.
Devils and Evil Spirits of Babylonia.   Thompson.
The Magic Art.   Frazer.
Magic : White and Black.   Hartmann.
Magica seu. 1557.
History of Life.   Faust.
Magica das vit.   1600.
Magica de Spectris.   1656.
History of Magic.   Waite.
Grand Grimoire.
Key to Physics.   Sibley.
Grimorium verum.
Magic and Mystery.   Thompson.

Devil Worship in France.   Waite.
Kabbala Denadch.   Mathers.
Book of Sacred Magic.   Mathers.
The Magus.   Barrett.
Talismanic Magic.   Barrett.
Illustrations of the Occult Sciences.   Sibley.
Selene und Vervandi.   Roscher.
Chronicle of Jerahmeel.   Gaster.
Book of Enoch.   Gaster.
Sword of Moses.   Gaster.
Occultists.   Shirley.
Conversations on Secrets and Mysteries.   Gabalis, 1700.
Witchcraft.   Wickwar.
Encyclopædia of Religion and Ethics.
Peintures et Gravures.   Breuil.
Des Sorciers et des Devineresses.   Molitor, 1489.
Œuvres complet.   Wier, 1660.
Demonology and Devil-lore.   Conway.
Folk-lore of Rome.   Busk.

INDEX

317